GOOD GIRL, BAD BLOOD

Also by Holly Jackson

A Good Girl's Guide to Murder series

A Good Girl's Guide to Murder
Good Girl, Bad Blood
As Good as Dead
Kill Joy (a Good Girl's Guide to Murder novella)

Five Survive

The Reappearance of Rachel Price

Not Quite Dead Yet

GOOD GIRL, BAD BLOOD

The Sequel to
A Good Girl's Guide to Murder

HOLLY JACKSON

Delacorte Press

For Ben,

and for every version of you these last ten years

Delacorte Press
An imprint of Random House Children's Books
A division of Penguin Random House LLC
1745 Broadway, New York, NY 10019
penguinrandomhouse.com
GetUnderlined.com

Library of Congress Cataloging-in-Publication Data is available upon request.
ISBN 978-1-9848-9640-7 (trade) — ISBN 978-1-9848-9642-1 (ebook) —
ISBN 978-1-9848-9643-8 (pbk.) — ISBN 979-8-217-11737-6 (deluxe edition)

Originally published in paperback and in slightly different form by Electric Monkey, an imprint of Egmont UK Limited, London, in 2020. Subsequently published in hardcover in the United States by Delacorte Press, an imprint of Random House Children's Books, a division of Penguin Random House LLC, New York, in 2021.

Closed old folder by vlntn/stock.adobe.com, older open folder with papers by vlntn/stock.adobe.com, tape roll by Igor Nikushin/stock.adobe.com, lined paper by macondos/stock.adobe.com, wooden background by LIGHTFIELD STUDIOS/stock.adobe.com, binder clip by gearstd/stock.adobe.com, Grunge metal texture by anammarques/stock.adobe.com, paper and stack of paper by LiliGraphie/stock.adobe.com, paper texture by Артём Ковязин/stock.adobe.com, open old notebook by Jakub Krechowicz/stock.adobe.com.

Manufactured in Italy
10 9 8 7 6 5 4 3 2 1
2025 Deluxe Edition

The authorized representative in the EU for product safety and compliance is
Penguin Random House Ireland, Morrison Chambers, 32 Nassau Street, Dublin D02 YH68, Ireland,
https://eu-contact.penguin.ie.

Random House Children's Books supports the First Amendment
and celebrates the right to read.

Fairview
Sycamore Rd
Blackfield Ln
Old Farm Rd
Main St
1
Weevil Road
Weevil Rd
Monroe
Lodge Park
Courtland
West Way
Beacon Cl
Thatcher Rd
Cedar Wy
Main St
Barrows Wood
Grove Pl
Fairview Dr
Gravelly Wy
Common Rd
Fairview Common
Highmoor
1
Cross Ln
Chalk Rd

AFTER AND BEFORE

You think you'd know what a killer sounds like.

That their lies would have a different texture, some barely perceptible shift. A voice that thickens, grows sharp and uneven as the truth slips beneath the jagged edges. You'd think that, wouldn't you? Everyone thinks they'd know, if it came down to it. But Pip hadn't.

"It's such a tragedy what happened in the end."

Sitting across from him, looking into his kind, crinkled eyes, her phone between them recording every sound and sniff and throat-clearing huff. She'd believed it all, every word.

Pip traced her fingers across the trackpad, skipping the audio file back again.

"It's such a tragedy what happened in the end."

Elliot Ward's voice rang out from the speakers once more, filling her darkened bedroom. Filling her head.

Stop. Click. Repeat.

"It's such a tragedy what happened in the end."

She'd listened to it maybe a hundred times. Maybe even a thousand. And there was nothing, no giveaway, no change as he slipped between lies and half-truths. The man she'd once looked to as an almost father. But then, Pip had lied too, hadn't she? And she could tell herself she'd done it to protect the people she loved, but wasn't that the exact same reason Elliot gave? Pip ignored that voice in her head; the truth was out, most of it, and that's the thing she clung to.

She kept going, on to the other part that made her hairs stand on end.

"And do you think Sal killed Andie?" asked Pip's voice from the past.

". . . he was such a lovely kid. But, considering the evidence, I don't see how he couldn't have done it. As wrong as it feels, I guess I think he must have. There's no other explanation—"

Pip's door pushed inward with a smack.

"What are you doing?" interrupted a voice from right now, one that lifted with a smirk because he knew damn well what she was doing.

"You scared me, Ravi," she said, annoyed, darting forward to pause the audio. Ravi didn't need to hear Elliot Ward's voice, not ever again.

"You're sitting here in the dark listening to that, but *I'm* the scary one?" Ravi said, flicking on the light, the yellow glow reflecting off the dark hair swept across his forehead. He pulled that face, the one that always got her, and Pip smiled because it was impossible not to.

She wheeled back from her desk. "How did you get in, anyway?"

"Your parents and Josh were on their way out, with a giant Tupperware full of fresh-baked cookies."

"Oh yes," she said. "They're from Costco, don't let my dad fool you. They're on neighborly welcome duties. A young couple just moved into the Chens' house down the street. Mom did the deal. The Greens . . . or maybe the Browns, can't remember."

It was strange, thinking of another family living in that house, new lives reshaping to fill its old spaces. Pip's friend Zach Chen had always lived there, four doors down, ever since Pip had moved here at age five. It wasn't a real goodbye; she still saw Zach at school every day, but his parents had decided they could no longer live in this town, not after *all that trouble.* Pip was certain they considered her a large part of *all that trouble.*

"Dinner's seven-thirty, by the way," Ravi said, his voice suddenly skipping clumsily over the words. Pip looked at him; he was wearing his nicest shirt, and . . . were those new shoes? She could smell aftershave too, as he stepped toward her, but he stopped short, didn't kiss her on the forehead nor run a hand through her hair. Instead he sat on her bed, fiddling with his hands.

"Meaning you're almost two hours early." Pip smiled.

"Y-yeah." He coughed.

Why was he being awkward? It was their first Valentine's Day, and Ravi had booked them a table at The Siren, out of town. Pip's best friend, Cara, was convinced Ravi was going to ask Pip to be his girlfriend tonight. She said she'd put money on it. The thought made something in Pip's stomach swell, spilling its heat up into her chest. But it might not be that: Valentine's Day was also Sal's birthday. Ravi's older brother would have turned twenty-four today, if he'd made it past eighteen.

"How far have you got?" Ravi asked, nodding at Pip's laptop, the audio-editing software Audacity filling the screen with spiky blue lines. The whole story was there, contained within those blue lines. From the start of Pip's project to the very end: every lie, every secret. Even some of her own.

"It's done," Pip said, dropping her eyes to the new USB microphone plugged into her computer. "I've finished. Six episodes. I had to use a noise-reduction effect on some of the phone interviews for quality, but it's done."

And in a green plastic file, beside the microphone, were the release forms she'd sent to everyone. Signed and returned, granting her permission to publish their interviews in a podcast. Even Elliot Ward had signed one from his prison cell. Two people had refused: Stanley Forbes from the town newspaper and, of course, Max Hastings. But Pip didn't need their voices to tell the story; she'd filled in the gaps with her production log entries, now recorded as monologues.

"You're finished already?" Ravi said, though he couldn't really be surprised. He knew her, maybe better than anyone else did.

It had been six weeks since Pip had stood at the front of the school assembly hall and told everyone what really happened. But the media still weren't telling the story right; even now they clung to their own angles because those were cleaner, neater. Yet the Andie Bell case had been anything but neat.

"If you want something done right, you have to do it yourself," Pip said, her gaze climbing the spiking audio clips. Right then, she couldn't decide whether this felt like something beginning or something ending. But she knew which she wanted it to be.

"So what's next?" asked Ravi.

"I export the episode files, upload them to SoundCloud on schedule, once a week, and then copy the RSS feed to podcast directories like iTunes and Stitcher. But I'm not quite finished," she said. "I need to record the intro over this theme song I found on AudioJungle. But to record an intro, you need a title."

"Ah," Ravi said, stretching out his back, "we're still titleless, are we, Lady Fitz-Amobi?"

"We are," she said. "I've narrowed it down to three options."

"Hit me," he said.

"No, you'll be mean about them."

"No, I won't," he said earnestly, with the smallest of smiles.

"OK." She looked down at her notes. "Option A is *An Examination into a Miscarriage of Justice.* Wha— Ravi, I can see you laughing."

"That was a yawn, I swear."

"Well, you won't like option B either, because that's *A Study of a Closed Case: The Andie Bell—* Ravi, stop!"

"Wha— I'm sorry, I can't help it," he said, laughing until his eyes were lined with tears. "It's just . . . of all your many qualities, Pip, there's one thing you lack—"

"Lack?" She spun her chair to face him. "I *lack* something?"

"Yes," he said, meeting her stony eyes. "Pizzazz. You are almost entirely pizzazz-less, Pip."

"I am not pizzazz-less."

"You need to draw people in, intrigue them. Have a word like 'kill' or 'dead' in there."

"But that's sensationalism."

"And that's exactly what you want, for people to actually listen," Ravi said.

"But all of my options are accurate and—"

"Boring?"

Pip threw a yellow highlighter at him.

"You need something that rhymes, or alliteration. Something with—"

"Pizzazz?" she said in her Ravi voice. "You think of one, then."

"Crime Time," he said. "No, oh, Fairview . . . maybe *Un-Fairview.*"

"Ew, no," said Pip.

"You're right." Ravi got up and started to pace. "Your unique selling point is, really, you. A seventeen-year-old who solved a case the police had long considered closed. And what are you?" he looked at her, squinting.

"Lacking, clearly," she said with mock irritation.

"A student," Ravi thought aloud. "A girl. Project. Oh, how about *Project Murder and Me*?"

"Nah."

"OK . . ." He chewed his lip and it made Pip's stomach tighten. "So something murder, or kill, or dead. And you are Pip, who's a student and a girl who's good at . . . Oh shit," he said suddenly, eyes widening. "I've got it!"

"What?" she said.

"I've literally got it," he said, far too pleased with himself.

"What is it?"

"A Good Girl's Guide to Murder."

"Noooo." Pip shook her head. "That's bad, way too try-hard."

"What are you talking about? It's perfect."

"Good girl?" she said dubiously. "I turn eighteen in two weeks; I won't contribute to my own infantilization."

"A Good Girl's Guide to Murder," Ravi said in his deep, movie-trailer voice, pulling Pip up from her chair and spinning her toward him.

"No," she said.

"Yes," he retorted, placing one hand on her waist, his warm fingers dancing up her ribs, making her glow.

"Absolutely not."

NEWSDAY

US > Culture > TV & Radio > Reviews

A Good Girl's Guide to Murder Review: The latest true-crime podcast obsession ends with a chilling finale

BENJAMIN COLLIS | MARCH 27

If you haven't yet listened to episode 6 of *A Good Girl's Guide to Murder,* look away now. Serious **spoilers** below.

Of course, many of us know how this mystery ended from when it exploded on the news last November, but the whodunit isn't the whole story here. The real story of *A Good Girl's Guide to Murder* has been the journey, from a seventeen-year-old sleuth's hunch about a closed case—the murder of teenager Andie Bell, allegedly by her boyfriend, Sal Singh—to the spiraling web of dark secrets she uncovers in her small town. The ever-shifting suspects, the lies, and the twists.

The final episode certainly isn't lacking in twists as it brings us the truth, starting with Pip's shocking revelation that Elliot Ward, her best friend's father, wrote the threatening notes Pip received during her investigation. Irrefutable proof of his involvement and truly a loss-of-innocence moment for Pip. She and Ravi Singh—Sal's younger brother and co-detective on this case—believed that Andie Bell might still be alive and Elliot had been keeping her the whole time. Pip confronted Elliot Ward alone and, in Ward's own words, the whole story unravels. An illicit relationship between student and teacher, allegedly initiated by Andie. "If true," Pip theorizes, "I think Andie wanted an escape from Fairview, particularly from her father, who allegedly, according to a source, was controlling and emotionally abusive. Perhaps Andie believed Mr. Ward could get her into Yale, like Sal, so she could get far away from home."

The night of her disappearance, Andie went to Elliot Ward's house. An argument ensued. Andie tripped, hitting her head against Ward's desk. But as Ward rushed to get a first-aid kit, Andie disappeared into the night. In the following days, as Andie was officially declared missing, Ward panicked, believing Andie must have died from her head injury and when police eventually found her body, there might be evidence that would lead to him. His only chance was to give the police a more convincing suspect. "He cried as he told me," Pip says, "how he killed Sal Singh." Ward made it look like suicide and planted evidence so that police would think Sal had killed his girlfriend and then himself.

But, months later, Ward was shocked to see Andie walking on the side of the road, thin and disheveled. She hadn't died after all. Ward couldn't allow her to return to Fairview, and that's how she ended up his prisoner for five years. However, in a twist truly stranger than fiction: the person in Ward's loft wasn't Andie Bell. "She looked so much like her," Pip claims, "she even told me she *was* Andie." She was actually Isla Jordan, a vulnerable young woman with an intellectual disability. All this time, Elliot had convinced himself—and Isla—that she *was* Andie Bell.

This left the final question of what had happened to the *real* Andie Bell. Our young detective beat the police to that too. "It was Becca Bell, Andie's little sister." Pip figured out that Becca had been sexually assaulted at a local house party (nicknamed calamity parties by attendees), and that Andie had sold drugs at these parties, including Rohypnol, which Becca suspected had played a part in her assault. When Andie was out *that night* with Ward, Becca allegedly found proof in her sister's room that Max Hastings had bought Rohypnol from Andie and was likely Becca's attacker (Hastings will soon face trial for several rape and sexual assault charges). But when Andie returned home, she didn't react the way that Becca had hoped; Andie forbade her sister from going to the police because it would get Andie in trouble. They started arguing and pushing each other, until Andie ended up on the floor, unconscious and vomiting. Andie's postmortem—performed last November when her body was finally recovered—showed that "the brain swelling from a head trauma was not fatal. Though it no doubt caused loss of consciousness and vomiting, Andie Bell died from asphyxiation, choking on her own vomit." Becca froze, allegedly watching Andie die, too shocked and too angry to save her sister's life. She hid Andie's body because she was scared no one would believe that her death had been an accident.

And there it is, our ending. "No angles or filters, just the sad truth of how Andie Bell died, how Sal was murdered and framed as her killer and everyone believed it." In Pip's scathing conclusion, she picks out everyone she finds at fault for the deaths of these two teenagers, naming and blaming: Elliot Ward, Max Hastings, Jason Bell (Andie's father), Becca Bell, Howard Bowers (Andie's drug dealer), and Andie Bell herself.

A Good Girl's Guide to Murder stormed to the top of the iTunes chart with its first episode six weeks ago, and it looks set to stay there for some time. With the final episode released last night, listeners are already clamoring for a season 2 of the hit podcast. But in a statement posted to her website, Pip said: "I'm afraid my detective days are over and there will *not* be a second season of *AGGGTM*. This case almost consumed me; I could only see that once I was out the other side. It became an unhealthy obsession, putting me and those around me in considerable danger. But I will finish *this* story, recording updates on the trials and verdicts of all those involved. I promise I will be here until the very last word."

ONE MONTH LATER . . .

THURSDAY

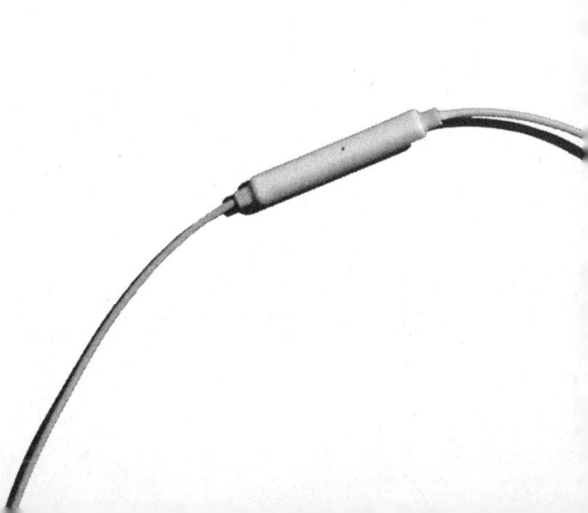

ONE

It was still there, every time she opened the front door. It wasn't real, she knew that, just her mind filling in the absence, bridging the gap. She heard it: dog claws skittering, rushing to welcome her home. But it wasn't, it couldn't be. It was just a memory, the ghost of a sound that had always been there.

"Pip, is that you?" her mom called from the kitchen.

"Hey," Pip replied, dropping her bronze-colored backpack in the hall, textbooks thumping together inside.

Josh was in the living room, sitting on the floor two feet from the TV, fast-forwarding through the ads on the Disney Channel. "You'll get square eyes," Pip remarked as she walked by.

"You'll get a square butt," Josh snapped back with a snort. A terrible retort, objectively speaking, but he was quick for a ten-year-old.

"Hi, darling, how was school?" her mom asked, sipping from a flowery mug as Pip walked into the kitchen and settled on one of the stools at the counter.

"Fine. It was fine." School was always fine now. Not good, not bad. Just fine. She pulled off her shoes, the leather unsticking from her feet and smacking against the tiles.

"Ugh," her mom said. "Do you always have to leave your shoes in the kitchen?"

"Do you always have to catch me doing it?"

"Yes. I'm your mother," she said, whacking Pip's arm lightly with her new cookbook. "Oh, and, Pippa, I need to talk to you about something."

The full name. So much meaning in that extra syllable.

"Am I in trouble?"

Her mom didn't answer the question. "Flora Green called me today. You know she's the new teaching assistant at Josh's school?"

"Yes. . . ." Pip nodded for her mother to continue.

"Joshua got in trouble today, sent to the principal." Her mom's brow knitted. "Apparently Camilla Brown's pencil sharpener went missing, and Josh decided to interrogate his classmates about it, finding evidence and drawing up a *persons of interest* list. He made four kids cry."

"Oh," Pip said, that pit opening up in her stomach again. Yes, she was in trouble. "OK, OK. Should I talk to him?"

"Yes, I think you should. Now," her mom said, raising her mug and taking a noisy sip.

Pip slid off the stool with a gritted smile and padded back toward the living room.

"Josh," she said lightly, sitting on the floor beside him. She muted the television.

"Hey!"

Pip ignored him. "So, I heard what happened at school today."

"Oh yeah. There's two main suspects." He turned to her, his brown eyes lighting up. "Maybe you can help—"

"Josh, listen to me," Pip said, tucking her dark hair behind her ears. "Being a detective is not all it's cracked up to be. In fact . . . it's a pretty bad thing to be."

"But I—"

"Just listen, OK? Being a detective makes the people around you unhappy. Makes you unhappy . . . ," she said, her voice withering away until she cleared her throat and pulled it back. "Remember Dad told you what happened to Barney, why he got hurt?"

Josh nodded, his eyes growing wide and sad.

"That's what happens when you're a detective. The people around you get hurt. And you hurt people, without meaning to. You have to keep secrets you're not sure you should. That's why I don't do it anymore, and you shouldn't either." The words dropped right into that waiting pit in her gut, where they belonged. "Do you understand?"

"Yes . . ." He nodded, holding on to the *s* as it grew into the next word. "Sorry."

"Don't be silly." She smiled, folding him into a quick hug. "You have nothing to be sorry for. So no more playing detective?"

"Nope, promise."

Well, that had been easy.

"Done," Pip said, back in the kitchen. "I guess the missing pencil sharpener will forever remain a mystery."

"Ah, maybe not," her mom said with a barely concealed smile. "I bet it was that Alex Davis, the little shit."

Pip snorted.

Her mom kicked Pip's shoes out of her way. "So, have you heard from Ravi yet?"

"Yeah." Pip pulled out her phone. "He said they finished about fifteen minutes ago. He'll be over to record soon."

"OK. How was today?"

"He said it was rough. I wish I could be there." Pip leaned against the counter, dropping her chin onto her knuckles.

"You know you can't, you have school," her mom said. It wasn't a discussion she was prepared to have again; Pip knew that. "And didn't you have enough after Tuesday? I know I did."

Tuesday, the first day of the trial at New Haven Superior Court, Pip had been called as a witness for the prosecution. Dressed in a new suit and a white shirt, trying to keep her hands from fidgeting so the jury wouldn't see. Sweat prickling down her back. And every second, she'd felt his eyes on her from the defendant's table, his gaze a physical thing, crawling over her exposed skin. Max Hastings.

The one time she glanced at him, she'd seen the smirk behind his eyes that no one else would see. Not behind those fake, clear-lens glasses, anyway. How dare he? How dare he stand up and plead not guilty when they both knew the truth? She had a recording, a phone conversation with Max admitting to drugging and raping Becca Bell. It was all right there. Max had confessed when Pip threatened to tell everyone his secrets: the hit-and-run and Sal's alibi. But it hadn't mattered anyway; the private recording was inadmissible in court. The prosecution had to settle for Pip's recounting of the conversation instead. Which she'd done, word for word . . . well, apart from the beginning, of course, and those same secrets she had to keep to protect Naomi Ward.

"Yeah, it was horrible," Pip said, "but I should still be there." She should; she'd promised to follow this story to all of its ends. But instead, Ravi would be there every day in the public gallery, taking notes for her. Because *school wasn't optional:* so said her mom and the new principal.

"Pip, please," her mom said in that warning voice. "This week is difficult enough as it is. And with the memorial tomorrow too. What a week."

"Yep," Pip agreed with a sigh.

"You OK?" Her mom paused, resting a hand on Pip's shoulder.

"Yeah. I'm always OK."

Her mom didn't quite believe her, she could tell. But it didn't matter because a moment later, there was a knock on the front door: Ravi's distinctive pattern. *Long-short-long.* And Pip's heart picked up to match it, as it always did.

File Name:

A Good Girl's Guide to Murder: The Trial of Max Hastings (update 3).wav

[Jingle plays]

PIP: Hello, Pip Fitz-Amobi here and welcome back to *A Good Girl's Guide to Murder: The Trial of Max Hastings*. This is the third update, so if you haven't yet heard the first two mini-episodes, please go back and listen to those first. We are going to cover what happened today, the third day of Max Hastings's trial, and joining me is Ravi Singh . . .

RAVI: Hello.

PIP: . . . who has been watching the trial unfold from the public gallery. Today started with the testimony from another of the victims, Natalie da Silva. You may well recognize the name; Nat was involved in my investigation into the Andie Bell case. I learned that Andie had bullied Nat at school, and had even sought and distributed indecent images of her on social media. I believed it could be a possible motive and, for a while, I considered Nat a person of interest. I was entirely wrong, of course. Today, Nat appeared in New Haven Superior Court to give evidence about how, on February 21, 2014, she was allegedly drugged and sexually assaulted by Max Hastings at a calamity party. But as I've explained before, due to Connecticut's ridiculous statute of limitations, Max cannot be charged for either rape or sexual assault because the alleged offenses happened more than five years ago in the cases of both Nat da Silva and Becca Bell. For these two victims, Max is instead being charged with kidnapping in the first degree, as the state has no statute of limitations for that crime. In Connecticut, the definition of kidnapping includes restraining someone with intent to inflict physical injury or sexual abuse, and therefore the state attorney general recommended these charges instead. Of course, the whole thing is disgraceful, but I won't start on my feelings about the statute of limitations again. I think I've previously made those very clear. So, Ravi, can you take us through how Nat's testimony went?

RAVI: Yeah. So the prosecutor asked Nat to establish a timeline of that evening: when she arrived at the party, the last instance she looked at the time before she began to feel incapacitated, what time she woke up in the morning and left the house. Nat said she has only a few hazy snatches of memory: someone leading her into the back room, away from the party, and laying her down on a sofa; her feeling paralyzed, unable to move, and then of someone lying down beside her. Other than that, she described herself as being blacked out. And then, when she woke up the next morning, she felt awful and dizzy, like it was the worst hangover she'd ever had. Her clothes were in disarray and her underwear had been removed.

PIP: And, to revisit what the prosecution's expert witness said on Tuesday about the effects of benzodiazepines like Rohypnol, Nat's testimony is very much in line with what you'd expect. The drug acts like a sedative and can have a depressant effect on the body's central nervous system, which explains Nat's feeling of being paralyzed. It feels almost like you're separated from your own body, like it just won't listen to you, your limbs aren't connected anymore.

RAVI: Right, and the prosecutor also made sure the expert witness repeated, several times, that a side effect of Rohypnol was "blacking out," as Nat said, or having anterograde amnesia, which means an inability to create new memories. I think the prosecutor wants to keep reminding the jury of this point because it will play a significant part in the testimonies of all the victims, the fact that they don't remember exactly what happened because the drug affected their ability to make memories.

PIP: The prosecutor also repeated that fact regarding Becca Bell. As a reminder, Becca recently changed her plea to guilty, despite a defense team who were confident that they could get her no jail time due to her being a minor at the time of Andie's death and the circumstances surrounding it. She accepted a four-year sentence, suspended after eighteen months, followed by two years' probation. Yesterday, Becca testified by video link from prison, where she will be for the next year and a half.

RAVI: Exactly. And like with Becca, today the prosecution was eager to establish that Nat had only one or two alcoholic drinks the night of the alleged attack, which couldn't possibly account for her level of intoxication. Specifically, Nat said she only drank one bottle of beer that night. And she stated who allegedly gave her that drink on her arrival: Max.

PIP: And how did Max react while Nat was testifying?

RAVI: From the gallery, I can only see his profile or the back of his head. But he appears to be acting the same way he has since Tuesday: this kind of calm, very still demeanor, eyes turned to whoever's on the witness stand as though he's really interested in what they're saying. He's still wearing those thick-rimmed glasses, and I'm 100 percent certain they aren't prescription lenses—I mean, my mom's an optometrist.

PIP: And is his hair still long and a little unkempt, like it was on Tuesday?

RAVI: Yeah, that seems to be the image he and his defense attorney have settled on. Expensive suit, fake glasses. Maybe they think his messy blond hair will be disarming to the jury or something.

PIP: Well, it's worked for certain recent world leaders.

RAVI: The courtroom sketch artist let me take a photo of her sketch today and said we could post it after the press has published it. You can see her impression of Max sitting there while his attorney, Christopher Epps, cross-examines Nat on the stand.

PIP: Yes, and if you'd like to look at the sketch, you can find it in the appendix materials on the website agoodgirlsguidetomurder-podcast.com. So, let's talk about the cross-examination.

RAVI: Yes, it was . . . pretty rough. Max's lawyer, Epps, asked a lot of invasive questions. What were you wearing that night? Did you dress promiscuously on purpose?—showing photos of Nat that night from social media. Did you have a crush on Max Hastings? How much alcohol would you drink on an average night? He also brought up her past criminal conviction for aggravated assault, implying that it made her untrustworthy. It was, essentially, a character assassination. You could see Nat getting upset, but she stayed calm, took a few seconds to breathe and have a sip of water before answering each question. Her voice was shaking, though. It was really hard to watch.

PIP: It makes me so angry that this kind of cross-examination of victims is allowed. It almost shifts the burden of proof onto them, and it isn't fair.

RAVI: Not fair at all. Epps then grilled Nat about not going to the police the next day, if she was sure she was assaulted and who the perpetrator was. That if she'd gone to the police within seventy-two hours, a urinalysis could have confirmed whether she had Rohypnol in her system, which, Epps claimed, was up for debate. Nat could only reply that she hadn't been sure afterward, because she had no memory. And then Epps said, "If you have no memory, how do you know you didn't consent to any sexual activity? Or that you even interacted with the defendant that night?" Nat replied that Max had made a loaded comment to her the following Monday, asking if she'd had a "good time" at the party because he had. Epps never let up. It must have been exhausting for Nat.

PIP: It seems this is Epps's tactic for Max's defense. To undermine and discredit each of us as witnesses. With me, it was his claim about how *convenient* it was that I had Max to use as a male patsy, to try to make Becca Bell and her alleged manslaughter sympathetic. That it was all part of the "aggressive feminist narrative" I've been pushing with my podcast.

RAVI: Yeah, that does seem to be the approach Epps is taking.

PIP: I guess that's the kind of aggressive strategy you get when your lawyer costs four hundred dollars an hour. But money is no issue for the Hastings family, of course.

RAVI: It doesn't matter what strategy Epps uses; the jury will see the truth.

File Name:

The Trial of Max Hastings Appendix: Courtroom Sketch.jpg

TWO

Words spliced, growing across the gaps like vines as Pip's eyes unfocused, until her handwriting was just one writhing blur. She was looking at the page, but she wasn't really there. It was like that now; giant holes in her attention that she slipped right into.

There was a time, not too long ago, she would have found a practice essay about Cold War escalation enthralling. She would have cared, *really* cared. That was who she was before, but something must have changed. Hopefully, it was just a matter of time until those holes filled back in and things went back to normal.

Her phone buzzed against the desk, Cara's name lighting up the screen.

"Good evening, Miss Sweet F-A," Cara said when Pip picked up, stating her initials in a terrible British accent. "Are you ready to Netflix and chill in the upside down?"

"Yep, C.W., two secs," Pip said, taking her laptop and phone to bed with her and sliding under the duvet.

"How was the trial today?" Cara asked. "Naomi almost went this morning, to support Nat. But she couldn't face seeing Max."

"I just uploaded the update." Pip sighed. "Makes me so angry that Ravi and I have to tiptoe around it when we record, saying 'allegedly' and avoiding anything that steps over the 'presumption of innocence' when we know he did it. He did all of it."

"Yeah, it's gross. But it's OK, it will be over in a week." Cara rustled in her covers, the phone line crackling. "Hey, guess what I found today?"

"What?"

"You're a meme. An actual meme that strangers are posting on Reddit. It's that photo of you with Detective Hawkins in front of all the press microphones. The one where it looks like you're rolling your eyes at him while he's talking."

"I *was* rolling my eyes at him."

"And people have captioned the funniest things. It's like you're the new 'jealous girlfriend' meme. This one has a caption of 'Me . . . ' by you, and beside Hawkins it says 'Men on the internet explaining my own joke back to me.' " Cara snorted. "That's when you know you've made it, becoming a meme. Have you heard from any more advertisers?"

"Yeah," Pip said. "A few companies have emailed about sponsorship. But . . . I still don't know if it's the right thing, profiting off what happened. I don't know, it's too much to think about, especially this week."

"I know, what a week." Cara coughed. "So tomorrow, you know . . . the memorial . . . would it be weird for Ravi and his parents if Naomi and I were there?"

Pip sat up. "No. You know Ravi doesn't think like that, you've spoken to each other about it."

"I know, I know. But I just thought, with tomorrow being about remembering Sal and Andie, now that we know the truth, maybe it would be weird for us to—"

"Ravi is the last person who'd ever want you to feel guilty for what your dad did to Sal. His parents too." Pip paused. "They lived through that, they know better than anyone."

"I know, it's just—"

"Cara, it's OK. Ravi would want you there. I'm pretty sure he'd say Sal would've wanted Naomi there. She was his best friend."

"OK, if you're sure."

"I'm always sure."

"You are. You should think about taking up gambling," Cara said.

"Can't. Mom's already too concerned about my 'addictive personality.' "

"Surely my and Naomi's fucked-uppedness helps to normalize you."

"Not enough, apparently," said Pip. "If you could try a bit harder, that would be great."

That was Cara's way of getting through the past six months, her new normal. Hiding behind the quips and one-liners that made others squirm and fall silent. Most people didn't know how to react when someone joked about their father who murdered a person and kidnapped another. But Pip knew exactly how to react: she crouched and hid behind the one-liners too so that Cara always had someone right there next to her. That was how she helped.

"Note taken. Although I'm not sure my grandma can cope with any more. You know, Naomi's had this new idea: apparently she wants to burn all of Dad's stuff. Grandparents obviously said no and got straight on the phone to our therapist."

"Burn it?"

"I know, right?" Cara said. "She'd accidentally summon a demon or something. I probably shouldn't tell Dad; he still thinks Naomi will turn up one day."

Cara visited her dad at the Bridgeport Correctional Center every two weeks. She said it didn't mean she'd forgiven him, but after all, he was still her dad. Naomi had not visited once and said she never would.

"So, what time does the memorial— Hold on, Grandpa's talking to me . . . Yes?" Cara called, her voice directed away from the phone. "Yeah, I know. Yeah, I am."

Cara's grandparents—her mom's parents—had moved into the house with her and Naomi last November so Cara had some doctor-ordered stability until she finished school. But April was almost over, and exams and the end of school were fast approaching. Too fast. And when summer arrived, Cara and Naomi's grandparents would put the Wards' house on the market and move the girls to their home in Warren Township, New Jersey. At least they'd be close when Pip started college at Columbia. But Fairview wouldn't be Fairview without Cara, and Pip quietly wished that summer would never come.

"OK," Cara said. "Good night, Grandpa."

"What was that?"

"Oh, you know, it's ten-thirty, so it's suuuuuper late and past 'lights-out' and I should have been in bed hours ago and not chatting with my 'girlfriends.' Plural. At this rate, I'll probably never have a girlfriend, let alone multiple, plus no one has said 'lights out' since, like, the 1700s," Cara huffed.

"Well, the light bulb was invented in 1879, so—"

"Ugh, please stop. Have you got it cued up?"

"Almost," Pip said, dragging one finger across the trackpad. "We're on episode four, right?"

This had started in December, when Pip first realized Cara wasn't sleeping. Not surprising, really: lying in bed at night is always when the worst thoughts come. And Cara's were worse than most. If only Pip could stop her from listening to them, distract her into sleep. When they were kids, Cara was always the first to go at sleepovers, her light snores disrupting the end of a cheesy horror film. So Pip tried to re-create those childhood sleepovers, calling Cara while they binge-watched Netflix together. It worked. As long as Pip was there, awake and listening, Cara eventually fell asleep, her breath whistling through the phone.

Now they did it every night. They'd started with shows Pip could legitimately argue had "educational value." But they'd watched so many that their standard had slipped somewhat. Still, at least *Stranger Things* had some historical quality.

"OK, ready?" Cara said.

"Ready." It had taken them several attempts to get the shows to run in exact synchronization; Cara's laptop had a slight delay, so she pressed play on *one* and Pip went on *go.*

"Three," Pip said.

"Two."

"One."

"Go."

FRIDAY

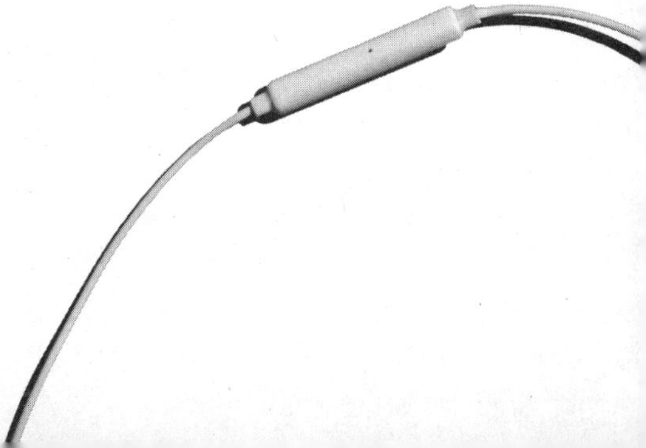

THREE

She knew his footsteps; knew them across carpet and hardwood floors, and knew them now across the gravel on the common parking lot. She turned and smiled at him, and Ravi's feet picked up in that small-stepped half run he always did when he spotted her. It made Pip glow every time.

"Hey, Sarge," he said, pressing the words into her forehead with his lips. His very first nickname for her, now one among dozens.

"You OK?" she asked, though she already knew he wasn't; he'd just oversprayed deodorant and it was following him around like a fog. That meant he was nervous.

"Yeah, a little nervous," Ravi said. "Mom and Dad are already there, but I wanted to shower first."

"That's OK. The ceremony doesn't start until seven-thirty," Pip said, taking his hand. "There are lots of people around the pavilion already, maybe a few hundred."

"Already?"

"Yeah. I walked through on my way home from school and the news crews were already setting up."

"Is that why you came in disguise?" Ravi smiled, tugging at the bottle-green jacket hood pulled over Pip's head.

"Just until we get past them."

It was probably Pip's fault they were here anyway; her podcast had reignited Sal's and Andie's stories in the media. Especially this week, the sixth anniversary of their deaths.

"How did court go today?" asked Pip, and then, "We can talk about it tomorrow if you don't want—"

"No, it's OK," Ravi said. "I mean, it wasn't OK. Today was one of the girls who lived in the same dorm as Max at college. They played her nine-one-one call from the morning after." Ravi swallowed the lump in his throat. "And in cross-examination, Epps went in on her, of course: no DNA profile lifted from the rape kit, no memory, that sort of thing. You know, watching Epps sometimes makes me reconsider whether I really want to be a criminal defense lawyer."

That was *The Plan* they'd worked out. Ravi had retaken the SAT in March, getting a score of 1580. But because of his low GPA, he'd applied to a local community college starting in the fall and would later transfer by articulation to Quinnipiac University to get his bachelor's degree. And from there, law school. "Quite the power couple," Ravi had remarked.

"Epps is one of the bad ones," Pip said. "You'll be a good one." She squeezed his hand. "Are you ready? We can wait here a little longer if you—"

"I'm ready," he said. "Just . . . I . . . Will you stay with me?"

"Of course." She pressed her shoulder into his. "I won't let go."

The sky was already darkening as they left the crunchy gravel behind for the soft grass of the common. To their right, little clusters of people were walking onto the green from the direction of Gravelly Way, all heading toward the pavilion on the south side of the common. Pip heard the crowd before she saw them—that low, living hum that only happens when you put hundreds of people into one small place. Ravi gripped her hand tighter.

They rounded a tight knot of whispering sycamore trees and the pavilion came into view, glowing a faint yellow; people must have started lighting the candles and tea lights laid out around the structure. Ravi's hand started to sweat against hers.

Pip recognized a few faces at the back as she and Ravi approached: Adam Clark, her new history teacher, standing beside Jill from the café, and over there, Cara's grandparents waving at her. She and Ravi pushed forward and, as eyes turned and met theirs, the crowd parted for Ravi, swallowing them, re-forming behind them to block the way back.

"Pip, Ravi." A voice pulled their attention to the left. It was Naomi, hair pulled back tight, like her smile. She was standing with Jamie Reynolds—the older brother of Pip's friend Connor—and, Pip realized with a stomach lurch, Nat da Silva. Nat's hair was so white that it almost set the air around her aglow. They had all been in the same grade as Sal and Andie.

"Hi," Ravi said, pulling Pip out of her thoughts.

"Hi, Naomi, Jamie," she said, nodding to them in turn. "Nat, hey." She faltered as Nat's pale blue eyes fell on her and her gaze hardened. The air around her lost its glow and turned cold.

"Sorry," Pip said. "I—I . . . just wanted to say I'm sorry you had to go through that, th-the trial yesterday, but you did amazingly."

Nothing. Nothing but a twitch in Nat's cheek.

"And I know this week and next must be awful for you, but we are going to get him. I know it. And if there's anything I can do . . ."

Nat's eyes slid off Pip like she wasn't really there at all. "OK," Nat said, a sharp edge to her voice as she faced the other way.

"OK," Pip said quietly, turning back to Naomi and Jamie. "We'd better keep moving. See you later."

She and Ravi moved on through the crowd, and when they were far enough, Ravi said in her ear, "Yeah, she definitely still hates you."

"I know." And she deserved it, really; she *had* considered Nat a murder suspect. Why wouldn't Nat hate her? Pip felt cold, but she packed away Nat's eyes into the pit in her stomach, alongside the rest of those feelings.

She spotted Cara's messy light brown topknot, bobbing above the heads in the crowd, and she maneuvered herself and Ravi toward it. Cara was standing with Connor, who was nodding in quick doubles as she spoke. Beside them, heads almost pressed together, were Ant and Lauren, who were now always Ant-and-Lauren, said in one quick breath, because one was never seen without the other. Not now that they were *together* together, unlike before when they must have been *pretend* together. Cara said it had apparently started at the calamity party they all went to last October, when Pip had been undercover. No wonder she hadn't noticed. Zach was standing on the other side of them, ignored, fiddling awkwardly with his liquid black hair.

"Hi," Pip said as she and Ravi broke through the outer circle of the group.

"Hey," came a quiet chorus of replies.

Cara turned to look up at Ravi, nervously picking at her collar. "I, um . . . I'm . . . How are you? Sorry."

Cara was never lost for words.

"It's OK," Ravi said, breaking free from Pip's hand to hug Cara. "It really is, I promise."

"Thank you," Cara said quietly, blinking at Pip over Ravi's shoulder.

"Oh, look," Lauren hissed, nudging Pip and indicating with a flash of her eyes. "It's Jason and Dawn Bell."

Andie and Becca's parents. Pip followed Lauren's eyes. Jason was wearing a smart wool coat, surely too hot for the evening, leading Dawn toward the pavilion. Dawn's eyes were down on the ground, on all those bodiless feet, her eyelashes mascara-clumped like she'd already been crying. She looked so small behind Jason as he pulled her along by the hand.

"Have you heard?" Lauren said, beckoning for the group to draw in tighter. "Apparently Jason and Dawn are back together. My mom says his second wife is divorcing him and apparently Jason has moved back into *that* house with Dawn."

That house. The house where Andie Bell died on the kitchen tiles and Becca stood by and watched. If those *apparentlys* were true, Pip wondered how much choice Dawn had had in the decision. From what she'd heard about Jason during her investigation, she wasn't sure how much choice anyone around him ever had. He certainly hadn't come out of her podcast looking so great. In fact, in a Twitter poll a listener made of "The Most Hateable Person in *AGGGTM,*" Jason Bell had received almost as many votes as Max Hastings and Elliot Ward. Pip herself had come in close fourth place. But she tried not to think about that.

"It's so weird they still live there," Ant said, widening his eyes like Lauren's. They fed off each other like that. "Eating dinner in the same room where Andie died."

"People deal with what they have to deal with," said Cara. "Don't think you can judge them by normal standards."

That shut Ant-and-Lauren up.

There was an awkward silence that Connor tried to fill. Pip looked away, immediately recognizing the couple standing next to them. She smiled.

"Oh, hi, Charlie, Flora." Her new neighbors from four doors down: Charlie with his rust-colored hair and well-trimmed beard, and Flora, who Pip had only ever seen wearing florals. She was the new teaching assistant at her brother's school, and Josh was more than a little obsessed with her. "Didn't see you there."

"Hello." Charlie smiled, dipping his head. "You must be Ravi," he said, shaking Ravi's hand, which hadn't yet found its way back to Pip. "We are both very sorry for your loss."

"It sounds like your brother was an amazing guy," Flora added.

"Thank you. Yeah, he was," said Ravi.

"Oh." Pip patted Zach's shoulder to bring him into the conversation. "This is Zach Chen. He used to live in your house."

"Lovely to meet you, Zach," Flora said. "We love the house so much. Was yours the back bedroom?"

A hissing sound behind Pip distracted her for a moment. Connor's brother, Jamie, had appeared beside him, and they were talking to each other in hushed tones.

"No, it's not haunted," Charlie was saying as Pip tuned back in to the conversation.

"Flora?" Zach turned to her. "Haven't you heard the pipes groaning in the downstairs bathroom? It sounds like a ghost saying *ruuuuun, ruuuuun.*"

Flora's eyes widened suddenly, her face draining as she looked at her husband. She opened her mouth to reply but started to cough and, excusing herself, stepped back from the circle.

"Look what you've started." Charlie smiled. "She'll be best friends with the bathroom ghost by tomorrow."

Ravi's fingers walked down Pip's forearm, sliding back into her hand as he gave her a look. Yes, they should probably move on and find his parents; it would start soon.

They said goodbye and continued toward the front of the gathering. Looking back, Pip could have sworn the crowd had doubled since they'd arrived; there might be nearly a thousand people here now. Almost at the pavilion, Pip saw for the first time the blown-up photographs of Sal and Andie resting against easels on opposite sides of the small building. Matching smiles etched into their forever-young faces. People had laid bouquets of flowers in orbiting circles underneath each portrait, and the candles flickered as the crowd shuffled their feet.

"There they are," Ravi said, pointing. His parents were at the front, on the right, the side Sal looked out over. There was a group of people around them, and Pip's family was close by.

Pip and Ravi passed right behind Stanley Forbes taking photos of the scene, the flash of his camera lighting up his pale face and dancing across his dark brown hair.

"Of course *he's* here," Pip said out of earshot.

"Oh, leave him alone, Sarge." Ravi smiled back at her.

Months ago, Stanley had sent the Singhs a four-page handwritten letter of apology, telling them he was ashamed of the way he'd spoken about their son. He'd printed another, public apology in the small-town newspaper he volunteered at, the *Fairview Mail.* And he'd also led the charge on fundraising to get a bench dedicated to Sal on the common, just up the path from Andie's. Ravi and his parents had accepted his apology, but Pip was skeptical.

"At least he said sorry," Ravi continued. "Look at all of them." He nodded at the group around his parents. "Their friends, neighbors. People who made their life hell. They've never apologized, just pretended like the last six years never even happened."

Ravi cut off as Pip's dad folded them both into a hug.

"Doing OK?" he asked Ravi, patting him on the back before he let go.

"Doing OK," Ravi replied, tousling Josh's hair in greeting and smiling at Pip's mom.

Ravi's dad, Mohan, came over. "I'm going in now to get a few things ready. I'll see you after." He tapped Ravi affectionately under the chin. "Look after Mom." Mohan walked up the stairs of the pavilion and disappeared inside.

* * *

The memorial started at 7:31 exactly, Ravi standing between Pip and his mom, Nisha, holding both of their hands. Pip circled her thumb in his palm as the town's first selectman, who'd helped organize the memorial, stepped up to the microphone at the top of the stairs to say "a few words." Well, he said far more than a few, going on about family values in the town and the *inevitability of truth,* praising the Fairview Police Department for all their "tireless work on this case." He wasn't even trying to be sarcastic.

Next up was Mrs. Morgan, now the principal of Fairview High School. Her predecessor had been forced by the board to resign early, in the fallout from everything Elliot Ward had done while working at the school. Mrs. Morgan spoke about Andie and Sal in turn, about the lasting impact their stories would have on the whole town.

Then Andie's best friends, Chloe Burch and Emma Hutton, walked out of the pavilion and up to the microphone. Clearly Jason and Dawn Bell had declined to speak at the vigil. Chloe and Emma did a joint reading, from Christina Rossetti's poem "Goblin Market." When they were done, they rejoined the quietly murmuring crowd, Emma sniffing and dabbing at her eyes with her sleeve. Pip was watching Emma when someone behind her bumped her elbow.

She turned. It was Jamie Reynolds, shuffling slowly through the crowd, a determined look in his eyes. The candles lit up a sheen of sweat breaking across his face.

"Sorry," he muttered distractedly, like he didn't even recognize her.

"It's OK," Pip replied, following Jamie with her eyes until Mohan Singh walked out of the pavilion and cleared his throat at the microphone, silencing the common. Not a sound, except the wind in the trees. Ravi gripped tighter, his fingernails pressing half-moons into Pip's skin.

Mohan looked down at the sheet of paper in his hand. He was shaking, the page fluttering in his grip.

"What can I tell you about my son Sal?" he started, a crack halfway through his voice. "I could tell you he was a straight-A student with a bright future ahead of him, but you probably already know that. I could tell you he was a loyal and caring friend who never wanted anyone to feel alone or unwanted, but you probably already know that too. I could tell you he was an incredible big brother and an amazing son who made us proud every day. I could share memories of him, as a grinning toddler who wanted to climb everything, as a teenager who loved early mornings and late nights. But instead, I will tell you just one thing about Sal."

Mohan paused, looked up to smile at Ravi and Nisha.

"If Sal were here today, he'd never admit to this and would probably be thoroughly embarrassed, but his favorite movie of all time, from age three to eighteen, was *Babe.*"

There was a light and tense laugh from the crowd. Ravi too, eyes starting to glaze.

"He loved that little pig. Another reason he loved the film was because it contained his favorite song. The one that could make him smile and cry, the one that made him want to dance. So I'm going to share a little of Sal and play that song for you now to celebrate his life, as we light and release the lanterns. But first, there's something I want to tell my boy, something I've waited six years to say out loud." The page quivered against the microphone like paper wings as Mohan wiped his eyes. "Sal. I'm sorry. I love you. You will never be truly gone; I will carry you with me through every moment. The big moments and the small, every smile, every laugh, every up and every down. I promise." He paused, nodded at someone off to the right. "Take it away."

From the speakers set up on both sides, the super-high-pitched voice of a mouse exclaimed: "And a one, and a two, and a three, hit it!"

The song started, a steady drum and the climbing melody sung by a squeaky mouse, until a whole chorus of other mice joined in.

Ravi was laughing now, and crying, and something between the two. And somewhere, behind them, someone started clapping in time to the song.

Now a few more.

Pip watched over her shoulder as the clapping caught on, passing up and down as it swelled through the swaying crowd. The sound was thunderous and happy.

People started singing along with the shrill mice, and—as they realized it was just the same few lyrics repeated—others joined in, struggling to hit those impossibly high notes.

Ravi turned to Pip, mouthing the words, and she mouthed them back.

Mohan walked down the steps, the page in his hand replaced with a Chinese lantern. The selectman carried another lantern down, passing it to Jason and Dawn Bell. Pip let Ravi go as he joined his mom and dad. Ravi was handed a small box of matches. The first one he struck was blown into a thin line of smoke by the wind. He tried again, sheltering the flame with his cupped hand, holding it under the lantern's wick until it caught.

The Singhs waited a few seconds for the fire to grow, filling the lantern with hot air. They each had two hands on the wire rim at the bottom, and when they were ready, when they were finally ready, they straightened up, arms above their heads, and let go.

The lantern sailed up above the pavilion, juddering in the breeze. Pip craned her neck to watch it go, its yellow-orange flicker setting the darkness around it on fire. A moment later, Andie's lantern crossed into view too, mounting the night as it chased Sal's across the endless sky.

Pip didn't look away. Her neck strained, sending stabs of pain down her spine, but she refused to look away. Not until those golden lanterns were little more than specks, nestling among the stars. And even beyond that.

SATURDAY

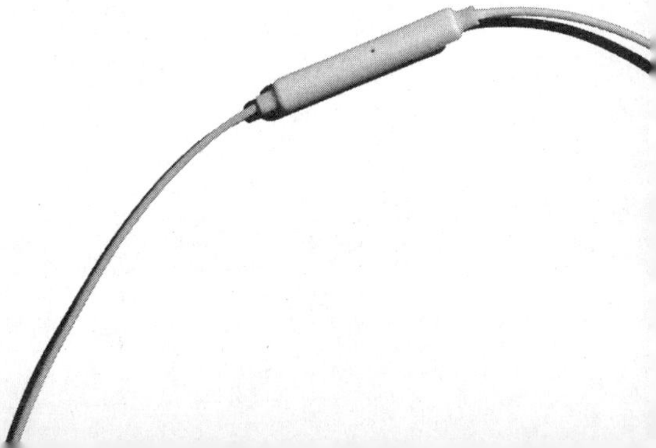

FOUR

Pip tried to fight them, her sinking eyelids. She felt fuzzy around the edges, ill-defined, like sleep had already taken her, but no . . . she really should get up off the sofa and do some revision. *Really.*

She was lying on the red sofa in the living room, in *Josh's Place* apparently, as he kept intermittently reminding her. He was on the rug, rearranging Legos while *Toy Story* played in the background. Her parents must still be out in the yard; her dad had enthusiastically told her this morning that they were painting the new shed today. Well, there wasn't much her dad *wasn't* enthusiastic about. But the only thing Pip could think of was the stalk of the solitary sunflower planted near there, over their dead dog's grave. It hadn't yet bloomed.

Pip checked her phone. It was 5:11 p.m. and there was a text waiting on the screen from Cara, and two missed calls from Connor twenty minutes ago; she must have actually fallen asleep for a bit. She swiped to open Cara's message: *Urgh, been throwing up literally all day and Grandma keeps trying to make me eat chicken soup. NEVER AGAIN. Thank you so much for coming to get me xx*

Cara's previous text, when Pip scrolled up, had been sent at 12:04 last night: *Polpp whertf ui i I traifng finds anfulpw ggind hekp me safd.*

Pip had called her immediately, whispering from her bed, but Cara was so drunk she couldn't speak in full sentences, not even half sentences or quarter, broken up by cries or hiccups. It took some time to understand where she was: a calamity party. She must have gone there after the memorial. It took even longer to coax out whose house the party was at: "Stephen Thompson's . . . I—I think." And where that was: "Hi-Highmoor somewhere . . ."

Pip knew Ant and Lauren were at that party too; they should have been looking out for Cara. But, of course, Ant and Lauren were probably too preoccupied with each other. And that wasn't even what worried Pip most. "Did you pour your own drinks?" she'd asked. "You didn't accept a drink from someone, did you?" So she had climbed out of bed and into her car, to "Highmoor somewhere" to find Cara and take her home. She didn't get back into bed until after one-thirty.

And today hadn't even been quiet to make up for it. Pip had taken Josh to soccer in the morning and stood in a cold field to watch the game, then Ravi came over at lunch to record another update on the Max Hastings trial. Afterward, Pip had edited and uploaded the mini-episode, updated her website, and replied to emails. So she'd sat down on the sofa for two minutes, in *Josh's Place,* just to rest her eyes. But two minutes had somehow become twenty-two, sneaking up on her.

She stretched out her neck and held up her phone to text Connor, when the doorbell rang.

"For God's sake," Pip said, getting up. One of her legs was still asleep and she stumbled over it, into the hallway. "How many frickin' Amazon deliveries does one man need?" Her dad had a serious next-day-delivery addiction.

She undid the security chain on the front door—a new rule in their house—and pulled it open.

"Pip!"

It wasn't the Amazon delivery guy.

"Oh, Connor, hey," she said, fully opening the door. "I was literally just texting you. What's up?"

It was only then that she noticed his eyes: the way they somehow looked both far off and urgent, too much white showing above and below the blue. And even though Connor had a pink-cheeked, freckle-faced complexion, his face was flushed red, a line of sweat trickling down his temple.

"Are you OK?"

He took a deep breath. "No, I'm not." His words cracked at the edges.

"What's wrong . . . do you want to come in?" Pip stepped back to clear the threshold.

"Th-thank you," Connor said, stepping past Pip as she shut and locked the door. His T-shirt was sticking to his back, damp and bunched up.

"Here." Pip led him into the kitchen and pointed him to one of the stools, her sneakers discarded beneath it. "Do you want some water?" She didn't wait for him to answer, filling up one of the clean glasses on the draining board and placing it in front of him with a thud that made him flinch. "Did you run here?"

"Yeah." Connor picked up the glass with both hands and took a large gulp that spilled water over his chin. "Sorry. I tried to call you and you didn't answer and I didn't know what to do other than just come here. And then I thought you might be at Ravi's instead."

"That's OK. I'm right here," Pip said, sliding onto the seat opposite him. Connor's eyes still looked strange and Pip's heart reacted, kicking around her chest. "What is it? What do you need to speak to me about?" She gripped the edges of her stool. "Has . . . has something happened?"

“Yes,” Connor said, wiping his chin on his wrist. He parted his lips and his jaw hung open and closed, chewing the air like he was practicing the words before he said them.

“Connor, what?”

“It’s my brother,” he said. “He . . . he’s missing.”

FIVE

Pip watched Connor's fingers as they slipped down the glass.

"Jamie's missing?" she said.

"Yes." Connor stared at her.

"When?" she asked. "When did you last see him?"

"At the memorial." Connor paused to take another gulp of water. "I last saw him at the memorial, just before it started. He never came home."

Pip's breath caught. "I saw him there after that. Maybe around eight, eight-fifteen. He was walking through the crowd." She pulled up the memory, unpicked it from everything else last night. Jamie knocking into her as he made his way to the other side of the crowd, his hurried apology, the way his jaw was set, determined. She'd thought it strange at the time, hadn't she? And the look in his eyes, not unlike Connor's now: somehow both distant and sharp. They looked very similar, even for brothers. They hadn't as kids, but Pip had watched it happen over the years, the gap closing. Jamie's hair was a couple of shades darker, closer to brown than blond. And Connor was all angles where Jamie was heavier, softer. But even a stranger could tell they were brothers. "Have you tried calling him?"

"Yes, hundreds of times," said Connor. "It goes straight to voice mail like it's off or . . . or it's dead." He stumbled over that last word, his head hanging between his shoulders. "Me and Mom spent hours calling anyone who might know where he is: friends, family. No one has seen him or heard from him. No one."

Pip felt something stirring, right in that pit in her stomach that never quite left her anymore. "Have you called all the local hospitals to see whether—"

"Yes, we called them all. Nothing."

Pip awakened her phone to check the time. It was five-thirty now, and if Jamie hadn't been seen since around eight last night, seen by *her,* that meant he'd been missing for over twenty-one hours already.

"OK," she said firmly, bringing Connor's eyes back to hers, "your parents need to go to the police station and file a missing persons report. You'll need—"

"We already did," Connor said, a hint of impatience creeping into his voice. "Me and my mom went down to the station a few hours ago, filed the report, gave them a recent photograph, all that. It was Nat da Silva's brother, Daniel, the officer who took the report."

"OK, good, so officers should be—"

Connor cut her off again. "No," he said. "No officers are doing anything. Daniel said that because Jamie is twenty-four, an adult, and has a history of leaving home without communicating with his family, there is very little the police can do."

"What?"

"Yeah, he gave us a reference number and just told us to keep calling Jamie's phone and anyone he's been known to stay with before. Said that almost all missing people return within forty-eight hours, so we just have to wait."

The stool creaked as Pip shifted. "They must think he's low risk. When a missing persons report is filed," she explained, "the police determine a risk assessment based on factors like age, any medical issues, whether the behavior is out of character, things like that. Then the police response depends on whether they think the case is low, medium, or high risk."

"I know how it might look to them," Connor said, the look in his eyes a little less far away now, "that Jamie's disappeared a couple of times before and he always comes back—"

"The first time was after he dropped out of college, wasn't it?" Pip said, scratching at the memory, how the air had been thick with tension in the Reynoldses' house for weeks after.

Connor nodded. "Yeah, after he and my dad had a huge argument about it, he stayed with a friend for a week and wouldn't answer any calls or texts. And it was two years ago when Mom actually filed a report because Jamie never returned from a night out in New York. He'd lost his phone and wallet and couldn't get home, so he just stayed on someone's couch for a couple of days. But . . ." Connor sniffed, wiping his nose on the back of his hand. "But something feels different this time. I think he's in trouble, Pip, I really do."

"Why?" she asked.

"He's been acting strange the last few weeks. Distant, kind of jumpy. Short-tempered. And you know Jamie, he's normally really chilled out. Well, lazy, if you ask my dad. But recently, he's seemed, at times, a little off."

And wasn't that how he had seemed last night when he knocked into Pip? That strange focus, like he could see nothing else, not even her. And why was he moving through the crowd right then, anyway? Wasn't that a little off?

"And," Connor continued, "I don't think he'd run off again, not after how upset Mom got last time. Jamie wouldn't do that to her again."

"I . . . ," Pip began. But she didn't really know what to say to him.

"So me and Mom were talking," Connor said, shoulders contracting like he was shrinking in on himself. "If the police won't investigate, won't contact the media or anything, then what can we do ourselves, to find Jamie? That's what I wanted to talk to you about, Pip."

She knew what was coming, but Connor didn't pause long enough for her to cut in.

"You know how to do this; everything you did last year where the police failed. You solved a murder. Two of them. And your podcast"—he swallowed—"hundreds of thousands of followers; that's probably more effective than any media connections the police have. If we want to find Jamie, spread the word that he's missing so people can come forward with any information they have, or sightings, you are our best hope of that."

"Connor—"

"If you investigate and release it on your show, I know we'll find him. We'll find him in time. We have to."

Connor trailed off. The silence that followed was alive and teeming; Pip could feel it crawling around her. She knew what he'd been about to ask. How could it have been anything else? She breathed out, and that thing that lived inside her twisted in her gut. But her answer was inevitable.

"I'm sorry," she said quietly. "I can't do it, Connor."

Connor's eyes widened, and he grew back out of his shoulders. "I know it's a lot to ask, but—"

"It's too much to ask," Pip said, glancing out the window, checking that her parents were still busy in the yard. "I don't do that anymore."

"I know, but—"

"Last time I almost lost everything: I ended up in the hospital, got my dog killed, put my family in danger, destroyed my best friend's life. It's too much to ask. I promised myself. I . . . I can't do it anymore." The pit in her stomach ripped wider still; soon it might even outgrow her. "I can't do it. It's not who I am."

"Pip, please . . ." He was begging now, words catching on their way up his throat. "Last time you didn't even really know them, they were already gone. This is Jamie, Pip. *Jamie.* What if he's hurt? What if he doesn't make it? I don't know what to do." Connor's voice finally cracked as the tears broke the surface of his eyes.

"I'm sorry, Connor, I am," Pip said, though the words hurt her to say. "But I have to say no."

"You aren't going to help?" He sniffed. "At all?"

She couldn't do it. She couldn't.

"I didn't say that." Pip jumped down from her stool to hand Connor a tissue. "As you can probably guess, I have a certain relationship with the local police now. I mean, I don't think I'm their favorite person, but I probably have some sway in matters like this." She scooped up her car keys from beside the microwave. "I'll go talk to Detective Hawkins right now, tell him about Jamie and why you're worried, see whether I can get them to rethink their risk assessment so that they'll actually investigate."

Connor slid from his stool. "Really? You'll do that?"

"Of course," she said. "I can't promise anything, but Hawkins is a good guy, really. Hopefully he sees sense."

"Thank you," Connor said, wrapping his awkward and angular arms around her quickly. His voice lowered. "I'm scared, Pip."

"It's going to be OK." She attempted a smile. "I'll give you a lift home on my way. Come on."

Stepping out into the early evening, the front door got caught in a cross breeze and slammed loudly behind them. Pip carried the sound with her, inside her, echoing around that hollow growing in her gut.

SIX

The russet-brick building was just starting to lose its edges to the gray evening sky as Pip climbed out of her small car. The white sign on the wall read "Fairview Police Station."

Pip walked through the main door into the blue-painted reception area. There was just one man waiting inside, asleep on one of the hard metal chairs against the back wall. Pip strode up to the desk and knocked on the glass, to get someone's attention in the attached office. The sleeping man snorted and shuffled into a new position.

"Hello?" The voice emerged before its owner did: the detention officer Pip had met a couple of times. The officer strolled out, slapping some papers down and then finally looking at Pip. "Oh, you're not who I was expecting."

"Sorry." Pip smiled. "How are you, Eliza?"

"I'm OK, love." Her kindly face crinkled into a smile, gray hair bunching at the collar of her uniform. "What brings you here this time?"

Pip liked Eliza, liked that neither of them had to pretend or dance around small talk.

"I need to talk to Detective Hawkins," she said. "Is he here?"

"He is right now." Eliza chewed her pen. "He's very busy, though. Looking to be a long night."

"Can you tell him it's urgent? Please," Pip added.

"Fine, see what I can do," Eliza sighed. "Take a seat, sweetheart," she said as she disappeared back into the office.

But Pip didn't take a seat. Her body didn't know how to be still right now. So she paced the width of the front desk, six steps, turn, six steps back, daring the squeak of her sneakers to wake the sleeping man.

The keypad-locked door leading to the offices and interview rooms buzzed open, but it wasn't Eliza or Richard Hawkins who emerged. It was two uniformed officers. Out first was Daniel da Silva, holding the door for another officer, Soraya Bouzidi, who was tying her tightly curled hair into a bun beneath her black peaked hat. Pip had first met them both at the police meeting in Fairview Town Hall last October, back when Daniel da Silva was a person of interest in Andie's case. Judging by the strained, tight-lipped smile he gave her now as he passed, he clearly hadn't forgotten that.

Soraya acknowledged Pip, throwing her a nod and a bright "Hello" before following Daniel outside to one of the patrol cars. Pip wondered where they were going and what had called them out. Whatever it was, they must think it more important than Jamie Reynolds.

The door buzzed again, but only opened a few inches. A hand was all that appeared through it, holding up two fingers toward Pip.

"You've got two minutes," Hawkins called, beckoning her to follow him down the corridor. She hurried over, sneakers shrieking as she did, the sleeping man snorting awake behind her.

Hawkins didn't wait to say hello; he strode down the hall in front of her. He was dressed in black jeans and a new jacket, padded and dark green. Maybe he'd finally thrown out that long wool coat he always wore when he was lead investigator on Andie Bell's disappearance.

"I'm on my way out," he said suddenly, opening the door to Interview Room 1 and gesturing her inside. "So I mean it when I say two minutes. What is it?" He closed the door behind them and leaned against it with one leg up.

Pip straightened and crossed her arms. "Missing person," she said. "Jamie Reynolds from Fairview. Case number four nine zero zero—"

"Yeah, I saw the report," Hawkins interrupted. "What about it?"

"Why aren't you doing anything about it?"

That caught him off guard. Hawkins made a sound somewhere between a laugh and a throat-clear, rubbing his hand across his stubbled chin. "I'm sure you know how it works, Pip. I won't patronize you by explaining."

"Jamie shouldn't be filed as low risk," she said. "His family believes he's in serious trouble."

"Well, family hunches aren't one of the criteria we trust in serious police work."

"And what about my hunches?" Pip said, refusing to let go of his eyes. "Do you trust those? I've known Jamie since I was nine. I saw him at Andie and Sal's memorial before he disappeared, and something definitely felt off."

"I was there," Hawkins said. "It was very emotionally charged. I'm not surprised if people weren't acting quite like themselves."

"That's not what I mean."

"Look, Pip," he sighed, dropping his leg and peeling away from the door. "Do you know how many missing persons reports we get every single day? Sometimes as many as twelve. We don't have the time or resources to chase up every single one. Especially not with all these budget cuts. Most people return on their own within forty-eight hours. We have to prioritize."

"So prioritize Jamie," she said. "Trust me. Something's wrong."

"I can't do that." Hawkins shook his head. "Jamie is an adult, and even his own mother admitted this isn't out of character. Adults have a legal right to disappear if they want to. Jamie Reynolds isn't missing;

he's just absent. He'll be fine. And if he chooses to, he'll be back in a few days."

"What if you're wrong?" Pip asked, knowing she was losing him. She couldn't lose him. "What if you're missing something, like with Sal? What if you're wrong again?"

Hawkins winced. "I'm sorry," he said. "I wish I could help, but I really have to go. We've got an actual high-risk case: an eight-year-old abducted from her backyard. There's nothing I can do for Jamie. It's the way it is, unfortunately." He reached for the door handle.

"Please," Pip said, the desperation in her voice surprising them both. "Please, I'm begging you."

His fingers stalled. "I'm—"

"Please." Her throat clenched like it did before she cried, breaking her voice into a million little pieces. "Don't make me do this again. Please. I can't do this again."

Hawkins wouldn't look at her, he just tightened his grip around the handle. "I'm sorry, Pip. My hands are tied. There's nothing I can do."

Outside, Pip stopped in the middle of the parking lot and looked up into the sky, clouds hiding the stars from her, hoarding them for themselves. It had just started to rain, cold droplets that stung as they fell into her open eyes. She stood there a while, watching the endless nothingness of the sky, trying to listen to what her gut was telling her. She closed her eyes to hear it better. *What do I do? Tell me what to do.*

She began to shiver and climbed into her car, wringing the rain from her hair. The sky had given her no answers. But there was someone who might, someone who knew her better than she knew herself. She pulled out her phone and dialed.

"Ravi?"

"Hello, trouble." The smile was obvious in his voice. "Have you been sleeping? You sound strange."

She told him; told him everything. Asked for help because he was the only one she knew how to ask.

"I can't tell you what to decide," he said.

"But could you?"

"No, I can't make that decision for you. Only you know, only you can know," he said. "But what I do know is that whatever you decide will be the right thing. That's just how you are. And whatever you choose, you know I'll be here, right behind you. Always. OK?"

"OK."

And as Pip said goodbye, she realized the decision was already made. Maybe it had always been made, maybe she'd never really had a choice and she'd just been waiting for someone to tell her that that was OK.

It was OK.

She searched for Connor's name and clicked the call button, her heart dragging its way to her throat.

He picked up on the second ring.

"I'll do it," she said.

SEVEN

The Reynoldses' house on Cedar Way had always looked like a face. The white front door and the wide windows on either side were the house's toothy smile. The mark where the bricks were discolored, that was its nose. And the two square windows upstairs were its eyes, staring down at you, sleeping when the curtains were closed at night.

The face usually looked happy. But as Pip stared at it now, it felt incomplete, like the house itself knew something inside was wrong.

Pip knocked, her heavy backpack digging into one shoulder.

"You're here already?" Connor said when he opened the door, moving aside to let her in.

"Yep, stopped by home to pick up my equipment and came straight here. Every second counts with something like this."

Pip paused to slip her shoes off, almost overbalancing when her bag shifted. "Oh, and if my mom asks, you fed me dinner, OK?"

Pip hadn't told her parents yet. She knew she'd have to, later. Their families were close, ever since Connor asked Pip over for a playdate in third grade. And her mom had seen a lot of Jamie recently; he'd been working at her real estate agency the past couple of months. But even so, Pip knew it would be a battle. Her mom would remind her how dangerously obsessed she got last time—as if she needed reminding—and tell her she should be studying instead. There just wasn't time for that argument now. The first seventy-two hours were crucial when someone went missing, and they'd lost twenty-three already.

"Pip?" Connor's mom, Joanna, had appeared in the hallway. Her fair hair was piled on top of her head and she looked somehow older in just one day.

"Hi, Joanna." That was the rule, always had been: Joanna, never Mrs. Reynolds.

"Pip, thank you for . . . for . . . ," she said, trying on a smile that didn't quite fit. "Connor and I had no idea what to do, and we just knew you were the person to go to. Connor says you had no luck trying again with the police?"

"No, I'm sorry," Pip said, following Joanna into the kitchen. "I tried, but they won't budge."

"They don't believe us," Joanna said, opening one of the top cupboards. It wasn't a question. "Tea?" But that was.

"No, thank you." Pip dropped her bag onto the kitchen table. She rarely drank tea anymore, not since the opening night of the town's winter carnival last year when Becca Bell had slipped Andie's remaining Rohypnol pills into Pip's cup. "Shall we get started in here?" she said, hovering beside a chair.

"Yes," Joanna said, losing her hands in the folds of her oversized sweater. "Best do it in here."

Pip settled into a chair, Connor taking the one beside her as she unzipped her bag and pulled out her computer, the two USB microphones and pop filters, the folder, a pen, and her bulky headphones. Joanna finally sat down, though she couldn't seem to keep still, shifting every few seconds and changing the position of her arms.

"Is your dad here? Your sister?" Pip directed the questions at Connor, but Joanna was the one who answered.

"Zoe's at college. I called her, told her Jamie's missing, but she's staying there. She seems to have come down on her father's side of things."

"What do you mean?"

"Arthur is . . ." Joanna exchanged a quick look with Connor. "Arthur doesn't think Jamie's missing, thinks he's just run off again and will be back soon. He seems very angry with the whole thing—with Jamie." She shifted again, scratching at a point just under her eye. "He thinks Connor and I are being ridiculous with all this—" She gestured to Pip's equipment. "He's gone to the supermarket, but he'll probably be back soon."

"OK," Pip said, making a mental note, trying to betray nothing with her face. "Do you think he'll talk to me?"

"No," Connor said firmly. "No point even asking."

The atmosphere in the room was tight and uncomfortable, and Pip's armpits prickled with sweat. "OK, before we do anything, I need to speak honestly with you both, give you . . . I guess, a kind of disclaimer."

They nodded, eyes wholly focused now.

"If you're asking me to investigate, to help find Jamie, we have to agree up front where this could potentially take us, and you need to be happy to accept that or I can't do it." Pip cleared her throat. "It might lead us to potentially unsavory things about Jamie, secrets he might have kept from you and wouldn't want exposed. I agree that releasing the investigation on my podcast is the fastest way to get media attention for Jamie's disappearance, bring in witnesses who might know something. It might convince the police to actually investigate. Or it might even get Jamie's attention if he really has just left, and bring him back. But with that, you have to accept that your private lives will be laid bare. Nothing will be off limits, and that can be hard to deal with." Pip knew that better than most.

The anonymous death and rape threats still came in weekly, comments and tweets calling her an ugly, hateful bitch. "Jamie isn't here to agree to this, so you need to accept, for him and for yourselves, that you're opening up your lives to be scrutinized, and it's possible you'll learn things you never would have wanted to know. That's what happened last time, so I . . . I just want to check you're ready for that. . . ." Pip trailed into silence, her throat dry, wishing she'd asked for a glass of water instead.

"I accept," Joanna said, her voice growing with each syllable. "Anything. Anything to get him home."

Connor nodded. "I agree. We have to find him."

"OK, good," Pip said, though she couldn't help but wonder whether the Reynoldses had just given her permission to blow up their family, like she had with the Wards and the Bells. They'd come to her, invited her in, but they didn't really understand the destruction that came in with her, hand in hand through that front door, which looked like a smile.

It was just then that the front door opened, heavy footsteps on the carpet, the rustling of a plastic bag.

Joanna jumped up, her chair screeching against the tiles.

"Jamie?" she shouted, running toward the hallway. "Jamie?"

"Just me," said a male voice. Not Jamie, and Joanna immediately deflated, like she'd just halved in size, holding on to the wall to keep the rest of her from disappearing too.

Arthur Reynolds walked into the kitchen, curly red hair with wisps of gray around the ears, a thick mustache that peppered out into well-trimmed stubble. His pale blue eyes looked almost colorless in the bright LEDs.

"Got more bread and—" Arthur broke off, his shoulders slumping as soon as he spotted Pip, laptop and microphones in front of her. "For God's sake, Joanna," he said. "This is ridiculous." He dropped the shopping bag on the floor and a can of plum tomatoes rolled under the table. "I'm going to watch TV," he said, marching out of the kitchen and into the living room. The door slammed behind him, ricocheting through Pip's bones. Of all her friends' dads, she would have said Connor's was the scariest. Maybe Ant's. But Cara's dad would have been the least, and look how that turned out.

"I'm sorry, Pip." Joanna came back to the table, picking up the lonely can on her way. "I'm sure he'll come round. Eventually."

"Should I . . . ," Pip began. "Should I be here?"

"Yes," Joanna said firmly. "Finding Jamie is more important than my husband's anger."

"Are you—"

"I'm sure," she said.

"All right." Pip unclipped a green folder and pulled out two sheets of paper. "I need you to sign release forms before we begin."

She handed Connor her pen, while Joanna fetched one from the counter. As they read through the forms, Pip reawakened her laptop, opened up Audacity and plugged in the USB microphones, then readjusted the foam pop filters over them.

Connor signed his name, and the microphones came alive, picking up the scratching of his pen, the blue sound wave spiking from the center line.

"Joanna, I'll interview you first, if that's OK?" Pip said.

"Sure." Joanna handed her the signed form.

Pip shot Connor a quick, close-lipped smile. He blinked vacantly back at her, not understanding the signal.

"Connor," she said gently, "you have to leave. Witnesses must be interviewed separately so they aren't influenced by anyone else's account."

"Right. Got it," he said, standing up. "I'll go upstairs, keep trying Jamie's phone."

He closed the kitchen door behind him, and Pip adjusted the microphones, placing one in front of Joanna.

"I'm going to ask you questions about yesterday," said Pip, "try to create a timeline of Jamie's day. But I'll also ask about Jamie in recent weeks, in case anything is relevant. Just answer as truthfully as you can."

"OK."

"Are you ready?"

Joanna breathed out, nodded. Pip slipped her headphones on, securing them around her ears, and guided the on-screen arrow toward the red record button.

The cursor lingered over it.

Pip wondered.

Wondered whether the moment of no return had already been and gone, or whether this was it, here, right now, hovering above that red button. Either way, going back didn't exist anymore, not for her. There was only forward. Only onward. She straightened up and pressed record.

File Name:

A Good Girl's Guide to Murder SEASON 2: Interview with Joanna Reynolds.wav

PIP: OK, before we get into the questions, Joanna, could you introduce yourself and Jamie a little?

JOANNA: OF COURSE, MY NAME IS—

PIP: Sorry, Joanna, you don't need to speak directly into the microphone. It picks you up just fine if you sit normally.

JOANNA: Sorry. My name is Joanna Reynolds. I'm Jamie's mom. I have three children, Jamie is the oldest, my first. He just turned twenty-four—his birthday was last week. We celebrated here, had Chinese takeout and a red velvet cake. Connor just managed to fit twenty-four candles on it. Oh, sorry, my other children: my daughter, Zoe, she's twenty-one, at college. And Connor, he's my baby, eighteen and in his last year of school. Sorry, that was terrible, should I try it again?

PIP: No, that's OK, it was perfect. This is just a raw interview; I'll edit all of this with sections of me talking and explaining in between so you don't need to worry about consistency or sounding polished or anything.

JOANNA: OK.

PIP: And some things I obviously already know the answer to, but I have to ask so we can present all the information in the episode. Like for example, I'm going to ask you: Does Jamie still live at home?

JOANNA: I understand. OK. Yes, Jamie still lives at home with me and my husband, Arthur, and my younger son, Connor.

PIP: And does he have a job currently?

JOANNA: Yes, you know he works with your mom, Pip.

PIP: I know, I just need you to say—

JOANNA: Oh, sorry, I forgot. Let me try again. Yes, Jamie is currently working part-time as a receptionist at a local real estate agency, Proctor and Radcliffe Homes. He's been there for almost three months now. It was very kind of your mom to give him the job, Pip; I'm very grateful. Since dropping out of college in his freshman year, Jamie's been struggling to find a job or keep the ones he does get. He's been a little lost the last couple of years, can't decide what he wants to do or what he's good at. We've tried helping him, but with Jamie, the more you push him toward something, the more he pulls away from it. That's why Arthur gets so frustrated with him. But I'm glad Jamie seems to be enjoying his job, at least for now.

PIP: And would you say Jamie struggles to commit to things? Is that why he dropped out of college?

JOANNA: Yes, I think that's part of the problem. He tried, he really did, but he found the pressure too much and just shut down, had a panic attack during one of his exams. I think some people just aren't made for that sort of academic environment. Jamie . . . he's a very sensitive boy . . . man. I mean, you know him, Pip. Arthur worries that he's oversensitive, but he's been like this since he was a child. A very sweet little boy, all the other mothers used to say so.

PIP: Yeah, he's only ever been nice to me; he was never Connor's scary older brother or anything. And everyone else seems to like him. Speaking of, who are Jamie's closest friends? Any in Fairview?

JOANNA: He still occasionally talks to one guy from college and I think he might have some internet friends too, he's always on that computer. Jamie's never been too good at friends; he makes fierce one-on-one friendships and falls in deep, so he's always devastated when they don't work out. I'd say his closest friend at the moment is Nat da Silva.

PIP: I know Nat.

JOANNA: Yes, of course. There's not many from their grade still living here in Fairview, apart from Naomi Ward and M-Max Hastings. Sorry, I shouldn't bring him up. But Nat and Jamie seem to have a lot in common. Nat also had issues at college and left early, and she's struggling to find a job she really wants because she's got a criminal record. I think they both feel left behind in this town, and it's nicer to be left behind with someone else. Everything that happened last year sort of brought them together too. Nat had been friendly with Sal Singh, and Jamie was friends with Andie Bell; he spent a lot of time with Andie during rehearsals for school plays. Jamie and Nat were just on the edge of everything that happened, and I think they bonded over it. They've become really close since last year, talk all the time. She's probably Jamie's only real friend at the moment. Though, truth be told, I think Jamie sees her in a different way from how she sees him.

PIP: What do you mean?

JOANNA: Well, oh god, Jamie is going to be furious I'm saying this. But I did agree nothing was off limits. . . . I know my son very well and he's never been good at hiding his feelings. I could always tell, by the way he talked about Nat, how he kept finding ways to bring her up in every single conversation, that he was enamored with her. Smitten. They spoke on the phone almost every day, always texting. But, of course, things were different after Nat got a new boyfriend a couple of months ago. I don't think Jamie ever mentioned the guy's name, but he was devastated. I found him crying in his room; he said it was because he had a stomachache, but I knew. It wasn't the first time I'd seen him like that. I knew it was because his heart was broken, and it was probably about Nat.

PIP: How long ago was this?

JOANNA: Must have been early March. There were a couple of weeks without much contact, I think. But they're still friends; in fact Jamie's always on his phone texting and it must be with Nat because he jumps up so none of us can see. I can hear him up late sometimes too, on the phone. By his voice, I can tell it's Nat he's talking to.

PIP: OK, thank you, I'll certainly talk to Nat as soon as I can. So Connor said to me that he's more worried about Jamie this time because he's been acting strangely the past few weeks, distant and short-tempered. Have you noticed the same thing?

JOANNA: He hasn't been quite himself the past couple of weeks. Up late, coming in at all hours, oversleeping and almost missing work. Snapping at his brother when they normally get on so well. I think it's partly everything with Nat, but also, like I said, feeling like he's been left behind, watching all the people he went to school and college with starting successful careers, settling down with partners, moving out of their parents' houses. Jamie's very self-conscious; he's told me before he often feels worthless, never quite good enough. He's been struggling with his weight too over the past six months or so. I told him it doesn't matter as long as he is healthy and comfortable in his skin, but . . . well, you know how the world tries to make anyone over a certain size feel ashamed of that. I think Jamie's been unhappy the past few weeks because he's comparing himself to everyone else, feeling like he'll never catch up. But I know he will.

PIP: Sorry, Joanna, I don't want to ask this, but you don't think . . . you don't think he could be at risk of harming himself?

JOANNA: No, absolutely not. Jamie wouldn't do that to me, to his family. He wouldn't. That's not what this is, Pip. He's missing. He's not dead. And we will find him, wherever he is.

PIP: OK, I'm sorry. Let's move on. Jamie went missing yesterday, Friday evening. Can you talk me through what happened during the day?

JOANNA: Yes. I woke up around nine; my hours on Friday are late, I don't start till eleven. Arthur was already at work—he commutes—and Connor had already walked to school. But Jamie was still fast asleep. I told him he was going to be late for work and he left the house around twenty past nine, said he would grab breakfast from the café on the way. Then I went to work. Arthur left work early, to get home in time for the memorial. He texted around five that he was home. I left work soon after and stopped by the supermarket and got home maybe six or six-thirty. Did a quick turnaround and then the four of us left for the memorial.

PIP: What was Jamie wearing that evening? I can't remember.

JOANNA: He was wearing jeans and his favorite shirt: it's burgundy and collarless. Like the Peaky Blinders, Jamie always says.

PIP: Shoes?

JOANNA: Oh, um, his sneakers. White.

PIP: Brand?

JOANNA: Nike, I think.

PIP: Did you drive to the memorial?

JOANNA: Yes.

PIP: And was Jamie acting strangely before the memorial at all?

JOANNA: No, not really. He was quiet, but he was probably just thinking about Andie and Sal. Everyone was quiet, in fact. I think we had an almost silent car ride. And when we arrived at the pavilion, around seven, Connor went to find his friends, you guys. And Jamie left too, said he was going to stand with Nat during the memorial. That was the last I saw him.

PIP: I saw him after that. He did find Nat; he was with her and Naomi. And after that he came over to talk to Connor briefly. He seemed fine to me, both times. And then during the memorial, before Ravi's dad spoke, Jamie walked past and knocked into me from behind. He seemed distracted, maybe even nervous. I don't know what he saw that made him want to struggle through the crowd right in the middle of the ceremony. But it had to be something.

JOANNA: When was that?

PIP: Maybe ten past eight.

JOANNA: So now *you're* the last person to see him.

PIP: I guess I am, for now. Do you know whether Jamie had any plans for after the memorial?

JOANNA: No, I thought he'd go home. But today Connor told me that Jamie mentioned seeing Nat, or something.

PIP: OK, I'll get that from Connor firsthand. Where did you go after the memorial?

JOANNA: Arthur and I went out for dinner, to Bobby's Bar & Grill—you know, the place near town hall—with some friends:

the Lowes—Ant's parents—and the Davises and the Morgans, you know, Mrs. Morgan and her husband. The date had been in the diary for ages.

PIP: And when did you and Arthur get home?

JOANNA: Well, we actually came back separately. I was driving, so I didn't drink, but some of our party who weren't supposed to be drinking said they needed one after the memorial. I said I'd drop the Lowes and the Morgans home so they could drink. Of course, that meant the car was full, but Arthur didn't mind walking home; it isn't far.

PIP: What time did you leave the restaurant?

JOANNA: I think we all left just before eleven. Everyone was tired and it felt wrong staying out too late enjoying ourselves, after the memorial. The Lowes live in town, as you know, but the Morgans are out in Springdale and, as Arthur says, I'm terrible when it comes to chatting, so I didn't get back until twelve-fifteen at least. Connor and Arthur were there, in bed. But no Jamie. I texted him before I went to sleep. Look, I'll read what I said. "Going to bed now, sweetie, will you be home soon?" That was at 12:36. Look. It never delivered. It hasn't gone through.

PIP: The text still hasn't gone through?

JOANNA: No. That's bad, isn't it? His phone is still off and it must have already been off before 12:36 . . . or something, something bad . . .

PIP: Please don't get upset, Joanna. OK, let's stop there.

File Name:

A Good Girl's Guide to Murder SEASON 2: Interview with Connor Reynolds.wav

PIP: Recording. You need to stop chewing your nails, though, Connor. The mike's picking it up.

CONNOR: Sorry.

PIP: So I wanted to focus on a comment you made earlier, that Jamie had been acting strangely the past few weeks. Short-tempered and distant. Can you give me specific instances and dates?

CONNOR: Yeah, I'll try. It's been the past couple of months, really, that Jamie's mood has seemed kind of erratic. He was fine, just normal Jamie, and then at the start of March he seemed really miserable and quiet, would hardly talk to anyone. A "black cloud hanging over him," to use my mom's words.

PIP: Your mom seems to think Jamie was upset when Nat da Silva got a new boyfriend, as they'd been getting so close. Could that have explained Jamie's mood then?

CONNOR: Yeah, maybe, that probably matches up timewise. So he was like that a couple of weeks and then, suddenly, he was OK again, smiling and joking, spending a lot of time on his phone. We have a "no phones with Netflix" rule, otherwise Mom just goes on Facebook and we have to rewind when she misses stuff. But I noticed Jamie was always on his, and not just on Reddit; it looked like he was typing, talking to someone.

PIP: And he seemed to be in a good mood during this period?

CONNOR: Yeah, definitely. For like a week and a half, he was good. Chatty, smiley. Normal Jamie. And then he switched back again, just as suddenly. I know exactly which day it was, because we all went to see the new *Sonic the Hedgehog* movie, and we went on March 27. Before we left, Jamie comes out of his room and says he's not coming, and I could tell from his voice he was trying not to cry. But my dad told him he had to come because we'd already bought the tickets. They got into a fight about it, and in the end Jamie did come. I sat next to him, could see him crying during the film. He didn't think anyone could see, because it was dark.

PIP: Do you know why he was so upset?

CONNOR: No idea. He carried on like that for a few days, locking himself in his room straight after work. One night I asked him if he was OK, and he just said, "Yeah, fine," though we both knew he wasn't. Jamie and me, we've always told each other everything. Everything. Up until recently. I don't know what happened to us.

PIP: And after those few days?

CONNOR: Well, then he kind of went back to normal. He seemed happy, not like *happy* happy, but better than before. And he was on his phone the whole time. I just wanted us to be close again, to play around like we always used to, so one day when he was typing away on his phone, a few weeks ago, I ran past and grabbed it, saying, "Who're you texting, then?" It was just a joke. I was teasing; I wasn't going to look, and he always does it to me. But Jamie didn't take it like that. He snapped. Pushed me up against the wall until I dropped his phone. I was never going to actually look at it, it was just a joke. But when he had me up against the wall like that, it . . . it didn't feel like my brother anymore. He said sorry afterward, said something about privacy, but it was . . . you know, it felt wrong. And I've heard him, up really late on the phone, in fact almost every night the past two weeks or so. And a couple of times over the past week, I heard him sneak out of his room once Mom and Dad had gone to bed. I don't know where he went. He did that last week, on the night of his birthday. I heard him sneak out before midnight. I waited up, listening. He came back in around two and when I mentioned it the next morning he said I must've been hearing things. And I woke up randomly at three a.m. this Monday night—well, Tuesday morning, I guess. I'm pretty sure it was Jamie sneaking back in that woke me.

PIP: I see.

CONNOR: But this is not normal Jamie. You know him, Pip, he's usually so easygoing, calm. But now his mood is suddenly up and down. He's keeping secrets and sneaking out. Getting angry. Something's wrong, I know it. My mom showed you the text, right? She sent it to Jamie around twelve-thirty last night and it's still not delivered. His phone's been off since before then. Or broken.

PIP: Or out of battery?

CONNOR: No. It was almost fully charged. I know because when we were in the car, I asked Jamie the time and he showed me his screen. It was at 88 percent or something. It's a newish phone, it wouldn't die that quickly. And why would he turn it off when he was out and about? Doesn't make sense.

PIP: Yes, the text not delivering at that time certainly is significant.

CONNOR: What do you think it means?

PIP: I can't speculate until I know more.

CONNOR: It means he's in trouble, doesn't it? You just don't want to say it, that someone's hurt him. Or taken him.

PIP: Connor, we don't know anything yet. I'm not ruling anything out, but we can't settle on conclusions without any evidence; that's not how this works. Let's move on to yesterday. Can you talk me through your day, your interactions with Jamie? Anything significant?

CONNOR: Um.

PIP: What?

CONNOR: Well, there was something.

PIP: Connor . . . ?

CONNOR: You won't tell my mom, will you?

PIP: Remember what you asked of me? When I release this, it will go out to hundreds of thousands of people. Your mom is going to hear it, so whatever it is, you need to tell me and then you need to tell her.

CONNOR: Shit, yeah. It's just . . . OK, so Jamie and my mom, they get on really well. They always have. I guess you might call him a mama's boy; they just click. But Jamie and Dad have a tricky relationship. Jamie's said to me before that he thinks Dad hates him, that Dad's constantly disappointed by him. They don't really talk anything through, they just let things build up until they occasionally explode into big arguments. And then once that's done and the awkwardness has gone, they go back to normal and the cycle resets. Well . . . they had one of their big arguments yesterday.

PIP: When?

CONNOR: At, like, five-thirty. Mom was at the supermarket. The argument ended before she got back, so she doesn't know about it. I was listening from the stairs.

PIP: What was it about?

CONNOR: The usual things they fight about. Dad telling Jamie he needs to suck it up and sort his life out, that he and Mom won't always be there to pick up the pieces. Jamie said he was trying, that Dad never notices when he's trying because he presumes Jamie's going to fail anyway. I couldn't hear the whole fight, but I remember Dad saying something like, "We aren't a bank, we are your parents." I don't know what that was about. I guess maybe Dad brought up that he thinks Jamie should pay rent to still live here. Mom thinks that's ridiculous and would never allow it, but Dad's always going on about "How else will he learn?" The last thing they said to each other before Mom came back was . . .

PIP: What?

CONNOR: Dad said, "You're a waste of space." And Jamie said, "I know."

PIP: Is that why everyone was quiet on the drive to the memorial? Your mom picked up on it.

CONNOR: Yeah. Oh god, she's gonna be so upset when I tell her.

PIP: You should tell her tonight, after I'm gone.

CONNOR: I guess.

PIP: So, back to last night. You arrive at the memorial, and you go off to find our friends, and Jamie goes off to find Nat. But then Jamie comes up to you at one point. When Zach and I were talking to my new neighbors, Jamie came and spoke to you.

CONNOR: Yeah.

PIP: What did he say?

CONNOR: He apologized. Said sorry about the argument with Dad; he knows I hate it when they fight. And then he told me that after the memorial, he was going to go to Nat da Silva's house for a bit;

spend the evening with her. I think they thought it was only right, to be in the company of someone else who knew Sal and Andie. He said he'd be back home that night, though. And as he walked off, the last thing he said to me was, "See you later." I don't think he'd lie to my face like that, if he knew he wasn't coming back. But Mom and I called Nat this morning. Nat never saw Jamie after the memorial. She doesn't know where he is.

PIP: And where did you go, after the memorial?

CONNOR: Well, me and Zach didn't want to go to the calamity party with Ant and Lauren, because they ignore everyone else anyway, so I went back to Zach's and we . . . we played *Fortnite,* so now the world knows that, then. And later Zach dropped me off at home.

PIP: What time?

CONNOR: We left Zach's just after eleven-thirty, so I must have been back around twelve. I was tired and went straight to bed, didn't even brush my teeth. And Jamie never came back. I went to bed without a second thought about Jamie. It's so stupid, really, how you take things like that for granted. I was stupid. I thought he'd come home. He was supposed to come home. And now he's . . .

EIGHT

"Photos?"

"Yes, recent photos of him," Pip said, looking between the two of them, the large kitchen clock counting the silence. But the ticks felt far too slow, as though she were somehow moving faster than time. A feeling she hadn't had in a while, one she missed. "I'm guessing you don't have any photos of Jamie from the memorial, what he was wearing?"

"No," Joanna said, unlocking her phone and flicking through her photos. "But I did take lots on Jamie's birthday last Thursday."

"One where his face shows clearly?"

"Here, have a look." Joanna passed her phone across the table. "There's several if you scroll left."

Connor moved his chair closer to look over Pip's shoulder at the screen. The first photo showed Jamie on his own, on the other side of the kitchen table from where Pip now sat. His dark blond hair was pushed to the side and he was grinning, an overly wide grin that stretched into his rosy cheeks, as his chin glowed orange from the lit candles on the birthday cake below. In the next photo he was bent low over the cake, cheeks puffed out to blow and the flames stretching away to escape from him. Pip swiped. Now Jamie was looking down at the cake, a long gray knife in his hand with a red plastic band between handle and blade. He was sticking the point of the knife into the center of the cake, parting the creamy white frosting. Next photo and the first slice was cut, Jamie looking up, smiling directly at the camera. Then the cake was gone, replaced by a present in Jamie's hands, the silver-spotted wrapping paper half ripped off.

"Oh yeah," Connor snorted, "Jamie's face when he realized Dad bought him a Fitbit for his birthday."

It was true; Jamie's smile did seem tighter, more strained here. Pip swiped again, but next was a video that started to play as her thumb brushed against it. Connor was in the frame now, the two brothers together, Jamie's arm draped across Connor's shoulders. The frame was swaying slightly, rustling sounds of breathing behind it.

"Smile, boys," Joanna was saying through the phone.

"We are," Jamie mumbled, trying not to ruin his smile for the photo.

"What's it doing?" Joanna's voice asked.

"For God's sake," Connor said, "she's accidentally taking a damn video again. Aren't you?"

"Oh, Mom." Jamie laughed. "Again?"

"I'm not," Joanna's voice insisted. "I didn't press that, it's this stupid phone."

"Always the phone's fault, isn't it?"

Jamie and Connor looked at each other, their laughs spiking into high-pitched giggles as Joanna grew more insistent that she hadn't pressed that. Arthur's voice saying, "Let me see, Jo." Then Jamie tightened his arm around Connor's neck, bringing his little brother's head down to his chest, where he messed up his hair with his other hand, Connor protesting through giggles. The frame dropped and the video ended.

"Sorry," Pip said, noticing how Connor had tensed in his chair and Joanna's eyes were so full she'd dropped her gaze to the floor.

"Can you please email me all of these, Connor? And any other recent photos?"

He coughed. "Yep, will do."

"All right." Pip stood up, packing her laptop and microphones into her bag.

"Are you going?" asked Connor.

"One last thing to do before I go," she said. "I need to search Jamie's room. Is that OK?"

"Yes. Yes, of course," Joanna said, also standing up. "Can we come too?"

"Sure," Pip said, waiting for Connor to open the kitchen door and lead them upstairs. "Have you already looked through it?"

"Not really," Joanna said, following them up the stairs, tensing when she heard Arthur coughing in the living room. "I went in there earlier when we first realized he was gone. I took a quick look to see if he'd slept here last night and left early in the morning. But no, the curtains were still open. Jamie's not the sort of person who opens his curtains in the morning or makes his bed." They paused outside the door to Jamie's darkened bedroom, which was ajar. "Jamie's a little messy," she said gently.

"That's fine," Pip said, nodding for Connor to go ahead. He pushed open the door, the room full of dark shapes until Connor flicked on the light, and the shapes became an unmade bed, a cluttered desk under the window, and an open closet spewing clothes onto the floor, piles like islands against the sea-blue carpet.

Messy was one word for it.

"Can I, um . . . ?"

"Yeah, do whatever you have to. Right, Mom?" said Connor.

"Right," Joanna said quietly, staring around the place from which her son was most missing.

Pip made a beeline for the desk, stepping over and between the small mountains of T-shirts and boxers. She ran her finger over the lid of the closed laptop in the middle of the desk, over the Iron Man sticker peeling at the edges. Gently, she opened the lid and clicked the on button.

"Do either of you know Jamie's password?" she asked as the computer purred into life, the blue Windows log-in screen jumping up.

Connor shrugged and Joanna shook her head.

Pip bent down to type *password1* into the box.

Incorrect Password

12345678

Incorrect Password

"What was your first cat called?" asked Pip. "That ginger one?"

"Peter Pan," said Connor.

Pip tried it. Incorrect.

She'd entered it wrong three times and now the password hint popped up beneath. In it, Jamie had written: *Get off my computer, Con.*

Connor sniffed, reading it.

"It's really important we get in," Pip said. "Right now this is our strongest link to Jamie and what he's been up to."

"My maiden name?" Joanna said. "Try Murphy."

Incorrect Password

"Football team?" asked Pip.

"Patriots."

Incorrect. Even with numbers replacing some vowels and trying 1 and 2 at the end.

"Can you keep trying?" Joanna asked. "It won't lock you out?"

"No, there's no limit on Windows. But guessing the exact password with the correct placement of numbers and capitals is going to be tricky."

"Can't we get around it some way?" said Connor. "Like reset the computer?"

"If we reboot the system, we lose all the files," Pip explained. "And, most important, the cookies and saved passwords on his browser, for his email and social media accounts. Those are what we really need to get into. Any chance you know the password to the email account Jamie's Windows is linked to?"

"No, I'm sorry." Joanna's voice cracked. "I should know these things about him. Why don't I know these things? He needs me and I'm no help to him."

"It's OK." Pip turned to her. "His password could be anything. We'll keep trying until we get in. Or I could try to contact a computer expert who might be able to brute-force it."

Joanna seemed to shrink again, hugging her own shoulders.

"Joanna," said Pip, standing up, "why don't you try some passwords while I keep searching? Try to think of Jamie's favorite places, favorite foods, vacations you've been on, anything like that. And try variations of each one, lowercase, capitals, replacing letters with numbers, a one or two at the end."

"OK." Her face seemed to brighten, just a little, at having something to do.

Pip moved on, checking the two desk drawers on either side. One held pens and a very old, dried-up glue stick. The other, a pad of A4 paper and a faded folder labeled *College Semester 1.*

"Anything?" Connor asked.

Pip shook her head, dropping to her knees to lean across Joanna's legs so she could reach the trash can beneath the desk. She pulled it out. "Help me with this," she said to Connor, fishing out the contents one by one. An empty can of deodorant. A crumpled receipt. Pip unfolded it: it was for a chicken mayo sandwich on Tuesday the twenty-first at 2:23 p.m. from the Stop & Shop on Main Street. Beneath that was a Cheetos bag: flamin' hot flavor. Sticking to the grease on the outside of the bag was a small slip of lined paper. Pip unpeeled it and spread it open. Written on the paper in blue ballpoint pen were the words *Hillary F Weiseman left 11*

She held the paper up to Connor. "Is this Jamie's handwriting?" Connor nodded. "Hillary Weiseman," Pip said. "Do you know her?"

"No," Connor and Joanna said at the same time. "Never heard that name," Joanna added.

"Well, Jamie must know her. Looks like this note was recent."

"Yes," Joanna said, "we have a cleaner, comes every two weeks. She's coming on Wednesday, so everything in that wastepaper basket is from the last ten, eleven days."

"Let's look up this Hillary, she might know something about Jamie." Pip pulled out her phone. On the screen was a text from Cara: *Ready for stranger things soon??* Shit. Pip quickly fired back: *I'm so sorry, I can't tonight, I'm at Connor's house. Jamie's gone missing. I'll explain tomorrow. Sorry!* Pip pressed send and tried to ignore the guilt, clicking on the browser and bringing up whitepages.com. She typed in *Hillary F Weiseman* and *Connecticut* and searched.

"Bingo," she said when it came up. "We have a Hillary F. Weiseman who lives in Fairview, Connecticut. But wait, it's saying her age is eighty-plus and she has no current address. Hold on. . . ." Pip opened another tab and Googled the name along with *Fairview* and *obituary*. The first result from the *Fairview Mail* gave her the answer she was looking for. "No, that can't be the right Hillary. She died in 2008, age eighty-four. Must be someone else with that name. I'll look into it later."

Pip spread the scrap of paper between her fingers and took a photo of it with her phone.

"You think it's a clue?" Connor asked.

"Everything's a clue until we discount it," she replied.

There was just one last thing left in the trash: an empty brown paper bag, scrunched up into a ball.

"Connor, without disturbing anything too much, can you search the pockets of all of Jamie's clothes?"

"For what?"

"Anything." Pip crossed to the other side of the room. She stopped and looked at the bed with its blue-patterned duvet, and her foot nudged something on the floor. It was a mug, the sugar-encrusted remains of coffee coating the bottom. But the remains weren't moldy yet. The handle had broken off and was lying a few inches away. Pip picked them up to show Joanna.

"Not just a little messy," Joanna said, quiet affection in her voice. "Very messy."

Pip placed the mug, handle inside, on the bedside table, where it had probably been knocked from in the first place.

"Just tissues and spare change," Connor reported back to her.

"No luck here," Joanna said, typing away at the keyboard, the clack of the enter key louder and more desperate each time she tried.

On the bedside table, now in addition to the broken mug, was a lamp, a battered copy of Stephen King's *The Stand,* and the cord of an iPhone charger. There was one drawer below, before the table split into four rickety legs, and Pip knew that that drawer would probably be where Jamie kept his more private items. She turned her back to block Connor and Joanna from seeing what she was doing, just in case, and pulled the drawer open. She was surprised to find there were no condoms or anything like that. There was Jamie's passport, a set of tangled white earphones, a bottle of multivitamins "with added iron," a bookmark shaped like a giraffe, and a watch. Pip's attention was immediately drawn to the last item, for one reason only: it couldn't have belonged to Jamie.

The delicate leather straps were a blush-pink color and the case was shiny rose gold, with a cuff of metallic flowers climbing up the left side of the face. Pip ran one finger over them, the petals spiking into it.

"What's that?" asked Connor.

"A ladies' watch." She spun around. "Is this yours, Joanna? Or Zoe's?"

Joanna came over to inspect the watch. "No, neither of ours. I've never seen it before. Do you think Jamie bought it for someone?"

Pip could tell Joanna was thinking of Nat, but if ever there was a watch less suited to Nat da Silva, it was this one. "No," Pip said. "It's not new, look—there are scratches along the case."

"Well, whose watch is it, then? That Hillary's?" said Connor.

"Don't know," Pip said, placing the watch carefully back in the drawer. "It could be significant; it could mean nothing. We just have to see. I think we're done, for now." She straightened up.

"OK, what next?" Connor said, eyes falling restlessly on hers.

"That's all we can do here for tonight," Pip said, looking away from the disappointment creasing Connor's face. Had he really thought she was going to solve this in just a few hours? "I want you two to keep trying to crack that password. Write down all the possibilities you try. Try Jamie's nicknames, favorite books, films, where he was born, anything you can think of. I'll research a list of typical password elements and combinations and give that to you tomorrow to help narrow it down."

"I will," Joanna said. "I won't stop."

"And keep checking your phone," Pip said. "If that message ever delivers to him, I want to know right away."

"What are you going to do?" Connor asked.

"I'm going to write down all the info I have so far, do some editing and recording, and draft the announcement for the website. Tomorrow morning, everyone is going to know that Jamie Reynolds is missing."

They both gave her quick, awkward hugs at the front door, and then Pip stepped out into the night. She looked over her shoulder as she walked away. Joanna had already gone inside, heading back to Jamie's computer, no doubt. But Connor was still there, watching her leave, looking like the scared little boy Pip once knew.

File Name:

Scrap of paper found in Jamie's trash can.jpg

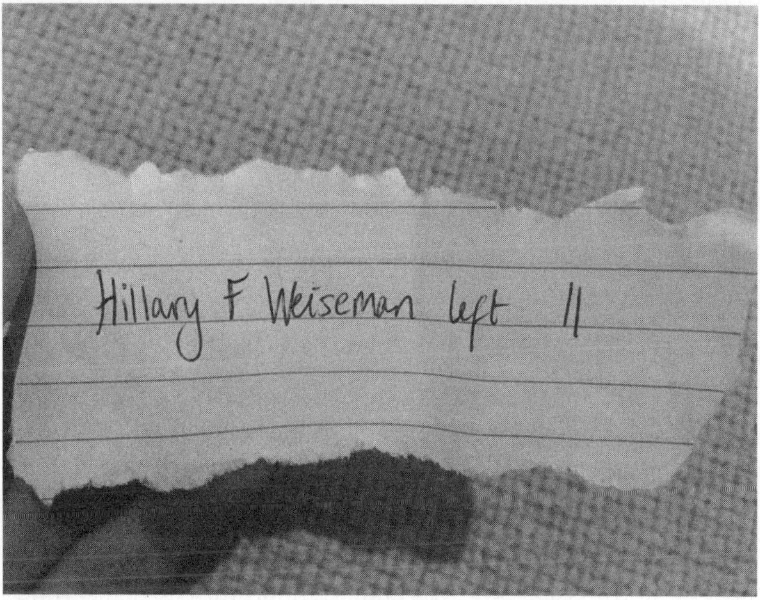

File Name:

A Good Girl's Guide to Murder SEASON 2, EPISODE 1: Intro.wav

PIP: I made a promise. To myself. To everyone. I said I would never do this again, never play the detective, never again lose myself to the world of small-town secrets. It wasn't me, not anymore. I would have stuck to it too; I know I would've. But something's happened and now I have to break that promise. Someone has gone missing. Someone I know. Jamie Reynolds from Fairview. He's the older brother of one of my closest friends, Connor. As I record these words, on Saturday, April 25, at 11:27 p.m., Jamie has been missing for twenty-seven hours. And no one is doing anything about it. The police have classified Jamie as a low-risk missing person and can't spare the resources to look for him. They think he's simply absent, not missing. And truthfully, I hope they're right. I hope this is nothing, that there is no case here. That Jamie has just left home to stay with a friend, neglecting to message his family or return their calls. I hope he's fine. . . . I hope he returns home in a couple of days, wondering what all the fuss is about. But there's no place for hope, not here, and if no one else will look for him, then I have to. So here it is: welcome to season 2 of *A Good Girl's Guide to Murder: The Disappearance of Jamie Reynolds.*

SUNDAY
2 DAYS MISSING

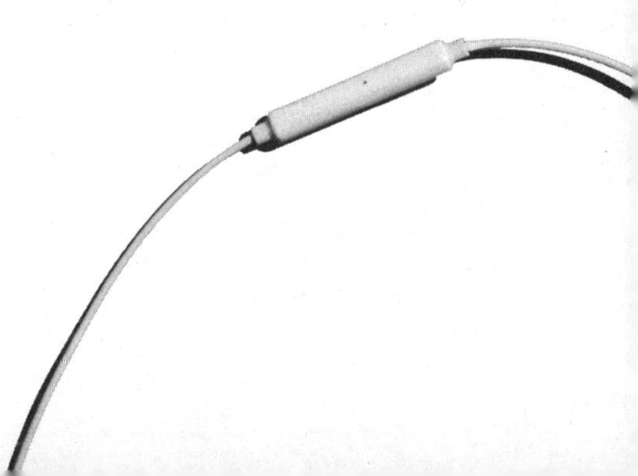

File Name:

Case Notes 1.docx

Initial thoughts:

- Jamie's behavior in the last several weeks seems significant: the mood changes, sneaking out late twice in the past week. But what has he been up to? It all seems connected in some way to his phone.
- Not appropriate to record this thought for podcast, but is it suspicious that Arthur Reynolds won't participate in the investigation? Or is this understandable given Jamie's history of disappearing without contact? Jamie and his dad have a tense relationship and had a big argument just before the memorial. Could this simply be a repeating pattern: argument with dad → run away without contact for a few days.
- But Connor and Joanna are convinced Jamie has not run off. They also don't believe Jamie would attempt to hurt himself, despite his recent mood swings.
- Joanna's undelivered text to Jamie at 12:36 a.m. is a key piece of evidence. This means Jamie's phone has been off since at least that time and has never been turned back on. This itself casts serious doubt on the "ran away" theory: Jamie would need his phone if he were contacting a friend to stay with or getting public transportation. So if something has happened to Jamie, if he's come to harm in any way, it must have happened by 12:36 a.m.
- Reynolds family movements post-memorial:

- Arthur walked home alone from Bobby's Bar & Grill, got in around 11:15 p.m. (my estimate)
- Joanna drove home, got in at 12:15 a.m. at the earliest
- Connor was dropped off by Zach Chen at approximately 12:00 a.m.

To-Do List:

- Announce 2nd season on website / social media
- Make Missing posters
- Get a notice printed in Monday's *Fairview Mail*
- Interview Nat da Silva
- Research Hillary F. Weiseman
- Record description of Jamie's bedroom search
- Have **The Conversation** with Mom and Dad

File Name:

Missing Poster.docx

MISSING

JAMIE REYNOLDS

WAITING FOR PHOTO FROM CONNOR

Age: 24
Height: 5'9"
Weight: 180 lbs
Hair: Short dark blond hair
Eyes: Blue

Last seen on Friday, April 24, around 8:00 p.m. at the memorial on Fairview Common. Wearing a collarless burgundy shirt, jeans, and white Nike sneakers.

URGENT APPEAL: If you have seen Jamie since the memorial or have any information as to his whereabouts, please call 475-555-0142 or email AGGGTMpodcast@gmail.com

Please send all photos and videos taken at the memorial on Friday to the above email address, to assist the investigation.

NINE

Pip waited on Main Street, the sun a pale and lazy yellow. Birds dawdled in the morning sky; even passing cars sounded half-asleep, their tires shushing against the road. There was no urgency in any of it. None. No trace that anything was wrong or amiss. Everything too quiet, too subdued, until Ravi turned the corner from Gravelly Way, waving and jogging over to her.

He hugged her and Pip tucked her nose under his chin. His neck was always warm, even when it had no business being so.

"You look pale," Ravi said, pulling back. "Did you manage to get any sleep last night?"

"Some," she said. And though she must have been tired, she didn't feel it, at all. In fact, she felt sharp for the first time in months, aligned inside her own skin. Head thrumming in that way she'd been missing. What was wrong with her? Her stomach tightened uncomfortably. "But every hour that passes makes it statistically less likely Jamie will ever be found. The first seventy-two hours are crucial—"

"Hey, listen to me." Ravi tilted her chin so she looked up at him. "You have to take care of yourself too. You can't think properly without sleep, and you're no good to Jamie like that. OK? It's going to be OK. We will find Sal—J-Jamie. I meant Jamie." He dropped his eyes.

"Ravi, I—" Pip began.

"It's nothing." He waved her off. "I meant Jamie. Pip, really, leave it alone. Anyway, have you had breakfast?"

"Coffee."

"Food?"

"No." There was no point lying to him, he could always tell.

"Right, well, I thought that would be the case," he said, pulling something out of his back pocket. A Cocoa Puffs cereal bar that he pushed into her hand. "Eat that, please, madam. Now."

Pip shot him a look of surrender and unpeeled the crackling wrapper.

"Breakfast of kings, that is," said Ravi. "Nice and softened by my ass-heat."

"Mmm, delicious," Pip said, taking a bite.

"So what's the plan?"

"Connor will be here soon," she said between bites. "And Cara. You three will head out with the Missing posters, and I'm going to the *Fairview Mail* office. Hopefully someone is in."

"How many posters did you print?" Ravi asked.

"Two hundred and fifty. Took forever, and Dad's gonna be pissed when he sees I used up all the ink."

Ravi sighed. "I could have helped you with those. You don't have to do everything yourself, remember. We're a team."

"I know. And I trust you with everything, *except* making the poster. Remember that email you almost sent to a law firm about work experience with the line 'I appreciate that you are very busty' instead of 'busy'?"

Ravi smirked despite himself. "Well, that's what I have a girlfriend for."

"For proofreading?"

"Yep, just that, nothing else."

Connor arrived a few minutes later, his hurried footsteps slapping against the sidewalk, cheeks redder than normal. "Sorry," he said. "I was helping Mom call the hospitals again. Nothing . . . Hi, Ravi."

"Hey," Ravi said, clapping one hand on Connor's shoulder, leaving it there for a few seconds as a look of silent understanding passed between them. "We'll find him," he said gently, indicating Pip with his head. "This one's too stubborn not to."

Connor attempted a smile.

"Right, these are for you." Pip pulled out the thick stack of Missing posters, split them in half, and handed them over. "The ones in plastic sleeves are for store windows and outside. Ones without are for posting through doors. Make sure you get them up all over Main Street and the roads by the common. And all your neighbors, Connor. Did you bring the stapler?"

"Yep, got two and some tape," he said.

"Good. We should get going." Pip nodded and left Connor and Ravi there, pulling out her phone to check the clock. The thirty-seven-hour mark had just ticked by, without any warning or fanfare. Time was creeping away from her, and Pip picked up her pace to catch it.

Someone was there: a hunched shape and a rattling of keys outside the small *Fairview Mail* office. Pip recognized her as one of the women who volunteered at the town paper.

The woman, unaware she was being watched, shuffled the bunch of keys and tried another.

"Hi," Pip said loudly, making the woman jump, as she'd suspected it might.

"Oh." The woman's yelp became a nervous laugh. "Oh, it's you. Can I help you with something?"

"Is Stanley Forbes in?" asked Pip.

"He should be." The woman finally located the correct key and slid it into the lock. "We've got the write-up of the memorial to sort out before we print today, so Stanley asked me to come in and help." She opened the door. "After you," she said, and Pip stepped over the threshold into the small front room.

"I'm Pip," she said, following the woman as they passed two tired sofas and headed for the back office.

"Yes, I know who you are," the woman said, shrugging off her jacket. And then, in a slightly less frosty tone: "I'm Mary, Mary Scythe."

"Pleased to meet you, again," Pip said, which wasn't exactly true. She figured Mary was one of those people who blamed Pip for all *The Trouble* last year in their nice, quaint town.

Mary pushed the door, revealing a small, square room, four computer desks lining its walls, as tight and claustrophobic as Pip remembered it. Guess that's what you got for a tiny town newspaper that ran mostly on donations from the family living in that mansion up Beecher Road.

Stanley Forbes was sitting at the desk against the far wall, his back to them, his dark brown hair in unkempt clumps, presumably from where his fingers had tunneled through. He paid them no attention, leaning toward his desktop screen, which, judging by the white-and-dark-blue stripes, was on Facebook.

"Hi, Stanley," Pip said softly.

He didn't turn. In fact, he hadn't moved at all, still scrolling down the page. He hadn't heard her.

"Stanley?" she tried again. Nothing, not even a flinch. He wasn't wearing headphones, was he? She couldn't see any.

"Honestly," Mary scoffed, "he does this all the time. Has the most selective hearing I've ever come across. Tunes the whole world out. Hey, Stan!" She barked that last part, and finally Stanley looked up, spinning his chair to face them.

"Oh, sorry, were you talking to me?" he said, his green-brown eyes jumping from Mary to settle on Pip.

"No one else in the room," Mary said irritably, dropping her handbag against the desk farthest from Stanley's.

"Hi," Pip said again, walking over to him, crossing the distance in just four large steps.

"H-hello," Stanley said, getting to his feet. He held out his hand, apparently to shake hers, but then evidently changed his mind and drew it back, then changed his mind again and re-extended the hand with an embarrassed laugh. He probably didn't know the appropriate way to greet Pip, given their fraught history and her being eighteen while he was at least in his late twenties.

Pip shook his hand just to make him stop.

"Sorry," Stanley said, returning the awkward hand to his side.

It wasn't just the Singhs he'd apologized to; Pip had also received a letter from Stanley a few months ago. In it he'd apologized for the way he'd talked down to her, and for Becca Bell taking Pip's number from his phone and using it to threaten Pip. He hadn't known at the time, but he was still sorry. Pip wondered how sincere he really was.

"What can I . . . ," Stanley began. "What do you—"

"I know the memorial will probably take up a lot of room in tomorrow's paper. But could you make space for this? I'm trying to spread the word to everyone in town." Pip dropped her backpack so she could take out the reserved Missing poster. She handed it over, watching Stanley read, his eyes furrowed and a hollow burrowing into his cheek as he chewed it from the inside.

"Missing, is he?" He looked down again. "Jamie Reynolds."

"Know him?"

"Don't think so," Stanley said. "Might recognize the face. Is he from Fairview?"

"Yep. Family live on Cedar Way. Jamie went to Fairview High, with Andie and Sal."

"Missing since when?" he asked.

"It says there." Pip's voice rose impatiently. Mary's chair creaked as she leaned closer to listen in. "Last seen around eight o'clock at the memorial, until I learn more about his movements. I saw you taking photos, could you email those to me?"

"Er, yes, OK. Police?" asked Stanley.

"A missing persons report has been filed," Pip replied. "Police response is nonexistent right now. So it's just me. That's why I need your help." She smiled, pretending like she didn't resent having to ask.

"Missing since the memorial?" Stanley thought aloud. "That's only, like, a day and a half, right?"

"Thirty-seven and a half hours," Pip said.

"That's not very long, is it?" He lowered the poster.

"Missing is missing," she countered. "And the first seventy-two hours are critical, especially if you suspect foul play."

"Do you?"

"Yes," she said. "The family does too. So will you help? Can you print that notice tomorrow?"

Stanley looked up for a moment, eyes spooling as he considered it. "Suppose I can move the article about the potholes until next week."

"Is that a yes?" Pip said.

"Yes, I'll make sure it goes in." He nodded, tapping the poster. "Though I'm sure he'll turn up OK."

"Thank you, Stanley." She returned his polite smile. "I really appreciate that." She pivoted on her heels to leave, but Stanley's voice stopped her before she reached the door.

"Mysteries always seem to find their way to you, don't they?"

TEN

The doorbell was shrill, splitting your ears the same way as a scream. Pip withdrew her finger, restoring quiet to the white-brick terraced house. She hoped this was the right house. This was the one they'd told her: number thirteen Beacon Close, dark red door.

An aggressively white BMW sports car sat in the drive, throwing the morning sun back into Pip's eyes, blinding her.

She was about to ring the bell again, when she heard a sliding bolt. The door swung inward and a man appeared in the gap, screwing his eyes against the brightness outside. This must be the new boyfriend, then. He was wearing a crisp white sweatshirt—black Adidas stripes up the sleeves—and a pair of dark basketball shorts.

"Yeah?" he said gruffly, voice crackling like he hadn't been awake long.

"Hello," Pip said brightly. The man had a tattoo across his throat, the gray ink stark against his white skin in symmetrical repeating shapes that looked a little like scales. A flock of birds emerged from the pattern, flying up the side of his face and into his brown close-shaved hair. Pip returned her gaze to his eyes. "Um, is Nat da Silva in? I just asked at her parents' house and her mom said she'd probably be here."

"Yeah, she's inside." He sniffed. "You a friend of hers?"

"Yes," Pip said, which was a lie, but it was easier to say than *No, she still hates me even though I keep trying to make her not hate me.* "I'm Pip . . . Fitz-Amobi. Can I come in? I need to talk to her about something urgent."

"Yeah, I guess. It's kinda early," he said, stepping back and gesturing for her to follow. "I'm Luke. Eaton."

"Nice to meet you." Pip closed the front door and followed Luke around the bend in the corridor, into the kitchen at the back.

"Nat, friend of yours," Luke said as they entered the room.

The kitchen was square, with counters in an L shape on one side, a large wood table on the other. On one end of the table was what looked like a stack of money, the pile weighted down by BMW car keys. At the other end sat Nat da Silva, a bowl of cereal in front of her. She was wearing what must have been one of Luke's sweaters, her bleached white hair brushed to one side.

She dropped her cereal-loaded spoon and it clattered noisily against the bowl.

"What do you want?" she said.

"Hi, Nat." Pip stood there awkwardly, trapped halfway between Luke in the doorway and Nat at the table.

"You already said what you wanted to say to me at the memorial," Nat said dismissively, picking the spoon back up.

"Oh, no, this isn't about the trial." Pip chanced one step toward Nat.

"What trial?" Luke said behind her.

"Nothing," Nat responded, the word spoken through a mouthful of cereal. "What is it, then?"

"It's Jamie Reynolds," Pip said. A breeze came through the open window, fluttering the lace curtain and rustling a couple of brown paper bags on the counter. Probably takeout bags. "Jamie's missing," she added.

Nat's eyebrows lowered, shadowing her blue eyes. "Missing?

His mom called me yesterday, asking if I'd seen him. He still hasn't turned up?"

"No, and his family is really worried. They filed a missing persons report yesterday, but the police aren't doing anything about it."

"My brother, you mean?"

Pip had walked right into that one.

"Well, no, I spoke to Detective Hawkins. He says there's nothing they can do. So the Reynoldses asked if I would investigate."

"For your podcast?" Nat said that last word full of spite, hardening the consonants, sharpening them to a point.

"Well, yes."

Nat swallowed another bite of cereal. "How opportunistic of you."

Luke snorted.

"They asked me to," Pip said quietly. "I'm guessing you won't want to do a recorded interview."

"Perceptive too," Nat said, milk dripping onto the table as another spoonful hovered between her mouth and the bowl.

"Jamie told his brother he was going to your house—your parents' house—after the memorial, to spend the evening with you."

"He was supposed to. He never showed up." Nat sniffed, glancing quickly up at Luke. "Never texted to say he wasn't coming. I waited. Tried calling him."

"So the last contact you had with Jamie was at the memorial, in person?"

"Yes." Nat crunched another mouthful. "Until just after Andie's friends spoke, when I noticed Jamie staring into the crowd on the other side, trying to see something. I asked him what was up, and he said, 'I've just seen someone.' "

"And?" Pip said when Nat paused for too long.

"Then he left, presumably to go talk to whoever it was," she said.

That's when Pip had last seen him too. Jostling her as he made his way to the other side of the crowd, a strange intensity on his face. But who was he moving toward?

"Do you have any idea who the 'someone' he spotted was?"

"No," Nat said, stretching her neck out with an audible crack. "Can't be somebody I know or he would've said their name. He's probably with whoever that *someone* is. He'll come home. Jamie's like that, very all or nothing."

"His family is convinced something has happened to him," Pip said, her legs starting to prickle from standing still too long. "That's why I need to work out his movements during and after the memorial. Find out who he interacted with on Friday night. Do you know anything that might help?"

She heard an inward breath behind her, from Luke, before he spoke. "Nat's right, Jamie's probably just staying with a friend. I'm sure this is a lot of trouble over nothing."

"Do you know Jamie?" Pip half turned to look at him.

"Nah, not really, only through Nat. They're good friends. If she says he's OK, then he's probably OK."

"Well, I—" Nat started.

"Were you at the memorial?" Pip asked Luke. "Did you see—"

"Nah, wasn't there." Luke clicked his tongue. "Never knew either of those kids. So no, didn't see Jamie. Didn't actually leave the house at all on Friday."

Pip nodded at him, then turned back to the kitchen table. As she did, she caught just the tail end of the expression on Nat's face. She was looking up at Luke, hand frozen in midair on its way back to the spoon, mouth slightly open like she'd started to speak but had forgotten how. Then her eyes flicked to Pip and the expression immediately dropped out, so fast that Pip wasn't sure she'd really seen it at all, nor what it might mean.

"So," Pip said, watching Nat more closely now, "was Jamie acting strange that night, or in the weeks before?"

"I don't think so," said Nat. "I haven't heard from him much lately."

"Have you been texting? Late-night phone calls?" asked Pip.

"Well, not . . . ," Nat started to say, but then she suddenly abandoned her cereal, sitting back with her arms crossed. "What is this?" she said, her voice jagged with anger. "Are you interrogating me? I thought I was just telling you when I last saw Jamie, but now it's sounding like you suspect me of something. Like last time."

"No, I'm not—"

"Well, you were wrong before, weren't you? Should learn from your mistakes." Nat pushed her chair back and it screeched on the tiles, cutting right through Pip. "Who made you the vigilante of this crappy town, anyway? Everyone else might be happy to play along, but I'm not." She shook her head and dropped her pale blue eyes. "You're leaving. Now."

"I'm sorry, Nat," Pip said. There was nothing else she could say; anything she tried only made Nat hate her more. And there was only one person to blame for that. But Pip wasn't that person anymore, was she? That yawning feeling opened up in her gut again.

Luke led Pip back down the hallway and opened the front door.

"You lied to me," he said as Pip passed, a hint of amusement in his voice. "Said you were friends."

She screwed her eyes against the glare from Luke's car, turned back and shrugged.

"Thought I was good at spotting liars." His grip tightened around the edge of the door. "Leave us out of it, whatever it is you're up to. You hear?"

"I hear."

Luke smiled at something and closed the door with a sharp click.

Walking away from the house, Pip pulled out her phone to check the time: 10:41 a.m. Thirty-eight and a half hours missing. Her home screen was piling up with notifications from Twitter and Instagram, more coming in as she watched. The scheduled post on her website and social media announcing the second season of the podcast had gone out at ten-thirty. So now everyone knew about Jamie Reynolds. There really was no going back.

A few emails had come in too. Another company inquiring about sponsorship. One from Stanley Forbes with twenty-two attachments, the subject line reading: *memorial pictures.* And one from two minutes ago: Gail Yardley, who lived on Pip's street.

Hello Pippa, it read. *I've just seen the Missing posters around town. I don't remember seeing Jamie Reynolds that evening, but I've had a quick look through my photographs from the memorial, and I've found him. You might want to take a look at this photo.*

File Name:

Case Notes 2.docx

It's unmistakably Jamie, standing there in Gail Yardley's photo. The metadata tells me the photo is time-stamped at 8:26 p.m., so here Jamie is, undisappeared, ten minutes after I last saw him.

Jamie is almost facing the camera, and that itself is the strangest thing about the photograph. Everyone else, every other face and every other pair of eyes are all turned up, looking at the exact same thing: the lanterns for Andie and Sal, hovering just over the roof of the pavilion during this sliver of time.

But Jamie is looking the wrong way.

His pale, freckled face is in the near darkness, at a slight angle to Gail's camera, looking at something behind her. Or someone. Probably the same someone he'd told Nat da Silva about.

And his face—there's something there I can't quite read. He doesn't look scared, per se. But it's something not far off. Concerned? Worried? Nervous? His mouth is hanging open, eyes wide with one eyebrow slightly angled up, like he could be confused about something. But who or what caused this reaction? Jamie told Nat he'd spotted someone, but why was it urgent enough for him to fight through the crowd during the middle of the memorial? And why is he standing there, presumably staring at that someone instead of joining them? There's something strange about this.

I've flicked through Stanley Forbes's photos. Jamie isn't in any of them, but I cross-referenced them against Gail's photograph, trying to find her in the crowd to see if I can work out who Jamie is looking at or at least narrow it down. Stanley has just one photo pointing that way, time-stamped before the memorial began. I can see the Yardleys standing on the left, a few rows from the front. I've zoomed in on the faces behind them, but the photo was taken from a distance and it's not very clear. From their police uniforms and shiny peaked hats, I can tell Daniel da Silva and Soraya Bouzidi are standing next to the Yardleys. That dark green blur beside them must be Detective Hawkins. I think I recognize a few of the pixelated faces behind as people from my grade, but it's impossible to tell who Jamie might have been looking at. Plus, this photo was taken an hour before the Jamie photo; the crowd might have shifted in that time.

- Record these observations later for episode 1.

The photo—coupled with Nat's evidence—has certainly opened up a lead to focus the investigation on. Who is the "someone" Jamie went to find in the crowd? They might know something about where Jamie went that night. Or what happened to him.

Other Observations

- Jamie must have been distracted by something or someone that night because he doesn't go to Nat's house as planned or even text her to say he isn't coming. Is what we see in this photo the start of that distraction?
- Jamie's recent late-night phone calls and constant texting haven't been with Nat da Silva, unless she just didn't want to say so in front of Luke (he is pretty intimidating).
- That expression on Nat's face when Luke said he hadn't left the house at all on Friday. Might be nothing. Might be

a "couple" thing between them that I don't understand. But her reaction seems significant to me. Most likely it has nothing to do with Jamie, but I should note down everything. (Do not mention in podcast—Nat hates me enough already.)

ELEVEN

The bell above the café door jangled, clattering around in Pip's head long after it should. An unwelcome echo that cut through all other thoughts, but she couldn't work at home, so the café had to do. Her parents must have seen the posters up around town by now. If Pip went home, she'd have to have *The Conversation* and there wasn't time for that now. Or she just wasn't ready.

More emails had come in with photos from the memorial attached, and the notifications from her announcement had reached into the thousands. Pip had just muted them, now that the trolls had found them. *I killed Jamie Reynolds,* said one of the gray blank profile pictures. Another: *Who will look for you when you're the one who disappears?*

The bell sounded again, but this time it was accompanied by Cara's voice.

"Hey," she said, pulling out the chair opposite Pip. "Ravi said you were here. Just saw him as I finished up with the posters on Chalk Road."

"You've run out?" asked Pip.

"Yeah. But that's not why I need to talk to you." Cara's voice lowered conspiratorially.

"What's up?" Pip whispered, following suit.

"So as I was putting up the posters, looking at Jamie's face, reading what he was wearing, I . . . I dunno." Cara leaned forward. "I know I was really drunk and don't remember much of that night, but I keep getting this feeling that . . . well, I think I saw Jamie there that night."

"What are you talking about?" Pip hissed. "At the calamity party?"

Cara nodded, leaning so far forward that she could no longer be actually sitting. "I mean, I don't have a clear memory of it. It's more like a déjà vu thing. But picturing him in that outfit, I swear he walked by me at the party. I was drunk, so maybe I didn't think anything of it at the time, or maybe I didn't realize but— Hey, don't look at me like that! I'm sure that maybe I maybe saw him there."

"Sure that maybe you maybe saw him there?" Pip repeated.

"OK, I'm obviously not sure." Cara frowned. "But I think he was." She finally sat back, widening her eyes at Pip, inviting her to speak.

Pip closed her laptop. "Well, OK, let's say you *did* see Jamie there. What the hell would Jamie be doing at a party full of eighteen-year-olds? He's twenty-four, and probably the only people he knows our age are us, Connor's friends."

"Dunno."

"Was he speaking to anyone?" Pip asked.

"I don't *know,*" Cara said, fingers going to her temples. "I think I only remember him walking past me at some point."

"But if he was there . . . ," Pip began, trailing off as her thoughts lost their shape.

"It's really strange," Cara finished for her.

"Really strange."

Cara paused to take a sip of Pip's coffee. "So what do we do about it?"

"Well, fortunately there are lots of other witnesses from the party who might be able to confirm what you think you saw. And if it's true, then I guess we know where Jamie went after the memorial."

Pip texted Ant and Lauren first, asking if they'd seen Jamie at the party. Ant's reply came two minutes later. He and Lauren were clearly together as he answered for both of them:

Nah we didn't, weren't there for long though. Why would Jamie have been there?

"Ant and Lauren not noticing something other than each other, how unlike them," Cara said sarcastically.

Pip texted back: *You have Stephen Thompson's number, right? Can I have it please. Urgent.*

The party had been at Stephen's house, and even though Pip still very much disliked him—from when she'd gone undercover at a calamity party last year to find information on the drug dealer Howie Bowers, and Stephen had forcibly tried to kiss her—she had to set that dislike aside for now.

When Ant finally sent Stephen's number through, Pip downed the rest of her coffee and called him, throwing a quick *shush* sign Cara's way. Cara pulled her fingers across her lips, zipping them shut but sliding closer to listen in.

Stephen picked up on the fourth ring with a confused-sounding "Hello?"

"Hi, Stephen," Pip said. "It's Pip Fitz-Amobi."

"Oh, hey," Stephen said, his tone changing. Softer and deeper.

Pip rolled her eyes at Cara.

"What can I do for you?" he asked.

"I don't know if you've seen any of the posters around town—"

"Oh, my mom actually just mentioned seeing those. Complained about them being 'unsightly.' " He made a sound Pip could only describe as a guffaw. "They have something to do with you?"

"Yeah," she said, in as bright a voice as she could muster. "So you know Connor Reynolds in our grade? Well, his older brother, Jamie, went missing on Friday night and everyone's really worried."

"Shit," Stephen said.

"You hosted a calamity party at your house on Friday night, didn't you?"

"Were you here?" Stephen asked.

"Unfortunately not," Pip said. Well, she'd been outside the house, to pick up a drunken, sobbing Cara. "But there are rumors that Jamie Reynolds was at the party, and I wondered if you remembered seeing him there? Or heard anyone else say they did?"

"Are you doing, like, a new investigate-y thing?" he asked.

She ignored the question. "Jamie's twenty-four, he's about five nine, has dark blond almost-brown hair and blue eyes. He was—"

"Yeah," Stephen cut her off. "Think I might have seen him. I remember walking past some guy I didn't know in the living room. He looked a little older; I assumed he was with one of the girls. Wearing a dark red shirt."

"Yes." Pip sat up straighter, nodding at Cara. "That sounds like Jamie. I'm sending a photo to you now. Can you confirm that's who you saw?" Pip lowered her phone to find Jamie's photo, the one from the poster, and sent it to Stephen.

"That's him." Stephen's voice was a little distant through the speaker; he must have been holding up his phone to look at the screen.

"Do you remember what time you saw him?"

"Uh, not really," he said. "I think it was early on, maybe nine, tenish, but I'm not sure. Only saw him that one time."

"What was he doing?" asked Pip. "Was he talking to anyone? Drinking?"

"No, didn't see him talking to anyone. Don't think he had a drink in his hand either. I think he was just standing there, watching. Kinda creepy when you think about it."

Pip felt like reminding Stephen that he was one to talk about creepy. But she held her tongue. "What time did people turn up at your place? The memorial finished around eight-thirty, did most people go straight to your house?"

"Yeah. I live, like, less than ten minutes away, so most people walked straight from the common. So you said you're, like, investigating again, right? Is this going on your podcast? Because"—Stephen lowered his voice to a whisper—"well, my mom doesn't know I had a party; she was away on a spa weekend. I blamed the smashed vases and drink stains on our dog. And the party got shut down by the police at like one; a neighbor must have called with a noise complaint. But I don't want my mom to find out about the party, so could you not—"

"Which police officer came to shut it down?" Pip interrupted.

"Oh, that da Silva guy. Just told everyone to go home. So you won't mention the party, right? On your podcast?"

"Oh, right, sure," Pip lied. Of course she was going to mention it, even better if it got Stephen "Gropey" Thompson in trouble. She thanked him and hung up. "You were right," she told Cara, dropping the phone.

"I was? Jamie was there? I helped?"

"He was and you did." Pip smiled at her. "Well, we have two eyewitness accounts, neither with an exact time, but I think we can be fairly certain Jamie went there after the memorial. Now I need to try to find photographic evidence, narrow down the time frame. What's the best way to get a message to everyone who was at the calamity?"

"Message everyone in that Facebook group for our grade?" Cara shrugged.

"Good idea." Pip reawakened her laptop. "I should tell Connor first. What the hell was Jamie doing there?" Her computer burred into life and Jamie's face popped up on-screen from the Missing poster document, his pale eyes staring right out into hers, holding her there as a cold shiver crept down the back of her neck. She knew him; this was Jamie. *Jamie.* But how well did you ever know anyone? She watched his eyes, trying to unpick the secrets that lay behind them. *Where are you?* she asked him silently, face to face.

Hi everyone,

As you might have seen from posters around town, Jamie Reynolds (Connor's older brother) went missing on Friday night after the memorial. I have recently learned that Jamie was seen at the calamity party at Stephen Thompson's house on Highmoor. I am making an urgent appeal for anyone who was there to please send me any photos or videos you took while at the party (I promise that none of these will make their way to parents/police at any time). This includes Snapchat/Instagram stories if you have those saved. Please send them in ASAP to the email address listed on my profile. I am posting Jamie's photograph below. If anyone remembers seeing him at the party or has any information at all on his whereabouts or movements Friday night, please get in contact with me via email or my phone number listed below.

Thank you,
Pip

12:58 p.m.

File Name:

A Good Girl's Guide to Murder SEASON 2: Phone interview with George Thorne.wav

PIP: George, I've just pressed record. I'll get you to sign a form at school tomorrow, but for now can I ask whether you consent to your voice being used in a published podcast?

GEORGE: Yes, that's fine.

PIP: OK, I've moved to the back of the café. Can you hear me better now?

GEORGE: Yep, much better.

PIP: OK. So you saw my message on Facebook. Let's go back over what you started to tell me. Can you go back to the beginning?

GEORGE: Yeah, so I saw him—

PIP: Sorry, before that. So on Friday night, you were where?

GEORGE: Oh, right. On Friday, after the memorial, I went to the calamity party at Stephen Thompson's. I wasn't drinking much because we've got a big soccer game next week, Ant's probably told you that. So I remember the whole night. And I saw him, I saw Jamie Reynolds in the living room. He was standing against one of the walls, not talking to anyone. I remember thinking to myself, I didn't know him, and, y'know, it's normally the same crowd from school who goes to calamities, so he stuck out to me. I didn't talk to him, though.

PIP: OK. Now let's go back to when you saw him next.

GEORGE: Right. So a little while later, I went outside to have a cigarette. There were only a few people out front. Jas and Katie M. were talking and Katie was crying about something. And Jamie Reynolds was out there too. I remember it very clearly. He was pacing up and down the sidewalk in front of the house and talking to someone on his phone.

PIP: Can you describe his demeanor while he was on the phone?

GEORGE: Yeah, well, he looked kind of . . . agitated. Like angry, but not quite. Maybe scared? His voice was kinda shaky.

PIP: And could you hear anything he was saying?

GEORGE: Only a little. As I was lighting up, I remember hearing him say, "No, I can't do that." Or words to that effect. And he repeated that a couple of times, like: "I can't do that, I can't." And by this time, he'd sort of caught my attention, so I was listening in while pretending to look at my phone. After a while, Jamie started shaking his head, saying something like, "I know I said anything, but . . . ," and sort of trailed off.

PIP: Did he notice you were there? That you were listening?

GEORGE: Don't think so. I don't think he was aware of anything other than what was going on at the other end of the phone. He was sort of plugging his other ear so he could hear whoever he was talking to better. He went quiet for a bit, like he was listening. Still pacing. And then he said, "I could call the police," or something like that. I definitely remember him mentioning the police.

PIP: Did he say it in a confrontational way, or like he was offering to help?

GEORGE: I don't know, it was hard to tell. So then he was quiet for a while, listening again, and he seemed to grow more jittery. I remember him saying something about a child.

PIP: A child? Whose child?

GEORGE: Don't know, I just heard the word. And then Jamie looked up and we accidentally made eye contact and he must have realized I was listening. So then, still on the phone, he started walking away from the house, down the street, and the last thing I heard him say was something like, "I don't think I can do it."

PIP: Which direction was he going?

GEORGE: Pretty sure he went right, heading toward Main Street.

PIP: And you didn't see him come back to the house?

GEORGE: No. I was out there for, like, another five minutes. He was gone.

PIP: Do you have any idea what time this happened?

GEORGE: I know exactly when it was, because right after Jamie left, like thirty seconds after, I texted this girl from Wilton High I've been talking to. Sent her this meme of SpongeBob. . . . You know what, that's irrelevant, but my phone says I sent it at 10:32 p.m. and it was literally right after Jamie walked away.

PIP: Ten-thirty-two? George, that's perfect. Thank you so much. Did you pick up any hints about the person Jamie was talking to? Could you tell whether it was a man or a woman?

GEORGE: No. No, I couldn't tell anything else, other than Jamie didn't much like what they were saying to him. Do you . . . do you think he's OK? Maybe I should have told someone what I saw sooner? If I'd texted Connor that night . . .

PIP: That's OK, you didn't know Jamie was missing until an hour ago. And your information has been incredibly helpful. Connor will really appreciate it.

TWELVE

They sat separated by two laptops on the kitchen island, the tapping of their keys in a pattern that fell in and out of unison.

"You're going too fast," Pip said to Ravi, peering at him over the top of her screen. "We need to look carefully at each one."

"Oh," he said sarcastically, making a face. "Didn't realize we were looking for clues in the night sky." He turned his laptop, showing her four consecutive photos of the Chinese lanterns floating against the darkness.

"Just checking, Grumpus."

"That's my name for *you,*" he said. "You aren't allowed to have it."

Pip went back to her screen, clicking through the photos and videos that had been emailed over by calamity-goers. Ravi was going through the memorial photographs. More than two hundred had been sent in already.

"Is this the best use of our time?" Ravi skipped quickly through another sequence of photos. "We know Jamie went to the calamity party after the memorial, and now we know he left there, alive and well, at ten-thirty. Shouldn't we be trying to track down his movements after that?"

"We know he left the calamity party," said Pip, "but we still don't know *why* he was there, which is strange enough by itself. And then add to that the phone conversation George heard. It's all behavior that's very out of character. I mean, you saw Connor's face when I told him. It's weird. There's no other word for it. Jamie's behavior starting from the memorial is weird. It has to be relevant to his disappearance somehow."

"I guess." Ravi returned his gaze to his laptop screen. "So we're thinking Jamie spotted 'someone'—whoever they are—at the memorial. He found them in the crowd and waited, then he followed them when they walked toward Highmoor and to the party. Gropey Stephen said it looked like Jamie was just standing there, watching?"

"I think so." Pip chewed her bottom lip. "That makes the most sense to me. Which means that 'someone' is most likely a person at school, in my grade or maybe a junior."

"Why would Jamie follow someone from your school?"

Pip picked up on the uneasiness in Ravi's voice, though he tried to disguise it. She felt an instinct to defend Jamie, but all she could say was "I really don't know." Nothing about it looked good. She was glad she'd sent Connor home with a four-page questionnaire about typical password elements, for him and his mom to try on Jamie's computer. It would be harder to talk about Jamie with him right there. But Pip was struggling to accept it too. They had to be missing something, something that would explain why Jamie had been at the party, who he was looking for. It must have been important for him to blow Nat off and ignore all her calls. But what?

Pip glanced at the time on the bottom right-hand corner of her screen. It was four-thirty. And with Jamie's new last-seen-alive-and-well time of 10:32 p.m., he'd now been missing for forty-two hours. Just six hours to go until the forty-eight-hour mark. The mark by which the majority of missing persons—almost 75 percent—had returned. But Pip had a feeling Jamie wouldn't be one of them.

And the next problem: Pip's parents were currently at the supermarket; her mom had texted to let her know. She'd avoided them all day, and Josh had gone with them, so he was bound to cause some delay with all his impulse buying (last time he'd persuaded Dad to buy two bags of carrot sticks, which went to waste when he remembered he didn't actually like carrots). But even with Josh's distractions, they'd be home soon, and there was no way they hadn't seen Jamie's Missing posters by now.

Well, there was nothing she could do, she'd just have to deal with it when they got back. Or maybe avoid it even longer by insisting Ravi never leave; her parents probably wouldn't yell at her in front of him.

Pip clicked through more of the photos sent in by Katie C., one of the six Katies in her grade. Pip had found evidence of Jamie in only two photos of the dozens she'd been through so far, and she wasn't even certain about one of them. It was just the lower part of an arm, peeking out behind a group of boys posing for a photo in the hallway. The disembodied arm wore a burgundy shirt that matched Jamie's, and the boxy black watch he'd had on too. So it probably was him, but it gave her no real information, other than Jamie had been walking through the party at 9:16 p.m. Maybe that was when he'd first arrived?

In the other photo you could at least see his face, in the background behind Jasveen, a girl in Pip's grade, who was sitting on a blue-patterned couch. The camera was focused on Jas, who was pouting in exaggerated sadness, presumably because of the huge red drink stain down the front of her once very white top. Jamie was standing several feet behind her, beside a darkened bay window. He was a little blurred, but Pip could pinpoint his eyes, staring diagonally out the left side of the frame. His jaw looked tense, like he was gritting his teeth. This must have been when Stephen Thompson saw him; he did look like he was watching someone. The metadata said the photo was taken at 9:38 p.m., so Jamie had been at the party for at least twenty-two minutes by this point. Had he stood there that whole time, watching?

Pip opened another email, from Chris Marshall in her AP U.S. History class. She downloaded the attached video file, replaced her headphones, and pressed play.

It was a series of stills and short video clips: it must have been Chris's story on either Snapchat or Instagram that he'd saved to his reel. There was a selfie of him and Peter-from-English downing two bottles of beer, followed by a short clip of some guy Pip didn't recognize doing a handstand while Chris cheered him on, voice crackling against the microphone. Next, a close-up of Chris's tongue, which had somehow turned blue.

Then another video clip, the sound exploding into Pip's ears, making her flinch. Voices screeched across each other, people loudly chanting "Peter, Peter," while others in the room booed and jeered and laughed. They were in what looked like a dining room, chairs pushed back from the table, which was set up with plastic cups assembled into two triangles on either side.

Beer pong. They were playing beer pong. Peter-from-English was on one side of the table, lining up a shot with a bright-orange ping-pong ball, one eye screwed shut as he focused. He flicked his wrist and the ball flew out of his hand, landing with a small splash into one of the outlying cups.

Pip's headphones vibrated with the screams that erupted around the room, Peter roaring in victory as the girl on the other side of the table complained about having to down the drink. But then Pip noticed something else, her eyes straying to the background. She paused the clip. Standing to the right of the bifold glass doors into the dining room was Cara, mouth wide as she cheered, a wave of dark liquid erupting from the top of her cup in this frozen moment of time.

And there was something else: in the bright yellow-lit corridor behind Cara, just disappearing beyond the door, was a foot. A sliver of leg in jeans the same color Jamie was wearing that night, and a white sneaker.

Pip scrolled the video back four seconds, back to before Peter's victory. She pressed play and immediately paused it again. There was a figure, out in the hallway. His edges were blurred because he was midstride, but he had dark blond hair and a shirt that looked dark red. He was looking down at the dark object clasped between his hands. A phone.

Pip un-paused it and watched as the figure walked quickly down the hallway, ignoring all the commotion in the dining room, eyes on his phone. Cara's head was turned, following his progress for half a second, before the ball landed in the cup and the screaming pulled her attention back into the room.

Four seconds.

It had to be Jamie. Had to be. The sighting lasted just four seconds. Then Jamie was gone, his white sneaker the very last trace of him.

"Found him," Pip said.

THIRTEEN

Pip dragged the cursor back and pressed play to show Ravi.

"That's him," he confirmed, resting his sharp chin on her shoulder. "That's when Cara saw him. Look."

"Who needs security cameras when you have Snapchat stories," Pip remarked. "Do you think he's walking down the hallway toward the front door?" She turned to watch Ravi's eyes as she played the clip again. "Or farther into the house?"

"Could be either," Ravi said. "Hard to tell without knowing the layout of the house. Do you think we can go round to Stephen's and see?"

"Doubt he'll let us in," she said. "He doesn't want his mom to know about the party."

"Hmm," said Ravi, "we might be able to look it up on a real estate site. Find photos or a floor plan or something."

The video kept playing beyond the beer pong, into another clip where Peter was hugging the toilet, throwing up into it while Chris giggled behind the camera, saying, "You all right, big man?"

Pip paused it so they didn't have to listen to any more of Peter's retching.

"Do you have a time for that Jamie sighting?" Ravi asked.

"No. Chris just sent me the saved story; it doesn't have time stamps for any individual part."

"Call him and ask." Ravi reached across Pip, dragging her laptop toward him. "I'll see if I can find the house listing online somewhere. What number is Stephen?"

"Nineteen Highmoor," Pip said, spinning her stool to face away from Ravi and taking out her phone. She had Chris's number in here somewhere. She knew she did, because they'd done a group project together a few months ago. Aha, there it was: *Chris M.*

"Hello?" Chris said when he picked up. The word trailed up like a question; clearly he hadn't saved her number.

"Hi, Chris. It's Pip."

"Oh, hey," he said. "I just sent you an email—"

"Yeah, thank you for that. That's actually what I wanted to ask you about. This clip here, of Peter playing beer pong, do you know what time it was taken?"

"Um, can't remember." Chris yawned on the other end of the line. "I was pretty drunk. But actually, hold on . . ." His voice grew echoey and distant as he put her on speaker. "I saved that story so I could abuse Peter with it, but I take videos in the actual camera app because Snapchat always crashes on me."

"Oh, that's great if it's on your camera roll," Pip said. "It'll have a time stamp."

"Crap," Chris hissed. "I must have deleted them all, sorry."

Pip's stomach dropped. But only for a second, crawling its way back up as she said: "Recently deleted folder?"

"Oh, good call." Pip could hear the fiddling of Chris's fingers against the device. "Yeah, here it is. Beer pong video was taken at 9:56 p.m."

"Nine-fifty-six," Pip repeated, writing the time down in the notebook Ravi had just slid across to her. "Perfect. Thank you so much, Chris."

Pip hung up, even though Chris was still speaking. She'd never been a fan of those straggling bits of talk that happened at the beginnings and ends of conversations, and she didn't have time to pretend right now. Ravi often referred to her as his little bulldozer.

"Hear that?" she asked him.

He nodded. "And I've found the old listing of Stephen's house on realtor.com, last sold in 2015. Photos don't give much away, but the floor plan is still up." He turned the screen back, showing her a black-and-white diagram of the ground floor of Stephen's house.

Pip reached for the screen, tracing her finger from the 16-by-12.5-inch box labeled *Dining Room,* out the bifold double doors, turning left down the corridor to follow Jamie's path. It led to the front door.

"Yes," she hissed. "He was definitely leaving the house at 9:56." Pip copied the floor plan and pasted it into Paint to annotate it. She drew an arrow down the corridor toward the front door and labeled it *Jamie leaves 9:56 p.m.* "And he's looking at his phone," Pip said. "Do you think he's about to call whoever George then sees him on the phone with?"

"Seems likely," Ravi said. "That would make it a pretty long phone call. Like, thirty minutes at least."

Pip drew a pair of forward and backward arrows outside the front door on the floor plan, as Jamie had paced the sidewalk on his phone. She labeled the time span of the phone call and then drew another arrow leading away from the house, when Jamie finally left.

"Have you ever considered becoming a professional artist?" Ravi said, looking over her shoulder.

"Oh, be quiet, it does the job," she said, poking the cleft in his chin. Ravi uttered a robotic *"Booooop,"* pretending to reset his face.

Pip ignored him. "Actually, this might help with that other Jamie sighting." She pulled up the photo of Jamie standing behind Jasveen and her stained top. She dragged it to the left to split-screen it beside the floor plan. "There's a sofa there, so this has to be the living room, right?"

Ravi agreed. "Sofa and a bay window."

"OK," Pip said. "And Jamie's standing just to the right of that window." She pointed to the bay window symbol in the floor plan. "But if you look at his eyes, he's looking away, to the left."

"She can solve murders, but can't tell her left from right." Ravi smiled.

"That's left," Pip insisted, glowering at him. "Our left, his right."

"OK, please don't hurt me." He held his hands up in surrender, his crooked smile stretching across his face. Why did he enjoy winding her up so much? And why did she like it when he did? It was maddening.

Pip turned back, placing her finger on the floor plan where Jamie had been standing, then drew her finger out, following Jamie's approximate eyeline. It brought her to a boxy black figure against the other wall. "What does that symbol mean?" she asked.

"That's a fireplace," said Ravi. "So Jamie was watching someone who was standing near that fireplace at 9:38 p.m. Likely the same someone he followed from the memorial."

Pip nodded, marking these new points and times on the annotated floor plan.

"So if I stop looking for Jamie," she said, "and instead look for photos taken near the fireplace around 9:38, I might be able to narrow down who that someone is."

"Good plan, Sarge."

"You get back to your job," she said, pushing Ravi away with her foot, back around the island. He went, but not before stealing her sock.

Pip heard just one click of his trackpad before he said, quietly, "Shit."

"Ravi, can you stop messing around—"

"I'm not," he said, and there was no trace of a smile on his face anymore. "Shit." He said it louder that time, dropping Pip's sock.

"What?" Pip slid off her stool and followed him to his side. "You found Jamie?"

"No."

"The someone?"

"No, but it's definitely *a* someone," Ravi said darkly as Pip finally saw what was on his screen.

The photograph was filled with a hundred faces, all looking up at the sky, watching the lanterns. The nearest people were lit with a ghostly silver glow, points of red eyes as the camera flash set them ablaze. And standing near the very back, where the crowd thinned out, was Max Hastings.

"No," Pip said, and the word carried on silently, breathing out until her chest felt ragged and bare. Not him.

Max was standing there, alone, in a black jacket that blended into the night, a hood hiding most of his hair. But it was unmistakably him, eyes bright red, face blank and unreadable.

Ravi slammed his fist down on the marble countertop, making the laptop and Max's eyes shudder. "Why the fuck was he there?" He sniffed. "He knew he wasn't welcome. By anyone."

Pip put a hand on Ravi's shoulder and felt the rage like a tremor beneath his skin. "Because he's the sort of person who does whatever he wants, no matter who he hurts," she said.

"I didn't want him there," Ravi said, staring Max down. "He shouldn't have been there."

"I'm sorry, Ravi." She trailed her hand down his arm, tucking it into his palm.

"And I have to look at him all day tomorrow. Listen to more of his lies."

"You don't have to go to the trial," she said.

"Yes I do. I'm not just doing it for you. I mean, I am doing it for you, I'd do anything for you." He dropped his gaze. "But I'm doing it for me, too. If Sal had ever known what a monster Max really was, he would have been devastated. Devastated. He thought they were friends. How *dare* he come." He slammed his laptop closed, shutting Max's face away.

"In just a few days, he won't be able to go anywhere for a long while," Pip said, squeezing Ravi's hand. "Just a few days."

He gave her a weak smile, running his thumb over her knuckles. "Yeah," he said. "Yeah, I know."

They were interrupted by the scratching sound of a key as the front door clacked open. Three sets of feet padded against the floorboards. And then:

"Pip?" Her mom's voice echoed, arriving in the kitchen just before she did. She looked at Pip with her eyebrows raised, whittling four angry lines down her forehead. She dropped the look for just a second to flash Ravi a smile before turning back to Pip. "I saw your posters," she said, steadily. "When were you going to tell us about this?"

"Uh . . . ," Pip began.

Her dad appeared, carrying four bags filled to the brim, clumsily walking through and breaking the eye contact between Pip and her mom as he dumped the groceries on the counter. Ravi took his opportunity in the brief interlude to stand and slide his laptop under his arm. He stroked the back of Pip's neck and said, "Good luck," before making his way to the door, saying his charmingly awkward goodbyes to her family.

Traitor.

Pip lowered her head, trying to disappear inside her plaid shirt, using her laptop as a shield between herself and her parents.

"Pip?"

File Name:

Annotated Floor Plan of Calamity Party.jpg

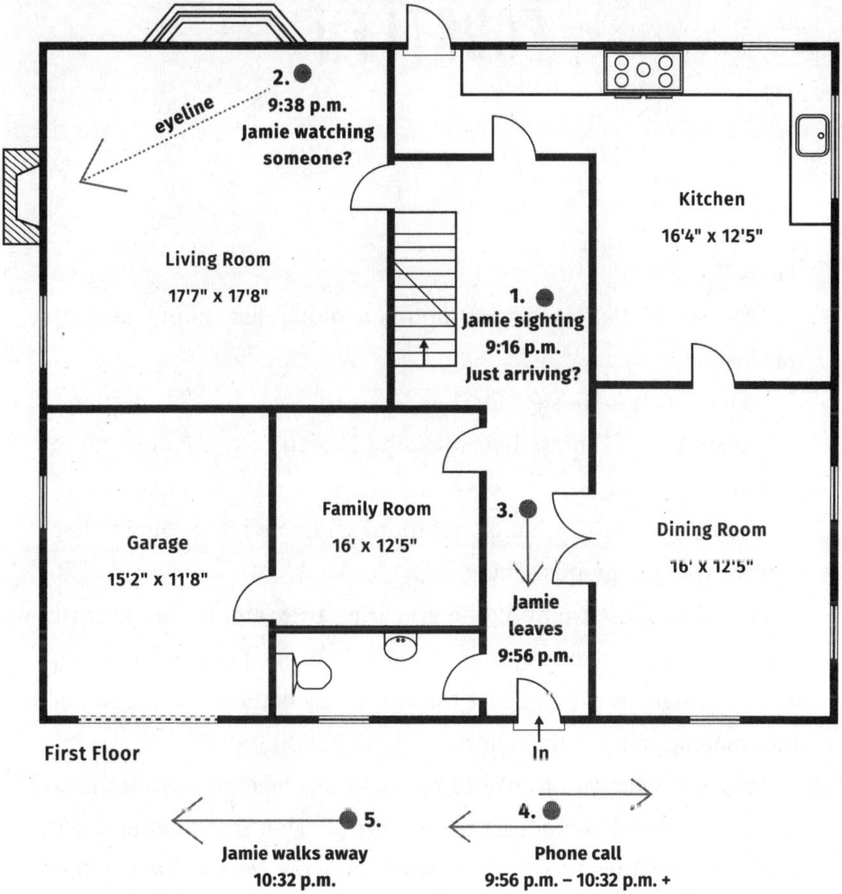

FOURTEEN

"Hello?"

"Yes, sorry." Pip closed her laptop, avoiding her mom's gaze. "I was just saving something."

"What are those posters for?"

Pip shuffled. "I think their meaning is pretty clear. Jamie's gone missing."

"Don't get smart with me," her mom said, one hand going to her hip: always a dangerous sign.

Pip's dad paused putting the groceries away and leaned against the counter, almost exactly in the middle between Pip and her mom, yet far enough away that he was safe from the battle. He was good at that: making camp in the neutral ground, building a bridge.

"Yes, it is what you think," Pip said, finally meeting her mother's eyes. "Connor and Joanna are really worried. They think something's happened to Jamie. So yes, I'm investigating his disappearance. And yes, I'm recording the investigation for season two of the show. They asked me to, and I said yes."

"But I don't understand," her mom said, even though she understood perfectly well. Another of her tactics. "You were done with all this. After everything you went through last time, the danger you put yourself in."

"I know—" Pip began, but her mom cut her off.

"You ended up in the hospital, Pippa, with an overdose. They had to pump your stomach. You were threatened by a now convicted killer." That was the only way Pip's mom referred to Elliot Ward now. She couldn't use the word, what he'd really been: a friend. "And Barney—"

"Mom, I know," Pip said, her voice rising, cracking as she fought to control it. "I know all the terrible things that happened last year because of me. I don't need your constant reminders. I know, OK? I know I was selfish, I know I was obsessive, I know I was reckless, and if I said sorry to you every day it still wouldn't be enough, OK?" Pip felt it, the pit in her stomach stirring, opening up to swallow her whole. "I'm sorry. I feel guilty all the time, so I don't need you to tell me. I'm the expert on my own mistakes. I understand."

"So why would you choose to put yourself through anything like that again?" her mom said, softening her voice and dropping the hand from her hip. Pip couldn't tell what that meant, whether it was a sign of victory or defeat.

A high, cartoonish giggling from the living room interrupted them.

"Joshua." Her dad finally spoke. "Turn the TV down, please!"

"But it's *SpongeBob* and it's only on fourteen!" a small voice shouted back.

"Joshua . . ."

"OK, OK."

The noise from the TV lowered until Pip could no longer hear it over the humming in her ears. Her dad settled back into his place, gesturing for them to continue.

"Why?" Her mom reiterated her last question, drawing a thick underline beneath it.

"Because I have to," Pip said. "And if you want to know the truth, I said no. That was my choice. I told Connor I couldn't do this again.

So yesterday, I went to speak to the police to get them to actually investigate Jamie's disappearance. I thought I could help that way. But they won't do anything for Jamie. They can't." Pip tucked her hands under her elbows. "The truth is, I had to do it, once the police said no. I didn't want to do it. But I can't *not* do it. The Reynoldses asked me. They came to me. And what if I'd said no? What if Jamie is never found? What if he's dead?"

"Pip, it is not your job to—"

"It isn't my job, but it feels like my responsibility," she said, cutting her mom off. "I know you'll both have a thousand arguments why that's not true, but I'm telling you the way it feels. It is my responsibility because I started something and I can't now take it back. Whatever it did to me, to all of us, I still solved a double murder case last year. Now I have six hundred thousand subscribers who will listen to me and I'm in a position to use that, to help people. To help Jamie. That's why I had no choice. I might not be the only one who can help, but I'm the only one here right now. This is Jamie, Mom. I couldn't live with myself if something happened to him and I'd said no because it was the easier choice. The safer choice. The choice my parents would want me to make. That's why I'm doing it. Not because I want to, because I have to. I've accepted that, and I hope you both can too."

Pip saw her dad out of the corner of her eye, nodding, the LED above drawing yellow streaks across the dark skin of his forehead. Her mom also saw it, turning to frown at him.

"Victor . . . ," she said.

"Leanne," he replied, stepping forward into no-man's-land. "Clearly she's not being reckless; she's put a lot of consideration into her decision. That's all we can ask of her, because it is her decision. She's eighteen now." He turned to smile at Pip, his eyes glazing in that way they did. The exact way he looked at her every time he told the story of how they'd met. Pip at four years old, stomping around this very house he was looking to buy, accompanying her mom to the showing because the childcare had fallen through. She'd followed them into each room, giving him a new animal fact in each one, despite her mother telling her to be quiet so she could inform the *nice man* about the high-spec kitchen. He always said it was both of them who stole his heart that day.

Pip returned his smile, and that hole in her stomach, it started to shrink just a little, freeing up more space for her around it.

"And what about the risks, Victor?" Pip's mom said, though her tone had changed now, the fight all but gone from it.

"Everything has risks," he said. "Even crossing the road. It's no different from if she were a journalist, or a police officer. And would we keep her from either of those things because of the potential risks? And also: I am very big. If anyone even thinks about hurting my daughter, I will rip off their head."

Pip laughed, and her mom's mouth twitched with a smile she didn't want to give into. The smile lost for now, though it gave a good fight.

"Fine," her mom said. "Pip, I'm not your enemy, I'm your mom. I only care about your safety and your happiness, the two things you lost last time. It's my job to protect you, whether you like it or not. So fine, I accept your decision. But I will be watching to make sure you don't become obsessive to the point where it's unhealthy, and you better believe me when I say there will be no missing school or neglecting your studies," she said, counting the points off on her fingers. "I'm sure everything is fine, but if there is any sign of danger, even the slightest hint, I want you to come straight to us. Promise me?"

"Thank you." Pip nodded, her chest releasing. "It won't be like last time, I promise." She wasn't that person anymore. She'd be good this time. She would. Things would be different, she told the yawning feeling that never left her. "But I should warn you: I don't think everything is fine. Put it this way: I don't think you'll see Jamie at work tomorrow morning."

Her mom's face flushed, and she dropped her gaze, tightening her lips into a line. Of all her mother's faces, Pip wasn't sure what this one meant. "Well," her mom said quietly, "all I'm saying is that Jamie is probably OK and I'm sure this will turn out to be nothing. That's why I don't want you to give too much of yourself to it."

"Well, I mean, hopefully it's nothing," Pip said, taking the bag of apples her dad handed her and placing them in the fruit bowl. "But there are a couple of red flags. His phone was turned off that night and hasn't been on since. And he was acting strangely that day—out of character."

Her mom placed a loaf of bread in the bread box. "Well, maybe acting strangely isn't that out of character for Jamie."

"Wait, what?" Pip stalled, pulling back from the box of oatmeal her dad was handing her.

"Oh, nothing," her mom said, busying herself with the canned tomatoes. "I shouldn't have said anything."

"Said anything about what?" Pip said, her heart jumping up to her throat, sensing her mom's unease. She narrowed her eyes at the back of her mom's head. "Mom? Do you know something about Jamie?"

File Name:

A Good Girl's Guide to Murder SEASON 2: Interview with Mom.wav

PIP: Mom, wait, hold on, I've set up the microphones now. Can you tell me what you were going to say? About Jamie?

[INAUDIBLE]

PIP: Mom, you . . . you have to come closer to the microphone. It can't pick you up from over there.

[INAUDIBLE]

PIP: Please can you just sit down and tell me what it is, whatever it is?

MOM: [INAUDIBLE] . . . need to get started on dinner.

PIP: I know, I know. This will only take a few minutes. Please? What did you mean by "acting strangely isn't that out of character for Jamie"? Are you talking about something that happened at work? Joanna said Jamie was working a later shift on Friday, before the memorial. Was he acting strangely then, is that what you mean? Please, Mom, this could really help the investigation.

MOM: No . . . it's . . . ah, no, I shouldn't. It's not my business. And this isn't the kind of thing I should be saying publicly anyway. I could get fired.

PIP: Jamie's missing. It's been almost two full days. He could be in danger. I don't think he'd care about what's anyone's business right now. And I'll edit out any details I need to, to protect you, obviously.

MOM: But Joanna—

PIP: She's the one who asked me to do this. She's accepted she might learn things about Jamie she wouldn't want to know.

MOM: Does Joanna . . . does Joanna think Jamie still works at Proctor and Radcliffe? Is that what he told her?

PIP: Yeah, of course, what do you mean? He does work there. He was at work on Friday before he went missing.

MOM: He's . . . Jamie doesn't work at the agency anymore. He left, maybe two and a half weeks ago.

PIP: He *left*? Did he quit? His family has no idea; they still think he works with you. He's been going to work every day. Why would he quit and lie about it?

MOM: He . . . he didn't quit.

PIP: What?

MOM: Pip . . .

PIP: Mom?

MOM: There was an incident. But I don't really want to talk about it; it has nothing to do with anything. My point was just that maybe Jamie disappearing isn't something so out of character, and why cause trouble for him when—

PIP: Mom, he's missing. Anything that happened in the past few weeks could be relevant. Anything. Joanna won't be angry if you tell, I know she won't. What was the incident? When?

MOM: Well . . . it must have been a Wednesday because Todd wasn't in, and Siobhan and Olivia were, but they were out on showings.

PIP: Wednesday two weeks ago? So that was the . . . eighth?

MOM: That sounds about right. I'd gone to lunch, went to see Jackie in the café, and left Jamie in the office alone. And when I got back . . . well, I must have been quicker than he expected because he . . .

PIP: What? What was he doing?

MOM: He had my key somehow. He must have taken it out of my purse earlier in the day and used it to unlock my desk drawer when I was out. I walked in on him taking the company credit card out of my drawer.

PIP: What?

MOM: He panicked when I came in. He was shaking. He tried several excuses as to why he was taking the card, said he needed the info so he could order more envelopes, then said Todd asked him to do something for him. But I knew he was lying, and Jamie knew I wasn't buying it. So then he just started apologizing, over and over again. Said he was sorry, he just needed the money and he said something . . . he said something like "I wouldn't have done this if it wasn't life or death."

PIP: "Life or death"? What did he mean by that?

MOM: I don't know. I'm guessing he wanted to take the card to an ATM and withdraw a few hundred dollars.

PIP: Can you take money out on a credit card?

MOM: Yes, you can. I mean, you wouldn't, under normal circumstances, but that's the impression I got. Jamie knew the PIN because I'd sent him out with that card to get office supplies before. I don't know why he needed the money, but clearly he was desperate. We'd never had any problems with Jamie before this. I'd offered him the job to help him out, to help Joanna and Arthur out because Jamie had been struggling to settle anywhere. He's a very sweet young man, has been since he was a kid. The Jamie I walked in on felt almost like a different person. He looked so scared. So sorry.

PIP: He must have been desperate, because he would've known that even if he'd managed to steal the cash, you'd have found out eventually. Why did he need money so urgently?

MOM: I never asked. I just told him to put the card down and return my key and I wouldn't call the police. I didn't need to make any more trouble for him; it looked like he had enough going on, whatever it was. And I would've felt too guilty, calling the police on one of my friend's children in trouble. You don't do that. So I told Jamie I wouldn't tell anyone what I had seen, but that he could no longer work at Proctor and Radcliffe and his contract would be terminated immediately. That I'd make up some other reason. I told him he needed to straighten out his life or I'd have to tell Joanna eventually. He thanked me for not calling the police, said thank you for the opportunity in the first place, and then he left. The last thing he said on his way out was "I'm so, so sorry, I wouldn't have done it if I didn't have to."

PIP: What did he need the money for?

MOM: He didn't say. But if he was willing to steal from the company and get caught, what else could he have needed the money for except, well, something . . . illegal?

PIP: Well, maybe. But that doesn't mean his disappearance two weeks later isn't suspicious or out of character. If anything, this makes me more certain Jamie's in trouble. That he's got himself mixed up in something dangerous.

MOM: I certainly never thought he'd be the sort to steal. Ever.

PIP: And the only reason he gave you was that it was life or death?

MOM: That's what he said, yes.

PIP: Whose life or death did he mean?

FIFTEEN

Pip was certain she could see the very moment Joanna's heart began to break. It wasn't when she told her and Connor about the calamity party, about Jamie following someone there. It wasn't when she said he'd left the party at ten-thirty and was witnessed on the phone, mentioning the police. It wasn't even when she told them Jamie had been lying to them for two weeks about still having his job, and how he'd lost it. No, it was precisely when she said those exact words: life or death.

Something instantly changed in Joanna: the way she held her head, the outline of her eyes, the way her skin slackened and paled like some of the life in her had slipped away, drifting out into the cold air of the kitchen. And Pip knew she'd just given voice to Joanna's very worst fears. Even worse than that, those words had come from Jamie himself.

"But we don't know what Jamie meant by that. It's possible he was exaggerating to minimize the trouble he was in, or to get my mom to sympathize with him," Pip said, looking from Connor to Joanna's broken eyes. Arthur Reynolds was not home. Apparently, he'd been out most of the day and neither Connor nor Joanna knew where he was. *Blowing off steam* was Joanna's best guess. "Do you have any idea what Jamie might have needed the money for?"

"Wednesday two weeks ago?" Connor said. "It's not like there were any birthdays or occasions coming up that he'd need money for."

"I doubt Jamie intended to steal money to buy birthday presents," Pip replied as gently as she could. "Do you know if he had any debts he might have needed to pay off? A phone bill? We know he was very attached to his phone in recent weeks."

"I don't think so." Joanna finally spoke. "He had a good salary at the agency; I'm sure that more than covered his phone bill. It's not like he's been spending more than usual. Jamie hardly ever buys anything for himself, not clothes or anything. I think his main expense would just be, well, lunch."

"OK, I'll look into it."

"Where has Jamie been going?" asked Connor. "When he told us he was going to work?"

"I'll look into that also," Pip said. "Maybe he was just getting out of the house so he wouldn't have to tell any of you what had happened. Maybe he was working on getting a new job before he told you he'd lost the last one? I know it was a point of contention between Jamie and his dad; maybe he was trying to avoid another argument about jobs."

"Yes," Joanna said, scratching her chin. "Arthur would have been angry about him losing another job. And Jamie hates confrontation."

"Going back to the calamity party," Pip said, steering the conversation, "do you have any idea who Jamie could have been on the phone with? Someone who might have asked him to do something?"

"No. It was none of us," Joanna said.

"Zoe?" asked Pip.

"No, she had no contact with Jamie that day. The only person I know Jamie calls regularly is Nat da Silva. Or it used to be."

"It wasn't her," Pip said. "She told me Jamie never turned up at her house as planned and ignored all her texts and calls."

"I don't know, then. I'm sorry," Joanna said in a small voice, like that was slipping away from her too.

"That's OK." Pip brightened hers to make up for it. "I'm guessing you would have told me, but any luck with the computer password?"

"Not yet," Connor said. "We've been working through that questionnaire, trying all variables with number replacements. Nothing so far. We're keeping a record of everything we've tried. I think we're over six hundred failed attempts now."

"OK, well, keep trying. Tomorrow I'll see if I can research and contact someone who can brute-force the password without damaging any of the data."

"Yep, will do." Connor fiddled with his own fingers. There was an open cereal box on the counter behind him, and two discarded bowls; Pip guessed that had been dinner. "Is there anything else we can be doing, other than the password? Anything?"

"Um, yeah of course," she said, scrambling to think of something. "I'm still going through all the videos and photos from the calamity party that people have sent me. As I said, I'm looking for people who were standing around the fireplace, from 9:38 p.m. until about 9:50 p.m. The only near hit I've found is a photo taken at 9:29 in the direction of the fireplace. There are about nine people in it, some in our grade, some the grade below. The photo might be too early to show whoever Jamie was watching, but it's something I . . . we can chase up tomorrow at school. Connor, I'll email you the photo and video files and you could look through them, too?"

"Yeah." He sat up straighter. "I'll do that."

"Perfect."

"I've been getting messages from people," Joanna said. "From friends and neighbors who've seen your Missing posters. I haven't left the house, been trying Jamie's computer and phone all day. Could I see the photo you used for the posters?"

"Yeah, sure." Pip swiped her finger across the trackpad to re-awaken her laptop. She navigated through her recent files, pulled up the photograph, and twisted the computer to face Joanna. "I went for this one," she said. "You can see his face clearly, and his smile isn't too wide, because I often think people look slightly different when they're *smiling* smiling. This was one you took before the birthday cake was lit, so no strange lighting from the candles. Is that OK?"

"Yes," Joanna said quietly, covering her mouth with her balled-up hand. "Yes, it's perfect." Her eyes filled as they flitted up and down her son's face, like she was scared to let her gaze settle on one spot for too long. What did she think she'd see if it did? Or was she studying his face, trying to remember every detail?

"I'm just going to the bathroom," Joanna said in a faraway voice, standing up shakily. She closed the kitchen door behind her and Connor sighed, deflated. He picked at the loose skin by his fingernails.

"She's gone upstairs to cry," he said. "Been doing it all day. I know what she's doing, and she must know I know. But she won't do it in front of me."

"I'm sorry."

"Maybe she thinks I'll lose hope if I see her crying."

"I'm sorry, Connor." Pip reached out to touch his arm, but he was too far across the table. She went for her laptop instead, pulling it back in front of her, Jamie's face staring out of the screen. "But we've made progress today, we have. We've filled in more of Jamie's timeline that night and have a couple of leads to look into."

Connor shrugged, looking at the time on his phone. "Jamie was last seen at 10:32 now, right? That means the forty-eight-hour mark is in fifty-seven minutes." He went quiet for a moment. "He's not coming back in the next fifty-seven minutes, is he?"

Pip didn't know what to say to that. She knew something she should say, something she should have told Connor yesterday: not to touch Jamie's toothbrush or his comb or anything that would have his DNA on it, in case it was ever needed. But now was not the time. She wasn't sure there would ever be a right time to say that. A line that could never be uncrossed.

Pip looked instead at her screen, at Jamie's half-smiling face, his eyes seeing out into hers as she saw into his, as though there weren't ten days between them. And then she realized: he was sitting exactly opposite her, at this very same table. She was here and Jamie was right there, like a crack in time had opened up across the polished wooden surface. Everything was the same as in the photograph behind him: the fridge door with a scattered collection of cheesy souvenir magnets, the cream-colored blind pulled one third of the way down behind the sink, the wooden chopping board propped up in the same place above Jamie's left shoulder, and the black cylindrical knife rack above his other shoulder, holding six different-sized knives with color-coded bands on their handles.

Well, actually—Pip's eyes flickered between the screen and up—the knife set behind Jamie in the photo was complete, all the knives tucked inside the rack: purple, orange, light green, dark green, red, and yellow. But now—Pip looked up again—one of the knives was missing. The one with the yellow band.

"What are you looking at?" Connor said. Pip hadn't noticed him standing behind her, watching over her shoulder.

"Oh, nothing," she said. "I was just looking at this photo, and I noticed one of the knives isn't here now. It's nothing," she repeated, waving her hand to dismiss the idea.

"It's probably in the dishwasher." Connor walked over and pulled open the dishwasher door. "Hmm," he said, abandoning it and moving to the sink instead. He clattered around in there, the sound of porcelain hitting porcelain making Pip flinch. "Someone probably put it in a drawer by accident. I'm always doing that," he said, but there was a frantic edge to his voice as he went about pulling out the drawers, their contents crashing around, drawers straining at their very limits.

Pip must have caught the dread from watching him, her heart spiking at every crash, and something cold made itself at home in her chest. Connor kept going, in a frenzy, until every drawer was open, like the kitchen had grown outward teeth, biting into the rest of the room. "Not here," he told her needlessly.

"Maybe you should ask your mom," Pip said, rising to her feet.

"Mom!" Connor shouted, turning his attention to the cupboards, opening each door until it looked like the kitchen was hanging upside down. It felt like it, too: Pip's stomach lurching, feet stumbling over themselves.

She heard Joanna thundering down the stairs.

"Calm down, Connor," Pip tried. "It's probably here somewhere."

"And if it isn't," he said, on his knees checking the cupboard under the sink, "what would that mean?"

What *would* it mean? Maybe she should have kept this observation to herself a little longer. "It would mean that one of the knives is missing."

"What's missing?" Joanna said, rushing into the room.

"One of your knives, the one with the yellow band," Pip said, dragging the laptop over to show Joanna. "Can you see? It was here in this photo taken on Jamie's birthday. But it's not in the rack now."

"It's not anywhere," Connor said, out of breath. "I've checked the whole kitchen."

"I can see that," Joanna said, closing some of the cupboards. She re-inspected the sink, removing all the mugs and glasses sitting in there, checking underneath. She looked over the drying rack, even though Pip could see from back here that it was empty. Connor was at the knife rack, removing each of the other knives, as though the yellow one could somehow be hiding underneath.

"Well, it's lost," Joanna said. "It's not in any of the places it should be. I'll ask Arthur when he gets back."

"Do you have any recent memories of using that knife?" Pip asked. She flicked through the photos from Jamie's birthday. "Jamie used the red knife to cut the cake on his birthday, but do you have any memories since that date, of using the yellow one?"

Joanna looked up to the right, eyes flitting in minuscule movements as she searched her memory. "Connor, what day this week did I make moussaka?"

Connor's chest was rising and falling with his breath. "Um, that was the day I came in late, after my guitar lesson, wasn't it? So Wednesday."

"Yes, Wednesday." Joanna turned to Pip. "I don't actually remember using it, but that's always the one I use for cutting eggplant, because it's the sharpest and widest. I would have noticed if it was gone, I'm sure."

"OK, OK," Pip said, buying herself some time to think. "So the knife likely went missing in the last four days."

"What does that mean?" Joanna said.

"It doesn't necessarily mean anything," Pip said tactfully. "It might have no correlation to Jamie at all. Might turn up somewhere around the house you haven't thought to look. Right now, it's just a piece of information about something out of the ordinary, and I want to know everything that's out of the ordinary, no matter what it is. That's all."

Yeah, she should have kept it to herself; the panic in both Joanna's and Connor's eyes confirmed that. Pip glanced at the brand of the knives and took a photo of the rack and empty slot with her phone, trying not to draw too much attention to what she was doing. Returning to her laptop, she Googled the brand and an image came up from the company's website, of all the different color-coded knives laid out in a row.

"Yes, those are the ones," Joanna said behind her.

"OK." Pip closed her laptop and slid it back into her bag. "I'll get those calamity files to you, Connor. I'll be looking through them until late, so if you find anything, text me right away. And I guess I'll see you tomorrow at school. Good night, Joanna. Sleep well."

Sleep well? What a stupid thing to say. Of course she wasn't going to sleep well.

Pip backed out of the room with a strained, toothless smile, hoping they couldn't read anything on her face, any imprint of the thought she'd just had. The thought she'd had before she could stop herself, looking at the online image of the six colored knives arranged in a line, her eyes circling the yellow one. The thought that if you wanted to use one of those knives as a weapon, that's the one you would choose. The missing one.

File Name:

Photographs of knife set last Thursday and today.jpg

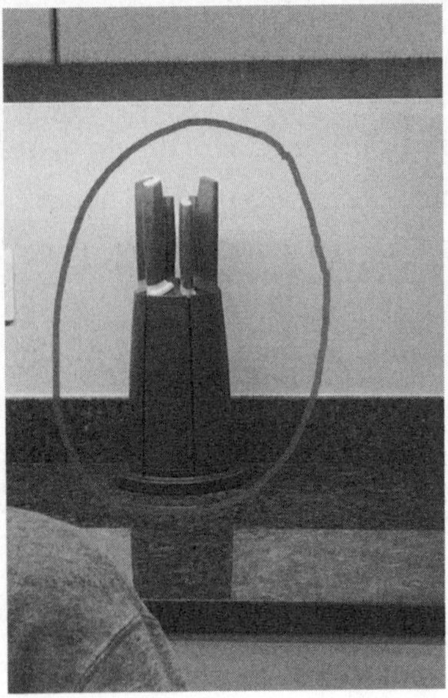

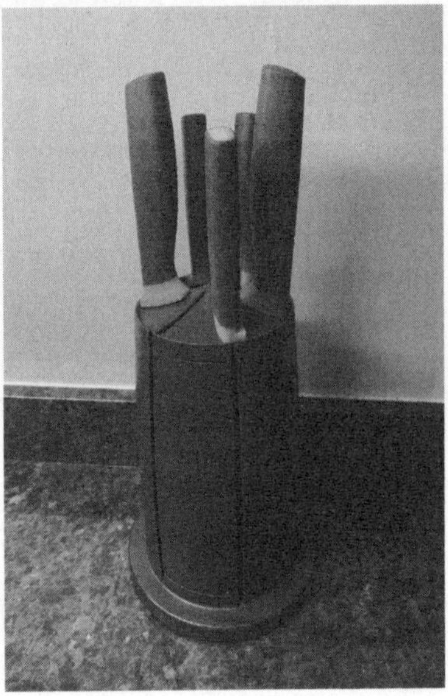

File Name:

Case Notes 3.docx

THE MISSING KNIFE:

Might be irrelevant. I'm desperately hoping it is, otherwise this case has taken a sinister turn I don't want to go down. But the timing does feel significant: that both Jamie and a knife from the Reynoldses' house go missing in the same week. How do you just lose a great big knife like that (a 6-inch chef's knife, the website says) around the house? You don't. It must have been taken out of the house at some point after Wednesday evening.

STRANGE BEHAVIOR:

Attempting to steal money from Mom's company is definitely out of character for the Jamie I know. The Reynoldses say so too, that he's never stolen anything before. What was his plan—take the card to an ATM and withdraw the maximum amount of cash (Google says this can be between $300 to $800)? And why was he so desperate for the money? Random thought: Could this have anything to do with that women's watch I found in Jamie's bedside table? It doesn't look new, but maybe he bought it secondhand? Or could that have been stolen, too?

And what did Jamie's "life or death" comment mean? I get chills thinking about it, looking back on it from the other side of his disappearance. Was he talking about himself or someone else? (Note: buying a secondhand women's watch probably doesn't fall under "life or death.")

Not telling his family about losing his job doesn't feel inherently suspicious to me. Of course he'd want to cover up the reason he was fired, but it also makes sense he wanted to hide the fact he was jobless again, given that so much of the tension between Jamie and his father has been about his noncommittal job-hopping, about not having enough ambition or drive.

On the topic of strange behavior—where was Arthur Reynolds today? OK, I understand that he doesn't believe Jamie is really missing, that he's likely run off after their big argument and will be back in a few days completely fine. Past experience supports this theory. But if your wife and younger son are so convinced something's wrong, wouldn't you start to entertain the possibility? It's clear Joanna is distraught; even if Arthur doesn't believe anything is wrong, wouldn't he stick around to support her? He still wants nothing to do with this investigation. Maybe he'll change his mind soon, now that we've passed the forty-eight-hour mark.

CALAMITY PARTY:

What was Jamie doing there? My working theory is that the "someone" he saw (and told Nat about) is likely a person in my grade or the grade below. Jamie spotted them at the memorial, and afterward, he followed this person as they walked (presumably with a group of friends) to Highmoor and the calamity party at Stephen Thompson's house. I suspect Jamie went inside (the sighting at 9:16 p.m.) because he wanted to talk to this "someone"—why else follow them? At 9:38 p.m. I believe Jamie was watching "someone" as they stood near the fireplace. A photo at 9:29 p.m. shows nine identifiable people around the fireplace.

Seniors: Elspeth Crossman, Katya Juckes, Struan Copeland, Joseph Powrie, Emma Thwaites, and Aisha Bailey.

Juniors: Yasmin Miah, Richard Willett, and Lily Horton.

The photo doesn't overlap with the Jamie sighting, but it's

the closest I have. I'll find them all at school tomorrow and see whether they know anything.

OPEN LEADS:

- More photos/videos from calamity party being sent in—go through them.
- Hillary F. Weiseman. The *only* Hillary F. Weiseman I can find is the 84-year-old who died in Fairview in 2008. Obit says she left behind one daughter and two grandsons, but I can't find any other Weisemans. Why was Jamie writing her name down within the last week and a half? What's the connection?
- Who was Jamie on the phone with at 10:32 p.m.? Long conversation—30+ mins? Same person he's been texting/talking to in recent weeks? Not Nat da Silva.
- The identity of "someone" and why Jamie followed them from the memorial to the calamity?
- Stealing money—why? Life or death?

MONDAY
3 DAYS MISSING

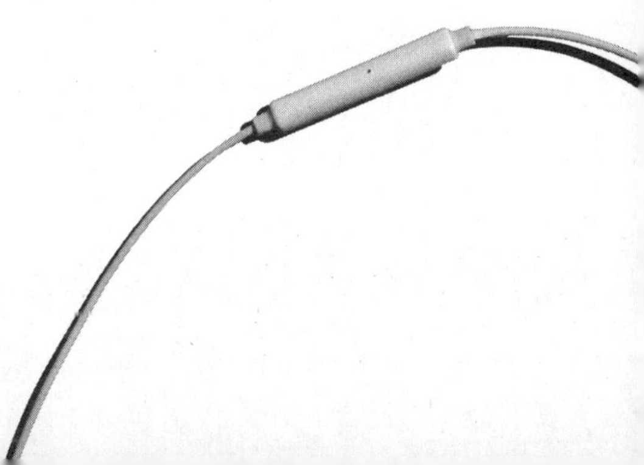

SIXTEEN

Pip didn't sit at the front anymore. That's where she used to sit, in this classroom, at this very time, when it was Elliot Ward standing at the front, talking them through the economic effects of World War II.

Now it was Mr. Clark, the new history teacher who'd come in after winter break to take Mr. Ward's place. He was young, maybe not even thirty, with brown feathered hair and a trimmed beard that was mostly ginger. He was eager, and more than a little enthusiastic about his PowerPoint slide transitions. Sound effects too. It was a little too early on a Monday morning for exploding hand grenades, though.

Not that Pip was really listening. She was sitting in the back corner. This was her place now, and Connor's was beside her; that hadn't changed. Except he'd been late today, and now he was jiggling his leg as he sat there, also not paying attention.

Pip's textbook was standing up on her desk, open to page 237, but she wasn't actually taking notes. The textbook was a shield, hiding her from Mr. Clark's eyes. Her phone was propped up against the page, earphones plugged in and the cable tucked up the front of her sweater, the wire snaking down one sleeve so the earbuds rested in her palm. Fully disguised. It must look to Mr. Clark like

Pip was resting her chin in her hand as she scribbled down dates and percentages, but really she was scrolling through calamity party files.

A new wave of emails with attachments had come in late last night and this morning. Word must have started to spread about Jamie. But still no photos in the location and time frame she needed. Pip glanced up: five minutes until the bell, long enough to go through another email.

The next one was from Hannah Revens, from Pip's English class.

Hey Pip, it said. *Someone told me this morning you're looking for Connor's missing brother and that he was at the calamity on Friday. This video is super embarrassing—apparently I sent it to my boyfriend at 9:49 when I was already super drunk—please don't show it to anyone. But there's a guy in the background I don't recognize. See you at school.*

A prickle of nervous energy crawled up the back of Pip's neck. The time frame, and a guy Hannah didn't recognize. This could be it: the break. Pip thumbed on to the attached file and pressed play.

The sound blared into her ear: loud music, chattering voices, bursts of jeering and cheering that must have come from the beer pong game in the dining room. But this video was taken in the living room. Hannah's face took up most of the frame as she pointed the phone down at herself from an outstretched arm. She was leaning against the back of a sofa, opposite the one Jasveen was sitting on at 9:38 p.m., the end of which was just visible in the background.

Hannah was on her own, the dog filter from Instagram applied to her face, pointy brown ears buried in her hair, following her as she swung her head around. The new Ariana Grande song was playing, and Hannah was lip-synching to it. *Very* dramatically. Air grabs and eyes screwed shut when the song demanded it.

This wasn't a joke, was it? Pip kept watching, searching the scene behind Hannah's head. She recognized two of the faces back there: Joseph Powrie and Katya Juckes. And judging by the positions of the sofas, they must have been standing in front of the fireplace, which hadn't quite made it into the shot. They were talking to a girl with her back to the camera. Long, dark straightened hair, jeans. That could be dozens of people Pip knew.

The clip was almost finished, the blue line creeping along the progress bar toward the end. Six seconds to go. And that was when two things happened at the exact same time. The girl with the long brown hair turned and started to walk away from the fireplace, toward Hannah's camera. Simultaneously, from the other side of the frame, a person crossed toward her, walking quickly, so all you really caught was the blur of their shirt and a head floating above. A burgundy shirt. Jamie.

As the two figures were about to meet, Jamie reached out to tap the girl on the shoulder.

The video ended.

"Shit," Pip whispered into her sleeve, drawing Connor's attention. She knew exactly who that girl was.

"What?" he hissed.

"Someone."

"Huh?"

The bell rang and the sound sliced right through Pip, making her wince. Her hearing was always more sensitive on not enough sleep.

"In the hall," she said, packing her textbook into her bag and untangling herself from the earphones. She stood up and shouldered her bag, missing whatever homework Mr. Clark was assigning them.

Being at the back of the room meant being last to leave, waiting impatiently for everyone else to spill out of the classroom. Connor followed Pip into the hall and she guided him over to the far wall.

"What is it?" Connor asked.

Pip unwound her earphones, jamming them one by one into Connor's pointy ears.

"Ouch, be careful, would you?" He closed his hands around his ears to keep the sound in as Pip held up her phone for him and pressed play. A tiny smirk flickered across his face. "Wow, that's embarrassing," he said after a few seconds. "Is that why you wanted to show m—"

"Obviously not," she said. "Wait for the end."

And when it came, his eyes narrowed and he said, "Stella Chapman?"

"Yep." Pip tugged the earphones out of his ears too hard, making him "ouch" again. "Stella Chapman must be the 'someone' Jamie spotted at the memorial and followed to the party."

Connor paused. "Stella? Why would Jamie know Stella? What do we do now?"

"Find her at lunch and talk to her. Ask how they know each other, what they talked about. Why Jamie followed her."

"OK, good," Connor said, and his face changed slightly, like the muscles beneath had shifted, loosened. "This is good, right?"

"Yeah," Pip said, though "good" might not be the right word. But at least they were finally getting somewhere.

"Stella?"

"Oh, hi," Stella replied, mouth full of Twix. She narrowed her almond-shaped brown eyes, her perfect cheekbones made even sharper by the bronzer she'd swiped over her tan skin.

Pip had known exactly where to wait for her. They were locker neighbors, Chapman just six places over from Fitz-Amobi, and they greeted each other most mornings, their hellos always bookended by the awful screech of Stella's locker door. Pip was ready for it this time, as Stella opened the door and deposited some books inside.

"What's up?" Stella's eyes trailed over Pip's shoulder to where Connor was standing, boxing her in. He looked ridiculous, hands on his hips like he was some kind of bodyguard. Pip flashed him an angry look until he stepped back and relaxed.

"You on the way to lunch?" asked Pip. "I was wondering if I could talk to you about something."

"Er, yeah, I'm heading to the cafeteria. What's wrong?"

"Nothing," Pip said casually, walking Stella down the hall. "Just wondered whether I could borrow you for a few minutes first. In here?" Pip halted, pushing open the door of a math classroom she'd already checked was empty.

"Why?" The suspicion was clear in Stella's voice.

"My brother's missing," Connor butted in, hands going to his hips again. Was he trying to look intimidating? Because it wasn't working for him at all. Pip glared at him again; normally he was good at reading her eyes.

"You might've heard that I'm looking into his disappearance?" Pip said. "I just have a few questions for you about Jamie Reynolds."

"I'm sorry." Stella shuffled uncomfortably, picking at the ends of her hair. "I don't know him."

"Bu—" Connor started, but Pip cut him off.

"Jamie was at the calamity party on Friday. It's currently the last time he was seen," she said. "I've found a video in which Jamie comes over to talk to you at the party. I just want to know what you talked about, even if you don't really know him. That's all."

Stella didn't answer, but her face said everything she wouldn't: her eyes widened, lines wrinkling her smooth forehead.

"We really need to find him, Stella," Pip said gently. "He could be in trouble, real trouble, and anything that happened that night might help us figure out where he's gone. It's . . . it's life or death," she said, refusing to look Connor's way.

Stella chewed her lip, eyes spooling as she made up her mind.

"OK," she said.

File Name:

A Good Girl's Guide to Murder SEASON 2: Interview with Stella Chapman.wav

STELLA: Is this OK?

PIP: Yes, great, I can hear you perfectly. So can we go over how you know Jamie Reynolds?

STELLA: I . . . um, I don't . . . know him.

CONNOR: [INAUDIBLE]

PIP: Connor, you can't talk while we're recording.

CONNOR: [INAUDIBLE]

STELLA: Um . . . I . . . I . . .

PIP: Actually, Connor, why don't you go on ahead to lunch? I'll see you there.

CONNOR: [INAUDIBLE]

PIP: No, really, I insist. *Connor.* I'll meet you there. Go on. Oh, and close the door please. Thank you. Sorry about that, he's just worried about his brother.

STELLA: Yeah, that's OK, I get it. I just didn't want to talk about his brother in front of him, y'know? It's weird.

PIP: I understand. It's better this way. So how do you know Jamie?

STELLA: I *really* don't know him. At all. That time on Friday, that was the first time I ever spoke to him. I didn't know who he was until I saw the posters on my way to school this morning.

PIP: Let me play this clip for you. Ignore Hannah's face. You see, in the background, you walk away from Katya and then Jamie comes over to you.

STELLA: Yeah, he did. It was, um . . . strange. Really strange. I think there must have been a misunderstanding or something. Or he was confused.

PIP: What do you mean? What did he want to talk to you about?

STELLA: Well, like you can see there, he tapped me on the shoulder, so I turned to him and he said, "Leila, it's you." And so I was like, "No, I'm Stella." But he carried on, he was like, "Leila, it's really you," and he wasn't listening when I said, "No, that's not me."

PIP: Leila?

STELLA: Yeah. He was pretty insistent, so then I was like, "Sorry, I don't know you," and began to walk away and he said something like, "Leila, it's me, Jamie. I almost didn't recognize you because you've changed your hair." So I was really confused at this point. And he also looked really confused, and then he asked me what I was doing at a high school party anyway. So I said to him, "I really think you have me confused with someone else." And he was like, "Leila, I know it's you from your photos. It's me, Jamie. We've been talking for weeks."

PIP: And then what did you say?

STELLA: Well, by this point he was freaking me out a bit, so I said to him, "My name is not Leila, it's Stella, and I don't know who you are or what you're talking about. Leave me alone or I'll scream." And then I walked away. That was it. He didn't say anything else or follow me. He actually looked really sad when I left, but I don't know why. I still don't understand what was going on, what he meant. If it was some, like, weird, creepy pickup tactic, I dunno. He's older, right?

PIP: Yes, he's twenty-four. So wait, let me get this straight: he calls you Leila multiple times, and says "It's me, Jamie" when you don't seem to recognize him. Then he comments that he knows you from your photos, but that you've changed your hair—

STELLA: Which I haven't. My hair's been the same since, like, forever.

PIP: Right, and then he also asks you "What are you doing at a high school party?"

STELLA: Yeah, basically those exact words. Why? What are you thinking?

PIP: Stella . . . on your social media, like on Insta, do you have a lot of pictures of yourself? Like selfies or photos where it's just you in the shot?

STELLA: Well, yeah, I do. Most of them. What's wrong with that?

PIP: Nothing. How many photos have you posted of just you?

STELLA: I don't know, tons. Why?

PIP: How many followers do you have?

STELLA: Not that many. Around eight hundred-ish? Why, Pip? What's wrong?

PIP: I, um, I'm thinking . . . it sounds to me like Jamie might have been talking to a catfish.

STELLA: A catfish?

PIP: Someone who's been using your photos, calls themselves Leila.

STELLA: Oh. Wait, you know, that actually makes a lot of sense, now that you've said it. Yeah, it definitely seemed as though Jamie thought he knew me and he expected me to know him too. And he said we'd been talking for weeks. Well, he and Leila had. Clearly never in real life, though.

PIP: And if it is a catfish, maybe they've edited your photos somehow, hence the "changed your hair" comment. I think Jamie spotted you at the memorial, well . . . he spotted who he thought was Leila, and it was the first time he'd seen her in real life, but he was confused because you looked different. I think he then followed you when you walked to the calamity party, waiting for an opportunity to speak to you. But he was also confused about why you were there, at a high school party, hanging around with eighteen-year-olds, so I'm guessing this Leila told him she was older, in her twenties.

STELLA: Yes, that makes total sense. That all fits. A catfish. It's so obvious now. Oh god, I feel bad about what I said now I know he wasn't trying to be creepy. And he looked so crushed afterward. He must have worked it out, right? Realized then that Leila wasn't real, that she'd been lying to him?

PIP: Seems like it.

STELLA: So he's missing now? Like *missing* missing?

PIP: Yeah, he's *missing* missing. Right after he found out someone's been catfishing him.

To: AGGGTMpodcast@gmail.com
Time: 2:41 p.m.
From: harryscythe98@yahoo.com
Subject: Sighting of Jamie Reynolds

Dear Pippa Fitz-Amobi,

Hello, my name's Harry Scythe. I'm a big fan of your podcast—great job with the first season!

I live in Fairview and work at the bookstore (where I'm emailing from now). I was working Friday afternoon, and after we closed up, me and a few work friends went to the memorial—we didn't really know Andie or Sal, but it's nice to show up, I think. And then we went to my buddy's house on Weevil Road for some takeout and beers.

Anyway, when we were leaving at the end of the night, I'm pretty sure we saw your guy, Jamie Reynolds, walking past. I'm like 98% sure it was him, and since seeing your posters this morning, I spoke to my friends and they think it was him too. So I thought I should let you know ASAP. Me and two of my friends who were also there are working now, so feel free to contact us/come in and talk, if this information is at all useful to your investigation.

Sincerely,
Harry

SEVENTEEN

The Book Cellar stood out along Main Street. It always had, as far back as Pip could remember. And not just because it had been her favorite place to go, dragging her mom in by the arm when she *needed* just one more book. But quite literally: the owner had painted the outside of the store a bright, cheerful purple, where the rest of the street was uniform in its clean white painted facades and redbrick walls. Apparently, it had caused a major uproar thirteen years ago.

Connor was lagging behind Pip on the sidewalk. He still wasn't on board with *this whole catfish theory,* as he'd phrased it. Even when she pointed out that, in Connor's own words, Jamie had been on his phone all the time in recent weeks.

"It fits everything we know so far," Pip continued, eyeing the bookstore up ahead. "Late-night phone calls. And Jamie's been protective about no one seeing his screen, which makes me think that his relationship with this Leila, this catfish, is a romantic one. Jamie was probably feeling vulnerable after the whole Nat da Silva situation, so it's easy to see how he might fall for someone online. Especially someone using Stella Chapman's photos."

"I guess. Just not what I expected." Connor dipped his head into his shoulder, a gesture that could either have been a nod or a shrug.

It wasn't the same, doing this with Connor. Ravi knew just what to say, what to pick out, how to push her into thinking clearly. And he jumped with her, hand in hand, into even her wildest conclusions. They just worked like that, teased out the best in each other, knowing when to talk and when to just be there. Ravi was still at the courthouse, but Pip had called him earlier, after Stella's interview. He'd been waiting around for Max's defense to start because the prosecution had just rested, and they'd talked through everything together—Jamie, Leila—until it all fit. But this was the third time she'd run the explanation by Connor, and each time he'd shrugged, making the doubts creep into Pip's mind. There wasn't time for doubts, so she tried to outrun them, hurrying along the sidewalk as Connor struggled to keep up.

"It's the only explanation that fits the evidence we have," Pip said. "Hunches have to follow the evidence, that's how this works." She turned her attention back to The Book Cellar, coming to a stop in front of the door. "When we're finished here with this potential sighting, we'll go back to my house and see if we can find this Leila online and confirm the theory. Oh"—she turned to Connor—"and let me do the talking, please. It works better that way."

"Yeah, fine," he said. "I said sorry about the Stella thing."

"I know. And I know you're just worried." She softened her face. "Just leave it to me. That's what I'm here for."

A bell jangled above the glass door as Pip pushed her way inside. She loved the smell here, an ancient kind of smell, stale and timeless. You could get lost in the labyrinth of dark mahogany bookshelves labeled with shining gold metal letters. Even as a child, she'd always found herself in front of the Crime shelves.

"Hi," came a deep voice from behind the counter. And then: "Oh, it's you. Hi."

The guy at the register sidestepped the counter and moved toward them across the store floor. He looked out of place here, as tall as the highest shelves and almost as wide; his arms were thick with muscle, and his near-black hair was tied back from his face in a small bun.

"I'm Harry," he said, holding his hand out to Pip. "Harry Scythe," he clarified when she shook it. "The one who emailed you."

"Yes, thank you so much for that," Pip said. "I came as fast as I could; we ran out as soon as the bell rang." A floorboard creaked under Connor's feet. "This is Connor Reynolds, Jamie's brother."

"Hello," Harry said, pivoting the outstretched hand to Connor now too. "I'm sorry about your brother, man."

Connor mumbled a few half-words.

"Could I ask you about what you saw on Friday night?" Pip asked. "Do you mind if I record us?"

"Yeah, yeah, that's fine. Hey, Mike," Harry called to a guy restocking shelves at the back. "Go get Soph from the office! All three of us were there when we saw him," he explained.

"Perfect. And could I set up the microphones here?" Pip gestured to the counter, beside the register.

"Sure, sure, it's always quiet from four until closing anyway." Harry cleared a pile of brown paper bags so Pip could set her backpack down. She pulled out her laptop and the two USB microphones.

Soph and Mike appeared from the back office. Pip had always been curious about what was back there, the sort of wonder that dies a little more each year you grow older.

They swapped new hellos and introductions and Pip instructed the three Book Cellar employees to gather around one microphone. She had to raise it on a stack of books to compensate for Harry's height.

When everyone was ready, Pip pressed record and nodded pointedly. "So after the memorial, Harry, you said you went to someone's house. Whose house?"

"Mine," said Mike, scratching his beard too hard, making the blue audio line spike on Pip's screen. He looked older than the other two, in his thirties at least. "On Weevil Road."

"How far up?"

"It's number fifty-eight, halfway up where the road bends."

Pip knew exactly where he meant. "OK, so you all spent the evening together?"

"Yep," Soph said. "Us and our friend Lucy. She's not in today."

"And did you all leave Mike's house at the same time?"

"Yeah, I was driving," said Harry. "I dropped Soph and Lucy home on my way."

"OK," Pip said, "and do any of you remember exactly what time you left the house?"

"It was, like, eleven-forty-five-ish, wasn't it?" Harry said, glancing at his friends. "I tried to work it back from the time I got home."

Mike shook his head. "Think it was just before that. I was already in bed at eleven-forty-five, 'cause I looked at my phone to set the alarm. I went straight to bed after seeing you all off and it takes me only five minutes to get ready, so I'm thinking it was closer to eleven-forty."

"Eleven-forty? That's great, thank you," Pip said. "And can you tell me about seeing Jamie? Where was he? What was he doing?"

"He was walking," Harry said, pushing back some flyaway strands of hair. "Pretty fast . . . with purpose, I mean. He was on the sidewalk on Mike's side of the road, so he crossed only a few feet behind us. He didn't even glance at us. Seemed totally focused on wherever he was going."

"Which direction was he going?"

"Up Weevil Road," said Mike, "away from the center of town."

"Did he go all the way up Weevil Road? Or could he have turned off, say, down Courtland or somewhere?" Pip asked, holding the headphones to her ears and glancing back to check that Connor was OK. He was watching intently, eyes tracking every spoken word.

"Don't know," Harry said. "We didn't see him after he passed us, we went the other way, to my car. Sorry."

"And you're certain it was Jamie Reynolds?"

"Yeah, I'm pretty sure it was him," Soph chimed in, leaning instinctively toward the microphone. "There was no one else walking around at that time, so I sort of noticed him more, if that makes sense. I knew it when Harry showed me your poster. I walked out the front door first, saw Jamie walking toward us, and then I turned around to say bye to Mike."

"What was Jamie wearing?" Pip asked. It wasn't a test, exactly, but she had to be sure.

"He had on a dark red, purply kind of shirt," Soph said, looking for confirmation in her friends' eyes.

"Yeah, burgundy color," Harry said. "Jeans. Sneakers. And maybe a black watch, I think. But I wasn't paying too much attention."

The watch hadn't been mentioned on the Missing poster, which meant this sighting had to be genuine. Pip unlocked her phone, scrolling to the photo of Jamie from the memorial. She held it up, and Soph and Harry nodded. But only Soph and Harry.

"I dunno," Mike said, stretching out one side of his mouth in a sort of wince. "I could've sworn he was wearing something darker. I mean, I only looked at him for a couple of seconds, and it was kinda dark. But I thought he was wearing something with a hood. Lucy thinks so too. And I swear I couldn't see his hands because they were in his jacket pockets. If he was just wearing a shirt, then where were his hands? But I got to the door last, so I only really saw the back of him."

Pip flipped her phone back, looking again at Jamie. "This is what he was wearing when he disappeared," she said.

"Ah, guess I just didn't get a good look," Mike conceded, shuffling back a half step.

"That's OK." Pip smiled reassuringly. "It's hard to remember small details you don't know will be significant later. Can you recall anything else about Jamie? His demeanor?"

"Nothing that really stuck out," Harry said, speaking across Soph. "Guess I noticed he was breathing pretty hard, but he just looked like a guy in a hurry to be somewhere."

In a hurry to be somewhere.

Pip's mind replayed those words, adding her own: *And now he was nowhere.*

"OK." She clicked stop on the recording. "Thank you all so much for your time."

EIGHTEEN

Pip returned to the scrap of paper in her hand, running her eyes over the list she'd scribbled thirty minutes ago:

Leila

Leyla

Laila

Layla

Leighla

Lejla

"This is impossible," Connor said, sitting back from Pip's desk in defeat, in a chair she'd borrowed from the kitchen.

Pip spun impatiently in her own chair, letting the breeze disturb the list in her hand. "Annoying our catfish chose a name with so many frickin' different spellings." They'd tried searching the name on Facebook and Instagram, but without a last name—or even knowing the correct form of the first name—the search results were numerous and useless. They'd tried reverse image-searching all of Stella Chapman's Instagram photos, but that hadn't led anywhere either. Clearly Leila's versions had been manipulated enough that the algorithm couldn't locate them.

"We're never going to find her," Connor said.

There was a faint triple knock at her bedroom door.

“Go away,” Pip said, scrolling down a page of Leighlas on Instagram. The door skittered open and Ravi stood there, lips pursed in affront, one eyebrow raised.

“Oh, not you.” Pip looked up, a smile breaking across her face. “I thought it was Josh again. Sorry. Hi.”

“Hi,” Ravi said, an amused half smile on his face as he raised both brows in greeting to Connor. He walked over to the desk and sat up beside the laptop, resting one foot on Pip’s chair, tucking it in under her thigh.

“How was the rest of the trial today?” Pip looked up at him as he wriggled his toes against her leg in a hidden hello that Connor couldn’t see.

“It was OK.” He narrowed his eyes to look at what they were doing on her screen. “Final victim gave her testimony this morning. And they presented Andie Bell’s burner phone to try to prove it was Max who regularly bought Rohypnol from her. Then the defense kicked off after lunch break, called Max’s mom to the stand first.”

“Oh, how’d that go?” asked Pip.

“Epps asked her about Max’s childhood, when he almost died of leukemia at age seven. His mom talked about his bravery during the illness, how *sensitive* and *caring* and *sweet* he was. How quiet and shy Max was in school after the all clear because he’d been held back a year. How he’s carried these traits into adulthood. She was pretty convincing,” he said.

“Well, I think that’s because she *is* convinced that her son isn’t a rapist,” Pip said. “Epps is probably ecstatic, that’s like hitting the gold mine. What’s better than childhood cancer to humanize your client?”

“My thoughts exactly,” Ravi said. “We’ll record the update later, yeah? What are we doing now? Looking for the catfish? That’s not how you spell Leila,” he added, pointing.

"It's one of the many ways," Pip sighed. "We're getting nowhere here."

"What about the sighting by the bookstore guy?" Ravi asked.

"Yeah, I think it's legit," she said. "Eleven-forty walking halfway up Weevil Road. Four eyewitnesses."

"Well," Connor said quietly, "they didn't agree on everything."

"No?" Ravi said.

"Slightly conflicting accounts on what Jamie was wearing," Pip said. "Two saw him in the burgundy shirt, two thought he was wearing something like a hoodie instead." She turned to Connor. "Small inconsistencies in eyewitness accounts are normal. Human memory isn't infallible. But four people swearing they saw your brother with otherwise matching accounts, we can trust that."

"Eleven-forty," Ravi thought aloud, "that's over an hour from the last sighting. And it doesn't take over an hour to walk from Highmoor to Weevil Road."

"No, it doesn't." Pip picked up his thread. "Jamie must have stopped somewhere in between. And I'm betting it has something to do with Leila."

"You think so?" Connor asked.

"He speaks to Stella at the calamity," Pip said. "Finds out Leila has been catfishing him. He's next seen outside with his phone, where he appears agitated and mentions calling the police. He had to be calling *his* Leila, confronting her with what he'd just found out. Jamie would have felt betrayed, upset, hence George's description of his behavior. What happens afterward, wherever Jamie was going, it has to be relevant to that. To Leila."

"She's had to explain that more than once, I can tell," Ravi said conspiratorially to Connor. "Heads-up: she hates doing that."

"I'm learning," Connor said.

Pip flashed Ravi an angry look. At least he could read her eyes, reacting right away. "She's also, annoyingly, always right, so . . ."

"Right, next plan," Pip said. "Make a Tinder profile."

"I just said you were always right," Ravi replied, voice shrill and playful.

"To catch a catfish." Pip whacked him on the knee. "We're not going to find Leila by blindly searching that name. At least on Tinder we can narrow down the search field by location. From Stella's interview, it didn't seem that Jamie was surprised at seeing Leila in Fairview, just specifically at the calamity party. That makes me think she told him she was local, they'd just never met up IRL because, well . . . catfish."

Pip downloaded the Tinder app on her phone and started making a new profile, her thumb hovering over the name box.

"What name should we use?" Ravi asked.

Pip looked up at him, the question already in her eyes.

"You want to put *me* on a dating site?" he said. "You're a weird kind of girlfriend."

"It's just easier because I already have photos of you. We'll delete the profile right after."

"Fine." Ravi smirked. "But you can't use this to win any future arguments."

"Right," Pip said, typing in the bio now. *"Enjoys mannish things like football and fishing."*

"Aha," Ravi said, "catfishing."

"You two," Connor remarked, flicking his eyes between them like he was watching a tennis match.

Pip clicked through settings to alter the preferences. "Let's keep it local, within a three-mile radius. We want it to show us women," she said, tapping the slider button beside that option. "And the age range . . . well, we know Jamie thought Leila was older than eighteen, so let's put the range between nineteen and twenty-six?"

"Yep, sounds good," Connor said.

"OK." Pip saved the settings. "Let's fish."

Ravi and Connor huddled forward, watching over Pip's shoulders as she swiped left through the potential matches. She skipped through about twenty before she recognized anyone: Soph from the bookstore. Pip kept swiping, on and on, names and faces blurring, her thumb starting to ache as Ravi began to fidget impatiently. And then, suddenly, another face she knew: Naomi Ward was grinning up at them. "We won't mention that to her," Pip said, continuing, moving Naomi's photo aside.

And there it was. She wasn't expecting it so soon; it crept up on her and she almost swiped past it, her thumb stalling just before it hit the screen.

Layla

"Oh my god," she said. "Layla, with an *a-y*. Twenty-five. Less than a mile away."

"Less than a mile away? Creepy," Connor said, shuffling closer for a better look.

Pip scrolled through the four photos on Layla's profile. They were pictures of Stella Chapman, stolen from her Instagram, but they'd been cropped, flipped, and filtered. And the main difference: Layla's hair was ash blond. It was done well; Layla must have played with the hue and layers on Photoshop.

"Reader. Learner. Traveler," Ravi read from her bio. *"Dog lover. And above all other things: Passionate Breakfaster."*

"Sounds approachable," Pip said.

"Yeah, she's right," said Ravi. "Breakfast is the best."

"It *is* a catfish, you were right," Connor spluttered over a sharp intake of breath. "Stella—but blond. Why?"

“Blonds have more fun, apparently,” Pip said, flicking through Layla’s photos again.

“Well, you’re brunette and you actively hate fun, so yeah. True fact,” said Ravi, affectionately scratching the back of Pip’s head.

“Aha.” She pointed to the bottom of the bio, where it said *Insta @LaylaylaylaM.* “Her Instagram handle.”

“Go to it,” Connor said.

“I am.” She opened the Instagram app and typed the handle into the search bar. Stella’s edited face peered up at them from the top result and Pip clicked on the profile.

Layla Mead. 32 posts. 503 followers. 101 following.

Most of the photos were ones taken from Stella’s page, her hair now a natural ashy blond but the same piercing smile and perfect hazel eyes.

“Stella does look old in most of these photos,” Connor said. “I don’t mean old, but, like, older, in her twenties.”

There were other photos without Stella: an overfiltered shot of the café on Main Street, looking cozy and inviting. And, farther down, a photo of the rolling fields near Ravi’s house, an orange setting sun clinging to the sky.

Pip scrolled down to check the very first post, a photo of Stella/Layla cuddling a beagle puppy. She’d captioned it: *Overhaul: new aesthetic oh and . . . puppy!*

“The first post was uploaded on February 16.”

“So that’s when Layla was *born,*” Ravi said. “Just over two months ago.”

Pip looked at Connor, and this time, he was able to read what she was going to say before she did.

“Yes,” he said. “That fits. Jamie must have started talking to her mid-March, that’s when his mood changed and he seemed happier again, always on his phone.”

"A lot of followers in that time. Ah"—Pip checked down the list of followers—"Jamie's on here. But most of them look like bots or inactive accounts. She probably bought her followers."

"Layla does not mess around," Ravi said, typing at Pip's computer, now in his lap.

"Hold on," Pip said, fixating on another name that had liked one of Layla's most recent photos. "Adam Clark." She stared at Connor, both widening their eyes in recognition.

Ravi picked up on the exchange. "What?" he asked.

"That's our new history teacher," Connor said as Pip clicked the name to double-check it was him. His profile was set to private, but the display picture was clearly him, a wide smile with small Christmas baubles attached to his ginger-flecked beard.

"I guess Jamie isn't the only person Layla's been talking to," Pip said. "Stella doesn't take history and Mr. Clark's new, so maybe he doesn't know he's talking to a catfish using Stella's photos. If he *is* talking to her, that is."

"Aha," Ravi said, spinning the laptop on the heel of his hand. "Layla Mead has a Facebook too. The very same pictures, the first also posted February 16." He turned the screen back and read on. "She did a status update that day saying: *New account because I forgot the password for my old one.*"

"A likely story, Layla," said Pip, returning to Layla's page and Stella-not-Stella's glittering smile. "We should try to message her, right?" She wasn't really asking, and all three of them knew it. "She's the person most likely to know what happened to Jamie. Where he is."

"You think she's definitely a she?" Connor asked.

"I mean, yeah. Jamie's been speaking on the phone with her."

"Oh, right. What are you going to message her, then?"

"Well . . ." Pip chewed her lip, thinking. "It can't come from me, or Ravi, or the podcast. Or even you, Connor. If she has anything to do with Jamie, she might know how we're connected to him and that we're looking into his disappearance. I think we have to be careful and approach her as a stranger just looking to talk. See if we can gradually work out who she really is, or what she knows about Jamie. Gradually. Catfish don't like to be caught out."

"We can't just make a new account, though, she'd be suspicious seeing zero followers," said Ravi.

"Damn, you're right," Pip muttered. "Um . . ."

"I have an idea?" Connor said, phrasing it like a question, the end of the sentence climbing up and away, abandoning him below. "It's, well, I have another Instagram account. An anonymous one. I'm, um, I'm into photography. Black-and-white photography," he said with an embarrassed shrug. "Not people, it's like birds and buildings and stuff. Never told anyone 'cause I knew Ant would be a dick about it."

"Really?" Pip said. "That could work. How many followers?"

"A good amount," he said, "and I don't follow any of you guys, so no connection there."

"That's perfect, good thinking." She smiled, holding out her phone. "Could you sign in on mine?"

"Yeah." Connor took her phone, tapping away at the keypad and handing it back.

"An.On.In.Frame," Pip read out the account's name, eyes sweeping down the first row of his grid, no farther, in case Connor didn't want to share. "These are really good, Con."

"Thank you."

Pip navigated her way back to Layla Mead's profile and clicked on the message button, bringing up a new private message page and an input box, waiting for her.

"OK, what do I say? What vocabulary do strangers typically use when they slide into the DMs?"

Ravi laughed. "Don't ask me," he said. "I've never slid into anyone's DMs."

"Connor?"

"Um, I don't know, maybe we should just go with a *Hey, how are you?*"

"Yeah, that works," Ravi said. "Innocent enough until we know how she likes to talk to people."

"OK," Pip said, typing it in, trying to ignore that her fingers were shaking. "Should I go for the flirty *Heyy,* double *y*?"

"Why not," Ravi said, and she knew immediately the pun he was attempting.

"Right. Everyone ready?" She looked at them both. "Should I press send?"

"Yes," Connor said, while Ravi shot her a finger gun.

Pip faltered, thumb hovering over the send button, reading back her words. She ran them through in her mind until they sounded misshapen and nonsensical.

Then she took a breath, and pressed send.

The message jumped to the top of the page, now encased in a grayed-out bubble.

"I did it," she said, exhaling, dropping the phone into her lap.

"Good, now we wait," Ravi said.

"Not for long," Connor said, leaning over to look at the phone. "It says *seen.*"

"Shit," Pip said, raising the phone again. "Layla's seen it. Oh my god." And as they watched, something else appeared. The word *Typing . . .* on the left side of the screen. "She's typing. Shit, she's already typing." Her voice felt tight and panicked, like it had outgrown her throat.

"Calm down," Ravi said, jumping off the desk so he could watch the screen too.

Typing . . . disappeared.

And in its place: a new message.

Pip read it and her heart dropped.

Hello Pip, it said.

That was all it said.

"Fuck." Ravi's grip stiffened on her shoulder. "How did she know it was you? How the fuck did she know?"

"I don't like this," Connor said, shaking his head. "Guys, I'm getting a bad feeling about this."

"Shhh," Pip hissed, though she couldn't hear if either of them was still talking, not over the hammering that now filled her ears. "Layla's typing again."

Typing . . .

And it disappeared.

Typing . . .

Again, it disappeared.

Typing . . .

And the second message appeared in a white box below.

You're getting closer :)

NINETEEN

Pip's throat closed in on her, trapping her voice inside, cornering the words until they gave up and scattered away. All she could do was stare at the messages, unravel them, and put them back together until they made some kind of sense.

Hello Pip.

You're getting closer :)

Connor was the first to find words. "What the fuck does that mean? Pip?"

Her name sounded strange, like it didn't belong to her, had been stretched out of shape until it no longer fit. Pip stared at those three letters, unrecognizable in the hands of this stranger. This stranger who was less than a mile away.

"Um" was all she had to offer.

"She knew it was you," Ravi said, his voice coaxing Pip back to herself. "She knows who you are."

"What does 'You're getting closer' mean?" Connor asked.

"To finding Jamie," Pip said. *Or finding out what happened to Jamie,* she thought, which sounded almost the same but was very, very different. And Layla knew. Whoever Layla was, she knew everything, Pip was sure of that now.

"That smiley face, though." Ravi shivered; she felt it through his fingers.

The shock had receded now, and Pip jumped into action. "I need to reply. Now," she said, typing out: *Who are you? Where's Jamie?* There was no point pretending anymore: Layla was one step ahead.

She pressed send but an error box appeared instead.

Unable to send message. User not found.

"No," Pip whispered. "Nononono." She thumbed back to Layla's page, but it was no longer there. The profile picture and bio were still displayed, but the grid was gone, replaced by the words *No Posts Yet* and a banner of *User not found* at the top. "No," Pip growled in frustration, the sound raw and angry in her throat. "She's disabled her account."

"What?" Connor said.

"She's gone."

Ravi hurried back over to Pip's laptop, refreshing Layla Mead's Facebook page. *The page you requested was not found.* "Fuck. She's deactivated her Facebook too."

"And Tinder," Pip said, checking the app. "She's gone. We lost her."

A quietness settled over the room, a quietness that wasn't the absence of sound but its own living thing, stifling the spaces between them.

"She knows, doesn't she?" Ravi said, his voice gentle, skimming just above the quiet instead of breaking through. "Layla knows what happened to Jamie."

Connor was holding his head, shaking it again. "I don't like this," he said, speaking to the ground. "I don't like this at all."

Pip watched him, transfixed by the movement of his head. "She knew it was me. I think Layla knows everything."

* * *

It was a fake smile, the one she put on for her dad later, as she walked Ravi to the front door.

"Done with your trial update, Pickle?" he asked, clapping Ravi gently on the back, her dad's way of saying goodbye reserved just for him.

"Yeah. Just uploaded it," Pip said.

Connor had gone home over an hour ago, after they'd run out of ways of asking one another the same questions. There was nothing more they could do tonight. Layla Mead was gone, but the lead wasn't dead. Not entirely. Tomorrow at school Pip and Connor would ask Mr. Clark what he knew about her; that was the plan. And tonight, once Ravi was gone, Pip would record about what had just happened, finish editing the interviews, and then it would go out later tonight: the first episode of season 2.

"Thanks for dinner, Victor," Ravi said, turning to give Pip one of their hidden goodbyes, a slight scrunching of his eyes. She blinked back at him and he reached for the catch on the front door, pulling it open.

"Oh," someone said, standing on the step right outside, fist floating in the air ready to knock.

"Oh," Ravi replied in turn, and Pip leaned to see who it was. Charlie Green, from four doors down, his rust-colored hair pushed back from his face.

"Hi, Ravi, Pip," Charlie said with an awkward wave. "Evening, Victor."

"Hello, Charlie," Pip's dad said in his bright, showy-offy voice, that booming one he always switched on in front of someone he considered a guest. Ravi had outgrown guest a while ago into something more, thank God. "How can we help you?"

"Sorry to disturb you," Charlie said, a slight nervous edge to his voice and his pale green eyes. "I know it's getting late, and it's a school night, it's just . . ." He trailed off, locking onto Pip's eyes. "Well, I saw your Missing poster in the newspaper, Pip. And I think I have some information about Jamie Reynolds. There's something I should show you."

Twenty minutes, her dad agreed, and twenty minutes was all it would take, Charlie had said. Now Pip and Ravi were following him down the darkened street, the orange streetlights stitching monstrous, overstretched shadows to their feet.

"You see," Charlie said, glancing back at them as they walked up the gravel path to his front door, "Flora and I, we have one of these doorbell cameras. We've moved around a lot, used to live in Scranton and we had a few break-ins there. So we installed the camera, for Flora's peace of mind, and it came with us here, to Fairview. I thought there's no harm in having extra security, no matter how nice the town, you know?"

He pointed the camera out to them, a small black device above the faded brass doorbell. "It's motion sensor, so it'll be recording us right now." Charlie gave it a small wave as he unlocked the door and showed them inside.

Pip already knew this house, from when Zach and his family lived here. She followed Charlie into what used to be the Chens' playroom, but now it looked like an office. There were bookshelves and an armchair beneath the front bay windows and, against the far wall, a wide white desk with two large computer monitors on it.

"Here," Charlie said, pointing them toward the computer.

"Nice setup," said Ravi, checking the screens like he had a clue what he was talking about.

"I work from home. Web design. Freelance," Charlie said in explanation.

"Cool," said Ravi.

"Yeah, mostly because I get to work in my pajamas," Charlie laughed. "My dad would probably say, 'You're twenty-seven now, get a real job.' "

"Older generations," Pip said disapprovingly, "they just don't understand the allure of pajamas. So what did you want to show us?"

"Hello." A new voice entered the room, and Pip turned to see Flora in the doorway, hair tied back and a smudge of flour on the front of her oversized shirt. She was holding a Tupperware stacked four rows high with brownies. "I just baked these, for Josh's class tomorrow. But I wondered if you guys were hungry. No nuts or pretend healthy things, I promise."

"Hi, Flora." Pip smiled. "I'm actually OK, thank you." Her appetite still hadn't returned; she'd had to force dinner down.

But a wide crooked smile appeared on Ravi's face as he sauntered over to Flora and picked up a brownie from the middle, saying, "Yes please, these look amazing."

Pip sighed: Ravi liked anyone who fed him.

"Have you shown them, Charlie?" Flora asked.

"No, I was just getting to it. Come look at this," he said, wiggling the mouse to bring life back to one of the screens. "So like I was saying, we have this doorbell camera, and it starts recording whenever it detects motion, sends a notification to the app on my phone. Whatever it records, it uploads to the cloud for seven days before it's wiped. When I woke up last Tuesday morning, I saw a notification on my app from the middle of the night. But I went downstairs and checked and everything looked fine, nothing out of place or missing, so I presumed it was just a fox setting off the camera again."

"Right," Pip said, moving closer as Charlie navigated through his files.

"But yesterday Flora noticed something of hers was missing. Can't find it anywhere, so I thought I'd check the doorbell footage, just in case, before it got wiped. I didn't think there'd be anything on it, but . . ." He double-clicked on a video file and it opened in a media player. Charlie clicked it into full screen and then hit play.

It was a 180-degree view of the front of the house, down the path to the gate they'd just come through, and over to the bay windows on either side of the front door. Everything was green, all light greens and bright greens, set against the darker green of the night sky.

"It's night vision," Charlie said, watching their faces. "This was taken at 3:07 a.m. on Tuesday morning."

There was movement by the gate. Whatever it was had set the camera off.

"Sorry, the resolution's not great," Charlie said.

The green shape moved up the front path, growing blurry arms and legs as it neared the camera. And as it walked right up to the front door, it grew a face, a face Pip knew, except for the absent black pinpoints for eyes. He looked scared.

"I don't know him, and I only saw his picture in the *Fairview Mail* today, but that's Jamie Reynolds, isn't it?" Charlie asked.

"It is," Pip said, her throat constricting again. "What's he doing?"

"Well, if you look to the window on the left, that's the one in here, this room." Charlie pointed to it on-screen. "I must have had it open during the day, for a breeze, and maybe I thought I closed it fully. But look, it's still open, just a couple of inches from the bottom."

As he said that, the green Jamie on-screen noticed it too, bending down in front of the window and creeping his fingers in under the gap. You couldn't see the back of his head; he had a dark hood pulled up over his hair. Pip watched Jamie pull at the window, sliding it up until the gap was large enough.

"What's he doing?" Ravi asked, leaning closer to the screen too, the brownie a thing of the past. "Is he breaking in?"

The question become irrelevant a half second later as Jamie

lowered his head and climbed through the window, his legs slipping in behind him, leaving just an empty dark green opening into the house.

"He's only in the house for a total of forty-one seconds," Charlie said, fast-forwarding the video to the point where Jamie's lighter green head reemerged from the window. He dragged himself outside, landing on one unsteady leg. But he looked the same as before he'd gone in: still scared, nothing in his hands. He turned back to the window, leaning into his elbows as he pushed it closed, right down to the sill. And then he walked away from the house, breaking into a run as he reached the gate and disappeared into the engulfing all-green night.

"What?" Pip and Ravi said together.

"We only found this yesterday," Charlie said. "And we discussed it. It's my fault for leaving the window open. And we're not going to go to the police and press charges or anything—seems like this Jamie guy has enough on his plate as it is. And what he took, well, what we *think* he took, it wasn't that valuable, only sentimental value, so—"

"What did he take?" Pip asked, her eyes flicking to Flora, instinct pulling her gaze to the empty spaces at Flora's wrists. "What did Jamie steal from you?"

"My watch," Flora said, putting the container of brownies down. "I remember leaving it in here the weekend before last, because it kept catching on the book I was reading. I haven't seen it since. And it's the only thing missing."

"Is this watch rose gold with light-pink leather straps, metal flowers on one side?" Pip asked, and immediately Charlie's and Flora's eyes snapped to each other in alarm.

"Yes," Flora said. "Yes, that's exactly it. It wasn't that expensive, but Charlie bought it for our first Christmas together. How did you . . . ?"

"I've seen your watch," Pip said. "It's in Jamie Reynolds's bedroom."

"O-oh," Charlie stuttered.

"I can make sure it's returned to you right away."

"That would be great, but no rush." Flora smiled kindly. "I know you must be very busy."

"But the strange thing is"—Charlie crossed the room, past a watchful Ravi, over to the window Jamie had climbed through just a week ago—"why did he only take the watch? It's clearly not expensive. And I leave my wallet in this room, with cash in it. There's my computer equipment too, none of that is cheap. Why did Jamie ignore all that? Why just a watch that's almost worthless? In and out in forty seconds and just the watch?"

"I don't know, that is strange," Pip said. "I can't explain it. I'm so sorry. This"—she cleared her throat—"this isn't the Jamie I know."

Charlie's eyes fell to the bottom ledge of the window, where Jamie's fingers had snuck through. "Some people are pretty good at hiding who they really are."

File Name:

A Good Girl's Guide to Murder SEASON 2, Episode 1 Outro.wav

PIP: There's one inescapable thing that haunts me about this case, something I didn't have to face last time. And that's time itself. As it passes, every minute and every hour, the chances of Jamie returning home safe and well get slimmer and slimmer. That's what the statistics say. By the time I've uploaded this episode and you're listening to it, we will have passed another important deadline: the seventy-two-hour mark from when Jamie was last seen. In normal police procedure, while investigating a *high-risk* missing persons case, the seventy-two-hour mark is a line in the sand, after which they quietly accept that they might not be looking for a person anymore, but a body. Time is in charge here, not me, and that's terrifying.

But I have to believe Jamie is OK, that we still have time to find him. Probability is just that: probable. Nothing is certain. And I'm closer than I was yesterday, finding the dots and connecting them. I think everything is linked. And if that's true, then it all comes back to one person: Layla Mead. A person who doesn't really exist.

Join us next time.

59:17 MB of 59:17 MB uploaded

**A Good Girl's Guide to Murder:
The Disappearance of Jamie Reynolds**

Season 2, Episode 1 successfully uploaded to SoundCloud.

TUESDAY
4 DAYS MISSING

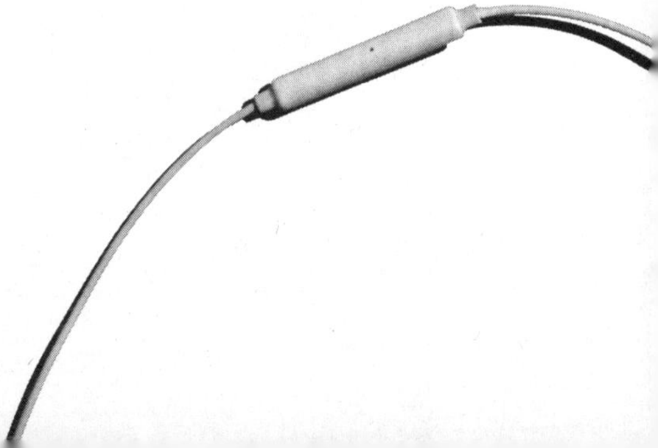

TWENTY

Jamie Reynolds is clearly dead.

The words jumped in and out of focus as Connor held the phone in front of Pip's eyes.

"Look," he said, his voice quivering, maybe with the effort of keeping up with her down this corridor, maybe with something else.

"I have," Pip said, slowing to divert around a group of chittering freshmen. "What was the one very important rule I gave you, Con?" She looked over at him. "Never read the comments. Ever. OK?"

"I know," he said, going back to his phone. "But that's a reply to your tweet with the episode link, and it's already got a hundred and nine likes. Does that mean a hundred and nine people really think my brother's dead?"

"Connor—"

"And there's this one, from Reddit," he continued, not listening to her. "This person thinks that Jamie must have taken the knife from our house on Friday evening, to defend himself, and therefore he must have known someone would try to attack him."

"Connor."

"What?" he said defensively. "*You* read the comments."

"Yes, I do. In case there are any tips or someone has spotted something I missed. But I know that the vast majority are unhelpful and that the internet is full of morons," she said, skipping up the first set of stairs. "Did you see Jamie carrying a huge knife around at the memorial? Or in any of the photos from the calamity? No. Because he couldn't have, he was wearing just a shirt and jeans. Not many places to hide a six-inch blade."

"You get a lot of trolls, huh?" Connor followed Pip as she pushed through the double doors on to the history floor. *"I killed Jamie and I'll kill you too, Pip."*

A student in the grade below was passing just as Connor said that. She gasped, mouth open in shock, hurrying away from them in the other direction.

"I was just reading something out," Connor called to explain, giving up as the girl disappeared through the opposite doors.

"Right." Pip stopped outside Mr. Clark's classroom, looking through the glass in the door. He was there, sitting at his desk even though it was break time. She guessed he was new enough that an empty classroom was still more welcoming than the staff room. "Come with me, but if I give you the eyes, that means you need to leave. Got it?"

"Yes, I get it now," Connor said.

Pip opened the door and gave Mr. Clark a small wave.

He stood up. "Hello, Pip, Connor," he said brightly, fidgeting like he wasn't sure what to do with his hands. One went to his wavy brown hair, the other settled in his pocket. "What can I do for you both? Is this about the final?"

"Um, it's actually about something else." Pip leaned against one of the tables at the front of the classroom, resting the weight of her backpack.

"What is it?" Mr. Clark said, his face changing, features rearranging beneath his heavy brows.

"I don't know if you've heard, but Connor's brother, Jamie, went missing last Friday and I'm looking into his disappearance. He was a former student here."

"Yes, yes, I saw that in the town newspaper yesterday," Mr. Clark said. "I'm very sorry, Connor, that must be very hard for you and your family. I'm sure the school guidance counselor would—"

"So." Pip cut him off; there were only fifteen minutes of break left, and time wasn't something she had to spare. "We're investigating Jamie's disappearance and we've traced a lead to a particular individual. And, well, we think you might know this individual. Might be able to give us some information on her."

"Well, I . . . I don't know if I'm allowed . . . ," he spluttered.

"Layla Mead," Pip said the name, watching Mr. Clark's face for a reaction. And he gave her one, though he tried to wrestle with it, shake it off. But he wasn't able to hide that flash of panic in his eyes. "So you *do* know her?"

"No." He fiddled with his collar like it was suddenly too small for him. "Sorry, I've never heard that name before."

He wanted to play it that way, did he?

"Oh, OK," Pip said, "my mistake." She stood up, heading toward the door. Behind her, she heard Mr. Clark breathe a sigh of relief. That was when she stopped, turned back. "It's just," she said, scratching her head like she was confused, "it's strange, then."

"Sorry?" said Mr. Clark.

"I mean, it's strange that you've never heard the name Layla Mead before, when you've liked several of her posts on Instagram." Pip looked up at the ceiling, like she was searching for an explanation. "Maybe you forgot about that?"

"I—I—I," he stammered, watching Pip warily as she stepped forward.

"Yeah, you must have forgot about it," she said. "Because I know you wouldn't intentionally lie about something that could help save a former student's life."

"My brother," Connor chimed in, and Pip hated to admit it, but his timing was perfect. And that glassy, imploring look in his eyes too: spot-on.

"Um, I . . . I don't think this is appropriate," Mr. Clark said, a flush of red appearing above his collar. "Do you know how strict they are now, after everything with Mr. Ward and Andie Bell? All these safeguarding measures, I shouldn't even be alone with a student."

"We aren't alone." Pip gestured to Connor. "And the door can stay wide open, if you want. All I care about is finding Jamie Reynolds alive. And to do that, I need to you to tell me everything you know about Layla Mead."

"Stop," Mr. Clark said, the red creeping above his beard into his cheeks now. "I am your teacher. Please stop trying to manipulate me."

"No one's manipulating anyone here," Pip said coolly, glancing back at Connor. She knew exactly what she was about to do, and that pit in her stomach knew too, reflooding with guilt. *Ignore it, just ignore it.* "Although I do wonder whether you knew Layla was using the photos of a current student here at Fairview: Stella Chapman?"

"I didn't know that at the time," Mr. Clark said, voice dipping into whispers. "I don't teach her, I only worked it out a few weeks ago when I saw Stella walking down the hall, and that was already after Layla and I had stopped talking. I unfollowed the Layla account immediately after."

"Still"—Pip pulled a face with gritted teeth, sucking in a breath between them—"I wonder if that would get you into hot water if anyone found out."

"Excuse me?"

"Here's what I suggest," she said, replacing her expression with an innocent smile. "You record an interview with me in which I use a plug-in to distort your voice. Your name will never be mentioned, and I'll bleep out any information that might potentially identify you. But you tell me everything you know about Layla Mead. If you do that, I'm sure no one will ever find out anything you wouldn't want them to."

Mr. Clark paused for a moment, chewing the inside of his cheek, glancing at Connor as though he could help. "Is that blackmail?"

"No, sir," Pip said. "It's just persuasion."

File Name:

A Good Girl's Guide to Murder SEASON 2: Interview with Adam Clark.wav

PIP: So let's start with how you and Layla met.

ANONYMOUS: [DISTORTED] We never met. Not in real life.

PIP: Right, but what was your first online communication? Who initiated contact? Did you match on Tinder?

ANONYMOUS: No, no, I'm not on there. It was Instagram. I have my account set to private so that [————BEEP————]. One day, I think near the end of February, this woman Layla requested to follow me. I checked out her profile, thought she looked nice, and clearly she was local to Fairview because she had photos from around town. I'd only been living here a couple of months then and hadn't really had a chance to meet any people outside of [—BEEP—]. I thought it might be nice to get to know someone new, so I approved her and followed her back. Liked a couple of her photos. I swear she looked a lot older than eighteen in her pictures.

PIP: Did you start messaging each other directly?

ANONYMOUS: Yes, I got a DM from Layla, something like "Hey, thanks for following me back." She said she thought she recognized me, asked if I lived in Fairview. I'm not going to go into all the particulars of our conversations, by the way.

PIP: Yes, I understand. So to clarify, the nature of your and Layla's conversations, would you say they were romantic? Flirtatious?

ANONYMOUS:

PIP: OK, no need to answer. Loud and clear. I don't want you to recount every conversation, I just want to know anything Layla said that might help me identify who she really is. Did you ever have a phone conversation with her?

ANONYMOUS: No. Only on Instagram. And really, we only spoke on and off for a few days. A week at most. It wasn't a big deal.

PIP: Did Layla tell you where she lives?

ANONYMOUS: Yes, Fairview. We didn't get to the point of swapping addresses, obviously. But she seemed to have local knowledge, talked about the amazing chicken burgers at Bobby's Bar & Grill.

PIP: Did she tell you anything else about herself?

ANONYMOUS: Said she was twenty-five. That she lived with her dad and worked in HR somewhere in New York, but she was on sick leave at the moment.

PIP: Sick? With what?

ANONYMOUS: I didn't ask. We hardly knew each other, that would have been rude.

PIP: Sounds like a classic catfish line to me. Did you suspect she wasn't who she said she was at any time?

ANONYMOUS: No. I had no idea, not until I saw Stella Chapman [————BEEP————] and I was very shocked that I'd been catfished. At least it hadn't gone on long.

PIP: So you only spoke for a week? What kind of things did you talk about? The clean stuff.

ANONYMOUS: She asked me a lot of questions about myself. *A lot,* in fact. I found it quite refreshing to meet someone so interested in me.

PIP: Really? What kinds of things did she ask?

ANONYMOUS: It wasn't like she was interviewing me or anything, her questions all occurred naturally during our conversations. Right at the start she wanted to know how old I was, asked me directly. I told her I was twenty-nine, and then she asked when I would turn thirty, and if I had any plans yet for the big birthday. She was chatty like that. Nice. And she was interested in my family too, asked if I still lived with any of them, if I had siblings, how my parents were. She would sort of avoid answering when I returned those questions, though. Seemed more interested in me. Made me think she didn't have such a good home life.

PIP: It seems like you two were hitting it off—why did you stop messaging after a week?

ANONYMOUS: She stopped messaging me. It felt completely out of the blue, to be honest.

PIP: She ghosted you?

ANONYMOUS: Yes, embarrassingly. I kept messaging after, like, "Hello? Where've you gone?" And nothing. Never heard from her again.

PIP: Do you have any idea why she ghosted you? Anything you might've said?

ANONYMOUS: I don't think so. I know what the last thing I said to her was, before she disappeared. She'd asked me what I did for a living, so I replied and told her that I was a [—BEEP—] at the [—BEEP—]. And then that was it, she never replied. I guess maybe she's one of those people who doesn't want to go out with a [–BEEP–]. Maybe she feels like she can do better, or something.

PIP: I know you didn't know she was a catfish at the time, but looking back now, did Layla let anything slip, any clues about her real identity? Her age? Any out-of-date slang she might have used? Did she mention Jamie Reynolds to you? Or any other people she interacts with in real life?

ANONYMOUS: No, nothing like that. I believed she was exactly who she told me she was. No slips. So if she's a catfish, then I guess she's a pretty damn good one.

TWENTY-ONE

Connor wasn't eating. He pushed the food around his plate, scoring deep lines through the untouched pasta with the points of his plastic fork.

Zach had noticed too; Pip accidentally caught his eye across the table as she watched Connor sitting there, silent in the deafening cafeteria. It was the comments, she knew. Strangers on the internet with their theories and their opinions. *Jamie Reynolds must be dead.* And: *He's definitely been murdered—seems he kind of deserved it, though.* Pip told Connor to ignore them, but it was clear he couldn't, their words skulking around him, leaving their mark.

Cara was sitting beside Pip, close enough that her elbow occasionally nudged Pip's ribs. She'd picked up on Connor's silence too, hence her attempt to bring up Connor's favorite topic: Area 51 conspiracies.

The only ones who hadn't noticed were Ant and Lauren. Ant was supposed to be Connor's best friend, but he had his back turned to him, straddling the bench as he and Lauren huddled and giggled about something. Pip couldn't say she was surprised. Ant hadn't seemed all that concerned about Connor yesterday either, only bringing Jamie up once. She knew it was an awkward situation and most people struggled with what to talk about, but you say sorry at least once. It's just what you do.

Lauren snorted at whatever Ant had whispered and Pip felt a flash of something hot under her skin, but she bit her lip and talked it down. This wasn't the time to pick a fight. Instead she watched as Cara pulled a KitKat from her bag and slowly slid it across the table, into Connor's eyeline. It broke his trance and he looked at Cara, the corners of his mouth twitching in a small, passing smile as he abandoned the fork and reached out to accept her offering.

Cara passed that same smile on to Pip. She looked tired. Three nights had gone by, three nights that Pip had been too busy to call her, to talk her to sleep. Pip knew she must be lying awake; the tint beneath Cara's eyes told her that. And now her eyes told her something else, widening and gesturing up just as someone behind Pip tapped her on the shoulder. She swiveled and looked up to see Tom Nowak standing there, giving her an awkward wave. Lauren's ex-boyfriend; they'd broken up last summer.

"Hi," he said, over the noise of the cafeteria.

"Urgh," Lauren immediately butted in. Oh, so *now* she paid attention. "What do you want?"

"Nothing," Tom said, shaking his long hair out of his eyes. "I just need to talk to Pip about something."

"Sure," Ant charged in, sitting up as tall as he could, crossing one arm in front of Lauren to grip the table. "Any excuse to come over to our table, right?"

"No, it's . . ." Tom trailed off with a shrug and turned back to Pip. "I have some information."

"No one wants you here. Go away," Ant said, and an amused smile spread across Lauren's face as she threaded her arm through his.

"I'm not talking to you," Tom said. He looked back at Pip. "It's about Jamie Reynolds."

Connor's head jerked up, his eyes blinking away that haunted look as he focused on Pip. She held up one hand and nodded, gesturing for him to stay put.

"Oh, sure," Ant said with a sneer.

"Be quiet, will you, Ant." Pip stood up and shouldered her heavy bag. "No one's impressed, except Lauren." She climbed over the plastic bench and told Tom to follow her as she headed toward the doors to the courtyard outside, knowing Connor would be watching them go.

"Let's talk over here," she said once they were outside, gesturing to the low wall. It had rained that morning and the bricks were still a little wet as she sat down, soaking into her pants. Tom spread out his jacket before joining her. "So what information do you have about Jamie?"

"It's about the night he went missing," Tom said with a sniff.

"Really? Have you listened to the first episode? I released it last night."

"No, not yet," he said.

"I only ask because we've built up a timeline of Jamie's movements last Friday. We know he was at the calamity party from 9:16 p.m. and left the area around 10:32 p.m., if that's where you saw him." Tom stared at her blankly. "What I mean is, I already have that information, if that's what you were going to tell me."

He shook his head. "Er, no, it's something else. I wasn't at the calamity party, but I saw him. After that."

"You did? After 10:32?" And suddenly Pip was hyperaware: the shrieking freshman boys playing soccer, a fly that had just landed on her bag, the wall pressing into her bones.

"Yes," Tom said. "It was after that."

"How long after?"

"Um, maybe fifteen minutes, or twenty." He screwed up his face in concentration.

"So around 10:50 p.m.?" Pip asked.

"Yeah. That sounds about right."

Pip sat forward, waiting for Tom to continue.

He didn't.

"And?" she said, starting to grow annoyed despite herself. "Where were you? Where did you see him? Was it somewhere near Highmoor, where the party was?"

"Yeah, it was that road, um, what's it called . . . oh, Cross Lane," he said.

Cross Lane. Pip knew only one person who lived on Cross Lane, with a bright-blue door and an angled front path: Nat da Silva and her parents.

"You saw Jamie on Cross Lane at ten-fifty p.m.?"

"Yeah, I saw him, in a burgundy shirt and white sneakers. I pacifically remember that."

"That's what he was wearing, *specifically*," Pip said, wincing at Tom's butchering of the word. "Why were you there at that time?"

He shrugged. "Just going home from a friend's house."

"And what was Jamie doing?" Pip asked.

"He was walking. Walked past me."

"OK. And was he on the phone when he walked past you?" she said.

"No, don't think so. No phone."

Pip sighed. Tom wasn't making this very easy for her.

"OK, what else did you see? Did it look like he was heading somewhere? Maybe a house?"

"Yeah." Tom nodded.

"Yeah, what?"

"A house. He was walking to a house," he said. "Like maybe halfway up the road."

Nat da Silva's house was about halfway up, Pip's thoughts intruded, demanding her attention. And Jamie had planned to go there, though Nat said he never showed up. Pip felt a thrumming in her neck as her pulse picked up. Palms growing sticky, and not from the rain.

"How do you know he was heading to a house?"

"Because I saw him. Go into a house," Tom said.

"Inside?" The word came out louder than she'd intended.

"Yes." He sounded exasperated, like *she* was the one making this difficult.

"Which house?"

"Ah," Tom said, scratching his hair, switching the part to the other side. "It was late, I wasn't looking at the numbers. Didn't see."

"Well, can you describe what the house looked like at all?" Pip was gripping the wall now, fingertips scraping against it. "What color was the front door?"

"Um"—Tom looked at her—"I think it was white."

Pip exhaled. She sat back from him, unhooked her fingers, and dropped her gaze. Not Nat da Silva's house, then. Good.

"Wait," Tom said suddenly, eyes settling on her again. "Actually no, I don't think it was white. No, I remember now . . . it was bl-blue. Yeah, blue."

Pip's heart reacted immediately, a beating in her ears, quick couplets that almost sounded like: *Nat-da Sil-va, Nat-da Sil-va, Nat-da Sil-va.*

She forced her mouth shut, and reopened it again to ask: "White brick house? Vine on one side?"

Tom nodded, more life in his face now. "Yeah, that's the one. I saw Jamie going into that house."

"Did you see anyone else? Who opened the door?"

"No. Just saw him go in."

Into Nat da Silva's house.

That had been the plan after all, for Jamie to go to Nat's house after the memorial. That's what he'd told Connor. That's what Nat had said to Pip. Except she also said he never showed up. That the last time she saw Jamie was when he walked away from her into the crowd to find "someone."

But Tom saw Jamie going into Nat's house at 10:50 p.m. After the calamity party.

So somebody was lying here.

And who would have reason to?

"Tom," she said, "would you mind if we went over this again, in a recorded interview?"

"Sure. No problem."

r/AGoodGirlsGuideToMurderPodcast

posted by u/hedeteccheprotecc 47 minutes ago

18

The Hillary F. Weiseman Lead?

I know Pip's been busy chasing Jamie's movements on that night. But I feel it would be a mistake for her to ignore this note in Jamie's trash can. We know the Reynoldses' cleaner comes once every two weeks on a Wednesday, so the note Pip found has to have been written/thrown away within the past ten days, coinciding with this time period in which Jamie is acting erratically (stealing, sneaking out).

Pip's research turned up only one Hillary F. Weiseman—an 84-year-old woman who lived in Fairview and died 12 years ago. So, yes, it's very strange that Jamie was recently writing down this old dead woman's name. But I'm wondering if the note doesn't refer to a person at all, but to a location. If Hillary Weiseman died there, then I'm guessing she's probably buried in a graveyard in the town. What if the note isn't referring to Hillary the person, but rather to her grave site as a meeting place? Look at the wording of the note again: *Hillary F Weiseman left 11.* What if that actually means the grave of Hillary F. Weiseman on the left side of the cemetery at 11 o'clock? A meeting time and place. What do you guys think?

59 comments Give Award Share Save •••

TWENTY-TWO

Pip tried not to look. She averted her eyes, but there was something about the house that dragged them right back. It could never be just a normal house, not after everything it had seen. It felt almost otherworldly, as though death clung to the air around it, making it shimmer in a way a house shouldn't, with its crooked roofline and stippled bricks swallowed by ivy.

The Bells' house. The place where Andie had died.

Through the living room window, Pip could see the back of Jason Bell's head, the TV flickering at the other end of the room. He must have heard their footsteps on the sidewalk because just then he snapped his head around and stared. He and Pip made eye contact for just a moment, and Jason's gaze soured when he recognized her. Pip recoiled and dropped her eyes as she and Ravi continued, leaving the house behind. But she still felt marked in some way by Jason's eyes.

"So," Ravi said, unaware; clearly he hadn't felt the same need to look at the house. "You got this idea from someone on Reddit?" he asked as they walked up the road where it wound to the church on top of the hill.

"Yeah, and it's a good theory," Pip said. "I should've thought of it."

"Any other good tips since the ep went out?"

"Nah," she said, the effort of the steep hill breaking up her voice as they turned a corner and the church appeared in the distance, nestled among the treetops. "Not unless you count the 'I saw Jamie in a McDonald's in Austin' tip. Or the one who saw him at Niagara Falls, the Canadian side, apparently."

They crossed the pedestrian bridge over the fast-moving road below, the sound of the cars like a rushing inside Pip's ears.

"OK," she said as they neared and the churchyard split into two on either side of the building, the wide path running through it. "The Redditor thinks the 'left' in the note might refer to the left-hand side. So let's check this way." Pip led Ravi off the path and onto the long stretch of grass to the left that wrapped around the hill. Everywhere they looked were flat marble plaques and standing gravestones in wavering rows.

"What's the name, Hillary . . . ?" asked Ravi.

"Hillary F. Weiseman, died 2008." Pip narrowed her eyes, studying the graves, Ravi beside her.

"So you think Nat da Silva lied to you?" he asked between reading names.

"Don't know," she said. "But they can't both be telling the truth; their accounts totally contradict each other. So either Nat da Silva or Tom Nowak is lying. And I can't help but think that Nat would have more reason to lie. Maybe Jamie did go to her house for a while that night, and she just didn't want to say so in front of her boyfriend in case it looked bad. He seems pretty scary."

"What's his name again? Luke?"

"Eaton, yeah. Or maybe she just didn't want to tell me she saw Jamie because she doesn't want to be involved. I didn't exactly treat her well last time. Or she could be lying because she's involved somehow. I got this weird feeling when I spoke to her and Luke about where they were Friday night, like I wasn't getting the full story."

"But Jamie was seen alive and well on Weevil Road almost an hour after that. So if he did go to Nat's, he was fine when he left."

"I know," Pip said. "So then why lie about it? What is there to hide?"

"Or Tom could be lying," Ravi said, bending down to get a closer look at the faded letters on a plaque.

"He could be," she sighed. "But why? And how could he have known that that house belonged to someone who's . . . well, a person of interest?"

"You going to talk to Nat again?"

"Not sure." Pip wound down another row of graves. "I should, but I'm not sure she'll talk to me again. She really hates me. And this week is hard enough for her anyway."

"I could go," Ravi said. "Maybe when Max's trial is over?"

"Yeah, maybe," Pip replied, but the thought that Jamie might still be missing by then made something in her sink. She quickened her pace. "We're going too slowly. Let's split up."

"No, but I really, really like you."

And Pip could feel his smirk, even though she wasn't looking at him.

"We are in a graveyard. Behave."

"They can't hear," he said, ducking from her frown. "OK, fine, I'll check this way." He traipsed up and over to the far side of the yard, starting at the other end to work back to her.

Pip lost him after a few minutes, behind an unkempt hedgerow, and it was like she was alone. Standing here in this field of names. There was no one else around; it was dead-of-night quiet, even though it was only six o'clock.

She reached the end of another row—still no sign of Hillary—when she heard a shout. Ravi's voice was faint as the wind carried it away from her, but she could see his waving hand above the hedges and hurried over.

"You found it?" she said, breathless now.

"'In loving memory of Hillary F. Weiseman,'" Ravi read out, standing over a black marble plaque with gold lettering. "'Died October 4, 2008. Beloved mother and grandmother. You will be missed dearly.'"

"That's her," Pip said, looking around. This part of the graveyard was almost closed in, sheltered by a row of hedges on one side and a cluster of trees on the other. "It's well covered here. You can't really be seen from any side, apart from the path up there."

Ravi nodded. "Would make a good secret meeting spot, if that's what it was."

"But with who? We know Jamie never met Layla in real life."

"What about those?" Ravi pointed to a small bouquet of flowers lying beside Hillary's grave.

They were dried out and dead, petals flaking away as Pip closed her fingers around the plastic packaging. "Clearly left here several weeks ago," she said, spotting a small white card in the middle of the bouquet. Blue ink bled down the paper, from the rain, but the imprint of the words was still legible.

"'Dear Mom, happy birthday! Miss you every day. Love from Mary, Harry, and Joe,'" she read out to Ravi.

"Mary, Harry, and Joe," Ravi said thoughtfully. "Do we know them?"

"No," she said. "But I looked on whitepages.com and couldn't find anyone living in Fairview now with the surname Weiseman."

"They aren't Weisemans, then. Probably have a different surname through marriage or something."

They heard a scuffling set of footsteps on the gravel path above, drawing closer. Pip and Ravi spun on their heels to see who it was. Pip felt a tightening in her chest, like she'd been caught somewhere she shouldn't be, as she watched a man cross into view from behind the canopy of wind-shivering willow. It was Stanley Forbes, and he looked just as shocked to see them, flinching with a sharp intake of breath when he spotted them there, hiding in the shadows.

"Crap, you scared me," he said, holding one hand to his chest.

"Are you allowed to say 'crap' near a church?" Ravi smiled, immediately breaking the tension.

"Sorry," Pip said, dead flowers still in her hand. "What are you doing here?" A perfectly fair question, she thought; there was no one else in the graveyard except them, and she and Ravi weren't exactly here for ordinary reasons.

"I'm, er . . ." Stanley looked taken aback. "I'm here to talk to the pastor about a story for next week's paper. Why are you here?" He returned the question, squinting so he could read the grave they were standing at.

Well, he'd caught them, Pip might as well give it a go. "Hey Stanley," she said, "you know most people in town, right? Because of the newspaper. Do you know the family of a woman named Hillary Weiseman? A daughter named Mary, and maybe two sons or grandsons named Harry and Joe?"

Stanley narrowed his eyes, like this was one of the stranger things he'd ever been asked after bumping into two people lurking in a graveyard. "Well, yes, I do. So do you. That's Mary Scythe. The Mary who volunteers at the paper with me. Harry and Joe are her sons."

And as he said that, something clicked in Pip's head.

"Harry Scythe. Does he work at The Book Cellar?" she asked.

"Yeah, I think so," Stanley said, shuffling his feet. "Does this have something to do with that disappearance you're looking into, Jamie Reynolds?"

"It might." She shrugged, reading something like disappointment on his face when she didn't elaborate. Well, sorry; she didn't want a small-town volunteer journalist chasing the story too, getting in her way. But maybe that wasn't entirely fair; Stanley had printed the Missing poster in the *Fairview Mail* like she'd asked, and it had brought people to her with information. "Um," she added, "I just wanted to say thank you for printing that notice in the paper, Stanley. You didn't have to, and it's really helped. So yeah. Thanks. For that."

"That's OK." He smiled, looking between her and Ravi. "And I hope you find him. I mean, I'm sure you will." He rolled up one sleeve to look at the time. "I better go, don't want to keep the pastor waiting. Um. Yeah. OK. Bye." He gave them a small, awkward wave, down by his waist, and walked off toward the church.

"Harry Scythe was one of the witnesses on Weevil Road," Pip told Ravi in a hushed tone, watching Stanley walk away.

"Huh, really?" Ravi said. "Small town."

"It is," Pip said, placing the dead flowers back by Hillary's grave. "It *is* a small town." She wasn't sure if this meant anything other than that. And she wasn't sure that coming here had explained anything about that scrap of paper in Jamie's wastepaper basket, other than he had possibly come here to meet someone, here under these same shadows. But it was too unclear, too vague to be a true lead.

"Come on. We should get the trial update done and out of the way," Ravi said, taking her hand and winding his fingers between hers. "Also, I can't believe you actually said thank you to Stanley Forbes."

He pulled a face at her, like he was frozen in shock, eyes crossing over each other.

"Stop." She nudged him.

"You actually being nice to someone." The stupid face continued. "Well done. Gold star for you, Pip."

"Shut up."

TWENTY-THREE

The Reynoldses' house stared her down, the top windows yellow and unblinking. But only for a second before the door swung inward and Joanna Reynolds appeared in the crack.

"You're here." Joanna ushered Pip inside as Connor appeared down the hall. "Thanks for coming straightaway."

"That's OK." Pip shrugged off her bag and took off her shoes. She and Ravi had just finished recording the update on Max Hastings's trial—discussing two witnesses for the defense, Max's male friends from college—when Joanna had called.

"It sounded urgent?" Pip said, looking between the two of them. She could hear the sounds of the television behind the closed door to the living room. Presumably Arthur Reynolds was in there, still refusing to have anything to do with this. But Jamie had been gone for four days now; when would his dad admit something might be wrong? Pip understood: it was hard to climb back out of the hole once you'd dug in your heels. But surely he was starting to worry?

"Yes, it is, I think." Joanna gestured for Pip to follow her down the hallway, turning to climb the stairs behind Connor.

"Is it Jamie's computer?" Pip asked. "Did you manage to get on?"

"No, not that," she said. "We've been trying. Tried more than seven hundred options now. Nothing."

"OK, well I tracked down and contacted two computer experts yesterday, so we'll see what they say." Pip moved up the stairs, trying not to catch Joanna's heels. "So what's wrong?"

"I've listened to the first episode you released last night several times already." Joanna spoke quickly, growing breathless halfway up the stairs. "It's the interview you did with the eyewitnesses from the bookstore, the ones who saw Jamie on Weevil at 11:40. There was something nagging at me about that interview, and I finally realized what it was."

Joanna led her into Jamie's chaotic bedroom, where Connor had switched on the light, waiting for them.

"Is it Harry Scythe?" Pip asked. "Do you know him?"

Joanna shook her head. "It's that part where they talked about what Jamie was wearing. Two witnesses thought they saw him in the burgundy shirt, the one we know he left the house in. But those were the first two to see him, as Jamie would have been walking toward them. The other two witnesses got to the door after, when Jamie would have already passed. So they saw him from behind. And they both thought that maybe he wasn't wearing a burgundy shirt, maybe he was wearing something darker, with a hood, and pockets because they couldn't see Jamie's hands."

"Yes, there is that discrepancy," Pip said. "But that can happen with small details in eyewitness accounts."

Joanna's eyes were alight now, burning a path across Pip's face. "Yes, and our instinct was to believe the two who saw him in the shirt, because that's what we presumed Jamie was wearing. But what if it's the other two who are right, the ones who saw him in a black hoodie? Jamie has a black hoodie," she said, "one with a zipper. He wears it all the time. If it was undone, maybe from the front you wouldn't see much of it and would focus on the shirt beneath."

"But he wasn't wearing a black hoodie when he left the house on

Friday," Pip said, looking to Connor. "And he wasn't carrying it with him; he didn't have a backpack or anything."

"No, he definitely didn't have it with him." Connor stepped in. "That's what I said at first. But . . ." He gestured back to his mom.

"But"—Joanna picked it up—"I've looked everywhere. Everywhere. In his wardrobe, his drawers, all these piles of clothes, his laundry basket, the ironing pile, the closets in our room, Connor's and Zoe's. Jamie's black hoodie isn't here. It's not in the house."

Pip's breath stalled in her chest. "It's not here?"

"We've, like, triple-checked everywhere it could be," said Connor. "Spent the last few hours searching. It's gone."

"So if they're right," Joanna said, "if those two eyewitnesses are right, and they saw Jamie wearing a black hoodie, then . . ."

"Then Jamie came back home," Pip said, and she felt a cold shiver, wandering the wrong way past her stomach, filling the hollows of her legs. "Between the calamity party and the sighting on Weevil Road, Jamie came back home. Back here," she said, looking around the room with new eyes: the hectic piles of clothes strewn about, maybe when Jamie had been frantically searching for the hoodie. The smashed mug by his bed, maybe that had happened by accident, in his haste. The missing knife downstairs. Maybe, if Jamie *was* the one who took it, maybe that's the real reason he returned home.

"Yes, exactly," Joanna said. "That's what I was thinking. Jamie came home." She said it with such hope in her voice, such undisguised wanting, her little boy back home, like the part that came after couldn't ever take that away from her, that he'd then left again and disappeared.

"So if he did come back and take his hoodie," Pip said, avoiding any mention of the missing knife, "it must have been between, say, ten-forty-five p.m., after walking back from Highmoor, and eleven-twenty-five-ish, because it would've taken at least fifteen minutes to get halfway down Weevil."

Joanna nodded, hanging on her every word.

"But . . ." Pip stopped herself and restarted, directing the question at Connor. It was easier that way. "But didn't your dad get home from the restaurant around eleven-fifteen?"

Joanna answered anyway. "Yes, he did. About then. Obviously, Arthur didn't see Jamie, so Jamie must have come and gone before Arthur got back."

"Have you asked him about that?" Pip said tentatively.

"Asked him what?"

"About his movements that night?"

"Yes, of course," Joanna said bluntly. "He got back from the restaurant around eleven-fifteen, as you said. No sign of Jamie."

"So Jamie must have come back earlier, right?" Connor asked.

"Right," Pip said, but that's not what she was thinking at all. She was thinking that Tom Nowak said he saw Jamie going into Nat da Silva's house on Cross Lane at ten-fifty p.m. And was there time to do both? To visit Nat, walk home, and leave again? No, not really, not without Jamie overlapping with Arthur. But Arthur said he was home at eleven-fifteen and hadn't seen Jamie. Something wasn't adding up here.

Either Jamie hadn't gone to Nat's at all, and came home earlier and left before eleven-fifteen, when his dad got home, or Jamie *had* gone to Nat's, briefly, then walked home, coinciding with the time his dad returned and Arthur just hadn't noticed Jamie was there, or when he left. Or Arthur *had* noticed, and for some reason he was lying about it.

"Pip?" Joanna repeated.

"Sorry, what was that?" Pip said, out of her head and back inside the room.

"I said, when I was looking for Jamie's black hoodie, I found something else." Joanna's eyes darkened as she approached Jamie's white laundry basket. "I looked through here," she said, opening the lid and retrieving an item of clothing from the top. "And this was about halfway down."

She held it up by the seams on the shoulders to show Pip. It was a gray cotton sweater. And down the front, about five inches below the collar, were small drops of blood, dried to a reddish brown. Seven stains in all, each one smaller than a quarter inch. And a longer smear of blood on the cuff of one sleeve.

"Shit." Pip stepped forward to get a better look at the blood.

"This is the sweater he wore on his birthday," Joanna said, and indeed Pip recognized it from the Missing posters all over town.

"You heard him sneak out late that night, didn't you?" Pip asked Connor.

"Yeah."

"And he didn't accidentally hurt himself at home that evening?"

Joanna shook her head. "He went into his bedroom and he was fine. Happy."

"These look like the blood dripped from above. It's not spatter," Pip said, circling one finger in front of the sweater. "The sleeve looks like it was wiped against a source of blood."

"Jamie's blood?" The color had gone from Joanna's face, drained away to somewhere unseen.

"Possibly. Did you notice if he had any cuts or bruises the next day?"

"No," Joanna said quietly. "None that I could see."

"It could be someone else's blood," Pip thought aloud, and immediately regretted it. Joanna's face folded, collapsing in on itself as a lone tear escaped and twisted around the contours of her cheek.

"I'm sorry, Joanna," Pip said. "I shouldn't have s—"

"No, it's not you," Joanna cried, carefully placing the sweater back on top of the basket. Two more tears broke free, racing each other to her chin. "It's just this feeling, like I don't even know my son at all. I'm not sure I recognize him."

Connor went to his mom, folded her into a hug. She had shrunk again, and she disappeared inside his arms, sobbing into his chest. An awful, raw sound that hurt Pip just to hear it.

"It's OK, Mom," Connor whispered down into her hair, looking to Pip, but she also didn't know what to say to make anything better.

Joanna reemerged with a sniff, wiping at her eyes in vain. She stared down at Jamie's sweater. "Jamie trying to steal from your mom, Pip, getting fired, and lying to us for weeks. Breaking into someone's home in the middle of the night to steal a watch he didn't need. Sneaking out. Coming back, possibly with someone's blood on his clothes, or his own. The missing knife. I don't recognize this Jamie," she said, closing her eyes like she could imagine her son back in front of her, the one she knew. "This isn't him, these things he's done. He's not this person; he's sweet, he's considerate. He makes me tea when I get home from work, he asks me how my day went. We talk, about how he's feeling, how I'm feeling. We're a team, me and him, we have been since he was born. I know everything about him—except clearly I don't anymore."

Pip found herself staring at the bloodied sweater too, unable to pull her eyes away. "There's more to all this than we understand right now," she said. "There has to be a reason behind it. He hasn't just changed after twenty-four years, flipped a switch. There's a reason, and I will find it. I promise."

"I just want him back." Joanna squeezed Connor's hand, meeting Pip's eyes. "I want our Jamie back. The one who still calls me Jomomma because he knows it makes me smile. That was his name for me, when Jamie was three and first learned I had a name other than

Mommy. He came up with Jomomma, so that I could have my own name back while still being his mom." Joanna sniffed and the sound stuttered all the way through her, shuddering in her shoulders. "What if I never get to hear him call me that again?"

But her eyes were dry, like she'd cried all she could cry and now she was empty. Hollow. Pip recognized the look in Connor's eyes as he wrapped an arm around his mom: fear. He squeezed tight, like that was the only way he knew how to stop his mom from falling apart.

This wasn't a moment for Pip to watch, to intrude on. She should leave them to their moment.

"Thank you for calling me over, about the hoodie," she said, walking slowly backward to Jamie's bedroom door. "We're getting one step closer, with every piece of information. I . . . I better get back to recording and editing. And I'll message those computer experts again." She glanced at the closed lid of Jamie's laptop as she reached the door. "Do you have any of those big Ziploc freezer bags?"

Connor screwed his eyes at her, confused, but he nodded nonetheless.

"Seal that sweater inside one of them," she said. "And keep it somewhere cool, out of sunlight."

"OK."

"Bye," Pip said, and it came out as barely a whisper as she left them, walking away down the hall. But after three steps, something stopped her. The fragment of a thought, circling too fast for her to catch. And when it finally settled, she retraced those three steps back to Jamie's door.

"Jomomma?" she said.

"Yes." Joanna lifted her gaze to Pip, like it was almost too heavy.

"I mean . . . did you try Jomomma?"

"Pardon?"

"For Jamie's password. Sorry," she said.

"N-no," Joanna said, glancing at Connor, a horrified look in her eyes. "I thought when you said to try nicknames, you meant nicknames *we* had for Jamie."

"That's OK. It really could be anything," Pip said, making her way over to Jamie's desk. "Can I sit?"

"Of course." Joanna came to stand behind her, Connor on the other side, as Pip opened the laptop. The dead screen mirrored back their faces, over-stretching them into the faces of phantoms. Pip pressed the power button and brought up the blue log-in screen, that empty white password box staring her down.

She typed it in—*Jomomma,* the letters mutating into small black circles as they entered the box. Pip paused, finger hanging over the enter button as the room suddenly went too silent. Joanna and Connor were holding their breath.

She pressed it and immediately:

Incorrect Password

Behind her, they both exhaled, someone's breath ruffling her half-up hair.

"Sorry," Pip said, not wanting to look back at them. "I thought it was worth a try." It had been, and maybe it was worth a few more, she thought.

She tried it again, replacing the *o* with a zero.

Incorrect Password

She tried it with a one at the end. And then a two. And then a one, two, three, and a one, two, three, four. Swapping the zero and the *o* in and out.

Incorrect Password

Capital *J.* Lowercase *j.*

Capital *M* for the start of "Momma." Lowercase *m.*

Pip hung her head, sighing.

"It's OK." Connor placed a hand on her shoulder. "You tried. Those experts will be able to do it, right?"

Yes, but one had replied to her email saying he couldn't look at it until the weekend, and the other hadn't responded at all. Clearly neither of them had time, which was all wrong because if anything, everyone else had all the time and Pip had none. Jamie had none.

But giving up was too hard, she'd never been good at that. So she tried one last thing. "Joanna, what year were you born?"

"Oh, sixty-six," she said. "Doubt Jamie knows that, though."

Pip typed in *Jomomma66* and pressed enter.

Incorrect Password. The screen mocked her, and she felt a flare of anger rise within her, itching in her hands to grab the laptop and throw it against the wall. That hot, primal thing inside that she never knew existed before a year ago. Connor was saying her name, but it didn't belong to this person sitting in the chair anymore. But she controlled the anger, pushed it back. Biting her tongue, she tried again, fingers hammering the keys.

JoMomma66

Incorrect Password

Fuck.

Jomomma1966

Incorrect

Fuck.

JoMomma1966

Incorr—

Fuck.

J0Momma66

Welcome Back

Wait, what? Pip stared at the place where *Incorrect Password* should be. But instead, there was a loading circle, spooling around and around, reflecting in the dark of her eyes. And those two words: *Welcome Back.*

"We're in!" She jumped up from the chair, a shocked half cough, half laugh escaping from her.

"We're in?" Joanna caught Pip's words, remolded them with disbelief.

"J0Momma66," Connor said, raising his arms in victory. "That's it. We did it!"

And Pip didn't know how it happened, but somehow, in a strange, confusing blur, they were hugging, all three of them in a chaotic embrace, the chirping sounds of Jamie's laptop waking up behind them.

TWENTY-FOUR

"Are you sure you want to be here for this?" Pip said, looking mainly at Joanna, her finger poised above the trackpad, about to pull up Jamie's browser history in Google Chrome. "We don't know what we might find."

"I understand," she said, hand tightly gripped on the back of the chair, not going anywhere.

Pip exchanged a quick look with Connor and he nodded that he was fine with that too.

"OK."

She clicked and Jamie's history opened in a new tab. The most recent entry was from Friday, April 24, at 5:11 p.m. He'd been on YouTube, watching an epic fail compilation video. Other entries for that day: Reddit, more YouTube, a series of Wikipedia pages that tracked back from Knights Templar to Slender Man.

She scrolled to the day before, and one particular result grabbed her attention: Jamie had visited Layla Mead's Instagram page twice on Thursday, the day before he'd gone missing. He'd also researched *nat da silva rape trial max hastings,* which had taken him to Pip's site, agoodgirlsguidetomurderpodcast.com, where it looked like Jamie had listened to her and Ravi's trial update that day.

Her eyes flicked down through the days: all the Reddit hits and

Wikipedia pages and Netflix binges. She was looking for something, anything that stuck out as unusual. *Actually* unusual, not Wikipedia unusual. She passed through Monday into the week before, and there was something that made her pause, something on Thursday the sixteenth, Jamie's birthday. Jamie had Googled *what counts as assault?* And then, after looking through a few results, he'd asked *how to fight.*

"This is weird," Pip said, highlighting the results with her finger. "These searches are from eleven-thirty on the night of his birthday. The night you heard him sneak out late, Connor, the night he came back with blood on his sweater." She glanced quickly at the gray sweater, still crumpled on the laundry basket. "Seems like Jamie knew he would get into an altercation that night. It's like he was preparing himself for it."

"But Jamie's never been in a fight before. I mean, clearly, if he had to Google how to do it," Connor said.

Pip had more to say on this, but another result lower down had just caught her eye. Monday the thirteenth, a few days earlier, Jamie had looked up *controlling fathers.* Pip's breath snagged in her throat, but she controlled her reaction, scrolling quickly past it before the others saw it.

But Pip couldn't unsee it. And now she couldn't stop thinking about Jamie and Arthur's explosive arguments, or Arthur's near-total lack of attention to the fact that his oldest son was missing, or the possible intersecting timelines of Jamie and Arthur that night. And suddenly, she was very aware that Arthur Reynolds was sitting in the room below her now, his presence like a physical thing, seeping up through the carpet.

"What's that?" Connor said suddenly, making her flinch.

She'd been distractedly running down the results, but now she stopped, eyes following the line of Connor's finger. Tuesday, April 7, at 1:26 a.m., there was an odd series of Google searches, starting with *brain cancer.* Jamie had clicked through to two results on WebMD, one for *brain tumors,* the other for *malignant brain tumor.* A few minutes later, Jamie had returned to Google, typing *inoperable brain tumor,* and clicking on to a cancer charity page. Then he'd asked Google one more thing that night: *brain cancer clinical trials.*

"Hmm," Pip said. "I mean, I know I look up all sorts of things online, and Jamie clearly does too, but this feels different from his general browsing. This feels sort of . . . targeted, deliberate. Do you know anyone who has brain cancer?" Pip asked Joanna.

She shook her head. "No."

"Did Jamie ever mention knowing someone who has?" She turned the question over to Connor.

"No, never."

And something Pip wanted to ask, but couldn't: Was it possible Jamie was researching brain tumors because he'd learned he had one? No, it couldn't be. Surely that wasn't something he could keep from his mom.

Pip tried to scroll farther, but she'd reached the end of the results. Jamie must have wiped his history from that point. She was about to move on when one last pair of search items jumped out at her, ones she'd glanced over and hadn't registered before, nestled quietly between the brain tumor results and videos of dogs walking on their hind legs. Nine hours after researching brain cancer, presumably after going to sleep and waking up the next day, Jamie had asked Google *how to make money quickly,* clicking on an article titled "11 Easy Ways to Make a Quick Buck."

It wasn't the strangest thing to see on the computer of a twenty-four-year-old who still lived at home, but the timing made it significant. Just one day after Jamie had searched that, Pip's mom caught him trying to steal her company credit card. This had to be related.

But why did Jamie wake up on Tuesday the seventh so desperate for money? Something must have happened the day before.

Crossing her fingers, Pip typed Instagram into the address bar. This was the most important thing: access to Jamie and Layla's private messages, a way to identify the catfish. *Please have Jamie's passwords saved, please please please.*

The Instagram home page popped up, logged in to Jamie Reynolds's profile.

"Yes," Pip hissed, but a loud buzzing interrupted her. It was her phone in her back pocket, vibrating loudly against the chair. She pulled it out. Her mom was calling and, glancing at the time, Pip knew exactly why. It was after ten on a school night, and now she was going to be in trouble for that. She sighed.

"Do you need to go, sweetie?" Joanna must have read the screen over her shoulder.

"Um, I probably should. Do you . . . would you mind if I take Jamie's laptop with me? That way, I can go through it all with a fine-tooth comb tonight, his social media accounts, and update you tomorrow on anything I find." Plus, she was thinking that Jamie probably wouldn't want his mom and little brother going through his private messages with Layla. Not if they were, you know . . . not for the eyes of a mother and a brother.

"Yes, yes, of course," Joanna said, brushing her hand against Pip's shoulder. "You're the one who actually knows what you're doing with it."

Connor agreed with a quiet "yeah," though Pip could tell he wished he could come with her, that real life didn't have to keep getting in the way. School, parents, time.

"I'll text you *as soon* as I find anything significant," she reassured him, turning to the computer to minimize the Chrome window, the blue robot-themed home screen reappearing. The computer ran Windows 10, and Jamie had it set up in app mode. That had confused her at first, before she'd spotted the Chrome app, tucked neatly beside the Microsoft Word square. She reached for the laptop lid to close it, running her eyes over the rest of the apps: Excel, Netflix, Hulu, Fitbit.

She paused before closing the laptop, something stopping her, the faintest outline of an idea, not yet whole. "Fitbit?" She looked at Connor.

"Yeah, remember my dad bought him one for his birthday. It was obvious Jamie didn't want it though, wasn't it?" Connor asked his mom.

"Well, you know, Jamie is impossible to buy presents for. Your father was just trying to be helpful. I thought it was a nice idea," Joanna said, her tone growing sharp and defensive.

"I know, I was just saying." Connor returned to Pip. "Dad set up the account for him and downloaded the app on his phone and on here, because he said Jamie would never get around to doing it himself, which is probably true. And Jamie *has* been wearing the Fitbit since, I think mostly to keep Dad off his—happy, I mean," he said, with a half glance in his mom's direction.

"Hold on," Pip said, the idea a fully formed thing now, solid, pressing down on her brain. "The black watch that Jamie had on the night he went missing, that's his Fitbit?"

"Yes," Connor said slowly, unsurely, but he could clearly tell Pip was going somewhere with this; he just wasn't with her yet.

"Oh my god," she said, voice cracking as it rushed out of her. "What type of Fitbit is it? Is it GPS-enabled?"

Joanna reeled back, like Pip's momentum had jumped right into her. "I still have the box, hold on," she said, running out of the room.

"If it has GPS," Connor said, breathless, though he wasn't the one running, "does that mean we can find out exactly where he is?"

He didn't really need Pip to answer that question. She wasted no time, clicking on the Fitbit app and staring at the colorful dashboard that opened up on the screen.

"No." Joanna was back in the room, reading from a plastic box. "It's a Charge HR, doesn't mention GPS, just says heart rate, activity tracker, and sleep quality."

But Pip had already found that out for herself. The dashboard on Jamie's computer had icons for step count, heart rate, calories burned, sleep, and active minutes. But below each of the icons were the same words: *Data not cleared. Sync & try again.* That was for today, Tuesday, April 28. Pip clicked on the calendar icon at the top and skipped back to yesterday. It said the same thing: *Data not cleared. Sync & try again.*

"What does that mean?" Connor asked.

"That Jamie's not wearing the Fitbit now," Pip said. "Or that it hasn't been in the proximity of his phone to sync the data."

But when she skipped past Sunday and Saturday and clicked on to the Friday he went missing, the icons burst into life, completed circles in thick bands of green and orange. And those words were gone, replaced by numbers: 10,793 steps walked that day, 1,649 calories burned. A heart rate graph that spiked up and down in bright blocks.

And Pip felt her own heart react, taking over, pulsating inside her fingers as it guided them along the trackpad. She clicked on the step count icon and it brought up a new screen, with a bar chart breakdown of Jamie's steps throughout the day.

"Oh my god!" she said, eyes on the very end of the graph. "There's data here from after the last time Jamie was seen. Look." She pointed to it as Joanna and Connor drew closer still, eyes circling. "He was walking, right up until midnight. So after eleven-forty-ish, when he was seen on Weevil Road, he did . . ." Pip highlighted the columns between 11:30 p.m. and 12:00 midnight to work out the specific number. "One thousand, eight hundred, and twenty-eight steps."

"What distance is that?" Joanna asked.

"Just Googling it," Connor said, tapping at his phone. "That's just under a mile."

"Why did he stop suddenly at midnight?" said Joanna.

"Because that data falls under the next day," Pip said, pressing the back arrow to return to Friday's dashboard. Before she flipped to Saturday, though, she noticed something in Jamie's heart rate graph and clicked the icon to zoom in.

It looked like Jamie's resting heart rate was around eighty beats per minute; that's where it stood for most of the day. Then, at five-thirty, there was a series of spikes up to around one hundred beats per minute. That's when Jamie and his dad had been arguing, according to Connor. It settled again for a couple of hours, but then started to climb back up through the nineties, as Jamie was following Stella Chapman, waiting to talk to her at the party. And then it got faster, during the time when George had seen Jamie on the phone outside, most likely to Layla. It stayed at that level, just over a hundred, as Jamie walked. Beyond 11:40 p.m., when he was seen on Weevil Road, his heart rate steadily grew faster, reaching 103 at midnight.

Why was it so fast? Was he running? Or was he scared?

The answers must lie in the early hours of Saturday's data.

Pip switched over to it and immediately the page felt incomplete compared with the day before, the colored circles barely filled in. Only 2,571 steps in total. She opened the step count menu fully and felt something heavy and cold dragging her stomach into her legs. Those steps all took place between midnight and around thirty minutes past, and then . . . nothing. No data at all. The graph dropped off completely: an entire line of zero.

But there was another, shorter period within that, where it looked like Jamie had taken no steps. He must have been standing still, or sitting. It happened just after midnight, and Jamie didn't move for a few minutes, but it wasn't for long, because just after five past, he was on the move again, walking right up until the point where everything stopped, just before 12:30 a.m.

"It just stops," Connor said, and that faraway look was back in his eyes.

"But this is amazing," Pip said, trying to bring his eyes back from wherever they'd gone. "We can use this data to try to track where Jamie went, where he was at just before twelve-thirty. The step count tells us that that's when the incident, whatever it was, happened, which fits, Joanna, with your text at 12:36 never being delivered. And it might also tell us *where* it happened. So from 11:40, when he's seen at the bend in Weevil Road, Jamie walks a total of two thousand and twenty-four steps before he stops for a few minutes. And then he walks another two thousand three hundred and seventy-five, and wherever that takes him is right where whatever happened, happened. We can use these figures to draw up a perimeter, working from that last sighting on Weevil Road. And then we search within that specific zone, for any sign of Jamie or where he went. This is good, I promise."

Connor tried a small smile, but it didn't convince his eyes. Joanna also looked afraid, but her mouth was set in a determined line.

Pip's phone rang in her pocket again. She ignored it and navigated back to the dashboard to look at Jamie's heart rate in that time span. It started already high, above one hundred, and, strangely, in that window of a few minutes when he wasn't moving, his heart was picking up faster and faster. At the point right before he started walking again, it spiked up to 126 beats per minute. It trailed off, but only slightly, as he walked those additional 2,375 steps. And then, in those last couple of minutes before half past the hour, Jamie's heart peaked up to 158 beats per minute.

And then, it flatlined.

Dropped from 158 straight to zero, and beat no more after that.

Joanna must have been thinking the same thing, because just then, a gasp, wretched and guttural, ripped through her, hands smacking to her face to hold everything in. And then the thought took Connor too, his mouth hanging open as his eyes flickered over that steep fall in the graph.

"His heart stopped," he said, so quietly that Pip almost didn't hear him, his chest juddering. "He's . . . is he . . . ?"

"No, no," Pip said firmly, holding up her palms, though it was a lie, because inside she was feeling the same dread. But she had to hide hers, that's why she was here. "That's not what it means. All this means is that the Fitbit was no longer monitoring Jamie's heart beat data, OK? He could have taken the Fitbit off, that's all this could be showing us. Please, don't think that."

But she could see from their faces that they weren't really listening to her anymore, both of their gazes fixed on that flatline, sailing along with it into nothingness. And that thought—it was like a black hole, feeding on whatever hope they had left, and nothing Pip could say, nothing she could think of to say, could possibly fill it in again.

File Name:

Case Notes 4.docx

I almost had a disaster, when I remembered you can't get into DMs on the desktop version of Instagram, only on the app. But it's OK: Jamie's associated email was still logged in on his laptop. I was able to send a reset password request from Instagram and then sign into Jamie's account from my phone. I went straight to Jamie's DMs with Layla Mead. There weren't *too* many of them; only over the course of about eight days. Judging from context, it looks like they met on Tinder first, then Jamie moved the conversation to Instagram and then they moved on to texting, where I can't follow them. The start of their conversation:

Found you . . .

so you did. i wasn't exactly hiding from you :)

how's your day been?

Yeah it's been good, thanks. I just made the best dinner this world has ever seen and I might possibly be the greatest chef.

And humble too. Go on, what was it?

Maybe you can make it for me some day.

I fear I may have talked this up a bit much. It was essentially mac and cheese.

Most of their messages are like that: long bouts of chatting/flirting. On the third day of messages, they discovered they both loved the show *Peaky Blinders* and Jamie professed his lifelong ambition to be a gangster from the 1920s. Layla does seem very interested in Jamie; she's always asking him questions. But there are a few strange moments I noticed:

didn't you say it was your birthday coming up soon?

Yeah it is

The BIG 30

So what are you gonna do for it?

A party? Invite all the family?

I'm not so much a party person tbh. I'll probably just have a chill one, hang with friends.

This one particularly caught my eye because I was confused as to why Layla thinks Jamie is six years older than he is: twenty-nine turning thirty. The answer comes lower down in their conversation. But when I first saw this exchange, I couldn't help but think of the similarities with what Mr. Clark said: that Layla was direct about asking his age, bringing it up a few times. And, strangely, he too is twenty-nine turning thirty. Could be a coincidence, but I felt it was at least worth making a note of.

Another weird thing is that Jamie (and Layla) keep making references to the fact that Jamie lives alone in a small house in Fairview, which isn't true at all. Again, this all became clearer when I reached the end of their conversation on Insta:

hope we can meet up one day.

Yeah sure. I'd really like that :)

Listen, Layla. I have to tell you something. It's not easy to say it, but I really like you. Really. I haven't felt like this about anyone ever and so I need to be honest with you. I'm not actually 29, I'm turning 24 in a few weeks. And I'm not a successful portfolio manager for a financial company in New York, that wasn't true. I'm working as a receptionist at a job a family friend got for me. And I don't own a house, I live at home still with my parents and my brother. I'm so sorry, my intention was never to deceive anyone, especially not you. I'm not even sure why I made up all those lies for my profile. I made it when I was in a really bad place, feeling very self-conscious about myself, my life or lack thereof, and so I think I just invented the person I want to be, instead of the real me. Which was wrong, and I'm sorry. But I hope to be that man one day, and meeting someone like you makes me want to try. I'm sorry, Layla, and I understand if you're angry with me. But, if it's OK, I'd really like to keep talking to you. You make everything better.

Which is veeeerrrryyyy interesting. So Jamie sort of catfished the catfish first. Lying on his Tinder profile about his age, his job, his living arrangements. He explained it best himself: it was insecurity. I wonder if these insecurities are related to what happened with Nat da Silva, feeling like he lost someone so important to him to an older guy like Luke Eaton. In fact, I wonder whether Luke *is* twenty-nine and that's why Jamie picked that age, as a sort of confidence boost, or a rationalization in his head of why Nat chose Luke and not him.

After that long message, Layla stops replying to Jamie for three days. During that time, Jamie keeps trying, until he finds something that works:

Layla, please talk to me.

Let me explain

I am very truly sorry

I would never want to upset you ever

I understand if you never talk to me again

But you haven't blocked me, so maybe there's a chance?

Layla please talk to me

I care about you a lot

I would do anything for you

Anything?

Oh my god hi Yes. Anything. I'd do anything for you. I swear. I promise

ok

hey what's your number? Let's move this over to texts

I'm so happy you're speaking to me again. I'm 475-555-0173

I don't know, there's something about this exchange that gives me chills. She ignores him for three days and then she just comes back with that "Anything?" It feels creepy (I mean *more* creepy than the fact that she's a catfish at all), but maybe those are just my residual feelings from my one small exchange with Layla. Who *is* Layla? Nothing here gives me any real identifying marks. She's very careful, good at being the right amount of vague. If only she'd given Jamie her phone number instead of asking for his, I'd be in a different position now: able to call Layla directly, or look up the number. But here I am, still hanging on those two questions. Who is Layla? And how is she involved in Jamie's disappearance?

OTHER NOTES

I looked up heart rate information—I just needed some context about what I was seeing in these graphs. But now I wish I hadn't. Jamie's heart rate spikes up to 126 in that initial stationary period at 12:02 a.m., and then it races up to 158 just before the data cuts out. But that range of beats per minute is what the experts might consider as the heart rate of someone who is experiencing a fight-or-flight response.

File Name:

Map with sightings and search area.jpg

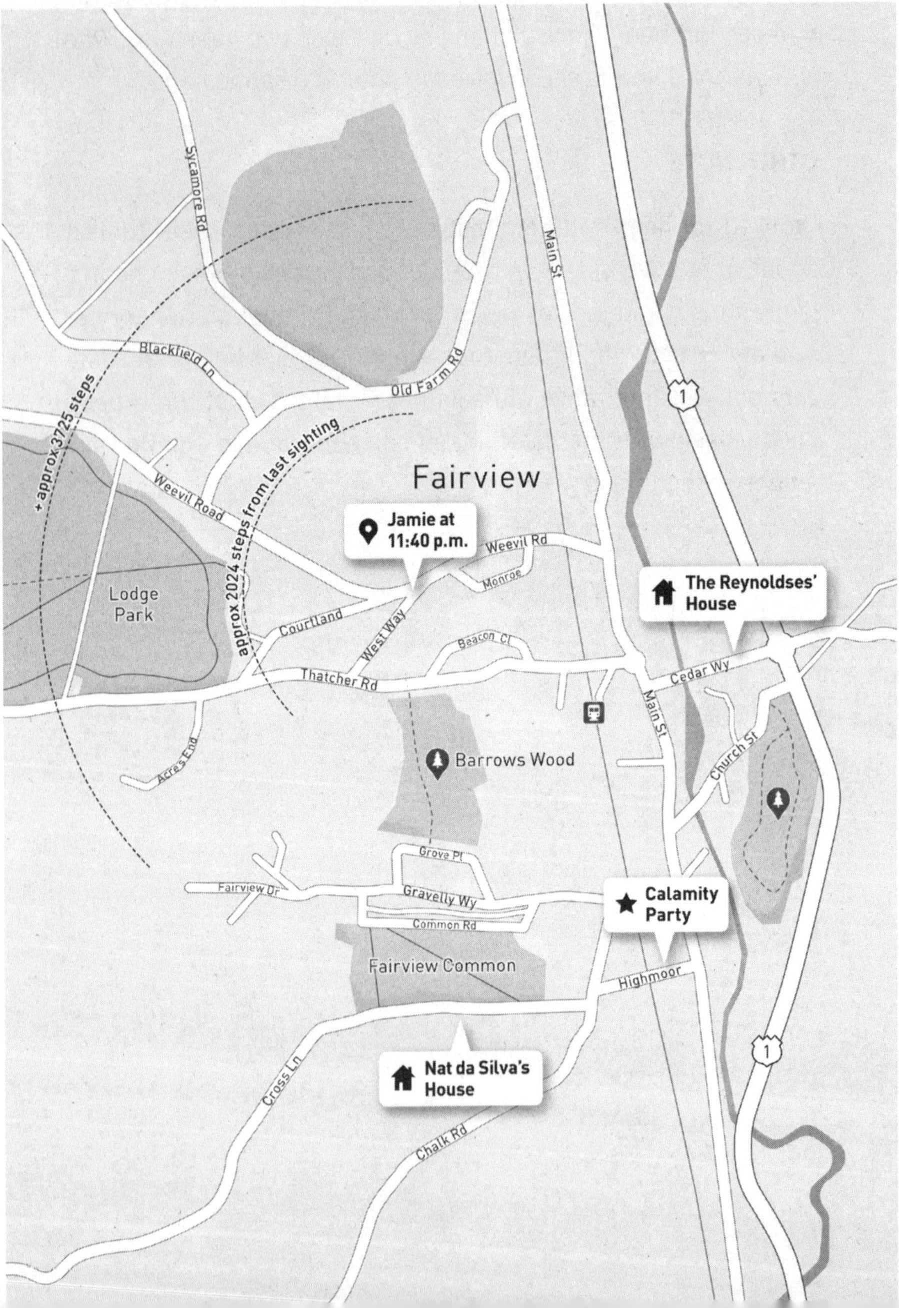

WEDNESDAY
5 DAYS MISSING

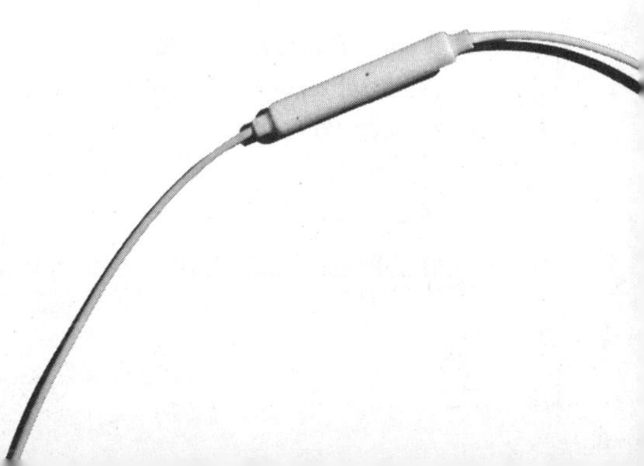

Search

Home

APRIL 29

Volunteer Search Party for Jamie Reynolds

Private · Hosted by Pip Fitz-Amobi

Interested | Going | •••

Today at 4:30 PM

Fairview High School, Fairview Drive, Fairview, CT 06820

Invited by Pip Fitz-Amobi

81 Going · 12 Maybe · 33 Invited

Hello everyone,

As you might have heard, Connor Reynolds's older brother, Jamie, has been missing for five days now, and I am looking into his disappearance for my podcast.

But I need your help! I've recently uncovered some information that provides an approximate area for Jamie's last known location. This area needs to be searched for any sign or clue as to where exactly Jamie was on Friday night and what might have happened to him. But the area is quite large, so I'm in desperate need of volunteers to help with the search.

If you would like to offer a hand, meet after school today for the briefing, 4:30 p.m., at the end of the parking lot. If we have enough volunteers, we'll be splitting into three search teams, led by me, Connor Reynolds, and Cara Ward. Please come find one of us to be assigned to a team.

Thank you, and please let me know if you intend to come.

TWENTY-FIVE

Every step Pip took was considered, careful, staring down at the forest floor and the mud that bunched up around the outline of her shoes. A record of her having been there, a trail of imprints that stalked her through the woods. But she was looking for someone else's prints: the jagged vertical lines on the soles of the Nike sneakers Jamie had been wearing when he disappeared.

And so was everyone else, eyes down and circling, searching for any of the signs Pip had mentioned in the briefing. Eighty-eight volunteers had turned up after school, most from her grade but a few juniors too. Thirty people on Connor's team, now searching the fields behind the school and knocking on doors at the far end of Thatcher Road, Acres End, and the lower part of Courtland, to ask residents if they'd seen Jamie between 12:02 and 12:28 a.m. Friday night. Twenty-nine people on Cara's team, who were farther north, combing through the fields and farmland up near Old Farm Road and Blackfield Lane. And twenty-nine people here with Pip, standing in a wide ant-line, staggered every six feet as they searched from one end of Lodge Park to the other.

Well, thirty people, now that Ravi had joined them. Max's trial had adjourned early today; it had been Max's turn on the stand and—Ravi told Pip reluctantly with a glint in his eyes that looked like hate—Max and his lawyer had done an all right job. They'd prepared an answer to everything the prosecution threw at Max in cross-examination. Closing remarks from both sides had followed and then the judge sent the jury off to deliberate.

"I can't wait to see his face tomorrow when he goes down. Wish I could record it for you," Ravi had said, using one foot to check inside a holly bush, reminding Pip of that time they were in these very woods, re-creating Andie Bell's murder to prove Sal didn't have time to be the killer.

Pip glanced up to her other side, exchanging a small, strained smile with Stella Chapman. But the face of Layla Mead stared back at her, sending a cold shiver down her back. They'd been out here for more than an hour already, and all the team had found was a tied baggie of dog shit and a crumpled bag of barbecue chips.

"Jamie!" someone down the line called.

The shouting had been going on for a while. Pip didn't know who'd started it, who first called out his name, but it had caught on, spreading sporadically up and down the line as they trudged on.

"Jamie!" she called in response. It was probably pointless, a literal shout into the void. Jamie couldn't still be here, and if he was, he'd no longer be able to hear his name. But at least it felt like they were actually doing something.

Pip stalled, breaking the line for a moment as she bent to check beneath a raised tree root. Nothing.

Her phone chimed, disturbing the crunching of their feet. It was a text from Connor: *OK, we split into threes to do the door knocking. Just finished Courtland and moving on to the fields. Found anything?*

"Jamie!"

Pip was relieved she didn't have to cover Courtland, the road where Max Hastings lived, even though his house was just outside the search zone. And no one would be home anyway; Max and his parents were staying in an expensive hotel near the courthouse for the duration of the trial. But still, she was glad she didn't have to go anywhere near that house.

Nothing yet, she texted back.

"Jamie!"

But as she pressed send, her screen was overtaken by an incoming call from Cara.

"Hey," Pip answered in an almost whisper.

"Hi, yeah," Cara said, the wind rattling against her microphone. "Um, someone on my team just found something. I've told everyone to stand back from it, set up a perimeter, as you'd say. But, um, you need to get here. Now."

"What is it?" Pip said, the panic riding her voice, twisting it. "Where are you?"

"We're at the farmhouse. The abandoned farmhouse on Sycamore Road. You know the one."

Pip did know the one.

"On my way," she said.

They were running now, her and Ravi, turning the corner onto Sycamore Road, the farmhouse set back and growing out of the small hill. Its dull-white painted bricks were cut through and sliced up by blackened timber, and the roof seemed to be curving inward now, in a way that roofs shouldn't do, like it could no longer quite hold up the sky. And just out of sight, behind the abandoned building, was the place where Becca Bell had hidden her sister's body for five and a half years. Andie had been right here all along, decomposing in the septic tank.

Pip tripped as they crossed from gravel to grass, and Ravi's hand skimmed hers instinctively, to pull her up. And as they neared, she saw the gathering of people, Cara's team, a colorful spattering of clothes against the dull colors of the farmhouse and the long-neglected land strewn with high tufts of weedy grass that tried to grab her feet.

Everyone was standing in a loose formation, all eyes trained on the same place: a small cluster of trees by the side of the house, the branches grown close to the building, like they were slowly reaching over to claim it as their own.

Cara was at the front of the group, with Naomi, waving to Pip as she shouted over her shoulder for everyone to get back.

"What is it?" Pip said, breathless. "What did you find?"

"It's over there, in the long grass at the bottom of those trees." Naomi pointed.

"It's a knife," said Cara.

"A knife?" Pip repeated the words, her feet following her eyes over to the trees. And she knew. She knew before she even saw it, exactly which knife it would be.

Ravi was beside her as she bent down to look. And there it was, half-concealed by the grass: a gray-bladed knife with a yellow band around the handle.

"That's the one missing from the Reynoldses' kitchen, isn't it?" Ravi asked, but he didn't need Pip to answer—her eyes told him enough.

She studied it through squinted eyes, not daring to get any closer. From here, a few feet away, the knife looked clean. Maybe a few flecks of dirt, but no blood. Not enough to be seen, at least. Pip sniffed, pulling out her phone to take a photo of the knife where it lay, then she drew back, beckoning Ravi to come with her.

"OK," she said, panic hardening into something like dread. But Pip could control dread, use it. "Cara, can you call Connor, tell him to let everyone on his team go and come over here, right now."

"On it," Cara said, phone already halfway to her ear.

"Naomi, when Cara's done, can you tell her to call Zach to dismiss my search team as well."

Pip and Ravi had left their team in the care of Zach and Stella Chapman. But they wouldn't find anything out there in the woods, because Jamie had come here. Jamie was here, carrying a knife he must have taken from his house. Here, at the outer limit of their search zone, which meant that his brief stop had been somewhere else, before he'd walked to the farmhouse. And here, right here, at 12:28 a.m., his Fitbit stopped recording his heart rate and step count. And there was a knife.

A knife was evidence. And evidence had to be dealt with in the correct way, without breaking the chain of custody. No one here had touched the knife, and no one would, not until the police arrived.

Pip dialed the number of the Fairview police station. She walked away from the gathering, plugging her other ear against the wind.

"Hello, Eliza," she said. "Yes, it's Pip Fitz-Amobi. Yep. Is anyone at the station? Uh-huh. Could you do me a favor and ask anyone who's free to come over to the farmhouse on Sycamore Road? Yes, that's where Andie B— No, this is about an open missing persons case. Jamie Reynolds. I've found a knife that's connected to his case, and it needs to be collected and documented as evidence. I know I'm supposed to call the other number. . . . Could you just, this one favor, Eliza, I swear, just this once." She paused, listening down the other end. "Thank you, thank you."

"Fifteen minutes," she said, when she rejoined Ravi. They might as well use those fifteen minutes, start trying to work out why Jamie might have come here.

"Can you keep everyone back from those trees?" she asked Naomi.

"Yeah, sure."

"Come on." Pip led Ravi toward the farmhouse entrance, the red-painted front door dangling from its hinges, like a mouth hanging open.

They stepped through, and the inside of the house wrapped them up in its dim light. The windows were fogged over by moss and grime, and the old carpet crunched under their feet, covered in stains. It even smelled abandoned in here: mildew and must and dust.

"When do we move in?" Ravi said, looking around in disgust.

"Like your bedroom is much better than this."

They continued down the hallway, the old, faded blue wallpaper peeling off and away in rolls that exposed the white underside, like small waves breaking up against the walls. An archway opened into a large space that once must have been a living room. There was a staircase on the far side, yellowing and peeling. Windows with limp, sun-bleached curtains that might have been floral-patterned in a previous life. Two old red sofas in the middle, brushed with gray, clinging dust.

As Pip stepped closer, she noticed a break in the dust on one of the sofa's cushions: a clearer, circular patch of the red material. As though someone had sat here. Recently.

"Look." Ravi drew her attention to the center of the room, where there were three small metal trash cans, upturned into stools. Scattered around them were food wrappers: Oreos, potato chip packages, empty Pringles cans. Discarded beer bottles and butts of hand-rolled cigarettes.

"Maybe not so abandoned after all," Ravi said, bending to pick up one of the butts, raising it to his nose. "Smells like weed."

"Great, and now you've put your prints on it, if this *is* a crime scene."

"Oh yeah," he said, and gritted his teeth, a guilty look in his eyes. "Maybe I'll just take this one home with me to dispose of." He pocketed it and straightened up.

"Why would people come here to hang out and smoke?" Pip said, studying the scene, questions surfacing from every corner. "That's rather morbid. Don't they know what happened here, that this is where Andie's body was found?"

"That's probably part of its charm," Ravi said, sliding into his movie-trailer voice. "*Old, abandoned murder house, the perfect place for a smoke and a snack.* Looks like whoever it is comes here pretty often and I'm guessing this is a nighttime activity. Maybe it's worth us coming back later tonight, staking out the place, see who comes here? They might be connected to Jamie's disappearance, or maybe they saw something last Friday."

"Stakeout?" Pip smiled. "All right, Sarge."

"Hey, *you're* Sarge. Don't you use my own names against me."

"Police are here!" Naomi called into the farmhouse as Pip and Ravi were showing Connor and Cara what they'd found inside.

"I'll go deal with them." Pip hurried back through the hallway and into the outside world. She screwed her eyes until they adjusted to the brightness. A police car had pulled up on the gravel road, doors on either side pushing open. Daniel da Silva stepped out from the driver's side, straightening his police cap, and Soraya Bouzidi from the other.

"Hi," Pip called, walking forward to greet them.

"Eliza said it was you," Daniel said, unable or unwilling to hide the disdain in his face. He didn't like Pip, not since she'd suspected him of being Andie's killer, and that was fine, because Pip didn't much like him either.

"Yep, it's me. Cause of all the trouble in Fairview since 2019," she said flatly, catching sight of Soraya smiling quickly. "Here, it's this way." She led them across the grass, pointing them toward the small huddle of trees.

Daniel and Soraya continued over to the long grass by the roots. Pip watched them looking down at the knife and then looking at each other.

"What is this?" Daniel called to her.

"It's a knife," she said. And then, more helpfully, "The same knife that's missing from a rack in the Reynoldses' house. Jamie Reynolds, remember, he's missing? Friends with your sister?"

"Yes, I—"

"Case number four nine zero zero one five two—"

"Yes, OK," Daniel interrupted. "What is all this?" He gestured to the students, still gathered a ways back from the farmhouse.

"That is a search team," Pip said. "When the police won't do anything, I guess you've gotta turn to high schoolers instead."

The muscles twitched in Daniel da Silva's cheek as he chewed on his tongue. "Right!" he shouted, clapping his hands loudly three times, surprising her. "Everyone go home! Now!"

The students disbanded immediately, breaking off into small, whispering groups. Pip gave them a grateful nod as they moved past the police and away to the road. But the Ward sisters didn't go, and neither did Connor or Ravi, standing in the entrance of the farmhouse.

"This knife is vital evidence to a missing persons case," Pip said, trying to regain control. "It needs to be collected and documented and handed over to the evidence clerk."

"Yes, I know how evidence works," Daniel said, darkly. "Did you put this here?" He pointed at the knife.

"No," she said, that hot primal feeling awakening again. "Of course I didn't. I wasn't even here when it was found."

"We'll take it," Soraya stepped in, placing herself between Daniel and Pip, disarming them. "I'll make sure it's correctly dealt with, don't worry." The look in her eyes was so different from Daniel's: kind, unsuspicious.

"Thank you," Pip said, as Soraya made her way back to the squad car.

When she was out of earshot, Daniel spoke again, not looking at Pip. "If I find out this isn't real, that you're wasting police time—"

"It's real," she said, the words crushed down to fit through her gritted teeth. "Jamie Reynolds is really missing. The knife is really here. And I know the police don't have the resources to make every case a priority, but please listen to me. Tell Hawkins. Something bad has happened here. I know it."

Daniel didn't respond.

"Do you hear me?" she said. "Foul play. Someone could be dead. And you're doing nothing. Something happened to Jamie, right here." She gestured toward the knife. "It has something to do with someone Jamie's been talking to online. A woman named Layla Mead, but that's not her r—"

And she stuttered to a stop, eyes circling his face. Because as soon as she'd said Layla's name, Daniel's reaction had been immediate. He sniffed, nostrils flaring, dropping his eyes like he was trying to hide them from her. A creep of pink spread across his cheeks as his wavy light-brown hair fell across his forehead.

"You know Layla," Pip said. "You've been talking to her too?"

"I have no idea what you're talking about."

"You've been talking to Layla," she said. "Do you know who she really is?"

"I haven't been talking to anyone," Daniel said in a low, rattling hiss that made the hairs on Pip's neck stand end up. "No one, you understand? And if I hear a word about this from you again . . ."

He ended the sentence there, leaving Pip to fill in the blank he'd left behind. He stepped back from her and straightened out his face just as Soraya was returning from the car, her hands covered by blue plastic gloves gripped around a paper evidence bag.

File Name:

Photograph of knife outside abandoned farmhouse.jpg

File Name:

Case Notes 5.docx

THE KNIFE

Found in a location that corresponds to Jamie's step count data, before his Fitbit stopped recording and his phone was turned off. I think this confirms it was Jamie who took the knife, which means he *had* to have gone home between the calamity party and the sighting on Weevil Road, to pick up his hoodie and the knife. But why did he need a weapon? What had made him so afraid?

If the theory is that Jamie did indeed return home, how does the timing work with Arthur Reynolds's movements? How did Jamie have enough time to visit Nat da Silva, walk home, and grab his hoodie and the knife, all before his dad got back at 11:15 p.m.? The timing isn't just tight, it's almost impossible. Something in my timeline isn't right, and that means someone is lying. I should try to talk to Nat again, maybe she'll be more honest with me about Jamie when her boyfriend isn't there?

DANIEL DA SILVA

He's been talking to Layla Mead; his reaction made that perfectly obvious. Is it possible he knows who she really is? He was clearly trying to hide any connection to her; is that because he knows something? Or is it just because he wouldn't want that information getting back to his wife, who's taking care of their new baby while Daniel has presumably been talking inappropriately to another woman online? I got the sense last year that this isn't out of character for Daniel.

And another observation, we now know of three people Layla

Mead has been talking to: Jamie, Adam Clark, and Daniel da Silva. And here's the slightly strange thing: all three of these men are in the 29-to-recently-30 range (well, not Jamie, but that's what his profile originally said). And they all look vaguely similar: white, with brownish hair. Is this a coincidence, or is there something to it?

THE FARMHOUSE

Jamie went there on Friday night. Well, at least, he was just outside. And clearly the place isn't as abandoned as we thought. We need to find out who goes there, and why, and whether they are connected to Jamie's disappearance.

STAKEOUT TONIGHT

I'm picking Ravi up just before midnight, meeting Connor and Cara there. I've just got to wait for Mom and Dad to fall asleep first. I parked my car down the road and told them I'd left it at school, so they won't hear me when I go. Need to remember to avoid the third stair down—that's the creaky one.

55:86 MB of 55:86 MB uploaded

A Good Girl's Guide to Murder:
The Disappearance of Jamie Reynolds

Season 2, Episode 2 successfully uploaded to SoundCloud.

TWENTY-SIX

Connor was already there when they pulled up, his eyes alive and glowing in the high beam of Pip's headlights. They were on Old Farm Road, right before the turn onto Sycamore. Ravi handed Pip the backpack, his hand lingering over hers, and then they climbed out of the car.

"Hey," Pip whispered to Connor. The midnight wind danced through her hair, throwing it across her face. "Did you get out OK?"

"Yeah," he said. "Don't think my mom was asleep, I could hear her sniffing. But she didn't hear me."

"Where's Cara?" Pip said, eyeing her friend's car parked thirty feet up the road.

"She's just inside the car, on the phone to her sister," Connor said. "Naomi must have noticed she'd snuck out. I don't think Cara was trying to be that quiet on her way out because, in her words, 'Both my grandparents are practically deaf.' "

"Ah, I see."

Ravi came to stand beside Pip, a shield between her and the biting wind.

"Have you seen the comments?" Connor said, his voice hardening. Was he angry? It was almost too dark to tell.

"Not yet," Pip said. "Why?"

"It's been, like, three hours since you released the episode and a theory on Reddit has already gone viral."

"Which one?"

"They think my dad killed Jamie." Yes, he was definitely angry, a sharp edge to his voice as he shot it toward her. "They're saying he took the knife from our house and followed Jamie down Weevil Road. Killed him, cleaned and dumped the knife, and hid his body temporarily. That he was still out when I got home around midnight, because I didn't 'actually see' my dad when I got in. And then he was absent last weekend because he was out disposing of Jamie's body. Motive: my dad hates Jamie because he's 'such a fucking disappointment.'"

"I told you not to read the comments," Pip said, calmly.

"It's hard not to when people are accusing my dad of being a fucking murderer. He didn't do anything to Jamie. He wouldn't!"

"I never said he did," Pip lowered her voice, hoping Connor would follow suit.

"Well, it's *your* podcast they're commenting on. Where do you think they got those ideas?"

"You asked me to do this, Connor. You accepted the risks that came with it." She felt the dead of night pressing in around them. "All I've done is present the facts."

"Well, *the facts* have nothing to do with my dad. If anyone's lying, it's Nat da Silva. Not him."

"OK." Pip held up her hands. "I'm not arguing with you. All I'm trying to do is find Jamie, OK? That's all I'm doing." Ahead, Cara had just stepped out of her car, a silent hand raised in greeting as she walked over.

But Connor hadn't noticed. "Yeah, I know." He also didn't notice Pip raising her eyebrows at him in warning. "But finding Jamie has nothing to do with my dad."

"Con—" Ravi began.

"No, my dad is not a killer!" Connor said, and Cara was standing right there, behind him.

Her eyes clouded over and her mouth stiffened, open around an unsaid word. Connor finally noticed her, too late, scratching his nose to fill the uncomfortable silence with something. Ravi suddenly became keenly interested in the stars overhead and Pip stuttered, scrambling for what to say. But it was only a few seconds until the smile flickered back onto Cara's face, a strain in it that only Pip would notice.

"Can't relate," she said offhandedly, with an exaggerated shrug. "Don't we have a stakeout to do? Or are we gonna stand here chit-chatting like lost lemons?"

It was a saying she'd picked up in recent weeks from her grandma. And an easy way out of this awkwardness. Pip grabbed it and nodded. "Yeah, let's go." It was best for all involved to gloss over those last thirty seconds like they'd never happened.

Connor walked stiffly beside her as they turned down the gravel road, the abandoned farmhouse facing them across the grass. And there was something else here, something Pip hadn't expected. A car pulled up roughly off the road, close to the building.

"Is someone here?" she said.

Her question was answered just a few seconds later as a white beam of light flashed behind the grimy windows of the farmhouse. Someone was inside, with a flashlight.

"What's the play?" Ravi said to Pip. "The indirect or direct approach?"

"What's the difference?" Connor asked, his normal voice returned to him.

"Indirect is stay out here, hidden, wait to see who it is when they leave," Ravi explained. "Direct is, well, march the hell inside now and see who it is, have a little chitchat. I'd lean toward a hider myself, but we've got an avid marcher here, so . . ."

"Direct," Pip said decisively, as Ravi well knew she would. "Time isn't on our side. Come on. Quietly," she added, because the direct approach didn't necessarily mean giving up the element of surprise.

They traipsed toward the house together, steps falling in line.

"Are we squad goals?" Ravi whispered to Pip. Cara heard and snorted.

"I said *quietly*. That means no jokes and no pig snorts." Which was exactly how each of them reacted to nervous energy.

Pip was the first to reach the open door, the silvery, spectral light of the moon on the walls of the hallway like it was lighting the way for them, guiding them toward the living room. Pip took one step inside and paused as a guffaw rang out up ahead. There was more than one person. And from their choral laughter, it sounded like two guys and a girl. They sounded young, and possibly high, holding on to the laughter long after they should.

Pip moved forward a few more silent steps, Ravi close behind her, holding his breath.

"I bet I can fit, like, twenty-seven of them in my mouth at once," one of the voices said.

"Oh, Robin, don't."

Pip hesitated. Robin? Was this the Robin she knew—the one in the year below who played soccer with Ant? The one she'd spied buying drugs from Howie Bowers last year?

She stepped into the living room. Three people were sitting on the upturned trash cans and it was light enough in here that they weren't just silhouettes detaching from the darkness; a flashlight was resting in the top drawer of a warped wooden sideboard, pointing its bright silver light at the ceiling. And there were three bright-yellow pinpricks at the ends of their lit cigarettes.

"Robin Caine," Pip said, making all three of them jump. She didn't recognize the other two, but the girl shrieked and almost fell off her stool, and the other boy dropped his cigarette. "Careful, you don't want to cause a fire," Pip said, watching the boy scramble to retrieve it while pulling up his hood to hide his face.

Robin's eyes finally focused on her and he said, "Urgh, not fucking you."

"It *is* fucking me, I'm afraid," Pip said, adding, "and Co.," as the others piled into the room behind her.

"What are you doing here?" Robin took a long drag on his joint. Too long, in fact, and his face reddened as he fought not to cough.

"What are *you* doing here?" Pip returned the question.

Robin held up the joint.

"I got that part. Do you . . . come here often?" she said.

"Is that a pickup line?" Robin asked, shrinking back immediately as Ravi straightened up to his full height beside Pip.

"The crap you've left behind answers my question anyway." Pip gestured to the collection of wrappers and empty beer bottles. "You know you're leaving traces of yourselves all over a potential crime scene, right?"

"Andie Bell wasn't killed in here," he said, returning his attention to his joint. His friends were deadly quiet, trying to look anywhere but at them.

"That's not what I'm talking about." Pip shifted her stance. "Jamie Reynolds has been missing for five days. He came here right before he disappeared. You guys know anything about that?"

"No," Robin said, quickly followed by the others.

"Were you here on Friday night?"

"No." Robin glanced down at the time on his phone. "Listen, you've really gotta go. Someone's turning up soon and you can't be here when he does."

"Who's that, then?"

"Obviously not going to tell you that," Robin scoffed.

"What if I refuse to leave until you do?" Pip said, kicking an empty Pringles can so that it skittered among the trio.

"You especially don't want to be here," Robin said. "He probably hates you more than most people because you basically put Howie Bowers in prison."

The dots connected in Pip's head.

"Ah," she said, drawing out the sound. "So this is a drug thing. Are you dealing now, then?" she said, noticing the large, black, overstuffed bag leaning against Robin's leg.

"No, I don't deal." He wrinkled his nose.

"Well, that looks like a lot more than *personal use* in there." Pip pointed at the bag, which Robin was now trying to hide from her, tucking it behind his legs.

"I don't deal, OK? I just pick it up from some guys in the city and bring it here."

"So you're, like, a mule," Ravi offered.

"They give me weed for free," Robin's voice rose defensively.

"Wow, you're quite the businessman," Pip said. "So someone's groomed you to carry drugs across state lines."

"No, fuck off, I'm not groomed." He looked down at his phone again, the panic reaching his eyes, swirling in the dark of his pupils. "Please, he'll be here any minute. He's already pissed this week 'cause someone skipped out on him; nine hundred dollars he'll never get back or something. You have to go."

And as soon as the last word left Robin's mouth, they all heard it: the sound of wheels crackling on gravel, the low hum of a car pulling in and cutting out, the tick of its cooling engine puncturing the night.

"Someone's here," Connor said needlessly.

"Ah, shit," Robin said, stubbing out his joint on the trash can beneath him. But Pip was already turning, passing between Connor and Cara, down the hall to the gaping front doorway. She stood there at the threshold, one foot curled over the ledge and into the night. She squinted, trying to sculpt the darkness into recognizable shapes. A car had pulled up in front of Robin's, a lighter-colored car but—

And then Pip couldn't see anything at all, blinded by the fierce white of the car's high beams.

She covered her eyes with her hands as the engine revved—and then the car sped off down Sycamore Road, disappearing in a cloud of dust and scattering pebbles.

"Guys!" Pip called to the others. "My car. Now. Run!"

She was already moving, flying across the grass and into the swirling dust of the road. Ravi overtook her on the corner.

"Keys!" he shouted, and Pip dug them out of her jacket pocket, throwing them into Ravi's hand. He unlocked the car and hurled himself into the passenger seat. When Pip slammed into the driver's side, climbing in, Ravi already had the keys in the ignition waiting for her. She turned them and flicked on the headlights, lighting up Cara and Connor as they sprinted over.

They flung themselves inside and Pip pulled away, accelerating before Cara had even shut the door behind her.

"What did you see?" Ravi asked as Pip rounded the corner, chasing after the car.

"Nothing." She pressed down on the gas pedal, hearing gravel kick up, dinging off the sides of her car. "But he must have spotted me in the doorway. And now he's running."

"Why would he run?" Connor asked, his hands gripping Ravi's headrest.

"Don't know." Pip sped up as the road dropped down a hill. "But running is something that guilty people do. Are those his taillights?" She squinted into the distance.

"Yeah," Ravi said. "God, he's going fast, you need to speed up."

"I'm already doing forty-five," Pip said, biting her lip and pushing her foot down a little harder.

"Left, he turned left there." Ravi pointed.

Pip swung around the corner, onto another narrow country lane.

"Go, go, go," said Connor.

And Pip was gaining on him, the white body of the car now visible against the dark hedgerows at the side of the road.

"Need to get close enough to read his license plate," Pip said.

"He's speeding up again," Cara said, face wedged between Pip's and Ravi's seats.

Pip accelerated, the speedometer needling over fifty, and up, and up, closing the gap between the cars.

"Right!" Ravi said. "He went right."

The turn was sharp. Pip took her foot off the pedal and pulled at the steering wheel. They flew around the corner, but something was wrong.

Pip felt the steering wheel escape from her, slipping through her hands.

They were skidding.

She tried to turn in to it, to correct it.

But the car was going too fast and it went. Someone was yelling but she couldn't tell who over the screaming of the wheels. They slid, left, then right, before spinning in a full circle.

They were all yelling as the car skidded to a stop, coming to rest facing the wrong way, its hood half embedded in the brambles that bordered the road.

"Fuck," Pip said, hitting her fist against the steering wheel, the car horn blaring for a split second. "Is everyone OK?"

"Yeah," Connor said, his breath heavy and his face flushed.

Ravi looked over his shoulder, exchanging a look with a shaken

Cara before passing it on to Pip. And Pip knew what was in their eyes, the secret the three of them knew that Connor never could: that Cara's sister and Max Hastings had been involved in a car accident when they were this age, Max convincing his friends to leave a severely injured man on the road. And that had really been the start of it all, how Ravi's brother was eventually murdered.

And they'd just come recklessly close to something like that.

"That was stupid," Pip said, that thing in her gut stretching out to take more of her with it. It was guilt, wasn't it? Or shame. She wasn't supposed to be like this this time, losing herself again. "I'm sorry."

"It's my fault." Ravi tucked his fingers around hers. "I told you to go faster. I'm sorry."

"Did anyone see the license plate?" Connor asked. "All I saw was the first letter and it was either an *N* or an *H*."

"Didn't see," Cara said. "But it was a sports car. A white sports car."

"A BMW," Ravi added, and Pip tensed, right down to the fingers gripping his hand. He turned to her. "What?"

"I . . . I know someone with a car like that," she said quietly.

"Well, yeah, so do I," he replied. "More than one someone probably."

"Yeah," Pip exhaled. "But the one I know is Nat da Silva's boyfriend."

THURSDAY

6 DAYS MISSING

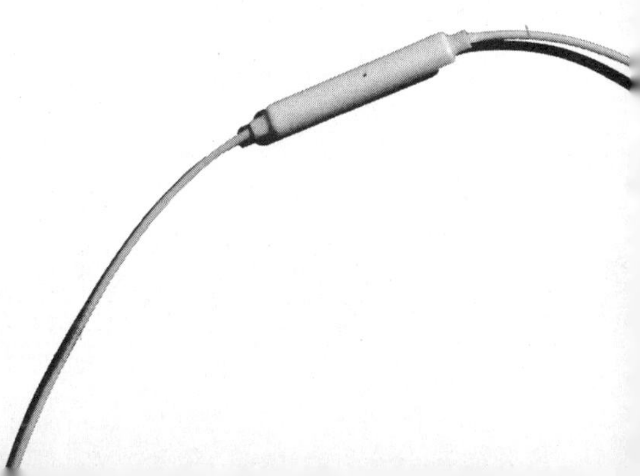

TWENTY-SEVEN

A yawn split Pip's face as she stared down at the toast in front of her. Not hungry.

"Why are you so tired this morning?" her mom asked, watching her over a mug of coffee.

Pip shrugged, flicking the toast around her plate. Josh was sitting opposite her, humming as he shoveled Cocoa Puffs into his mouth, swinging his legs under the table and kicking her accidentally on purpose. She didn't react, pulling her knees up to sit cross-legged on the chair instead. The radio was on in the background, tuned to WNPR, as always. A song was just ending, the hosts talking over the fading drums.

"Are you taking too much on with this Jamie thing?" her mom said.

"It's not a thing, Mom," Pip said, and she could feel herself growing irritable, wearing it like a layer beneath her skin, warm and unstable. "It's his life. I can be tired for that."

"OK, OK," her mom said, taking the empty bowl away from Josh. "I'm allowed to worry about you."

Pip wished she wouldn't. She didn't need anyone's worry; Jamie did.

A text lit up Pip's phone, from Ravi. *Just leaving for court to wait for deliberation. How are you?*

Pip stood and scooped up her phone, grabbing her plate with the other hand and sliding the toast into the trash. She felt her mom's eyes on her. "Not hungry yet," she explained. "I'll take a cereal bar to school."

She had taken only a few steps down the hall when her mom called her back.

"I'm just going to the bathroom!" she replied.

"Pip, get in here now!" her mom shouted. And it was a real shout, a sound Pip rarely heard from her, rough and panicked.

Pip felt instantly cold, all feeling draining from her face. She spun back, socks sliding on the oak floor as she sprinted into the kitchen.

"What, what, what?" she said quickly, eyes darting from a confused-looking Josh to her mom, who was reaching over to the radio and turning up the volume.

"Listen," she said.

". . . a dog walker discovered the body at about six a.m. yesterday morning in the trees beside I-95, between Fairview and Stamford. Officers are still at the scene. The deceased is as yet unidentified but has been described as a white male in his early twenties. The cause of death is currently unknown. A spokesperson for Fairview Police Department has said—"

"No." The word must have come from Pip, but she didn't remember saying it. Didn't remember moving her lips, nor the scrape of the word against her narrowing throat. "No no nonono." She didn't feel anything except numb, her feet a solid weight sinking into the ground, her hands detaching from her finger by finger.

"P . . . i . . . p?"

Everything around her moved too slowly, like the room was floating, because it was right there with her in the eye of the panic.

"Pip!"

And everything snapped back into focus, into time, and she could hear her heart battering in her ears. She looked up at her mom, who mirrored back her terrified eyes.

"Go," her mom said, hurrying over and turning Pip by her shoulders. "Go! I'll call school and tell them you'll be late."

"Up next, one of my favorite songs from the eighties, we have 'Sweet Dreams' . . . "

"He—he c-can't be—"

"Go," her mom said, pushing her down the hall, just as Pip's phone started buzzing with an incoming call from Connor.

It was Connor who opened the door, his eyes rubbed red and a twitch in his upper lip.

Pip stepped inside without a word. She gripped his arm, above the elbow, for a long, silent second. And then she let go, saying, "Where's your mom?"

"Here." His voice was just a croak as he led Pip into the cold living room. The daylight was wrong in here, too harsh, too bright, too alive. And Joanna was huddled against it, wrapped in an old blanket on the sofa, her face buried in a tissue.

"Pip's here," Connor said in barely more than a whisper.

Joanna glanced up. Her eyes were swollen and she looked different, like something beneath her face had broken.

She didn't speak, just held out her arms, and Pip stumbled forward to lower herself onto the sofa. Joanna wrapped her arms around her and Pip held her back, feeling Joanna's racing heart in her own chest.

"We need to call Detective Hawkins at the police station," Pip said, pulling back. "Ask if they've identified the—"

"Arthur's on the phone to them now." Joanna shuffled over to clear a space between them for Connor. And once Connor had settled, his leg pressing into hers, Pip could hear the sound of Arthur's voice, growing louder as he left the kitchen and walked toward them.

"Yes," he said, entering the room with the phone to his ear, blinking as his gaze settled on Pip. His face looked gray, mouth in a tense line. "Jamie Reynolds. No, *Reynolds,* with an *r.* Yes. Case number? Um . . ." His eyes darted to Joanna. She began to push herself up from the sofa, but Pip cut in.

"Four nine zero," she said. Arthur repeated the numbers after her into the phone. "Zero one five. Two nine three."

Arthur nodded at her. "Yes. Missing since last Friday night." He chewed his thumb. "The body found by the I-95, do you know who it is yet? No. No, don't put me on hold aga—"

He leaned against the door, closing it and resting his head against one finger, pushing his skin into folds. Waiting.

And waiting.

It was the worst wait Pip had ever had in her life. Her chest was so tight she had to force the air through and out of her nose. And with every breath she thought she might be sick, swallowing down the bile.

Please, she kept thinking, no idea who she was thinking it to. Just someone. Anyone. *Please, please don't let it be Jamie. Please.* She'd promised Connor. She'd promised she'd find his brother. She promised she'd save him. *Please. Please, not him.*

Her eyes slipped from Arthur back to Connor beside her.

"Should I be here?" she mouthed.

But Connor nodded and took her hand, their palms clammy, sticking together. Pip saw him take his mother's hand, too, on the other side.

Waiting.

Arthur's eyes were closed, the fingers on his free hand pressing into his eyelids, so hard it must have hurt, his chest rising in stuttering movements.

Waiting.

Until . . .

"Yes?" Arthur said, his eyes snapping open.

Pip's heartbeat was so loud, so fast, it felt like that was all she was: a heart and the empty skin around it.

"Hello, Detective," said Arthur. "Yes, that's what I'm calling about. Yes."

Connor gripped Pip's hand even tighter, crushing her bones together.

"Yes, I understand. So is—" Arthur's hand was shaking at his side. "Yes, I understand that."

He went quiet, listening to the other end of the phone.

And then his face dropped.

Cracked in two.

He doubled forward, the phone going limp in his fingers. Other hand up to his face as he bawled into it. A high, inhuman sound that racked his entire body.

Connor's hand went slack against Pip's, his jaw falling open.

Arthur straightened up, tears spilling down into his bared mouth.

"It's not Jamie," he said.

"What?" Joanna stood up, clutching her face.

"It's not Jamie," Arthur said again, choking on a sob, putting his phone down. "It's someone else. His family just identified him. It's not Jamie."

"It's not Jamie?" Joanna said, like she didn't dare believe it yet.

"It's not him," Arthur said, staggering forward to pull her to him, crying down into her hair. "It's not our boy. Not Jamie."

Connor unstuck from Pip, his cheeks flushed and tear-streaked, and he folded himself around his parents. They held each other and they cried, and it was a cry of relief and grief and confusion. They'd lost him for a while. For a few minutes, in their heads and in hers, Jamie Reynolds had been dead.

But it wasn't him.

Pip held the sleeve of her shirt to her eyes, tears falling hot, soaking into the fabric.

Thank you, she thought to that invisible person in her head. *Thank you.*

They had another chance.

She had one last chance.

File Name:

A Good Girl's Guide to Murder SEASON 2: Interview with Arthur Reynolds.wav

PIP: OK, recording. Are you OK?

ARTHUR: Yes. I'm ready.

PIP: So why didn't you want to be interviewed or involved before now?

ARTHUR: Honestly? I was angry. In my head, I was convinced Jamie had run away again. And he knows how worried we were the first time he did that. I didn't want to indulge Joanna and Connor's idea that Jamie was really missing because I didn't think he was. I didn't want to believe something was wrong. Seems I preferred to be angry at Jamie instead. But I was wrong, I think. It's been too long. And if he was out there, Jamie would've heard about your podcast by now. He would have come home if he could.

PIP: And why did you think Jamie had run off again? Is it because you had a big argument, right before the memorial?

ARTHUR: Yes. I don't want to argue with him, I just want what's best for him. I want to push him to make smart decisions for his life, to do something that he loves. I know he's capable of that. But he's seemed stuck the past few years. Maybe I go about it the wrong way. I just don't know how to help him.

PIP: And what were you arguing about last Friday?

ARTHUR: It's just . . . it had been simmering for a while. He recently asked if he could borrow a lot of money, and I don't know, he just said something that set me off about money and responsibility and finding a career. Jamie didn't want to hear it.

PIP: When did he ask you to borrow money?

ARTHUR: Oh, it was . . . Joanna was out at tennis, so it must have been a Tuesday. Yes, Tuesday, April 7.

PIP: Did Jamie say what he wanted the money for?

ARTHUR: No, that's the thing. He wouldn't tell me. Just said it was really important. So of course I told him no. It was a ridiculous amount.

PIP: If you don't mind me asking, how much did Jamie want to borrow?

ARTHUR: Nine hundred dollars.

PIP: Nine hundred?

ARTHUR: Yes.

PIP: Nine hundred exactly?

ARTHUR: Yes. Why? What's wrong?

PIP: It's just . . . I've heard that exact figure recently, about someone else. A guy named Luke Eaton, he mentioned losing nine hundred dollars this week. And I think he's involved in dr— You know what, I'll look into it. So after you left Bobby's Bar & Grill Friday night, what time did you get home?

ARTHUR: I don't remember looking at the time specifically, but it was definitely before eleven-thirty. Maybe around twenty past.

PIP: And the house was empty, right? You didn't see Jamie?

ARTHUR: No, I was alone. I went to bed, but I heard Connor get in later.

PIP: And there's no way Jamie could've snuck in before then? Like, just after you got back?

ARTHUR: Not possible. I was sitting here, in the living room, for a while. I would have heard the front door.

PIP: I believe Jamie came back here, for his hoodie and the knife, so he must have arrived and left again before you got home. Do you know anything about the knife?

ARTHUR: No. I didn't even know it was missing until Joanna told me.

PIP: So where were you all last weekend when Jamie was first missing? Connor mentioned you weren't at home much.

ARTHUR: I was out driving, looking for him. I thought I'd find him somewhere, just blowing off steam. And that I could talk to him, fix things, get him to come home. But he wasn't anywhere.

PIP: Are you OK, Mr. Reynolds?

ARTHUR: No. I'm terrified. Terrified that the last thing I did was argue with my son. The last words I said to him were in anger. I never told him I loved him, and I'm scared I'll never get the chance again. Jamie came to me, asked me for help, and I sent him away. *Life or death,* that's what Jamie said to your mom about the money, wasn't it? And I said no to him. I'm his dad, he's supposed to be able to turn to me for anything. He asked me for help and I said no. What if this whole thing is my fault? If I had only said yes to him, maybe . . . maybe . . .

TWENTY-EIGHT

The trees shivered on Cross Lane, recoiling from Pip as she walked beneath them, chasing her morning shadow, never catching up to it.

She'd dropped Connor at school once everyone had calmed down, leaving her car there. But she hadn't gone inside with him. Her mom had already called the school to say Pip would be late, so she might as well make use of it. And it couldn't be avoided any longer: she had to speak to Nat da Silva. At this point, all roads led back to her.

Even the one Pip was walking on right now.

Her eyes fixated on the painted blue front door as she stepped up the concrete path, following it as it bent to run alongside the house.

She took a breath to steel herself and pressed the bell in two short mechanical bursts. She waited, fidgeting nervously with her unbrushed hair, her heartbeat not yet back to normal.

A shape grew out of the frosted glass, blurred and slow as it approached the door.

It opened with a clack and Nat da Silva stood there, her white-blond hair pushed back from her face, deep streaks of eyeliner holding up her pale blue eyes.

"Hello," Pip said, as brightly as she could.

"Fuck's sake," said Nat. "What do you want now?"

"I need to ask you some things, about Jamie," she said.

"Yeah, well, I already told you everything I know. I don't know where he is and he still hasn't been in contact with me." Nat reached for the door to close it again.

"They found a body," Pip blurted, trying to stop her. It worked. "It wasn't Jamie, but it could have been. It's been six days, Nat, without any contact. Jamie's in real trouble. And you might be the person who knows him best. Please." Her voice cracked. "Not for me. I know you hate me and I understand why. But please help me, for the Reynoldses' sake. I just came from their house, and for twenty minutes we all thought Jamie was dead."

It was subtle, almost too subtle to notice, but there was a softening in Nat's eyes. Something flickered across them, glassy and sad.

"Do you . . . ," she said, slowly. "Do you really think he's not OK?"

"I'm trying to stay hopeful, for his family," Pip said. "But . . . I don't know."

Nat relaxed her arm, chewing on her pale bottom lip.

"Have you and Jamie still been talking in recent weeks?" Pip asked.

"Yeah, a bit," Nat said.

"Did he ever mention someone named Layla Mead to you?"

Nat looked up, thinking, teeth moving farther down her lip, meeting the skin of her chin. "No. Never heard that name before."

"OK. And I know you said before that he didn't, but did Jamie come to your house after the memorial as planned? Around ten-fifty p.m.?"

"No." Nat tilted her head, short white hair skimming down into her eyes. "I told you, last time I saw him was at the memorial."

"It's just . . . ," Pip began. "Well, an eyewitness saw Jamie go into your house at that time. He said Cross Lane and described your house exactly."

Nat blinked, and that softness in her eyes was gone.

"Well, I don't care what your fucking eyewitness said. He's wrong," she said. "Jamie never came here."

"OK, I'm sorry." Pip held up her hands. "I was just asking."

"Well you've already asked that, and I've already answered. Is there anything else?" Nat's hand glided to the door again, tightening around the edge.

"There's one last thing," Pip said, nervously eyeing Nat's fingers on the door. Last time she was here like this, Nat had slammed it in her face. *Tread carefully, Pip.* "Well, it's your boyfriend, Luke Eaton."

"Yeah, I know his name," Nat spat. "What about him?"

"It's, um . . ." Pip didn't know which way to approach it, so she went with fast. "Um, so I guess Luke is involved with drugs—has a kid collect them from a gang in the city—and I presume he then distributes to various dealers in the county."

Nat's face tightened.

"And the place where he picks the drugs up from . . . it's the abandoned farmhouse where Andie's body was found. But it's also the last place Jamie was, before something happened to him. So there's a possible connection to Luke."

Nat shifted, her knuckles whitening from her grip on the door.

"But there's more," Pip carried on, giving Nat no room to speak. "The kid Luke uses to transport the drugs said that Luke was angry this week because he'd lost nine hundred dollars. And that's the exact amount of money Jamie asked to borrow from his dad a couple of weeks ago—"

"What point are you trying to make?" Nat said, the downward tilt of her head shadowing her eyes.

"Just that maybe Luke also loans people money, and he loaned Jamie money for something but Jamie couldn't pay it back, so he asked his dad, and then he was desperate enough to try stealing it from work, saying it was life or death . . ." Pip paused, daring to glance up at Nat. "And I wondered, when I spoke to you both before, you seemed to react when Luke said he was home all night, so I just wondered—"

"Oh, you just wondered, did you?" There was a quiver in Nat's top lip and Pip could feel the rage coming off her, like heat. "What is wrong with you? These are people's lives. You can't just fuck around with them for your own entertainment."

"I'm not, it's for—"

"I have nothing to do with Jamie. And neither does Luke," Nat shouted, stepping back. "Just leave me the fuck alone, Pip." Her voice shook. "Please. Leave me alone."

And her face disappeared behind the door as it slammed shut, the sound echoing down into that pit in Pip's stomach, staying with her as she walked away.

It was when she turned on to Gravelly Way, heading back to school, that she first had the feeling. A creeping up her neck like static on her skin. And she knew what it was, had felt this before. Eyes. Someone watching her.

She stopped on the sidewalk, looked over her shoulder. There was no one behind her on Chalk Road, except a man she didn't know pushing a stroller, and his eyes were down.

She checked in front of her, running her eyes along the windows of the houses that lined the street, bearing down on her. There wasn't a face in any of them, pushed up against breath-fogged glass. She scanned the cars parked along the road. Nothing. No one.

Pip could've sworn she felt it. Or maybe she was just losing her mind.

She continued on toward school, holding on to the straps of her bag. It took her a while to realize she wasn't hearing her own footsteps. Not just her own, anyway. There was another set, stepping faintly in between hers, coming from the right. Pip looked up.

"Morning," a voice called from across the road. It was Mary Scythe from the *Fairview Mail,* with a black Labrador at her side.

"Good morning," Pip returned the greeting, but it sounded empty even to her own ears. Luckily her ringing phone excused her. She turned away and swiped to answer.

"Pip," Ravi said.

"Oh god," she said, falling into his voice, wrapping herself up with it. "You won't believe what's happened this morning. It was on the news that they found a body, a white male in his twenties. So I panicked, went to the Reynoldses' house, but they called in and it wasn't Jamie, it was someone else—"

"Pip?"

"—and Arthur finally agreed to talk to me. And he told me that Jamie asked him to borrow nine hundred dollars, the exact amount Robin said Luke had just lost this week, so—"

"Pip?"

"—that's too coincidental to be nothing, right? So I just went to see Nat and she insists Jamie didn't go there after—"

"Pip, I really need you to stop talking and listen to me." And now Pip heard it, the edge in Ravi's voice, new and unfamiliar.

"What? Sorry. What?" she said, her feet slowing to a stop.

"The jury just returned their verdict," he said.

"Already? And?"

But Ravi didn't say anything, and she could hear a click as his breath caught in his throat.

"No," she said, her heart picking up on that click before she did, throwing itself against her ribs. "Ravi? What? No, don't say . . . it can't . . ."

"They found him not guilty, on all charges."

And Pip didn't hear what he said next because her ears flooded with blood, a rushing sound, like a windstorm trapped inside her head. Her hand found the brick wall beside her and she leaned into it, lowering herself down to sit on the cold concrete sidewalk.

"No," she whispered, because if she said it any louder, she would scream. She still might scream; she could feel it clawing at her insides, fighting to get out. She grabbed her face and held her mouth shut, fingernails digging into her cheeks.

"Pip," Ravi said, gently. "I'm so sorry. I couldn't believe it. I still can't. It isn't fair. This isn't right. If there was anything I could do to change this, I would. Anything. Pip? Are you OK?"

"No," she said through her hand. She would never be OK again. This was it; the worst thing that could have happened. She'd thought about it, had had bad dreams about it, but she'd known it couldn't really happen. It wouldn't happen. But it just did. And the truth no longer mattered. Max Hastings, not guilty. Even though Pip had his voice on a recording, admitting to it all. Even though she knew he was guilty, beyond any doubt. But no, she and Nat da Silva and Becca Bell and those two women from college: they were the liars now. And a serial rapist had just walked free.

Her mind turned to Nat.

"Oh god, Nat," she said, removing her hand. "Ravi, I have to go, I have to go back to see Nat. Make sure she's OK."

"OK, I lo—" he said, but it was too late. Pip had already pressed the red button, pushing herself up from the ground as she turned back down Gravelly Way.

She knew that Nat hated her. But she also knew that Nat shouldn't be alone when she heard the news. No one should be alone for something like that.

Pip sprinted, her sneakers slapping uncomfortably against the sidewalk, juddering up through her body. Her chest hurt, like her heart wanted to give out already, give up. But she ran, pushing herself harder as she turned the corner onto Cross Lane, back to that blue door.

She knocked this time, forgetting about the bell because her mind was already stuttering, rewinding the last few minutes. It couldn't have happened, could it? This couldn't be real. It didn't feel real.

Nat's silhouette emerged again in the frosted glass, and Pip tried to read it, study it, work out if Nat's world had already been blown apart.

She opened the door, jaw clenching as soon as she saw Pip standing there.

"What the fuck, I told you to . . ."

But then she must have noticed the way Pip was breathing. The horror that must be written all over her face.

"What is it?" Nat said quickly, pulling the door open fully. "Is Jamie OK?"

"H-have you heard?" Pip said, and her voice sounded strange to her, not her own. "The verdict?"

"What?" Nat narrowed her eyes. "No, no one's called me yet. Are they done? What . . . ?"

And Pip could see the moment it happened, the moment Nat read what was on her face. The moment her eyes changed.

"No," she said, but it was more a breath than a word.

She stumbled back from the door, hands snapping up to her face as she gasped, her eyes glazing over.

"No!" The word was a strangled yell this time, choking her. Nat fell back into the wall in the hallway, slamming against it. A picture frame dropped from its hook, the glass cracking as it hit the floor.

Pip darted forward inside the house, catching Nat by the arms as she slid down the wall. But she lost her footing and they slid down together, Nat to the floor, Pip to her knees.

"I'm so sorry," Pip said. "I'm so, so, so sorry."

Nat was crying, the tears stained as they ran through her makeup, black tears chasing each other down her face.

"This can't be real," she cried. "It can't be real. Fuck!"

Pip sat forward, wrapping her arms around Nat. She thought Nat would pull away from her, push her off. But she didn't. She leaned into Pip, arms climbing up and around her neck as she held on. Tight. Her face buried into Pip's shoulder.

Nat screamed, the sound muffled, burrowing into Pip's shirt, her breath hot and jagged as it spread down, into Pip's skin. And then the scream broke open and she cried, shaking the both of them with the force of it.

"I'm so sorry," Pip whispered.

TWENTY-NINE

Nat's scream never left her. Pip could feel it there, slinking around beneath her skin. Feel it simmering as she walked into history class eighteen minutes late and Mr. Clark said, "Ah, Pip. What time do you call this? Do you think your time is more valuable than mine?"

And she'd replied, "No, sir. Sorry, sir," quietly, when really all she wanted to do was let the scream out, tell him that yes, it probably was. She'd taken her place next to Connor at the back of the room, her grip tightening on her pen until it snapped, pieces of plastic scattering between her fingers.

The lunch bell rang and they followed it out of the room, she and Connor. He'd heard about the verdict from Cara because Ravi had texted her, worrying when he hadn't heard back from Pip. "I'm sorry," was all Connor said as they headed toward the cafeteria. That's all he could say, all Pip could say too, but there was no amount of sorrys that could ever fix this.

They found the others at their usual table, and Pip slotted in beside Cara, squeezing her hand once in greeting.

"Have you told Naomi?" Pip asked her.

Cara nodded. "She's devastated, can't believe it."

"Yeah, that sucks," Ant said loudly, cutting in as he tore into his second sandwich.

Pip turned to him. "And where were you yesterday, during the search party?"

Ant rearranged his eyebrows, looking affronted as he swallowed. "It was Wednesday, I was at soccer," he said, not even looking at Connor.

"Lauren?" Pip said.

"Wh . . . My mom made me stay in to study for French." Her voice was high and defensive. "I didn't realize you expected us all to be there."

"Your best friend's brother is missing," Pip said, and she felt Connor tensing beside her.

"Yeah, I get that." Ant flashed a quick smile at Connor. "And I'm sorry, but I don't think Lauren or I are going to change that."

Pip wanted to carry on picking at them, keep feeding the scream under her skin, but she was distracted by someone behind Ant, her eyes pulling her up. Tom Nowak, loudly laughing at a table with his friends. Either Tom or Nat had to be lying about the night Jamie went missing, and now Pip knew, in her gut, which one of them it was.

"Excuse me," Pip said, though she was already gone, skirting around their table and across the loud chaos of the cafeteria.

"Tom," she said, and then again, louder than the boys' guffawing.

Tom put down his open bottle of Coke, twisting to look up at her. Pip noticed some of his friends on the opposite bench whispering and elbowing each other.

"Hey, what's up?" he said, his cheeks indented with a laid-back smile, and Pip's rage flared at the sight of it.

"You lied to me, didn't you?" she said, but it wasn't a question and she didn't wait for an answer. At least he'd surrendered the fake smile now. "You didn't see Jamie Reynolds on Friday night. I doubt you were anywhere near Cross Lane. You just said that street because it was near the site of the calamity party, and then the rest was my fault. I accidentally led the witness. You saw my reactions to that road name, to the color of the front door, and you used those to manipulate me. Made me believe in a narrative that never even happened."

People were watching now from nearby tables, a wave of half turned heads and the prickle of unseen eyes.

"Jamie didn't go to Nat da Silva's house that night and you were never a witness. You're a liar." Her lip curled up, baring her teeth at him. "Well done, good job, Tom, you got yourself on the podcast. What were you hoping to achieve with that?"

Tom stuttered, raising his finger as he scrambled for words.

"Internet fame, is that it?" Pip spat. "You got a SoundCloud you want to promote or something? What the fuck is wrong with you? Someone is missing. Jamie's life is at stake, and you decide to waste my time."

"I didn't—"

"You're pathetic," she said. "And guess what? You already signed the consent form for me to use your name and likeness, so this will also be going on the podcast. Good luck being universally hated by the entire internet."

"No, you're not allowed to—" Tom began.

But the rage took hold of Pip's hand, guiding it as she reached over to snatch Tom's open bottle of Coke. And without a second thought—without even a first thought—Pip upturned the bottle over his head.

A cascade of fizzing brown liquid fell over Tom, soaking into his hair and over his face, eyes screwed shut against it. There were gasps around the room, titters of laughter, but it was a few seconds before Tom himself could react through the shock.

"You bitch!" He stood up, hands to his eyes to clear them.

"Don't fucking cross me again," Pip said, dropping the empty bottle at Tom's feet with a clatter that echoed around the now almost-quiet room.

She walked away, flicking droplets of Coke from her hand, a hundred eyes following her as she went, but none of them, not any of them, would meet hers.

Cara was waiting for her by the usual spot, at the double doors near their English classroom, the second-to-last class of the day. But as Pip crossed the hall toward her, she noticed something: a quieting of voices as she passed, people gathering to talk behind their hands, looking her way. Well, they couldn't *all* have been in the cafeteria at lunch. And anyway, Pip didn't care what they thought. Tom Nowak was the one who should be walking through whispers, not her.

"Hey," she said, arriving at Cara's side.

"Hey, um . . ." But Cara was acting strangely too, scrunching her mouth in that way she did when something was wrong. "Have you seen it yet?"

"Seen what?"

"The WiredRip article." Cara glanced down at the phone in her hand. "Someone linked to it on the Facebook event you made for Jamie."

"No," Pip said. "Why, what does it say?"

"Um, it . . ." Cara trailed off. She looked down, thumbs tapping away at her phone and then she held it out on her open hand, offering it to Pip. "I think you should just read it."

WIREDRIP.com

News > Quizzes > TV & Movies > Videos > What's Hot > More v

Season 2 of A Good Girl's Guide to Murder podcast may not be all it seems. . . .

A *Good Girl's Guide to Murder* made an explosive return to our ears this week, with the first episode of a new mystery released on Tuesday. Jamie Reynolds, 24, has gone missing from host Pip Fitz-Amobi's hometown. The police won't look for him, so Pip has stepped up to the plate, uploading episodes during the course of her investigation.

But is there a real reason the police aren't looking for Jamie?

A source close to Pip has told us, exclusively, that this entire season of the podcast is, in fact, a setup. Jamie Reynolds is the older brother of one of Pip's closest friends, and our source says that Jamie's disappearance has been plotted by the three of them, to create a thrilling new season for the podcast and capitalize on the popularity of the first. Jamie's incentive in playing along with his own disappearance is financially motivated, with Pip promising the brothers a large payout once the season airs and she has secured new, major sponsorship deals.

So what do you think—is Jamie Reynolds even missing at all? Are we being duped by the teen queen of true crime? Let us know your thoughts in the comments below.

THIRTY

Another corridor lined with eyes. Circling.

Pip kept her head down as she stumbled through, toward her locker. It was the end of the day, clearly enough time for that article to have spread around the entire school.

But she couldn't get to her locker. A group of sophomores was standing in front of it, talking in a tight circle of bumping backpacks. Pip drew to a stop and stared at them, until one of the girls noticed her there, eyes widening as she elbowed her friends, shushing them. The group immediately disbanded, scattering away from her, leaving their whispers and giggles behind.

Pip opened her locker and placed her political science textbook inside. As she withdrew her hand, she noticed the small, folded piece of paper that must have been pushed through the gap above the door.

She reached for it, opened it.

In large black printed letters it read: *This is your final warning, Pippa. Walk away.*

The scream inside her flashed again, climbing up her neck. How imaginative: the exact same note Elliot Ward had left in her locker last October.

Pip's hand tightened into a fist around the note, screwing it up. She dropped the ball of paper to the floor and slammed her locker shut.

Cara and Connor were standing just behind it, waiting for her.

"Everything OK?" Cara asked, her face soft with concern.

"I'm fine," Pip said, turning to walk with them down the hall.

"Have you seen?" Connor said. "People online are actually believing it, saying they thought it was all a little too elaborate. That it felt scripted."

"I told you," Pip said. Her voice came out dark, remolded by her anger. "Never read the comments."

"But—"

"Hey," Ant's voice called as they turned the corner past the chemistry classrooms. He, Lauren, and Zach were just behind them, coming from the other direction.

They waited for the others to catch up and slot between them, Ant's steps falling in line with Pip's.

"Whole school's talking about you," he said, and out of the corner of her eye, Pip could see him watching her.

"Well, the whole school is full of idiots," Cara said, hurrying to walk on Pip's other side.

"Maybe." Ant shrugged, with a glance at Lauren. "But we were just thinking that, I don't know, it does seem kind of convenient."

"What seems convenient?" Pip said, and there was a growl in her voice. Maybe no one else could hear it, but she did.

"Well, the whole Jamie thing," Lauren spoke up now.

"Oh, really?" Pip shot her a warning look, trying to hurt her with her eyes. "Connor, has it felt convenient to you that your brother is missing?"

Connor's mouth opened, but he was unsure how to answer, and all that came out was a croak between *yes* and *no.*

"You know what I mean, though," Ant continued. "Like, the whole catfish thing, so you don't actually have to name a culprit because it's someone who doesn't really exist. Everything happening the night of the memorial for Andie and Sal. The missing knife, and you just happening to find it by that creepy farmhouse. It is all a little . . . convenient, isn't it?"

"Shut up, Ant," Zach said quietly, falling back to keep his distance like he sensed something was coming.

"What the fuck?" Cara stared incredulously at Ant. "Say the word 'convenient' one more time and I will end you."

"Whoa." Ant chuckled, holding up his hands. "I'm just saying."

But Pip couldn't hear what he was *just saying,* because her ears were ringing, a hiss like static, broken up by her own voice asking her: *Did you plant the knife? Could you have planted the knife? Is Jamie missing? Is Layla Mead real? Is any of this even real?*

And she didn't know how she was still walking because she couldn't feel her feet. She could feel only one thing. The scream had wound itself around her throat now, pulling tighter and tighter as it chased its own end.

"I won't be mad," Ant was saying. "To be honest, if this *is* all made up, I think it's a genius idea. Except, you know, that you got caught. And that you didn't tell me and Lauren."

Cara snapped, "So you're essentially calling both Connor and Pip liars? Grow up, Ant, and stop being such a dick all your life."

"Hey," Lauren chimed in now. "*You're* the one being a dick."

"Oh, really?"

"Guys . . . ," Connor said, but the word was lost as soon as he uttered it.

"So where *is* Jamie?" Ant said. "Holed up in some Super 8 somewhere?"

And Pip knew that he was just prodding her, but she couldn't control it, she couldn't—

The double doors swung inward at the end of the corridor, and the principal, Mrs. Morgan, stepped through. Her eyes narrowed, then lit up.

"Ah, Pip!" she shouted down the hall. "I need to speak to you, urgently, before you go home!"

"Busted," Ant whispered, making Lauren snort. "Go on, it's over now, *good girl*. Might as well tell us the truth."

But everything had turned to fire behind Pip's eyes.

Her feet twisted.

Her arms swung out.

Hands against Ant's chest, she shoved him, pushing him with all her strength across the width of the hall.

He crashed into a bank of lockers.

"What the—"

Pip's elbow drew up, her forearm against Ant's neck, holding him in place. She stared him in the eyes, though hers had burned to ash, and she finally let it out.

She screamed into his face. It ripped at her throat and tore at her eyes, feeding itself from that never-ending pit in her stomach.

Pip screamed, and they were all that existed. Just her and the scream.

THIRTY-ONE

"Suspended?"

Pip sank into the stool in the kitchen, avoiding her dad's eyes.

"Yes." Her mom was standing on the other side of the room, Pip in the middle. Talking around her, over her head. "For three days. What about Columbia, Pippa?"

"Who was the other student?" Dad asked, voice softening where her mom's had grown harder, sharper.

"Anthony Lowe."

Pip glanced up, catching the face her dad pulled: bottom lip rolled up over the top, eyes crinkling like he wasn't surprised.

"What's that look for?" her mom said.

"Nothing." Her dad rearranged his face, untucking his lip. "Just never really liked the kid that much."

"How is that helpful right now, Victor?" her mom snapped.

"Sorry, it's not," he said, exchanging a look with Pip. It was quick, but it was enough, and she felt a little less alone out there in the middle of the room. "Why did you do it, Pip?"

"I don't know."

"You don't know?" her mom said. "You shoved him against a locker with your arm on his throat. How do you not know how that happens? You're lucky that Cara, Zach, and Connor were there and defended you to Mrs. Morgan, told her Ant provoked you, otherwise you would have been expelled."

"How did he provoke you, Pickle?" her dad asked.

"Called me a liar," she said. "The internet thinks I'm a liar. A jury of twelve peers thinks I'm a liar. My own friends think I'm a liar. So I guess I'm a liar now, and Max Hastings is the good guy."

"I'm sorry about the verdict," her dad said. "That must be really hard for you."

"Harder for the people he drugged and raped," she said.

"Yes, and it's unfair and awful," her mom said with a frown. "But that's not an excuse for your violent behavior."

"I'm not making an excuse. I'm not asking for forgiveness," Pip said, flatly. "It happened and I don't feel guilty. He deserved it."

"What are you saying?" her mom said. "This isn't like you."

"What if it is?" Pip rose from the stool. "What if this is exactly like me?"

"Pip, don't shout at your mother," her dad said, crossing over to her mom's side, abandoning her in the middle.

"Shouting? Really?" Pip said, really shouting now. "That's what we're focusing on? A serial rapist walked free today. Jamie has been missing six whole days and might be dead. Oh, but the real problem is that I'm *shouting*!"

"Calm down, please," he said.

"I can't! I can't calm down anymore! Why should I?"

Her phone was facedown on the floor. She hadn't looked at it for an hour, sitting here underneath her desk, her fingers hooked around her toes. Her head was pressed against the cool wood of the desk leg, eyes hiding from the light.

She hadn't gone down for dinner, said she wasn't hungry, even though her dad came up and said they didn't have to talk about it, not in front of Josh. But she didn't want to sit there at the table, in a fake truce midargument. An argument that couldn't end, because she wasn't sorry, she knew that. And that's what her mom wanted from her.

She heard a knock at the front door, a knock she knew: *long-short-long.* The door opened and closed, and then the footsteps she knew too, the scuff of Ravi's sneakers on the wood floor before he took them off and lined them up neatly by the doormat.

And the next thing she heard was her mom's voice, passing by the stairs. "She's in her room. See if you can talk any sense into her."

Ravi couldn't find her as he stepped into the room; not until she said, quietly, "I'm down here."

He bent down, knees clicking as his face came into view.

"Why aren't you answering your phone?" he said.

Pip looked at her facedown phone, out of arm's reach.

"Are you OK?" he said.

And she wanted, more than anything, to say no, to slide out from under the desk and fall into him. To stay there, in his gaze, wrap herself up in it and never set foot outside again. To let him tell her it was all going to be OK, even though neither of them knew it would be. She wanted just to be the Pip she was with Ravi for a while. But that Pip wasn't here right now. And maybe she really was gone.

"No," she said.

"Your parents are worried about you."

"Don't need their worry," she sniffed.

"I'm worried about you," Ravi said.

She put her head against the desk leg again. "Don't need yours either."

"Can you come out and talk to me?" he said gently. "Please?"

"Did he smile?" she asked. "Did he smile when they said 'Not guilty'?"

"I couldn't see his face." Ravi offered his hand to help Pip out from under the desk. She didn't take it, crawling out on her own and standing up.

"I bet he smiled." She ran her finger along the sharp edge of the desk, pressing in until it hurt her.

"Why does that matter?"

"It matters," she said.

"I'm sorry." Ravi tried to hold her eyes, but her gaze kept slipping away. "If there was anything I could do to change it, I would. Anything. But there's nothing we can do now. And you getting suspended because you're so angry about Max . . . he's not worth any of that."

"So he just wins?"

"No, I . . ." Ravi abandoned his sentence, stepping over to her, his arms out to pull her in and wrap her up. And maybe it was because Max's angled face flashed into her head, or maybe she didn't want Ravi to get too close to the after-scream still thrumming inside her, but she pulled away from him.

"Wha—" His arms fell back to his sides, his eyes darkening, deepening. "What are you doing?"

"I don't know."

"So what is it, you just want to hate the whole world right now, including me?"

"Maybe," she said.

"Pip—"

"Well, what's the point?" Her voice snagged against her dried-out throat. "What was the point in everything we did last year? I thought I was doing it for the truth. But guess what? The truth doesn't matter. It doesn't! Max Hastings is innocent and I'm a liar and Jamie Reynolds isn't missing. *That's* the truth now." Her eyes filled. "What if I can't save him? What if I'm not good enough to save him? I'm not good, Ravi, I—"

"We will find him," Ravi said.

"I *need* to."

"And you think I don't?" he said. "I might not know him like you do, and I can't explain it, but I need Jamie to be OK. He knew my brother, was friends with him and Andie at school. It's like it's happening all over again six years later, and this time I actually have a chance, a small chance, to help save Connor's brother where I had no hope of saving my own. I know Jamie isn't Sal, but this feels like some kind of second chance for me. You aren't on your own here, so stop pushing people away. Stop pushing me away."

Pip's hands gripped the desk, bones pushing through her skin. He needed to get away from her, in case she couldn't control it again. The scream. "I just want to be alone."

"Fine," Ravi said, scratching the phantom itch at the back of his head. "I'll go. I know you're only lashing out because you're angry. I'm angry too. And you don't mean it, you know you don't mean it." He sighed. "Let me know when you remember who I am. Who you are."

Ravi moved over to the door, his hand stalling in the air before it, head slightly cocked. "I love you," he said angrily, not looking at her. He slammed the handle down and walked out, the door juddering behind him.

THIRTY-TWO

Makes me sick.

That's what the text said. From Naomi Ward.

Pip sat up on her bed, clicking on the photo Naomi sent with the message.

It was a screenshot, from Facebook. A post from Nancy Tangotits: the name of Max Hastings's profile. A photo, of Max, his mom and dad, and his lawyer, Christopher Epps. They were gathered around a table in a lavish-looking restaurant with marble pillars and giant stone vases filled with tropical plants in the background. Max was holding up the phone to get them all in the frame. And they were smiling, all of them, glasses of champagne in their hands.

He'd tagged them in at the Plaza Hotel in New York, and the caption read: *Celebrating . . .*

The room immediately started to shrink, closing in around Pip. The walls took an inward step and the shadows in the corners stretched out to take her. She couldn't be here. She needed to get out before she suffocated inside this room.

She stumbled out of her door, phone in hand, tiptoeing past Josh's room to the stairs. He was already in bed, but he'd come in to see her earlier, with a whispered, "Thought you might be hungry," leaving her a box of Cracker Jack he'd smuggled from the kitchen. "Shhh, don't tell Mom and Dad."

Pip could hear the sounds of her parents watching television in the living room, waiting for their show to start at nine. They were talking, a muffled drone through the door, but she could hear one word clearly: her own name.

Quietly, she stepped into her sneakers, scooped up her keys, and slipped out of the front door, shutting it silently behind her.

It was raining, hard, spattering against the ground and up against her ankles. That was fine, that was OK. She needed to get out, clear her head. And maybe the rain would help: water down the rage until she was no longer ablaze, just the charred parts left behind.

Pip ran across the road, into the woods on the other side. It was dark here, pitch dark, but it covered her from the worst of the rain. And that was fine too, until something unseen rustled through the undergrowth and scared her. She returned to the road, safe along the moonlit sidewalk, soaked through. She should have felt cold—she was shivering—but she couldn't really feel it. And she didn't know where to go. She just wanted to walk, to be outside where nothing could shut her in. So she walked, to the end of Thatcher Road and back, stopping before she reached her house, turning and walking the road again. Up and down and back again, chasing her thoughts, trying to unravel their ends.

Her hair was dripping by her third time coming back. She stopped dead. There was movement. Someone walking down the front path of Zach's house. But it wasn't Zach's house, not anymore. The figure was Charlie Green, carrying a filled black bag toward the garbage can left out near the path.

He jumped when he saw Pip emerging from the dark.

"Ah, Pip, sorry," he said, laughing, dropping the bag in the trash can. "You scared me. Are you—" He paused, looking at her. "God, you're soaking. Why aren't you wearing a jacket?"

She didn't have an answer.

"Well, you're almost home now. Get in and get dry," he said kindly.

"I—I . . . ," she stuttered, her teeth chattering. "I can't go home. Not yet."

Charlie tilted his head, his eyes searching out hers.

"Oh, OK," he said awkwardly. "Well, do you want to come to our place, for a little while?"

"No. Thank you," she added hastily. "I don't want to be inside."

"Oh, right." Charlie shuffled, glancing back at his house. "Well, uh . . . do you want to sit on the porch, get out of the rain?"

Pip was about to say no but, actually, maybe she was feeling cold now. She nodded.

"OK, sure," Charlie said, beckoning for her to follow him down the path. They stepped onto the covered front steps and he paused. "Do you want a drink or something? A towel?"

"No thank you," Pip said, sitting down on the dry middle step.

"Right." Charlie nodded, pushing his reddish hair back from his face. "So, um, are you OK?"

"I . . . ," Pip began. "I've had a bad day."

"Oh." He sat down, on the step below hers. "Do you want to talk about it?"

"I don't really know how," she said.

"I, er, I listened to your podcast, and the new episodes about Jamie Reynolds," he said. "You're really good at what you do. And brave. Whatever it is that's bothering you, I'm sure you'll find a way."

"They found Max Hastings not guilty today."

"Oh." Charlie sighed, stretching out his legs. "Shit. That's not good."

"To put it lightly." Pip sniffed, wiping rain from the end of her nose.

"You know," he said, "for what it's worth, the justice system is supposed to be this purveyor of right and wrong, good and bad. But sometimes, I think it gets it wrong almost as much as it gets it right. I've had to learn that, too, and it's hard to accept. What do you do when the things that are supposed to protect you fail you like that?"

"I was so naive," Pip said. "I practically handed Max Hastings to them, after everything came out last year. And I truly believed it was some kind of victory, that the bad would be punished. Because it was the truth, and the truth was the most important thing to me. It's all I believed in, all I cared about: finding the truth, no matter the cost. And the truth was that Max was guilty and he would face justice. But justice doesn't exist, and the truth doesn't matter, not in the real world, and now they've just handed him right back."

"Oh, justice exists," Charlie said, looking up at the rain. "Maybe not the kind that happens in police stations and courtrooms, but it does exist. And when you really think about it, those words—good and bad, right and wrong—they don't really matter in the real world. Who gets to decide what they mean: those people who just got it wrong and let Max walk free? No"—he shook his head—"I think we all get to decide what good and bad and right and wrong mean to us, not what we're told to accept. You did nothing wrong. Don't beat yourself up for other people's mistakes."

Pip turned to him, her stomach clenching. "But that doesn't matter now. Max has won."

"He only wins if you let him."

"What can I do about it?" she asked.

"From listening to your podcast, sounds to me like there's not much you can't do."

"I haven't found Jamie." She picked at her nails. "And now people think he's not really missing, that I made it all up. That I'm a liar and I'm bad and—"

"Do you care?" Charlie asked. "Do you care what people think, if you know you're right?"

She paused, her answer sliding back down her throat. Why did she care? She was about to say she didn't care at all, but hadn't that been the feeling in the pit of her stomach all along? The pit that had been growing these past six months. Guilt about what she did last time, about her dog dying, about not being good, about putting her family in danger, and every day reading the disappointment in her mom's eyes. Feeling bad about the secrets she was keeping to protect Cara and Naomi. She *was* a liar, that part was true.

And worse, to make herself feel better about it all, she'd said it wasn't really her and that she'd never be that person again. That she was different now . . . good. That she'd almost lost herself last time and it wouldn't happen again. But that wasn't it, was it? She hadn't almost lost herself, maybe she'd actually been meeting herself for the very first time. And she was tired of feeling guilty about it. Tired of feeling shame about who she was. She bet Max Hastings had never felt ashamed a day in his life.

"You're right," she said. And as she straightened up, untwisted, she realized the pit in her stomach, the one that had been swallowing her from inside out, it was starting to go. Filling in until it was hardly there at all. "Maybe I don't have to be good, or other people's versions of good. And maybe I don't have to be likable." She turned to Charlie, her movements quick and light despite her water-heavy clothes. "Fuck likable. You know who's likable? People like Max Hastings who walk into a courtroom with fake glasses and charm their way out. I don't want to be like that."

"So don't," Charlie said. "And don't give up because of him. Someone's life might depend on you. And I know you can find him, find Jamie." He turned a smile to her. "Other people might not believe in you, but, for what it's worth, your neighbor from four doors down does."

She felt it grow on her face: a smile. Small, flickering out after a moment, but it had been there. And it had been real. "Thank you, Charlie." She'd needed to hear that. All of it. Maybe she wouldn't have listened if it had come from anyone close to her. There'd been too much anger, too much guilt, too many voices. But she was listening now. "Thank you." She meant it. And the voice in her head thanked him too.

"No problem."

Pip stood up, out into the downpour, staring up at the moon, its light quivering through the sheets of rain. "I have to go do something."

THIRTY-THREE

Pip sat in her car, halfway down Courtland. Not outside his house, just a little farther up, so no one would see. Her thumbs on her phone, she played the audio clip one last time:

"Max, at a calamity party in March 2014, did you drug and rape Becca Bell?"

"What? No, I fucking didn't."

"MAX, do not lie to me or I swear to god I will ruin you! Did you put Rohypnol in Becca's drink and have sex with her?"

"Yes, but, like . . . it wasn't rape. She didn't say no."

"Because you drugged her, you vile rapist gargoyle. You have no idea what you've done."

Pip's ears rang, trying to push away his voice and listen to her own. Good and bad didn't matter here. There were only winners. And Max only won if she let him. That was justice.

So she did it.

She pressed the button, uploading the audio of that phone call to her website, reposting it on the podcast's Twitter account. Alongside the post, she wrote: *Max Hastings trial final update. I don't care what the jury believes: he is guilty.*

It was done; it was gone.

There was no going back now. This was her, and it was OK.

She dropped her phone onto the passenger seat and picked up the can of paint she'd taken from the garage, tucking the brush into her back pocket. She opened the door, reaching back for the final item—a hammer from her dad's toolbox—before stepping silently out of the car.

She walked up the road, passing one house, two, three, four, until she stopped, looking up at the Hastings family's sprawling home, with its painted white front door. They were out, all of them, at their fancy dinner at the Plaza. And Pip was here, outside their empty house.

Up the drive, past the large oak tree, coming to a stop before the front door. She set the paint can on the ground and bent down to use the end of the hammer to pry open the lid. The can was half full, the paint a dull green. Pip pulled out the brush and dipped it inside, spooling off the excess.

No going back. She took one breath and then stepped up, pressing the brush against the front door. She reached high, looping it up and down, crouching to pick up more paint when the lines ran dry.

The letters were shaky and dripping, spreading out from the door to the light-colored bricks on either side. She went back over the words, deeper and darker, and when she was done, she dropped the brush on the path, a small spatter of paint where it landed. She picked up the hammer, twirling it between her fingers, feeling its weight in her hands.

She crossed to the left side of the house, to the window there. She readied her arm and the hammer, held it back. Then she swung with full force into the window.

It shattered. A sprinkling of broken glass fell inside and out, like glitter, like rain, dusting the tops of her sneakers. She tightened her grip on the hammer, glass crunching under her feet as she approached the next window. Pulled back and smashed it, the sound of the tinkling glass lost beneath the rain. And the next window. First swing, cracked. Second swing, exploded. Past the front door and the words she'd painted there, to the windows on the other side. One. Two. Three. Until all six windows at the front of the house were destroyed. Broken open. Exposed.

Pip's breath was heavy in her chest now, right arm aching as she stepped backward down the drive. Her hair was matted and wet, whipping across her face as she looked up at the destruction. Her destruction.

And painted across the front, in the same forest-green shade as the Amobis' new shed, were the words:

RAPIST
I WILL GET YOU

Pip read them, and read them again; looked around at what she'd done.

And she checked, down inside herself, under her skin, but she couldn't find it. The scream was no longer there, waiting for her. She'd beaten it.

Can you come outside? she texted, the rain pattering against her screen, the phone no longer recognizing her thumb.

Read, it said beneath her message a few seconds later.

She watched from outside as the light in Ravi's bedroom clicked on, and the curtain twitched for just a second.

Pip followed his progress as the hall light turned on in the upper middle window, and then the downstairs hall light, glowing through the glass in the front door. It was broken up now by Ravi's silhouette as he made his way toward it.

The door opened and he stood there against the light, wearing just a white T-shirt and navy sweatpants. He looked at her, then up at the rain in the sky, and he walked outside, his feet bare, slapping against the path.

"Nice night," he said, squinting against the droplets running down his face.

"I'm sorry." Pip looked at him, her hair sticking to her face in long, dark streaks. "I'm sorry I took it out on you."

"That's OK," he said.

"No, it's not." She shook her head. "I had no right to be angry at you. I think I was angry at me, mostly. And it's not just everything that happened today. I mean, it *is* that, but also I've been lying to myself for a while now, trying to separate myself from that person who became so obsessed with finding Andie Bell's killer. Trying to convince everyone else it wasn't really me so I could convince myself. But I think, now, that that *is* me. And maybe I'm selfish and maybe I'm a liar and maybe I'm reckless and obsessive and I'm OK with doing bad things when it's me doing them and maybe I'm a hypocrite, and maybe none of that is good, but it feels good. It feels like me, and I hope you're OK with all that because . . . I love you too."

She had barely finished speaking, but Ravi's hand was against her face, cupped around her cheek, his thumb rubbing the rain from her bottom lip. He moved his fingers down to lift her chin and then he kissed her. Long and hard, their faces wet against each other, both trying to fight a smile.

But the smile broke eventually, and Ravi drew back. "You should have just asked me. I know exactly who you are. And I love her. I love you. Oh, by the way, I said it first."

"Yeah, in anger," said Pip.

"Ah, that's just because I'm so brooding and mysterious." He pulled a face with puckered lips and too-serious eyes.

"Um, Ravi?"

"Yes, Um Pip."

"I need to tell you something. Something I just did."

"What did you do?" He dropped the face into one that was actually serious. "Pip, what did you just do?"

FRIDAY
7 DAYS MISSING

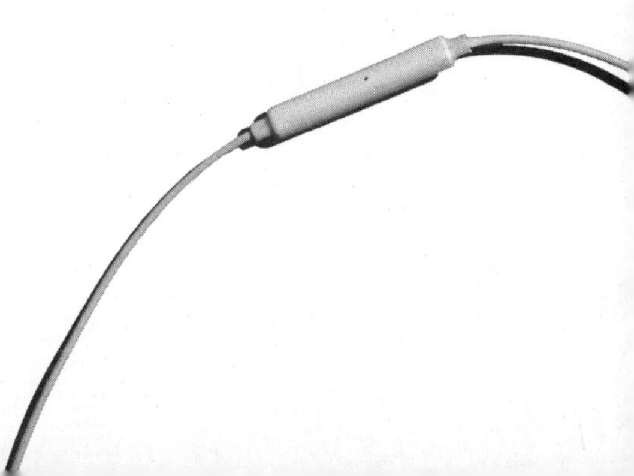

THIRTY-FOUR

Pip's alarm went off for school, chirping from her bedside table.

She yawned, sticking one foot outside the duvet. Then she remembered that she was suspended, so she tucked the foot back inside and leaned over to snooze the alarm.

But even through one sleepy eye, she saw the message waiting on her phone. Received seven minutes ago, from Nat da Silva.

Hi it's Nat. I need to show you something. It's about Jamie. About Layla Mead.

Her eyes hadn't even unstuck yet, but Pip sat up and kicked off the duvet. Her jeans were still damp from last night as she pulled them on, with a long-sleeved white T-shirt from the top of the laundry basket; it probably had one more use in it.

She was just fighting a brush through her rain-tangled hair when her mom came in to say goodbye before work.

"I'm taking Josh to school now," she said.

"OK." Pip winced as the brush caught in a knot. "Have a good day."

"We need to have a real conversation this weekend about what's going on with you." Her mom's eyes were stern, but her voice was trying not to be. "I know you're under a lot of pressure, but we agreed that wouldn't happen this time."

"No pressure, not anymore," Pip said, the knot coming loose. "And

I'm sorry about getting suspended." She wasn't, not one bit. Ant deserved it, as far as she was concerned. But if that's what her mom needed to hear to leave it alone, then lying it was. Her mom had the best intentions, Pip knew, but right now, those best intentions would only get in her way.

"That's OK, sweetie," her mom said. "I know the verdict must have hit you hard. And everything with Jamie Reynolds. Maybe it's best if you stay home today, get some studying done. Some normality."

"OK, I'll try."

Pip waited, listening at her bedroom door to the sounds of her mom telling Joshua to put his shoes on the correct feet and ushering him outside. The car engine, wheels on the drive. She gave them a three-minute head start, and then she left.

Nat's face appeared in the crack, her eyes swollen, white hair pushed back and broken up by visible finger tracks.

"Oh, it's you," she said, pulling the door fully open.

"I got your message," Pip said, her chest constricting as she met Nat's sad eyes.

"Yeah." Nat stepped back. "You should, um, you should come in." She beckoned Pip over the threshold before closing the door and leading her down the corridor to the kitchen. The farthest Pip had ever been invited inside this house.

Nat took a seat at the small kitchen table, gesturing for Pip to take the one opposite. She did, sitting awkwardly at its very edge. Waiting, the air thickening between them.

Nat cleared her throat, rubbed one eye. "My brother told me something this morning. He said Max Hastings's house was vandalized last night, and someone painted *Rapist* across his door."

"Oh . . . r-really?" said Pip, swallowing hard.

"Yeah. But apparently they don't know who it was, don't have any witnesses or anything."

"Oh, that's a . . . that's a shame." Pip coughed.

Nat looked pointedly at her, something different, something new in her eyes. And Pip knew that she knew.

Then something else happened; Nat reached out across the table and took Pip's hand. Held on to it.

"And I saw you uploaded that audio file," she said, her hand shifting around inside Pip's. "It's already getting a lot of attention, huh? You're going to get in trouble for that, aren't you?"

"Probably," said Pip.

"I know how that feels," Nat said. "That anger. Like you just want to set fire to the world and watch it burn."

"Something like that."

Nat tightened her grip on Pip's hand and then she let it go, drawing hers back flat against the table. "I think we're alike, you and me. I didn't before. I wanted to hate you so badly, I really did. I used to hate Andie Bell that much, for a while it felt like the only thing I had. And you know why I wanted to hate you so much? Apart from you being a pain in the ass." She tapped her fingers. "I listened to your podcast, and it made me not hate Andie quite so much anymore. In fact, I felt sorry for her, so I hated you even harder instead. But I think I've been hating the wrong people all along." She sniffed, with a tiny smile. "You're OK," she said.

"Thanks," Pip said, Nat's smile passing to her and then out the open window.

"And you were right." Nat picked at her fingernails. "About Luke."

"Your boyfriend?"

"Not anymore. Not that he knows it yet." She laughed, but there was no joy in it.

"What was I right about?"

"What you noticed, when you asked where we were the night Jamie went missing. Luke said he was home all night, alone." Nat paused. "He was lying, you were right."

"Did you ask him where he was?" said Pip.

"No. Luke doesn't like to be asked questions." Nat shifted in her chair. "But after Jamie never showed up and was ignoring my calls, I went over to Luke's house to see him. He wasn't there. And his car was gone."

"What time was this?"

"Around midnight. Then I went back home."

"So you don't know where Luke was?" Pip leaned forward, elbows on the table.

"I do now." Nat withdrew one of her hands to pull her phone out, laying it on the table. "Last night, I was thinking about what you said yesterday, that maybe Luke had something to do with Jamie's disappearance. So I, uh, looked through his phone while he was asleep. Went through his texts. He's been talking to a girl." She laughed again, small and hollow. "Her name is Layla Mead."

Pip felt the name creeping along her skin, climbing up her spine, jumping rung to rung.

"You said Jamie's been talking to her too," Nat said. "I stayed up till four, listening to your two episodes. You don't know who Layla is, but Luke does." She ran her fingers through her hair. "That's where he was, the night of Jamie's disappearance. Meeting Layla."

"Really?"

"That's what his messages say. They've been talking for several weeks; I scrolled back and read every message. Looks like they met on Tinder, so that's great for me. And the messages are, you know, explicit. Also great for me. But they hadn't met yet, not until last Friday night. Here." She unlocked her phone, thumbing on to the photos app. "I took two screenshots and sent them to my phone. I was already thinking of showing you, because, you know . . . you came back so I didn't have to be alone. And when I heard about Max's house, that's when I decided to message you. Here." She put the phone into Pip's waiting hands.

Pip's eyes trailed down the first screenshot: Luke's messages on the right in blue boxes, Layla's on the left and in gray.

I've been thinking about you . . .

Yeah? Been thinking bout you too

Nothing good I hope :)

You know me

I'd like to.

I don't wanna wait anymore. Wanna meet tonight?

All right where?

Parking lot in Lodge Park

Pip's breath stuttered at Layla's last message. The parking lot at Lodge Park; her search party team had walked through that parking lot on Wednesday. It fell inside their zone.

She glanced up quickly at Nat before swiping to the second screenshot.

A parking lot?

I won't be wearing much . . .

When?

Come now.

Then, ten minutes later, at 11:58 p.m.:

Are you coming?

Almost there.

And then much later, at 12:41 a.m., from Luke:

What the fuck, I'm gonna kill you

Pip's eyes shot up to Nat's.

"I know," she said, nodding. "No more messages from either of them after that. But he knows who Layla is, and you think she had something to do with Jamie?"

"Yeah, I do," Pip said, sliding Nat's phone back across the table. "I think she had everything to do with Jamie."

"I need you to find him," Nat said, and there was quiver to her lip now that wasn't there before, a sheen to her dried-out eyes. "Jamie, he . . . he's really important to me. And I—I just need him to be OK."

It was Pip who reached across the table now, taking Nat's hand in hers, her thumb hovering above the sharp ridges of Nat's knuckles. "I'm trying," she said.

THIRTY-FIVE

Ravi was jittery, moving too much, disturbing the air beside Pip as they walked.

"How scary did you say this guy is again?" he asked, his fingers finding their way into the pocket of Pip's jacket and hooking on.

"Pretty scary," she said.

"And he's a drug dealer."

"Think he's higher up than that," she said as they turned on to Beacon Close.

"Oh good," Ravi said. "Howie's boss. Are we going to blackmail this one too?"

Pip shrugged, pulled a face at him. "Whatever works."

"Great. Cool," Ravi said. "Really love that new motto, covers all bases. Yep. Cool. This is all fine. Which house is he?"

"Number thirteen." Pip pointed out the house with the white BMW parked outside.

"Thirteen?" Ravi squinted at her. "Oh, fabulous. Another good sign, that is."

"Come on," Pip said, suppressing a smile, patting him twice on the backside as they walked up the path alongside the car, the one they'd chased on Wednesday night. Pip glanced at it, and back at

Ravi, then pressed her finger into the doorbell. The sound was shrill and piercing.

"I bet everyone dreads the day they get a knock at the door from Pip Fitz-Amobi," Ravi whispered.

The door pulled open sharply, and Luke Eaton stood before them, wearing the same black basketball shorts and a gray T-shirt that clashed with the color of the tattoos scaling the pale skin of his neck.

"Hello. Again," he said gruffly. "What is it this time?"

"We need to ask you some questions, about Jamie Reynolds," Pip said, standing as tall as she could.

"Shame," Luke said, itching one leg with the foot of the other. "I really don't like questions."

He slapped his hand forcefully against the door.

"No, I—" Pip said, but it was too late. The door slammed shut before her words could make it through the gap. "Fuck," she said loudly, an urge to hit the door with her fist.

"I didn't think he'd talk . . ." But Ravi's voice trailed off as he watched Pip crouch by the door, pushing her fingers against the mail slot to hold it open. "What are you doing?"

She drew her face close to the small rectangular opening and shouted through it: "I know Jamie owed you money when he went missing! If you talk to us, I'll give you the nine hundred dollars he owes you!"

She straightened up, the mail slot closing with a metallic clang. Ravi narrowed his eyes angrily at her, mouthing, "What?"

But Pip didn't have time to offer an answer, because Luke was pulling the door open again, his jawbone protruding and retreating as he chewed on an answer.

"All of it?" he said with a click of his tongue.

"Yes." The word rushed out of her, breathy but firm. "All nine hundred. I'll get it to you next week."

"In cash," he said, eyes alighting on hers.

"Yes, OK," she said, nodding, "by the end of next week."

"All right." He pulled the door fully open. "You've got a deal there, Sherlock."

Pip stepped over the threshold, Ravi right behind her as Luke closed the door, shutting them all in inside this too-narrow corridor. Luke passed them, his arm brushing against Pip's as he did, and she couldn't tell whether it had been intentional or not.

"In here," he barked over his shoulder, leading them into the kitchen.

There were four chairs, but no one sat down. Luke leaned against the counter, knees cocked and careless, tattooed arms out wide anchoring him there. Pip and Ravi stood together, at the entrance, toes in the kitchen, their heels left behind in the corridor.

Luke opened his mouth to speak, but Pip couldn't let him take charge, so she rushed out her question first.

"Why does Jamie owe you nine hundred dollars?"

Luke dropped his head and smiled, licking the front of his teeth.

"Was it something to do with drugs, did he buy from—"

"No," Luke said. "Jamie owed me nine hundred dollars because I lent him nine hundred dollars. He came to me a little while ago, desperate to borrow money. Guess Nat mentioned to him I did that sometimes. So I helped him out—with a high interest rate, of course," he added with a dark laugh. "Told him I'd beat the shit out of him if he was late paying me back, and then the fucker goes missing, doesn't he?"

"Did Jamie say what he needed the money for?" Ravi asked.

Luke turned his attention to Ravi. "I don't ask people's business, because I don't care."

But Pip's mind had jumped instead to when, not why. Was Luke's threat a little stronger than he was letting on, something Jamie might have considered life or death? Had he asked his dad to borrow money and then tried to steal from Pip's mom's office because he was scared of what Luke would do to him if he couldn't pay him back on time?

"When did Jamie borrow money from you?" said Pip.

"Dunno." Luke shrugged, his tongue between his teeth again.

Pip worked out the timeline in her head. "Was it Monday the sixth? Tuesday the seventh? Before then?"

"No, after," Luke said. "Pretty sure it was a Friday, so must have been three weeks ago today. He's officially late repaying me now."

The pieces rearranged themselves in Pip's head: no, Jamie borrowed the money *after* asking his dad and trying to steal the credit card. So going to Luke must have been a last resort, and something else had been life or death. She glanced at Ravi, and from the quick movement of his eyes, back and forth, she knew he was thinking the same.

"OK," Pip said. "Now I need to ask you about Layla Mead."

"Of course you do." He laughed. What was so funny?

"You went to meet Layla, last Friday, around midnight."

"Yes, I did," he said, looking off guard for only a moment, then drumming his fingers on the counter, the sound unsettling Pip's heartbeat.

"And you know who she really is."

"Yes, I do."

"Who is she?" Pip said, her voice desperate, giving her away.

Luke smiled, showing too many of his teeth.

"Layla Mead *is* Jamie."

THIRTY-SIX

"What?" Pip and Ravi said together, eyes swivelling to find each other.

Pip shook her head. "That's not possible," she said.

"Well, it is." Luke smirked, clearly enjoying their shock. "I was messaging Layla that night, agreed to meet her at Lodge Park parking lot, and who was there waiting for me? Jamie Reynolds."

"B-but, but . . ." Pip's brain stalled. "You saw Jamie? You met him, just after midnight?" The exact time, she was thinking, that Jamie's heart rate had first spiked.

"Yep. Fucking freak clearly thought he was being clever, having one over on me. Pretending to be a girl to lead me on. Maybe he did it to try take Nat away from me, don't know. I'd kill him if he was still here."

"What happened?" Ravi said. "What happened in the parking lot with Jamie?"

"Not much," Luke said, running a hand over his close-shaved head. "I got out of the car, called Layla's name, and it's Jamie instead who walks out of the trees."

"And?" Pip said. "What happened, did you talk?"

"Not really. He was acting all weird, like, scared, which he should've been, fucking with me." Luke licked his teeth again. "Had both his hands in his pockets. And he only said two words to me."

"What?" Pip and Ravi said together again.

"I can't even remember exactly what it was, something strange. It was like 'child broomstick' or 'child brown sick,' I dunno, couldn't really hear the second part. And after Jamie said it, it was like he was watching me, waiting for a reaction," Luke said. "So obviously I was like, 'What the fuck?' and when I said that, Jamie turned and bolted, without another word. I chased after him, woulda killed him if I caught him, but it was dark, I lost him in the trees."

"And?" Pip pressed.

"And nothing." Luke straightened up, cracking the bones in his gray-patterned neck. "Didn't find him. Went home. Jamie goes missing. So I'm thinking someone else he was fucking with got to him after. Whatever happened to him, he deserved it. Fucking fat loser."

"But Jamie went to the abandoned farmhouse, right after meeting you," Pip said. "I know you use that place to pick up your, er, business items. Why would Jamie go there?"

"I don't know. I wasn't there that night. But it's isolated, secluded, best place in town for conducting any private business. Except now I have to find a new drop-off point, thanks to you," he growled.

"Are . . . ," Pip said, but the rest of the sentence died before she even knew what it was.

"That's all I know about Layla Mead, about Jamie." Luke dipped his head and then raised one arm, pointing down the corridor behind them. "You can go now."

They didn't move.

"Now," he said, louder. "I'm busy."

"OK," Pip said, turning to go, telling Ravi with her eyes to do the same.

"A week today," Luke called after them. "I want my cash by next Friday and I don't like to be kept waiting."

"Got it," Pip said, two steps away. But then the broken thought floating around her head rearranged and reached its end, and she doubled back. "Luke, are you twenty-nine?" she asked.

"Yeah." His eyebrows lowered, reaching for each other across the bridge of his nose.

"And do you turn thirty soon?"

"Couple of months. Why?"

"No reason." Pip shook her head. "Thursday. I'll have your money." And she walked back down the hall and out the front door Ravi was holding open for her, an urgent look in his eyes.

"What was that?" Ravi said, when the door was firmly shut behind them. "Where are you going to get nine hundred dollars from, Pip? He's clearly a dangerous guy, you can't just go around and—"

"Guess I'm accepting one of those sponsorship deals. ASAP," Pip said, turning to look at the lines of sun skimming across Luke's white car.

"You're gonna give me a heart attack one day," Ravi said, taking her hand, leading her around the corner. "Jamie can't be Layla, right? Right?"

"No," Pip replied before she'd even thought about it. And then, after she had: "No, he can't be. I've read the messages between the two of them. And the whole Stella Chapman thing. And Jamie was on the phone with Layla outside the calamity party; he had to have been on the phone to a real person."

"What, so maybe Layla sent Jamie there, to meet Luke?" Ravi said.

"Yeah, maybe. Maybe that's what they were talking about on the phone. And Jamie must have had the knife with him when he met Luke, probably in his hoodie pocket."

"Why?" Lines of confusion drew across Ravi's forehead. "None of this makes sense. And what the hell is 'child broomstick'? Is Luke messing with us?"

"Doesn't seem like the kind to mess around. And remember, George heard Jamie on the phone saying something about a child too."

They headed toward the train station, where Pip had parked her car earlier, so her mom wouldn't see it if she was driving up and down Main Street.

"Why'd you ask his age?" Ravi said. "Looking to trade me in for an older model?"

"It's too many now to be a coincidence," she said, more to herself than to Ravi. "Adam Clark, Daniel da Silva, Luke Eaton, and even Jamie too—only because he lied about his age—but every single person Layla has spoken to is twenty-nine or recently thirty. And more than that, they're all white guys, with brownish hair, living in the same town."

"Yeah," Ravi said, "so Layla has a type. A very, *very* specific type."

"I don't know." Pip looked down at her sneakers, still damp from last night. "All those similarities, asking lots of questions. It's like Layla's been looking for someone. Someone specific, but she doesn't know who."

Pip looked at Ravi, but her eyes escaped from her, breaking away to the side, to someone standing right on the other side of the road. Outside the new Starbucks that had opened there. Neat black jacket, messy blond hair falling into his eyes. Sharp, angled cheekbones.

He was back.

Max Hastings.

Standing with two guys Pip didn't recognize, talking and laughing in the street.

Pip emptied out and refilled with a feeling that was black and cold and red and burning. She stopped walking and stared.

How dare he? How dare he stand there, laughing, in this town? Out where anyone could see him?

Her hands tightened into fists, nails digging into Ravi's palm.

"Ouch." Ravi escaped her grip and looked at her. "Pip, wha—?" Then he followed her eyes across the road.

Max must have felt it, her gaze, because at that exact moment, he looked up, over the street and the idling cars. Right at her. Into her. His mouth settled into a line, pulling up at one end. He raised one arm, his hand open palm-out in a small wave, and the line of his mouth was a smile.

Pip felt it growing inside her, sparking, but Ravi exploded first.

"Don't you look at her!" he screamed at Max, over the top of the cars. "Don't you dare look at her, you hear me?"

Heads turned in the street. Mutters. Faces in windows. Max lowered his arm, but the smile never once left his face.

"Come on," Ravi said, retaking Pip's hand. "Let's get out of here."

Ravi lay on Pip's bed, throwing a pair of her balled-up socks in the air and catching them. Throwing always helped him think.

Pip was at her desk, laptop asleep in front of her, digging one finger through her small jar of pins, letting them jab her.

"One more time," Ravi said, his eyes following the socks up to the ceiling and down to his hand.

Pip cleared her throat. "Jamie walks to the parking lot in Lodge

Park. He's carrying the knife. He's nervous, scared, his heart rate tells us that. Layla has potentially set this up, told Luke to be there. We don't know why. Jamie says two words to Luke, studies him for a reaction, and then runs off. He then goes to the abandoned farmhouse. His heart spikes higher. He's even more scared, and the knife somehow ends up in the grass by the trees. And Jamie's Fitbit is removed, or it breaks or . . ."

"Or his heart stops." Catch and throw.

"And then his phone is turned off a few minutes later and never turns on again," Pip said, lowering her head so her hands could take its weight.

"Well," Ravi began, "Luke wasn't exactly quiet about wanting to kill Jamie, because he thinks he's the one who catfished him. Isn't it possible he chased Jamie to the farmhouse?"

"If Luke was the one who hurt Jamie, I don't think he would've talked to us at all, not even for nine hundred bucks."

"Fair point," Ravi said. "But he did lie initially; he could have told you about seeing Jamie when you first talked to him and Nat."

"Yeah, but, you know, Luke went out there to cheat on Nat, and Nat was sitting in the room with us. Plus, I'm guessing he prefers not to be associated with missing people, given his line of work."

"OK. But the words Jamie said to Luke, they have to be important somehow." Ravi sat up, squeezing the socks in his hands. "They are the key."

"Child broomstick? Child brown sick?" Pip looked at him, skeptical. "They don't sound very *key.*"

"Maybe Luke misheard. Or maybe they have another meaning we can't see yet. Look them up." Ravi gestured toward her laptop.

"Look them up?"

"It's worth a try, Grumpus."

“Fine.” Pip pressed the power button to awaken her laptop. She double-clicked on Chrome, bringing up a blank Google page. “OK.”

She typed in *child broomstick* and pressed enter. “Yep, as I suspected, we’ve got a lot of Halloween costumes for small witches and Quidditch players. Not very helpful.”

“What did Jamie mean?” Ravi wondered aloud, sock-ball back in the air. “Try the other one.”

“Urgh, fine, but I’m telling you now, I’m not clicking on images for this one,” Pip said, clearing the search bar and typing in *child brown sick.* She pressed enter and the top result, as expected, was a website about kids’ health, with a page titled *Vomiting.* “See, I said this was pointle—”

The word got caught halfway up her throat, stalling there as Pip’s eyes narrowed. Just below the search bar, Google was asking her: *Did you mean: Child Brunswick.*

“Child Brunswick.” She said it quietly, sounding out the words on her lips. They felt familiar somehow, pushed together like that.

“What’s that?”

Ravi slid off the bed and padded over as Pip clicked on Google’s suggestion and the page of results changed, replaced by articles from all of the large news outlets. Pip’s eyes skimmed down them.

“Of course,” she said, looking at Ravi, searching for the same recognition in his eyes. But his were blank. “Child Brunswick,” Pip said, “that’s the name the media gave to the unnamed kid involved in the Scott Brunswick case.”

“The what case?” he asked, reading over her shoulder.

“Have you not listened to *any* of the true-crime podcasts I’ve recommended?” she said. “Practically all of them have covered this case, it’s one of the most notorious in the whole country. Happened, like, twenty years ago.” She looked up at Ravi. “Scott Brunswick was a serial killer. He killed children. And he made his young son, Child Brunswick, help him lure out the victims. You've really never heard of this?"

Ravi shook his head.

"Look, read about it," Pip said, clicking on one of the articles.

THE FIND-IT

HOME > TRUE CRIME > AMERICA'S MOST INFAMOUS SERIAL KILLERS > SCOTT BRUNSWICK "THE MONSTER OF ROCHESTER"

By Oscar Stevens

Between 2000 and 2001, the city of Rochester, New York, was struck by a string of horrific child murders. In the space of just thirteen months, six children disappeared: Jessica Moore, age 11; Megan French, age 10; Edward Keller, age 9; Patrick Evans, age 9; Charlotte Long, age 10, and Emily Nowell, age 8. Their burned remains were later discovered buried along the shore of Lake Ontario, all within one mile of each other. The cause of death in each case was blunt force trauma.[1]

Emily Nowell, the youngest and final victim of the Monster of Rochester, was found three weeks after her disappearance in March 2001, but it would take police two more months to track down her killer.[2]

Police zeroed in on Scott Brunswick, a 41-year-old forklift driver who had lived in Rochester his whole life.[3] Brunswick was a close match to a police composite sketch released after an eyewitness saw a man driving late at night in the area where the bodies were later found.[4] His vehicle, a white Toyota van, also matched the witness's description.[5] Searches of Brunswick's home uncovered trophies he had kept from each of the victims: one of their socks.[6]

But there was very little forensic evidence tying Brunswick to the murders.[7] And when the case was brought to trial, the prosecution relied on circumstantial evidence and their key witness: Brunswick's son, who was ten years old at the time of the final murder.[8] Brunswick, who lived alone with his only child, had used his son in committing the murders; he directed the boy to approach potential victims in public places—a playground, a park, a public swimming pool, and a shopping mall—and to lure them away on their own, to where Brunswick was waiting in his van to abduct them.[9] [10] [11] The son also assisted in the disposal of the bodies.[12]

The trial of Scott Brunswick began in September 2003 and the son—nicknamed Child Brunswick by the press at the time—now 13, gave testimony that was essential in securing a unanimous guilty verdict.[13] Scott Brunswick was sentenced to life without the possibility of parole. But just seven weeks into his sentence at the maximum security Sullivan Correctional Facility in New York state, Brunswick was beaten to death by another inmate.[14] [15]

For his role in assisting the murders, Child Brunswick was charged by a juvenile court to serve a five-year custodial sentence in a juvenile detention center.[16] When he turned eighteen, a parole board decision recommended his release on lifetime probation. Child Brunswick was given a new identity under a witness-protection-style program and a worldwide injunction was imposed on the media, preventing the publication of any details about Child Brunswick or his new identity.[17] The attorney general stated that this was because there was a risk of "vigilante-type retaliation against this individual if his real identity became known, because of the role he played in his father's horrendous crimes."[18]

THIRTY-SEVEN

Connor stared at them both, his eyes narrowing, darkening, creasing the skin on his freckled nose. He'd come straight here when Pip texted him that she had an urgent update—walked out of school right in the middle of biology class.

"What are you saying?" he asked, nervously swiveling in the desk chair.

Pip leveled her voice. "I'm saying that, whoever Layla Mead really is, we think she's been looking for Child Brunswick. And not just because Jamie said that name to Luke. Child Brunswick was ten at the time of the final murder in March 2001, and he was thirteen in September 2003, when the trial began. That means that right now, Child Brunswick would be twenty-nine or recently turned thirty. Every single person Layla has spoken to, including Jamie because he lied about his age, has been twenty-nine turning thirty soon, or recently thirty. And she's been asking them lots of questions. She's trying to work out who Child Brunswick is, I'm sure of it. And for some reason, Layla thinks this person is in our town."

"But what has this got to do with Jamie?" Connor asked.

"Everything," Pip said. "I think he's involved in this because of Layla. He goes to meet Luke Eaton, a meeting Layla set up, and says the words 'Child Brunswick' to him, looking for a reaction. A reaction Luke doesn't give."

"Because he's not Child Brunswick?" Connor said.

"No, I don't think he is," Pip said.

"But then"—Ravi stepped in—"we know that after meeting Luke, Jamie went immediately to the abandoned farmhouse, and it's there that whatever happened . . . happened. So we were theorizing that maybe . . ." He glanced at Pip. "Maybe he went to meet someone else. Someone else Layla thought could be Child Brunswick. And this person . . . did react."

"Who? Who else is there?" Connor said. "Daniel da Silva or Mr. Clark?"

"No." Pip shook her head. "I mean yes, those are the two other people we know Layla was talking to. But one is a police officer and the other is a teacher. Child Brunswick couldn't be either of those things, and I think Layla would've worked that out when talking to them. As soon as Adam Clark told her he was a teacher, she stopped talking to him, wrote him off. It's someone else."

"So what does this mean?"

"I think it means that if we find Child Brunswick"—Pip tucked her hair behind her ears—"we find Jamie."

"This is crazy. How on earth do we do that?" Connor said.

"Research," Pip said, dragging her laptop across the duvet and onto her lap. "Find out everything we can about Child Brunswick. And why Layla Mead thinks he's here."

"Which isn't easy when there's a worldwide injunction on publishing anything about him," Ravi said.

She and Ravi had already started, reading through the first full page of article results, noting down any details they could find, which, as yet, was nothing but Child Brunswick's age range. Pip had printed out Scott Brunswick's mug shot, but he didn't look like anyone she recognized. He had pale white skin, stubble, light wrinkles, brown eyes and hair: he was just a man. No trace of the monster he had really been.

Pip returned to her search and Ravi to his, Connor joining in on his phone. It was another ten minutes until one of them spoke.

"Found something," Ravi said, "in the anonymous comments on one of these old articles. Unconfirmed rumors that, in December 2011, Child Brunswick was living in Amherst and he revealed his true identity to an unnamed female friend. She told people, and he had to be moved somewhere else and given another new identity. Lots of people complaining in the replies about *waste of taxpayers' money.*"

"Write it down," Pip said, reading through yet another article that was essentially a reworded version of the first one.

She was next to find something, reading off the screen: " 'December 2016, a man from Atlanta received a suspended jail sentence of nine months after admitting to contempt of court by publishing photos that he claimed were of Child Brunswick as an adult.' " Pip took a breath. "The claim was false and the attorney general expressed his concern, saying that the order in place is not just to protect Child Brunswick but also members of the public who might be incorrectly identified as being him and consequently placed in danger."

Not long after, Ravi got up from the bed, unbalancing Pip. He ran his fingers through her hair before going downstairs to make them all sandwiches.

"Anything new?" he asked when he returned, handing plates to Pip and Connor, two bites already missing from his own sandwich.

"Connor found something," Pip said, skimming down another page of results for the search term *Child Brunswick Fairview CT.* The first few pages of results had been articles about her from last year, the "child detective from Fairview" who'd solved the Andie Bell case.

"Yeah," Connor said, releasing his chewed-up lip to speak. "On a subreddit for a podcast that covered the case, someone in the comments said they'd heard rumors of Child Brunswick living in Scranton, Pennsylvania. Posted a few years ago."

"Scranton?" Ravi said, resettling behind his laptop. "I was just reading a news story about a man in Scranton who committed suicide after an online mob spread false rumors that he was Child Brunswick."

"Oh, he's probably who the rumors were about," Pip said, typing that into her notes and returning to her search. She was now on the ninth page of Google results, and she clicked on the link third from the top, a post on 4chan where the OP briefly outlined the case, ending with the line: *And Child Brunswick is out there right now, you might have walked past him and never knew it.*

The comments below were varied. Most contained violent threats about what they'd like to do to Child Brunswick if they ever found him. A few people posted links to articles they'd already found and read. One commenter said in response to a particularly graphic death threat: *You know he was just a small child when the murders happened, his dad forced him to help.* To which another commenter had replied: *he still should of been locked up for life, probably just as evil as his dad, bad seed and all that—it's in the blood.*

Pip was about to hit backspace out of this particular dark corner of the internet when a comment almost at the bottom of the page caught her eye. From four months ago:

Anonymous · Sat 29 Dec 11:26:53
I know where Child Brunswick is. He's in Fairveiw CT—you know that town that's been in the news a lot recently where that girl solved the old Andie Bell case

Pip's heart kicked up at the sight of it, echoing around her chest as her eyes doubled back over the reference to her. The typo in Fairview: that must be why this hadn't come up sooner in the search results.

She scrolled down to read more in the thread.

Anonymous • Sat 29 Dec 11:32:21

Where did you hear this?

Anonymous • Sat 29 Dec 11:37:35

My friend's cousin is in prison. At the Osborn Correctional Institute. Apparently his new cellmate is from that town and says he knows exactly who Child Brunswick is. Said they used to be friends and CB told him his secret a couple years ago

Anonymous • Sat 29 Dec 11:39:43

Really? :)

Pip's breath shortened, barely reaching her throat anymore. She tensed and Ravi felt it, his dark eyes falling on her. Connor started to speak from the other side of the room and Pip shushed him so she could think.

Osborn Correctional Institute.

Pip knew someone at that prison. That was where Howie Bowers had been sent after pleading guilty to his drug-related charges. He started his sentence in early December. This comment *had* to be about him.

Which meant Howie Bowers knew exactly who Child Brunswick was. And that meant . . . wait . . . Pip's mind stalled, peeling back the months, shedding them, searching for a hidden memory.

She closed her eyes. Focused.

And she found it.

"Shit." She let the computer slide from her lap as she stood up, darting toward the desk and her phone lying on it.

"What?" Connor asked.

"Shit, shit, shit," she muttered, unlocking her phone and thumbing into her photo library. She swiped down to scroll it back, through April, and March, and Josh's birthday, and all the haircut photos Cara had needed her advice on, and back through January and the Reynoldses' New Year's Eve party, and Christmas, and New York with her friends to see the lights, and her first dinner out with Ravi, and November, and screenshots of the first articles about her, and pictures from her three-day stay in the hospital, and the photos she'd taken of Andie Bell's planner when she and Ravi broke into the Bell house and, oh, hey, she'd never noticed Jamie's name scribbled there in Andie's handwriting. Back even farther, and then she stopped.

October 2. The collection of photos she'd used as leverage to get Howie Bowers to talk to her last year. The photos he'd made her delete and she later restored, just in case. A younger Robin Caine seen handing over money to Howie in exchange for a paper bag. But that wasn't it. It was the photos she'd taken just minutes before those.

Howie Bowers standing against the fence. Someone walking out of the shadows to meet him. Someone who handed over an envelope of money, but he wasn't buying anything. In a beige coat and shorter brown hair than he had now. Cheeks flushed.

Stanley Forbes.

And though the figures in her photos were static, unmoving, their mouths were open and Pip could almost recall the conversation she'd overheard seven months ago.

"This is the last time, do you hear me?" Stanley had spat. *"You can't keep asking for more; I don't have it."*

And Howie's response had been almost too quiet to hear, but Pip could have sworn it was something like: *"But if you don't pay me, I will tell."*

Stanley had glared at him, replying: *"I don't think you would dare."*

Pip had captured that very moment here, Stanley's eyes filled with desperation and anger, closing in on Howie.

And now she knew why.

Ravi and Connor were both watching her silently as she glanced up.

"And?" Ravi asked.

"I know who Child Brunswick is," she said. "He's Stanley Forbes."

THIRTY-EIGHT

They sat there, silent. And Pip could hear something hiding beneath the silence, an imperceptible hum in her ears.

Nothing they'd found could disprove it.

Stanley mentioned being twenty-five in an article about house prices four years ago for the *Fairview Mail,* placing him right within the correct age range. He didn't seem to have any personal social media profiles, which ticked another box. And something else Pip recalled, from last Sunday morning:

"He doesn't always recognize his own name. I said 'Stanley' last week and he didn't react. His colleague says he does it all the time, has selective hearing. But maybe it's because he hasn't had this name long, not as long as he lived with his original name."

And they'd agreed; there were too many signs, too many coincidences for it not to be true. Stanley Forbes was Child Brunswick. He'd told his friend Howie Bowers, who then turned on him and used the secret to extort money from him. Howie told his new cellmate, who told his cousin, who told his friend, who then put the rumor on the internet. And that's how Layla Mead, whoever she was, whatever she wanted, found out that Child Brunswick was living in Fairview.

"So what does this mean?" Connor said, opening a tear through the thickening silence.

"If Layla had narrowed her Child Brunswick suspects down to two," Ravi said, talking with his fingers, "and sent Jamie to confront them both that night, that means Stanley was the one Jamie met at the farmhouse where he disappeared. Meaning . . ."

"Meaning Stanley knows what happened to Jamie. He's the one who did it," Pip said.

"But why is Jamie involved in all of this?" Connor asked. "This is crazy."

"We don't know, and right now it's not important." Pip stood, and the fizzing nervous energy dripped down into her legs. "What's important is finding Jamie, and Stanley Forbes is how we do that."

"What's the plan?" Ravi said, standing too, the bones in his knees cracking.

"Should we call the police?" Connor also stood up.

"I don't trust them," Pip said. And she never would again, not after all of this, not after Max. They didn't get to be the only ones who decided right or wrong. "We need to get into Stanley's house," she said. "If he took Jamie, or"—she glanced at Connor—"or hurt him, the clues to where Jamie is will be in that house. We need to get Stanley out so we can get in. Tonight."

"How?" Connor asked.

And the idea was already there, ready, like it had only been waiting for Pip to find her way. "*We* are going to be Layla Mead," she said. "I have another SIM card I can put in my phone, so Stanley won't recognize my number. We text him, as Layla, telling him to meet us at the farmhouse later tonight. Just like she must have messaged him last week, but instead it was Jamie he saw there. I'm sure Stanley wants the chance to meet the real Layla, to find out who knows his identity and what she wants. He'll come. I know he will."

"You're gonna need your own Andie Bell burner phone one of these days," Ravi said. "OK, lure him out to the farmhouse and then we all break in while he's gone, look for anything that leads us to Jamie."

Connor was nodding along.

"No," Pip said, stalling them, drawing their attention back to her. "Not all of us. One person needs to run lead on the distraction at the farmhouse, keep Stanley out long enough to give the others a chance to look. Let them know when he's on the way back." She met Ravi's eyes. "That will be me."

"Pip—" he began.

"Yes," she cut across him. "I will be lookout at the farmhouse, and you two will be the ones to go to Stanley's house. He's two doors down from Ant on Acres End, right?" She turned the question to Connor.

"Yeah, I know where he lives."

"Pip," Ravi said again.

"My mom will be home soon." She closed her fingers around Ravi's arm. "So you need to go. I'll tell my parents I'm going to yours for the evening. Let's all meet halfway down Weevil at nine, give us time to send the message and get ready."

"OK." Connor blinked pointedly at her, then stepped out of the room.

"Don't tell your mom," Pip called after him. "Not yet. We keep this a closed circle, just the three of us."

"Got it." He took another step. "Come on Ravi."

"Er, just give me two seconds." Ravi nodded his chin up at Connor, signaling for him to continue down the hall.

"What?" Pip looked at Ravi as he stepped in close, his breath in her hair.

"What are you doing?" he said, gently, flicking his gaze between her eyes. "Why are you volunteering for lookout duty? I'll do it. You should be the one who goes into Stanley's house."

"No, I shouldn't," she said, and her cheeks felt warm, standing this close to him. "Connor needs to be there, it's his brother. But so do you. Your second chance, remember?" She brushed away a strand of hair caught in Ravi's eyelashes, and he held her hand, pressing it against his face. "It should be you. You find him, Ravi. You find Jamie, OK?"

He smiled at her, interlocking his fingers with hers for a long moment, outside of time. "Are you sure? You'll be on your own—"

"I'll be fine," she said. "I'm just the lookout."

"OK." He dropped their hands and pressed his forehead against hers. "We're going to find him," he whispered. "It's going to be OK."

And Pip, for a moment, dared to believe him.

It's Layla.

Meet me at the farmhouse at 11

:)

Read 10:18 PM

I'll be there.

THIRTY-NINE

Backlit by the moon, the abandoned farmhouse glowed silver around its ragged edges, the light piercing its cracks and crevices and the holes upstairs where the windows once were.

Pip stood about sixty feet back from the house, hidden inside a small huddle of trees on the other side of the road. She watched the old building, trying not to flinch when the wind hissed through the leaves, her mind creating words out of the voiceless sounds.

Her phone lit up, vibrating in her hand, Ravi's name on the screen.

"Yeah?" she said quietly as she picked up.

"We're parked down the street," Ravi said in a hushed tone. "Stanley just walked out the front door. He's getting in his car." Pip listened as Ravi moved his mouth away from the phone, whispering unheard things to Connor beside him. "OK, he just drove past. He's on his way to you."

"Got it," she said, her fingers tensing around the phone. "You two get inside as fast as you can."

"On our way," Ravi replied over the sound of a car door quietly closing.

Pip listened to his and Connor's feet on the sidewalk, up the front path, her heart beating in time with their hurried steps.

"No, there's no spare key under the mat," Ravi said, to both her and Connor. "Let's go round the back, before anyone sees us."

Ravi's breath crackled down the line as he and Connor circled the small house, two miles away from her but under the very same moon.

A rattling sound.

"Back door's locked," Pip heard Connor say, faintly.

"Yeah, but the lock's right there by the handle," said Ravi. "If I break the window, I can reach in and unlock it."

"Do it quietly," said Pip.

Rustles and grunts down the phone as Ravi removed his jacket and wrapped it around his fist. She heard a thump, and then another, followed by the pitter-patter of broken glass.

"Don't cut yourself," Connor said.

Pip listened to Ravi's heavy breath as he strained.

A click.

A creaking sound.

"OK, we're in," he whispered.

She heard one of them crunching over the fallen glass as they stepped inside—and that's when two yellow eyes blinked open into the night at her end. Headlights, growing as they sped along Old Farm Road toward her.

"He's here." Pip lowered her voice below the wind as a black car turned up Sycamore Road, wheels churning against the gravel until the car ground to a halt off the side of the road. Pip had left hers farther up Old Farm Road so Stanley wouldn't see it.

"Stay low," Ravi told her.

The car door swung open and Stanley Forbes stepped out, his white shirt clawing the darkness away. His brown hair fell unkempt into his face, hiding it in shadows as he shut the door and turned toward the glowing farmhouse.

"OK, he's in," Pip said, as Stanley entered through the gaping front entrance and stepped into the darkness beyond.

"We're in the kitchen," Ravi said. "It's dark."

Pip held the phone closer to her mouth. "Ravi, don't let Connor hear this, but if you find anything of Jamie's, his phone, his clothes, don't touch them yet. Those are evidence, if this doesn't go the way we want it to."

"Got it," he said, and then he sniffed loudly or gasped and Pip couldn't tell which.

"Ravi?" she said. "Ravi, what's wrong?"

"Fuck," Connor hissed.

"Someone's here," Ravi said, his breath quickening. "We can hear a voice. There's someone here."

"What?" Pip said, fear rising up her throat, pulling it closed.

And then, through the phone and through Ravi's panicked breaths, Pip heard Connor shout.

"Jamie. It's Jamie!"

"Connor, wait, don't run!" Ravi shouted after him, the phone lowering away from his voice.

Just rustling.

And running.

"Ravi?" Pip hissed.

A muffled voice.

A loud thump.

"Jamie! Jamie, it's me, it's Connor! I'm here!"

The phone crackled and Ravi's breath returned.

"What's going on?" Pip said.

"He's here, Pip," Ravi said, his voice shaking as Connor shouted in the background. "Jamie's here. He's OK. He's alive."

"He's alive?" she said, the words not quite clicking in her head.

And beneath Connor's shouts, now breaking up into frantic sobs, Pip could hear the faint edges of a muffled voice. Jamie's voice.

"Oh my God, he's alive," she said, the words cracking in half in her throat as she stepped back against a tree. "He's alive," she said, just to hear it again. Tears stung at her eyes, so she closed them. And she thought those words, harder than she'd ever thought anything in her life: *Thank you, thank you, thank you.*

"Pip?"

"Is he OK?" she asked, wiping her eyes on her sleeve.

"We can't get to him," Ravi said. "He's locked in a room, the downstairs bathroom, I think. It's locked and there's a padlocked chain outside too. But he sounds OK."

"I thought you were dead," Connor was crying. "We're here, we're going to get you out!"

Jamie's voice rose, but Pip couldn't make out the words.

"What's Jamie saying?" she said, angling to watch the farmhouse again.

"He's saying . . ." Ravi paused, listening. "He's saying that we need to leave. We need to leave because he's made a deal."

"What?"

"I'm not going anywhere without you!" Connor shouted.

But something in the darkness pulled Pip's attention away from the phone. Stanley was reemerging from the shadows, walking back down the hallway toward the outside.

"He's leaving," Pip hissed. "Stanley's leaving."

"Fuck," Ravi said. "Text him as Layla, tell him to wait."

But Stanley had already crossed the rotted threshold, turning back to his car.

"It's too late," Pip said, blood rushing through her ears as she made the decision. "I'll distract him. You get Jamie out now, get him somewhere safe."

"No, Pip—"

But the phone was in her hand by her side now, her thumb on the red button as she ran out from behind the trees and across the road, scattering gravel around her feet. Onto grass and Stanley finally looked up, catching her movement in the moonlight.

He stopped.

Pip slowed, walking up to him just outside the gaping front door.

Stanley's eyes were narrowed, trying to cut through the darkness.

"Hello?" he said, blindly.

And when Pip was near enough for him to see, his face crumpled, lines crawling eye to eye.

"No," he said, his voice breathy and raw. "No, no, no. Pip, it's you?" He stepped back. "You're Layla?"

FORTY

Pip shook her head.

"I'm not Layla," she said, the words dented by the fast beating of her heart. "I sent that text to you tonight, but I'm not her. I don't know who she is."

Stanley's face reshaped in the shadows, but all Pip could really see were the whites of his eyes and the white of his shirt.

"D-d-do you . . . ," he stuttered, voice almost failing him. "Do you know . . . ?"

"Who you are?" Pip said gently. "Yeah, I know."

His breath shuddered, his head dropping to his chest. "Oh," he said, eyes unable to meet hers.

"Can we go inside and talk?" Pip nodded to the entrance. How long would Ravi and Connor need to break open the chain and the door and get Jamie out? At least ten minutes, she thought.

"OK," Stanley said in barely more than a whisper.

Pip went first, watching over her shoulder as Stanley followed her along the dark corridor, his eyes down and defeated. In the living room, Pip crossed through the wrappers and beer bottles over to the wooden sideboard. The top drawer was open and the large flashlight Robin and his friends used was propped up against it. Pip reached for it, glancing up at the dark room filled with nightmare silhouettes,

Stanley lost among them. She flicked the flashlight on, and everything grew edges and color.

Stanley screwed his eyes against the light.

"What do you want?" he asked, his hands fiddling nervously. "I can pay you, once a month. I don't earn a lot, the town paper is mostly voluntary, but I have another job, at the gas station. I can make it work."

"Pay me?" Pip said.

"T-to not tell anyone," he said. "To keep my secret."

"Stanley, I'm not here to blackmail you. I won't tell anyone who you are, I promise."

Confusion crossed his eyes. "But then . . . what do you want?"

"I just wanted to save Jamie Reynolds." She held up her hands. "That's all I'm here for."

"He's OK," Stanley sniffed. "I kept telling you he's OK."

"Did you hurt him?"

The sheen over Stanley's brown eyes hardened into something like anger.

"Did *I* hurt *him*?" he said, voice louder now. "Of course I didn't hurt him. He tried to kill me."

"What?" Pip's breath stalled. "What happened?"

"What happened is that this woman, Layla Mead, started talking to me through the *Fairview Mail*'s Facebook page," Stanley said, standing against the far wall. "We eventually exchanged numbers and started texting. For weeks. I liked her . . . at least, I thought I liked her. And last Friday, she messaged me late, asking me to meet her here." He paused to glance around at the old, peeling walls. "I arrived, but she wasn't here. I waited for ten minutes, outside the door. And then someone turned up: Jamie Reynolds. And he looked strange, panting like he'd just been running. He came up to me, and the first thing he said was 'Child Brunswick.' " Stanley broke into a small, crackling cough. "And obviously I was in shock, I've been living here over eight years, and no one has ever known, except . . ."

"Except Howie Bowers?" Pip offered.

"Yeah, except him." Stanley sniffed. "I thought he was my friend, that I could trust him. Same thing I thought about Layla. So, anyway, I start to panic, and then the next thing I know, Jamie lunges at me with a knife. I managed to get out of the way and knock the knife out of his hands. And then we were fighting, out by those trees beside the house, and I'm saying, 'Please, please don't kill me.' And as we're fighting, I push Jamie off, into one of the trees, and he hits his head, falls to the ground. I think he lost consciousness for a few seconds and after that he seemed a little dazed, concussed maybe.

"And then . . . I didn't know what to do. I knew if I called the police and told them someone had just tried to kill me because they knew my identity, that was it. I'd have to go. A new town, a new name, a new life. And I didn't want to go. This is my home. I like my life here. I have friends now. I never had friends before, ever. And living here, being Stanley Forbes, it's the first time I've been almost happy. I couldn't start over again somewhere new as a new person, it would kill me. I've already done that once before, when I was twenty-one and told the girl I loved who I was. She called the police on me and they moved me here, gave me this name. I couldn't go through that, starting everything again. I just needed time to think about what to do. I was never going to hurt him."

He looked up at Pip, his eyes shining with tears, straining like he was willing her to believe him. "I helped Jamie up and led him to my car. He seemed tired, dazed still. So I said I was taking him to the hospital. I took his phone from him and turned it off, in case he tried to call anyone. Then I drove back to my house and helped him inside. I took him to the downstairs bathroom—it's the only room with a lock on the outside. I . . . I didn't want him to get out. I was scared he might try to kill me again."

Pip nodded and Stanley continued.

"I just needed time to think about what I could do to fix the situation. Jamie was saying sorry through the door and asking me to let him out, that he just wanted to go home, but I needed to think. I panicked that someone might trace where he was from his phone, so I smashed it with a hammer. After a few hours, I put a chain across the door handle and the pipe outside the wall so I could open the door a little without Jamie being able to get out. I passed him a sleeping bag and some cushions, some food, and a cup so he could fill it up with water from the sink. Told him I needed to think and shut him in again. I didn't sleep at all that night, thinking. I still thought Jamie *was* Layla, that he'd spoken to me for weeks as her so he could lure me into a trap and kill me. I couldn't let him go in case he tried to kill me again, or told everyone who I was. And I couldn't call the police. It was impossible.

"The next day, I had to go to work at the gas station; if I don't turn up or I call in sick, my parole officer asks questions. I couldn't raise suspicions. I got home that evening and I still had no idea what to do. I made dinner and opened the door to pass it through to Jamie, and that's when we started talking. He said he had no idea what Child Brunswick even meant. He'd only done what he did because a girl called Layla Mead told him to. The same Layla I'd been speaking to. He fell for her hard. She gave him all the same lines as she did to me: that she had a controlling father who wouldn't let her out much, and she had an inoperable brain tumor." He sniffed. "Jamie said it went further with him, though. She told him there was a clinical trial her dad wouldn't let her participate in and she had no way of paying for it and would die if she didn't. Jamie was desperate to save her, thought he loved her, so he gave her twelve hundred dollars in cash for the trial, said he had to borrow most of it. Layla instructed him to leave the money by a gravestone in the churchyard, that she would collect it later when she could get away from her dad. And she made him do other things too: break into someone's house and steal a watch that had belonged to her dead mother, because her dad had given it to the Salvation Army and someone else had bought it. Told Jamie to go beat up someone on his birthday night because this guy was trying to make sure she wouldn't get into the clinical trial that would save her life. Jamie fell for it all."

"And Layla sent him on that Friday night?"

Stanley nodded. "Jamie said he found out Layla had been catfishing him, using someone else's photos. He called her right away and she told him she had to use fake photos because she had a stalker. But that everything else was real, just not the pictures.

"Then she told him that her stalker had just messaged her, threatening to kill her tonight because he'd found out about her and Jamie being together. She told Jamie she didn't know who her stalker was, but she'd narrowed it down to two men, and she was sure they'd go through with the threat. She said she would message them both and set up a meeting in a remote place, and then she asked Jamie to kill her stalker, before he killed her. She told him to say the words 'Child Brunswick' to both men, and that her stalker would know what they meant, that he would be the one to react.

"Jamie told her he wouldn't do it, at first. But she convinced him. In his mind it was either he do this or lose Layla forever, and it would be his fault. But he says at the moment he attacked me, he didn't want to do it. Said he was actually relieved when I knocked the knife out of his hands."

And Pip could see it all, played the scene through in her mind. "So,

Jamie has spoken to Layla on the phone?" she asked. "She's definitely a woman?"

"Yes," Stanley said. "But I still didn't entirely trust him. I thought he still might be Layla and was lying to me so I'd let him out, and then he'd either kill me or tell. So after this conversation with him—we talked most of Saturday night—we made a deal. We would work together to try to find out who Layla really was, if she wasn't Jamie and she did really exist. And when—*if*—we found her, I would offer Layla money to keep my secret. And Jamie would keep my secret in exchange for me not telling the police he had attacked me. We agreed Jamie would stay in the bathroom until we'd found Layla and I knew I could trust him. It's hard for me to trust people.

"And then the next morning, when I'm at the *Fairview Mail* office, you come to see me about Jamie and I see all the Missing posters up around town. So then I knew we had to find Layla quickly and work out a cover story of where Jamie had been, before you got too close. That's what I was doing at the church that day, I was looking for Hillary F. Weiseman's grave too, to see if it led me to Layla. I thought it would take us only a day or two, and everything would be fine, but we still don't know who she is. I've listened to your episodes and know Layla messaged you. I knew then that it couldn't be Jamie, that he was telling me the truth."

"I haven't worked out who she is either," Pip said. "Or why she's done this."

"I know why. She wants me dead," Stanley said, wiping one eye. "A lot of people want me dead. I've lived every day looking over my shoulder, waiting for something like this to happen. I just want to live. A quiet life, maybe do some good with it. And I know I'm not good, I haven't been. Like the things I said about Sal Singh, the way I treated his family. When it was all happening, here where I lived, I looked at what Sal had done, what I thought he'd done, and I saw my dad. I saw a monster like him. And, I don't know, it seemed a chance to make amends somehow. I was wrong; I was horribly wrong." Stanley wiped the other eye. "I know it's not an excuse, but I haven't grown up in the best places, around the best people. I learned everything from them, but I'm trying to unlearn all those things, those views, those ideas. Trying to be a better person. Because the worst thing I could be is anything like my dad. But people think I'm exactly like him, and I've always been terrified that they're right."

"You aren't like him," Pip said, taking a step forward. "You were just a child. Your father made you do those things. It wasn't your fault."

"I could have told someone. I could have refused to help him." Stanley pulled at the skin on his knuckles. "He probably would have killed me, but at least those kids would have lived. And they would have made better lives than I've made of mine."

"It's not over, Stanley," Pip said. "We can work together, find out who Layla is. Offer her money or whatever she wants. I won't tell anyone who you are. Jamie won't, either. You can stay here, in this life."

A small glimmer of hope flashed across Stanley's eyes.

"Jamie is probably telling Ravi and Connor what happened right now and then—"

"Wait, what?" Stanley said, and in one blink, the hope was all gone. "Ravi and Connor are in my house right now?"

"Um"—she swallowed—"yes. Sorry."

"Did they break a window?"

The answer was written on Pip's silent face.

Stanley's head dropped between his shoulders and he breathed out all his air in one go. "Then it's already over. The windows are fitted with a silent alarm that alerts the local police station. They'll be there in fifteen minutes." He drew one hand up, holding his face before it fell any further. "It's over. Stanley Forbes is finished. Gone."

Pip's words staled in her mouth. "I'm so sorry," she said. "I didn't know; I was just trying to find Jamie."

He looked up at her, attempted a weak smile. "It's OK," he said quietly. "I never really deserved this life anyway. This town was always too good for me."

"I don—" But the word never made it out of her mouth, crashing instead against her gritted teeth. She'd heard a noise, nearby. The sound of shuffling footsteps.

Stanley must have heard it too. He turned, walking backward toward Pip.

"Hello?" a voice called down the hall.

Pip swallowed, forcing it down her throat. "Hello," she replied as whoever it was approached. They were just a shadow among shadows until they walked into the circle of light given off by the flashlight.

It was Charlie Green in a zipped-up jacket, a light smile on his face as his gaze landed on Pip.

"Ah, I thought it must be you," he said. "I saw your car parked on the road and then I saw the light on in here and thought I should check. Are you all right?" he asked, eyes dropping to Stanley for just a moment before flicking back.

"Oh yes." Pip smiled. "Yes, we're all fine here. Just talking."

"OK, good," Charlie said with an outward breath. "Actually, Pip, could I borrow your phone quickly? Mine's dead and I need to message Flora something."

"Oh yeah," she said. "Yeah, sure." She pulled her phone out of her jacket pocket, unlocked it, and walked the few steps over to Charlie, offering the phone to him on her outstretched hand.

He picked it up, his fingers scratching lightly against her palm.

"Thank you," he said, looking down at the screen as Pip walked back to where she'd been, beside Stanley. Charlie's grip tightened around the phone. He lowered it, slipped it into his front pocket and pushed it down.

Pip watched him do it and she didn't understand, she didn't understand at all, and she couldn't hear her thoughts because her heart was too loud.

"Yours too," Charlie said, turning to Stanley.

"What?" Stanley said.

"Your phone," Charlie said calmly. "Slide it over to me, now."

"I d-don't—" Stanley stuttered.

Charlie's jacket rustled as he swung one hand behind him, tensing his mouth into a sharp line, his lips disappearing. And when he brought the hand back out, there was something in it.

Something dark and pointed. Something he held up in his trembling grip and pointed at Stanley.

It was a gun.

"Slide your phone over to me, now."

FORTY-ONE

The phone scraped against the old floorboards as it skittered past the wrappers and beer bottles, spinning as it came to rest near Charlie's feet.

The gun was still in his right hand, pointed shakily at Stanley.

He took a step forward, and Pip thought he was going to pick the phone up, but he didn't. He raised his foot and brought the heel of his boot down hard, shattering the screen. The light inside the phone blinked out and died as Pip flinched from the sudden sound, her eyes fixed on the gun.

"Charlie . . . what are you doing?" she said, her voice shaking like his hand.

"Come on, Pip," he said with a sniff, eyes following the line of the gun. "You've worked it out by now."

"You're Layla Mead."

"I'm Layla Mead," Charlie repeated, a look on his face that was either a grimace or a jittery smile, Pip couldn't tell which. "Can't take all the credit, though. Flora did the voice when I needed her to."

"Why?" Pip said, and her heart was so fast it was like one held note.

Charlie's mouth twitched with his answer, gaze darting between her and Stanley. But the gun never moved to follow his eyes. "The surname is Flora's too. You want to know what mine used to be? Nowell. Charlie Nowell."

Pip heard the intake of Stanley's breath, saw the abject look in his eyes.

"No," he said quietly, barely audible. But Charlie heard him.

"Yes," he said. "Little Emily Nowell, the final victim of the Monster of Rochester and his son. She was my sister, my twin sister. Do you remember me now?" he shouted at Stanley, jerking the gun. "Do you remember my face? I never remembered yours, and I hated myself for it."

"I'm sorry. I'm so sorry," Stanley said.

"Don't give me that," Charlie screamed, the tendons sticking up like tree roots on his reddening neck. "I was listening to you talking, giving her your sob story." He indicated his head at Pip. "You want to know what he did?" he asked her, but it wasn't a question. "I was eight years old, out in the playground with my sister, Emily. My mom was at the far end, talking to the other parents. I was teaching Emily how to use the big swings when this boy comes up to us and asks if we want to play hide-and-seek. We say yes, of course, because he's slightly older and, ah, isn't that just the best thing when you're a kid." Charlie's hand danced as he spoke, the gun shifting around with it. "The boy tells me to count first, that he and Emily will go hide. So I do. I go to the slide and cover my eyes and count to sixty. No peeking, no cheating. And when I'm done, I can't find them anywhere. My mom can't find them anywhere. But they find Emily three weeks later, mutilated and burned." Charlie blinked, so hard the tears fell from his eyes straight to his collar, leaving his face untouched. "I covered my eyes and counted slowly to sixty while you abducted my sister."

"I'm sorry," Stanley cried, his hands up, fingers splayed. "I'm so sorry. I think about her the most, your sister, I—"

"Don't you dare!" Charlie shouted, spit foaming at the edges of his mouth. "Get her out of your ugly head! You were the one who chose her, not your dad. It was you! You picked her! You helped abduct six kids knowing exactly what would happen to them; you even helped him do it. But, oh, the government just hands you a brand-new shiny life, wipes all of that away. You want to know what my life has been like?" His breath growled in his throat. "Three months after they found Emily's body, my dad hanged himself. I was the one who found him, after school. My mother couldn't cope and turned to alcohol and drugs to numb everything out. I almost starved. Within a year I was removed from her care and sent from foster family to foster family. Some were kind to me, some weren't. By seventeen, I was living on the streets. But I turned my life around, and there was only one thing that got me through all that. Neither of you deserved to live after what you did. Someone already got to your father, but they let you walk free. But I knew that one day I would find you and I would be the one to kill you, Child Brunswick."

"Charlie, please just put the gun down and we—" Pip said.

"No." Charlie didn't look at her. "I've waited nineteen years for this moment. I bought this gun nine years ago knowing that one day I'd use it to kill you. I've been ready; I've been waiting. I've followed every single tip and rumor about you on the internet. I've lived in ten different towns in the last seven years, looking for you. And a new version of Layla Mead came with me to each one, finding the men who fit your age and description, getting close to them until one might confide in me who they really were. But you weren't in any of those other towns. You were here. And now I've found you. I'm glad that Jamie failed. It's right that I do it. This is how it's meant to be."

Pip watched Charlie's finger flexing and tensing on the trigger. "Wait!" she shouted. *Just buy some time, keep him talking.* If the police were at Stanley's house now, with Ravi and Connor and Jamie, maybe Ravi would send them here. *Please, Ravi, send them here.* "What about Jamie?" she asked quickly. "Why get him involved?"

Charlie licked his lips. "The opportunity presented itself. I started talking to Jamie because he fit the Child Brunswick profile. Then I found out he'd lied about his age, and I discounted him. But he was so eager. He'd fallen for Layla in a way none of the others have before, kept messaging saying he'd do anything for her. And it got me thinking"—he sniffed—"my whole life, I accepted that I would be the one to kill Child Brunswick and most likely forfeit my life in return, end up with the life sentence *he* should have had. But Jamie made me think: if I just wanted Child Brunswick dead, what if I could get someone else to do it for me? And then I could go on and have a life afterward, me and Flora. She really pushed for that, for a chance for us to stay together. She's known I've had to do this since we met at eighteen; she's followed me around the country looking for *him,* helping me. I owed her to at least try.

"So I started to test Jamie, see what I could get him to do. Turns out it was a lot," he said. "Jamie withdrew twelve hundred dollars in cash and left it in the graveyard at night for Layla. He beat up a stranger, though he'd never been in a fight in his life before. For Layla. I invented some story to make him break into my own house in the middle of the night and steal a watch, and he did it. For Layla. I was escalating each time, and I think it would have worked, I think I could have got him to the point where he would have killed for Layla. But everything went wrong at the memorial. I guess that's what happens when you bring an entire town together on one field.

"I've run this Layla scheme nine times before. I quickly learned that it's best to use photos of a local girl, manipulate them slightly. Men were always less suspicious when they could see photos taken in places they recognized, and a face that looked vaguely familiar to them. But it backfired here, and Jamie found out Layla wasn't real. And he wasn't ready yet; I wasn't ready yet. But I had to try the plan that night, while Jamie was still under Layla's thumb.

"But I didn't know who Child Brunswick was. I'd narrowed it down to two suspects: Luke Eaton and Stanley Forbes. Both the right age, the right appearance, neither had jobs that ruled them out, neither ever mentioned any family and avoided questions about their childhood. So I had to send Jamie to both of them. I knew it had all gone wrong when I heard Jamie was missing. I suppose you killed him?" he said to Stanley.

"No," Stanley whispered.

"Jamie's alive. He's fine," Pip said.

"Really? That's good. I was feeling guilty about what might have happened to him," Charlie said. "And then of course after everything went wrong, I couldn't make any more moves to find out which one of them was Child Brunswick. But that's OK, because I knew *you* would." He turned his face, gave Pip a small smile. "I knew you would find him for me. I've been watching you, following you. Waiting for you. Pushing you in the right direction when you needed help. And you did it," he said, steadying the gun. "You found him for me, Pip. Thank you."

"No," she shouted, stepping in front of Stanley with her hands up. "Please don't shoot."

"PIP, GET AWAY FROM ME!" Stanley screamed at her, pushing her back. "Don't come near me. Stay back!"

She stopped, her heart so wild and fast it felt like her ribs were caving in on her, bony fingers closing around her chest.

"Back!" Stanley screamed, tears chasing down his pale face. "It's OK, get back."

Pip did, four more steps away, turning to Charlie. "Please don't do this! Don't kill him!"

"I have to," Charlie said, narrowing his eyes along the sight of the gun. "This is exactly what we talked about, Pip. Where the justice system gets it wrong, it's down to people like you and me to step in and set things right. And it doesn't matter if people think we're good or not, because we know we're right. We're the same, you and me. You know it, deep down. You know this is right."

Pip didn't have an answer for him. Didn't know what to say other than: "PLEASE! Don't do this!" Her voice ripped at her throat, words cracking as she forced them out. "This isn't right! He was just a child. A child scared of his own father. It's not his fault. He didn't kill your sister!"

"Yes he did!"

"It's all right, Pip," Stanley said to her, barely able to talk because he was shaking so hard. He held one trembling hand up and out, to comfort her, to keep her back. "It's OK."

"No, please!" she screamed, folding in on herself. "Charlie, please don't do this. I'm begging you. Please! Don't!"

Charlie's eyes twitched.

"Please!"

His gaze shifted from Stanley to her.

"I'm begging you!"

He gritted his teeth.

"Please!" she cried.

Charlie looked at her, watched her crying. And then he lowered the gun.

Took two heavy breaths.

"I—I'm not sorry," he said quickly.

He lifted the gun and Stanley gasped.

Charlie fired.

The sound ripped the earth out from under Pip.

"NO!"

He fired again.

And again.

And again.

Again.

Again.

Until they were just empty clicks.

Pip screamed, watching Stanley stagger back off his feet, falling hard against the floor.

"Stanley!" She ran to him, skidding to her knees beside him. Blood was already overflowing the wounds, sprays of red on the wall behind him. "Oh my God."

Stanley was gulping at the air, a strange whine in his throat. Eyes wide. Scared.

Pip heard a rustle behind her and whipped her head around. Charlie had lowered his arm, watching Stanley writhing on the floor. Then his eyes met Pip's. He nodded, just once, before he turned and ran out of the room, his heavy boots careening down the corridor.

"He's gone," Pip said, looking down at Stanley. And in just those few seconds, the blood had spread, seeping out until there were only small channels of white shirt between the red.

Stop the bleeding, need to stop the bleeding. She looked over him: one gunshot in his neck, one in his shoulder, one in his chest, two in his stomach, and one in his thigh.

"It's OK, Stanley," she said, pulling off her jacket. "I'm here, it's going to be OK." She tore at the seam of one sleeve, biting it until she ripped a hole and pulled it free. Where was the most blood? His leg; must have hit the artery. Pip slid the sleeve under Stanley's leg, his warm blood coating her hands. She made a knot above the wound, pulling it as tight as she could and double-knotting it to keep the material in place.

Stanley was watching her.

“It’s OK,” she said, pushing the hair back from her eyes, a smear of wet blood on her forehead. “It’s going to be OK. Help will come.”

She ripped off the other sleeve, bunched it up, and held it to the gushing wound in his neck. But there were six holes in Stanley, and she only had two hands.

He blinked slowly, his eyes slipping shut.

“Hey,” she said, grabbing his face. His eyes snapped open again. “Stanley, stay with me, keep talking to me.”

“It’s OK, Pip,” he croaked as she tore more strips of fabric from her jacket, balling them up and stuffing them against the other wounds. “This was always going to happen. I deserve it.”

“No, you don’t,” she said, pressing her hands against the hole in his chest and the hole in his neck. She could feel the pulses of blood pushing against her.

“Jack Brunswick,” he said quietly, eyes circling hers.

“What?” Pip said, pushing down as hard as she could, his blood pooling in the webs of her fingers.

“It was Jack, that was my name,” he said, with a heavy, slow blink. “Jack Brunswick. And then I was David Knight. Then Stanley Forbes.” He swallowed.

“That’s good, keep talking to me,” Pip said. “Which name did you like best?”

“Stanley.” He smiled weakly. “Silly name, and he wasn’t much, he wasn’t always good, but he was the best of them. He was trying.” There was a crackling sound from his throat; Pip felt it in her fingers. “I’m still his son, though, whatever my name is. Still that boy that did those things. Still rotten.”

“No, you aren’t,” Pip said. “You’re better than him. You are better.”

“Pip . . .”

And as she looked at him, a shadow crossed over his face, a

darkness from above, something smothering the light of the flashlight. Pip glanced up and that was when she smelled it too. Smoke. Rolling black smoke creeping out across the ceiling.

Now she could hear them too. The flames.

"He set it on fire," she said to herself, her stomach falling away from her as she watched smoke pour in from the hallway across from where the kitchen must be. And she knew, knew it would only be minutes until the whole house went up.

"I need to get you out of here," she said.

Stanley blinked silently up at her.

"Come on." Pip let go of him, pushing up to her feet. She slipped in the blood at Stanley's side, staggering over his legs. She bent down and picked up his feet, pulling him, dragging him.

Holding his shoes up by her hips, gripping his ankles, Pip twisted around, facing forward so she could see where they were going as she dragged Stanley behind her. She tried not to look back at the trail of red following him.

Out in the hall, and the room off to the right was filled with fire: an angry, roaring vortex up every wall and across the floor, spilling through the open doorway into the narrow hallway. Flames were licking along the old, peeling wallpaper. And above her head, the exposed insulation in the ceiling was burning, dropping ash down on them.

The smoke was getting lower and darker. Pip coughed, breathing it in. And the world started spinning around her.

"It's going to be OK, Stanley," she called over her shoulder, ducking her head down, out of the smoke. "I'll get you out."

It was harder dragging him, out here on the carpet. But she dug in her heels and she pulled as hard as she could. The fire was growing on the wall beside her—hot, too hot—and it felt like her skin was blistering and her eyes were burning. She turned her face away from it and pulled.

"It's OK, Stanley!" She had to scream over the flames now.

Pip coughed with every breath. But she didn't let go of him. She held on and she pulled. And when she reached the threshold, she sucked the clean, cold outside air into her lungs, dragging Stanley out onto the grass, just as the carpet behind them started to catch.

"We're out, Stanley," Pip said, dragging him farther through the unkempt grass, away from the burning house. She bent and laid his feet down gently, turning her eyes back to the fire. Smoke was billowing out of the holes where the upstairs windows once were, blocking out the stars.

She coughed again and looked down at Stanley. The wet blood glistened in the light from the flames, and he wasn't moving. His eyes were closed.

"Stanley!" She crashed down beside him, grabbing his face again. But this time his eyes didn't open. "Stanley!" Pip lowered her ear to his nose, listening for his breath. It wasn't there. She placed her fingers on his neck, just above the gaping hole. Nothing. No pulse.

"No, Stanley, please no." Pip settled on her knees, placing the heel of one hand in the middle of his chest, right beside one of the holes. She covered her hand with the other, straightened up, and started to push down. Hard.

"Don't, Stanley. Please don't go," she said, keeping her arms straight, compressing his chest.

She counted to thirty and then pinched his nose, placed her mouth over his, and breathed into him. Once. Twice.

Returned her hands to his chest and pressed down.

She felt something give way beneath her palm, a crunching sound. One of his ribs cracking.

"Don't go, Stanley." She watched his unmoving face as she pushed all of her body weight into him. “I can save you. I promise. I can save you.”

Breathe. Breathe.

There was a flash in the corner of her eye as the flames exploded, the downstairs windows shattering outward as whirls of fire and smoke climbed up and out, engulfing the outside of the farmhouse. It was incredibly hot, even twenty feet away, and there was a line of sweat running down Pip’s temple as she pushed. Or was that Stanley’s blood?

Another crack under her hand. Another rib gone.

Breathe. Breathe.

“Come back, Stanley. Please. I’m begging you.”

Her arms were aching already, but she kept going. Push and breathe. She didn’t know for how long; time didn’t seem to exist anymore. Just her and the crackling heat of the flames and Stanley.

one	seven	fourteen	twenty-one	twenty-eight
two	eight	fifteen	twenty-two	twenty-nine
three	nine	sixteen	twenty-three	thirty
four	ten	seventeen	twenty-four	*breathe*
five	eleven	eighteen	twenty-five	*breathe*
six	twelve	nineteen	twenty-six	
	thirteen	twenty	twenty-seven	

The first thing she heard was the siren.

Thirty and breathe. Breathe.

And then the slamming of car doors, voices shouting that she couldn’t understand because words didn’t exist here. Only *one* to *thirty* and *breathe.*

Someone’s hand was on her shoulder, but she shrugged it off. It was Soraya. Daniel da Silva stood over them, the fire mirrored back in his horrified eyes. And as he watched, there was a thunderous, end-of-the-world crash as the roof collapsed, caving into the flames.

"Pip, let me take over," Soraya said gently. "You're tired."

"No!" Pip shouted, breathless, sweat falling into her open mouth. "I can keep going. I can do this. I can save him. He's going to be OK."

"Paramedics and the fire department will be here any minute," Soraya said, trying to catch Pip's eye. "Pip, what happened?"

"Charlie Green," she gasped between presses. "Charlie Green, from number twenty-two Thatcher Road. He shot Stanley. Call Hawkins."

Daniel stepped back to speak into his radio.

"Hawkins is already on his way," Soraya said. "Ravi told us where to find you. Jamie Reynolds is safe."

"I know."

"Are you hurt?"

"No."

"Let me take over."

"No."

The next siren wasn't far behind, and then two paramedics were around her in their dark uniforms and their purple-gloved hands.

One paramedic asked Soraya for Pip's name. She bent low so Pip could see her face.

"Pip, I'm Julia. You're doing really well, sweetheart. But I'm going to take over compressions from here, OK?"

Pip didn't want to; she couldn't stop. But Soraya dragged her back and she didn't have the strength to fight her and the purple-gloved hands replaced hers on Stanley's sunken chest.

Pip collapsed in the grass and watched his pale face, glowing orange from the fire.

Another siren. The fire truck pulled up to the side of the farmhouse and people peeled out of it. Was any of this real anymore?

"Is there anyone else inside?" someone was shouting down at her.

"No." But her own voice felt detached from her.

The paramedics swapped over.

Pip glanced behind her and a small crowd was there. When had that happened? People standing in coats and bathrobes, watching the scene. Other uniformed officers had arrived, helping Daniel da Silva push the onlookers back, cordon off the area.

And how long was it after that, that she heard his voice? She didn't know.

"Pip!" Ravi's voice fought over the flames to reach her. "Pip!"

She pushed up to her feet and turned, saw the horror on Ravi's face as he looked across at her. She followed his eyes down. Her white top was fully soaked through with Stanley's blood. Her hands red. Smudges up her neck and across her face.

Ravi sprinted toward her, but Daniel caught him, pushed him back.

"Let me through! I need to see her!" Ravi yelled in Daniel's face, struggling against him.

"You can't, this is an active crime scene!" Daniel shoved him back, into the growing crowd. Held his arms out to keep Ravi there.

Pip's eyes returned to Stanley. One of the paramedics had withdrawn, speaking into her radio. Pip could catch only a few words over the noise of the fire and all of that fog inside her head. "Medical control . . . twenty minutes . . . no change . . . call it . . ."

It took a moment for those words to work their way into her head and make any kind of sense.

"Wait," Pip said, the world moving too slowly around her.

The paramedic nodded to the other. She sighed quietly and pulled her hands away from Stanley's chest.

"What are you doing? Don't stop!" Pip charged forward. "He's not dead, don't stop!"

She crashed toward Stanley, lying there, still and bloodied in the grass, but Soraya caught her arm.

"No!" Pip screamed at her, but Soraya was stronger, pulling Pip into her arms and wrapping her up inside them. "Let me go! I need to—"

"He's gone," Soraya said quietly. "There's nothing we can do, Pip. He's gone."

And then things really came undone time skipping other words half heard and half understood: *coroner* and *hello can you hear me?*

Daniel is trying to talk to her and all she can do is scream at him.

"I told you! I told you someone was going to end up dead. Why didn't you listen to me?"

Someone else's arms on her. Stopping her.

Detective Hawkins is here now and where did he come from? His face doesn't move much and is he dead too, like Stanley? Now he's in the front of the car driving, and Pip, she's in the back watching the fire recede

away as they drive. Her thoughts are no longer in straight lines, they

cascade

away from her

like ash.

The police station is cold, that must be why she is shivering. A back room she hasn't seen before. And Eliza is here: "I need to take your clothes, darling."

But they won't come off when she pulls, they have to

be peeled off, the skin underneath no longer hers, streaky and pink from blood. Eliza seals the clothes and all that's left of Stanley inside a clear evidence bag. Looks at Pip. "I'm going to need your bra too."

Because she's right, that's soaked red as well.

Now Pip's wearing a new white T-shirt and gray sweatpants, but they aren't hers and whose are they, then? And *be quiet* because someone is talking to her. It's Detective Hawkins: "It's just to rule you out," he says, "to eliminate you." And she doesn't want to say but she already feels eliminated.

"Sign here."

She does.

"Just a gunpowder residue test," says a new person Pip doesn't know. And he's placing something sticky, adhesive against her hands and her fingers, sealing them away in tubes.

Another *sign here.*

"To rule you out, you understand?"

"Yes," Pip says, letting them place her fingers into the soft ink pad and against the paper. Thumb, forefinger, middle, the swirling lines of her fingerprints like little galaxies of their own.

"She's in shock," she hears someone say.

"I'm fine."

A different room and Pip is sitting alone, a clear plastic cup of water between her hands, but it ripples and shakes, warning her of an earthquake. Wait . . . we don't get those here. But the earthquake comes all the same because it's inside her, the shakes, and she can't hold the water without spilling.

A door slams nearby but before the sound reaches her, it has changed.

It's a gun. It fires two three six times and, oh, Hawkins is in the room again, sitting across from her, but he can't hear the gun. Only Pip can.

He asks questions.

"What happened?"

"Describe the gun."

"Do you know where Charlie Green went? He and his wife are gone. Their belongings look packed up in a hurry."

He has written it all down too. Pip has to read it, re-remember it all.

Sign at the bottom.

And after, Pip asks a question of her own: "Did you find her?"

"Find who?"

"The eight-year-old abducted from her yard?"

Hawkins nods. "Yesterday. She's fine, was with her father. Domestic dispute."

And "Oh," is all Pip can say   to that.

She's left alone again, listening to the gun no one else can hear. Until there's a soft hand on her shoulder and she flinches. An even softer voice, "Your parents are here to take you home now."

Pip's feet follow the voice dragging   the rest of her with them. Into the waiting room, too bright, and it's her dad she sees first. She can't think what to say to him or Mom but that doesn't matter because all they want to   do is   hold her.

Ravi is behind them.

Pip goes to him and his arms pull her into his chest. Warm. Safe. It's always safe here and Pip breathes out, listening to the sound of his heart. But   oh no, the gun is in there too,   hiding beneath   every beat.

Waiting for her.

It follows Pip as they leave. Sits beside her in the dark car. It tucks itself up into bed with her. Pip shakes and she blocks her ears and she tells the gun to go away.

But it won't go.

SUNDAY
16 DAYS LATER

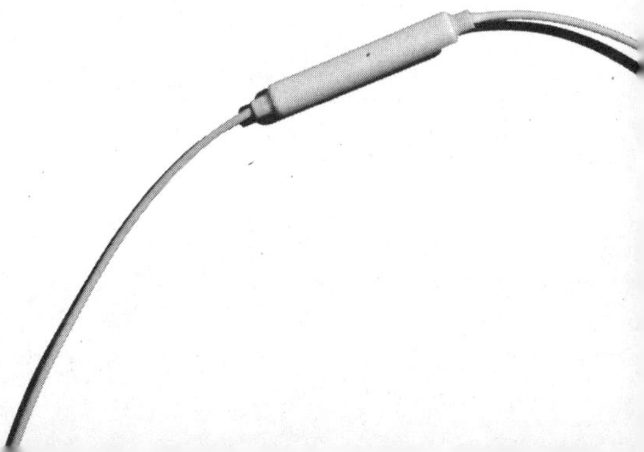

FORTY-TWO

They were dressed in black, all of them, because that's how it was supposed to be.

Ravi's fingers were entwined with hers, and if Pip held them any tighter, they would break, she was sure of it. Crack in half, like ribs.

Her parents were standing on her other side, hands clasped in front of them, eyes down, her dad breathing in time with the wind in the trees. She noticed everything like that now. On the other side were Cara and Naomi Ward, and Connor and Jamie Reynolds. Connor and Jamie were both wearing black suits that didn't quite fit, too small here, too long there, as though they'd both borrowed them from their father.

Jamie was crying, his whole body shuddering with them inside that ill-fitting suit. Face reddening as he tried to swallow the tears down, glancing across at Pip, over the coffin.

A solid pine coffin with unadorned sides measuring eighty-four inches by twenty-eight by twenty-three, with white satin lining inside. Pip had been the one to choose it. Stanley had no family, and his friends . . . they all disappeared after the story came out. All of them. No one stepped up to claim him, so Pip had, arranging the whole funeral. She'd chosen a burial, against the funeral director's *professional opinion.* Stanley died with his ankles in her hands, scared and bleeding out while a fire raged around them. She didn't think he'd want to be cremated, burned, like his father had done to those six kids.

A burial, that's what he would have wanted, Pip insisted. So they were outside, on the left-hand side of the churchyard, beyond Hillary F. Weiseman. The petals of the white roses atop his coffin shivered in the wind. It was positioned over an open grave, inside a metal frame with straps and green carpeting like fake grass, so it didn't look like exactly what it was: a hole in the ground.

Members of the police force were supposed to have been here, but Detective Hawkins had emailed Pip last night, saying he'd been advised by his supervisors that attending the funeral would be "too political." So here they were, just the eight of them, and most only here for Pip. Not for him, the one lying dead in the solid pine coffin. Except Jamie, she thought, catching his rubbed-red eyes.

The priest's collar was too tight, the flesh of his neck bunching over it as he read out the sermon. Pip looked beyond him, at the small gray headstone she'd picked out. A man with four different names, but Stanley Forbes was the one he chose, the life he'd wanted, the one who was trying. So that was the name engraved over him, forever.

STANLEY FORBES

June 7, 1990 – May 1, 2020

You Were Better

"And before we say our final prayer, Pip, you wanted to say a few words?"

The sound of her name caught her off guard and she winced, her heart spiking, and suddenly her hands were wet but it didn't feel like sweat, it was blood, it was blood, it was blood. . . .

"Pip?" Ravi whispered to her, giving her fingers a gentle squeeze. And no, there was no blood, she'd only imagined it.

"Yes," she said, coughing to clear her voice. "Yes. Um, I wanted to say thank you, everyone, for coming. And to you, Father Renton, for the service." If Ravi weren't holding her hand still, it would be shaking, fluttering on the wind. "I didn't know Stanley all that well. But I think, in the last hour of his life, I got to know who he truly was. He—"

Pip stopped. There was a sound, carrying on the breeze. A shout. It came again, louder this time. Closer.

"Murderer!"

Her eyes shot up and her chest tightened. There was a group of about fifteen people marching past the church toward them. Painted signs held up in their hands.

"You're mourning a child killer!" a man yelled.

"I—I—I . . . ," Pip stuttered, and she felt the scream again, growing in her stomach, burning her inside out.

"Keep going, Pickle." Her dad was behind her, his warm hand on her shoulder. "You're doing so well. I'll go talk to them."

The group was nearing, and Pip could recognize a few faces among them now: Leslie from the Stop & Shop, and Mary Scythe from the *Fairview Mail,* and was that . . . was that Ant's dad, Mr. Lowe, in the middle?

"Um," she said, shakily, watching her dad hurrying away up the path toward them. Cara gave her an encouraging smile, and Jamie nodded. "Um. Stanley, he . . . when he knew his own life was in danger, his first thought was to protect me and—"

"Burn in hell!"

She tightened her hands into fists. "And he faced his own death with bravery and—"

"Scum!"

She dropped Ravi's hand and she was gone.

"No, Pip!" Ravi tried to hold on to her, but she slipped out of his grasp and away, pounding up the grass. Her mom was calling her name, but that wasn't her right now. Her teeth bared as she flew down the pathway, her black dress flailing behind her knees as she took on the wind. Her eyes flickered across their signs painted in dripping red letters:

Killer Spawn

Monster of Fairview

Charlie Green = HERO

Child Brunswick Rot in Hell

Not in OUR town!

Her dad looked back and tried to catch her as she passed, but she was too fast, and that burning inside her too strong.

She collided into the group, shoving Leslie hard, her cardboard sign clattering to the ground.

"He's dead!" she screamed at them all, pushing them back. "Leave him alone, he's dead!"

"He shouldn't be buried here. This is *our* town," Mary said, pushing her sign toward Pip, blocking her sight.

"He was your friend!" Pip snatched the sign out of Mary's hands. "He was your friend!" she roared, bringing the poster board down with all her strength against her knee. It broke cleanly in two and she threw the pieces at Mary. "LEAVE HIM ALONE!"

She started toward Mr. Lowe, who flinched away from her. But she didn't make it. Her dad had grabbed her from behind, pulled her arms back. Pip reeled up against him, her feet kicking out toward them, but they were all backing away from her. Something new on their faces. Fear maybe, as she was dragged away.

Pip's eyes blurred with angry tears as she looked up, arms locked behind her, her dad's calming voice in her ear. The sky was a pale and creamy blue, pockets of soft clouds floating across. A pretty sky for today. Stanley would have liked that, she thought, as she screamed up into it.

SATURDAY
6 DAYS LATER

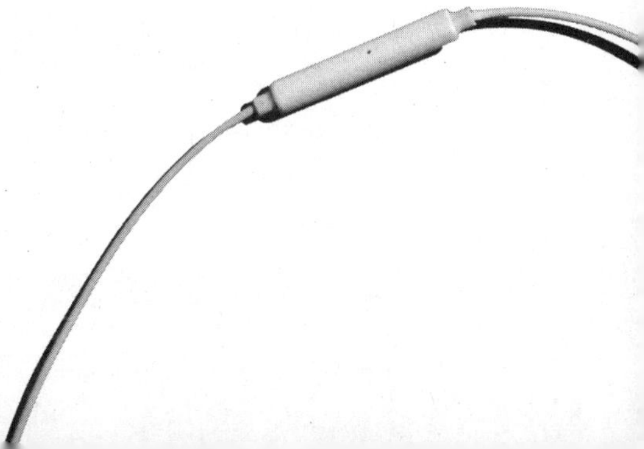

FORTY-THREE

The sun climbed up her legs in leaflike patches, reaching through the tall willow tree in the Reynoldses' yard.

The day was warm, but the stone step she sat on was cool through the back of her new jeans. Pip blinked against the shifting beams of light, watching them all.

"A get-together," Joanna Reynolds's message had said, but Jamie joked it was a *Surprise, I'm not dead* barbecue. Pip had found that funny. She hadn't found much funny the past few weeks, but that had done it.

The dads were hovering around the barbecue, and Pip could see her dad eyeing the unflipped burgers, itching to take over from Arthur Reynolds. Mohan Singh was laughing, tilting his head back to drink his beer, the sunlight making the bottle glow.

Joanna was leaning over the picnic table nearby, removing plastic wrap from the tops of bowls: pasta salad and potato salad and actual salad. Dropping serving spoons into each one. On the other side of the yard, Cara stood talking with Ravi, Connor, and Zach. Ravi was intermittently kicking a tennis ball, for Josh to chase.

Pip watched her brother, whooping as he cartwheeled after the ball. A smile on his face that was pure and unknowing. Ten years old, the same age Child Brunswick was when . . . Stanley's dying face flashed into her mind. Pip screwed her eyes shut, but that never took him away. She breathed, three deep breaths, like her mom told her to do, and reopened her eyes. She shifted her gaze and took a shaky sip of water, her hand sweating against the glass.

Nisha Singh and Pip's mom were standing with Naomi Ward, Nat da Silva, and Zoe Reynolds, words unheard passing from one to another, smiles following along behind them. It was nice to see Nat smiling, Pip thought. It changed her, somehow.

And Jamie Reynolds, he was walking toward her, wrinkling his freckled nose. He sat down on the step beside her, his knee grazing hers as he settled.

"How are you doing?" he asked, running one finger over the rim of his beer bottle.

Pip didn't answer the question. "How are you?" she said instead.

"I'm good." Jamie looked at her, a smile stretching into his pink-tinged cheeks. "Good, but . . . I can't stop thinking about him." The smile flickered out.

"I know," said Pip.

"He wasn't what people expected," Jamie said quietly. "You know, he tried to fit a whole mattress through the gap in the bathroom door so I would be comfortable. And he asked me every day what I'd like for dinner, despite being scared of me. Of what I almost did."

"You wouldn't have killed him," Pip said. "I know."

"No," Jamie sniffed, looking down at the smashed Fitbit still on his wrist. He'd said he would never take it off; he wanted it there, as a reminder. "I knew I couldn't do it, even when the knife was in my hand. And I was so scared. But that doesn't make it any better. I told the police everything. But without Stanley, they don't have enough to charge me. Doesn't feel right somehow."

"Doesn't feel right that we're both here and he's not," Pip said, her chest tightening, filling her head with the sound of cracking ribs. "We both led Charlie to him, in a way. And we're alive and he's not."

"I'm alive because of you," Jamie said, not looking at her. "You and Ravi and Connor. If Charlie had worked out that it was Stanley before that night, he might have killed me, too. I mean, he set a building on fire with you inside."

"Yeah," Pip said, the word she used when no other would fit. But she didn't agree. She didn't think Charlie had been trying to kill her; that wasn't it. He'd wanted her to get out and leave Stanley there to die.

"They're going to find him eventually," Jamie said. "Charlie Green, and Flora. They can't run forever. The police will catch them."

That's what Hawkins had said to Pip that night: *We will get him.* But one day had turned into two had turned into three weeks.

"Yeah," she said again.

"Has my mom stopped hugging you yet?" Jamie asked, trying to bring her out of her thoughts.

"Not yet," she said.

"She hasn't stopped hugging me either," he laughed.

Pip's eyes followed Joanna as she handed a plate to Arthur at the grill.

"Your dad loves you, you know," Pip said. "I know he doesn't always show it in the right way, but I saw him, the moment he thought he'd lost you forever. And he loves you, Jamie. A lot."

Jamie's eyes filled, sparkling in the dappled sunlight. "I know," he said over a new lump in his throat. He coughed it down.

"I've been thinking," Pip said, turning to face him. "All Stanley wanted was a quiet life, to learn to be better, to try to do some good with it. And he doesn't get to do that anymore. But we're still here, we're alive." She paused, meeting Jamie's eyes. "Can you promise me something? Can you promise me you'll live a good life? A full life, a happy one. Live well, and do it for him, because he can't anymore."

Jamie held her eyes, a quiver in his lower lip. "I promise," he said. "And you too?"

"I'll try." She nodded, wiping her eyes with her sleeve just as Jamie did the same. They laughed.

Jamie took a quick sip of his beer. "Starting today," he said, "I think I'm going to apply to the ambulance service, to work as a trainee paramedic."

Pip smiled at him. "That's a good start."

They watched the others for a moment, Arthur dropping a load of hot-dog buns and Josh rushing to pick them up, shouting, "Five-second rule!" Nat's laugh, high and unguarded.

"And," Jamie continued, "with the final episodes out, I guess you've already kinda told the whole world I'm in love with Nat da Silva. So I guess I should tell her myself sometime. And if she doesn't feel the same, I move on. Onward and upward. And no more strangers on the internet."

He raised his beer bottle out toward her. "Live well," he said.

Pip lifted her glass of water and clinked it against Jamie's bottle. "For him," she said.

Jamie hugged her, a quick, teetering hug, different from Connor's clumsy hugs. Then he stood up and walked across the yard to Nat's side. His eyes were different when he looked at her, fuller somehow. Brighter. A dimpled smile stretched across his face as she turned to him, the laugh still in her voice. And Pip swore, maybe just for a second, she could see the same look in Nat's eyes.

She watched the two of them joking around with Jamie's sister, and she didn't even notice Ravi walking over. Not until he sat down, hooking one of his feet under her leg.

"You OK, Sarge?" he said.

"Yeah."

"You want to come over and join everyone?"

"I'm fine here," she said.

"But everyone is—"

"I said I'm fine," Pip said, but it wasn't her saying it, not really. She sighed, looked across at him. "I'm sorry. I don't mean to snap. It's . . ."

"I know," Ravi said, closing his hand over hers, sliding his fingers in between hers in that perfect way they slotted together. They still fit. "It will get better, I promise." He pulled her in closer. "And I'm here, whenever you need me."

She didn't deserve him. Not even one little bit. "I love you," she said, looking into his dark brown eyes, filling herself with them, pushing everything else out.

"I love you too."

Pip shuffled, leaning over to rest her head on Ravi's shoulder as they watched the others. Everyone had now encircled Josh as he tried his best to teach them all how to floss, straight jerking arms and locking hips everywhere.

"Oh god, Jamie, you're so embarrassing," Connor giggled, as his brother somehow managed to hit himself in the groin, bending double. Nat and Cara clutched each other, falling to the grass with laughter.

"Look at me, I can do it!" Pip's dad was saying, because of course he was. Even Arthur Reynolds was trying, still at the grill, thinking nobody could see him.

Pip laughed, watching how ridiculous they all looked, the sound a small croak in her throat. And it was OK, to be out here on the sidelines, with Ravi. Separate. A gap between everyone and here. A barricade around her. She would join them when she was ready. But for now, she just wanted to sit, far back enough that she could see them all in one go.

* * *

It was evening. Her family had eaten too much at the Reynoldses' house and were dozing downstairs. Pip's room was dark, her face underlit by the ghostly white light of her laptop. She sat at her desk, staring at the screen. Studying for finals, that's what she'd told her parents. Because she lies now.

She finished typing in the search bar and pressed enter.

Most recent sightings of Charlie and Flora Green.

They'd been spotted nine days ago, security footage of them withdrawing money from an ATM just outside of Madison. The police had verified that one; she'd seen it on the news. But here—Pip clicked—someone had commented on an article posted to Facebook, claiming they'd seen the couple yesterday at a gas station near Wichita, driving a new car: a red Nissan Juke.

Pip ripped the top sheet from her pad of paper, screwed it up, and threw it behind her. She hunched over, checking back to the screen as she scribbled the details down on a fresh page. Returned to her search.

"We're the same, you and me. You know it, deep down," Charlie's voice intruded, speaking inside her head. And the scariest thing was, Pip didn't know if he was wrong. She couldn't say how they were different. She just knew they were. It was a feeling beyond words. Or maybe, just maybe, that feeling was only hope.

She stayed there, clicking through for hours, jumping from article to article, comment to comment. And it was with her too, of course. It always was.

The gun.

It was here now, beating within her chest, knocking against her ribs. Aiming with her eyes. It was in nightmares, and crashing pans, and heavy breaths, and dropped pencils, and thunderstorms, and closing doors, and too loud, and too quiet, and alone and not, and the ruffle of pages, and the tapping of keys and every click and every creak.

The gun was always there.

It lived inside her now.

ACKNOWLEDGMENTS

To the best agent in the world, Sam Copeland. Thank you for always being there and for sharing in all of this with me: the lows and the many highs. And for answering all my "quick questions," which are, in fact, eighteen paragraphs long.

To everyone at Delacorte Press and Random House Children's Books, thank you so much for all the incredible work you've done to help me bring this book to life. To Kelsey Horton—my superstar editor—I couldn't have done it without you! Thank you for being the most incredible cheerleader for this book and this series, and for holding my hand throughout the entire process. One of the memories I will treasure FOREVER is the moment I found out *AGGGTM* had hit the *New York Times* list while on the phone with you and Beverly. I think my exact words were "Are you sure?" repeated ten thousand times. You were, in fact, very sure. And of course, massive thanks to Beverly Horowitz for all your support and for the incredible opportunities you have given me—I will be eternally grateful. Thank you to the genius Casey Moses and Christine Blackburne for the beautiful cover again: it is perfect, and I am so happy that your incredible work is the first thing readers will see of the book. Thank you to Barbara Marcus, Emma Benshoff, Kimberly Langus, Elizabeth Ward, and Jenn Inzetta and all the publicity and marketing team. I had so much fun working on book one with you guys, and I'm so excited to see all the amazing things you have planned for *GG, BB.* A big thank you to Nick Martorelli and the audiobook team: I'm still in awe of your work and wish the audiobook could follow me around like a soundtrack to my life. And a special thank-you to Priscilla Coleman for the incredible courtroom sketch in this book!

A huge thank-you to everyone who helped make *A Good Girl's Guide to Murder* a success. It's because of all of you that I have been able to continue Pip's story. To the bloggers and reviewers who shouted about the book online, I can never thank you enough for everything you've done for me. Thank you to the booksellers around the country for your amazing support and enthusiasm for the first book; it has truly been a dream come true to be able to walk into a bookstore and see my own book on the shelves or tables inside. And thank you to everyone who picked up the book and took it home; Pip and I are back because of you.

As Pip and Cara know, there ain't nothing stronger than the friendship of teenage girls. So thank you to my friends, my flower-huns, who have been with me since I was a teenage girl: Ellie Bailey, Lucy Brown, Camilla Bunney, Olivia Crossman, Alex Davis, Elspeth Fraser, Alice Revens, and Hannah Turner. (Thanks for letting me steal parts of your names.) And to Emma Thwaites, my oldest friend, thanks for helping me hone my storytelling skills with all those terrible plays and songs we wrote throughout our childhood, and to Birgitta and Dominic too.

To Gaye, Peter, and Katie Collis for again being among the very first readers of my new book and for always being such great cheerleaders. In an alternate universe, this book would have been called *Good Girl, Badass* *wink face*.

Thanks to everyone in my family who read and supported the

first book, with special shout-outs to Daisy and Ben Hay and Isabella Young. Good to know murder enthusiasm runs in the family.

To my mum and dad for giving me everything, including my love of stories. Thank you for always believing in me, even when I didn't. To my big sister, Amy, for all your support (and your cute kids), and my little sister, Olivia, for actually getting me out of the house while writing this book and probably keeping me sane. To Danielle and George—nope, sorry, you're still too young for this book. Try again in a few years.

The biggest thanks, as ever, go to Ben for quite literally keeping me alive while I wrote this book over an intense three months. And thank you for being the very willing model for Jamie Reynolds's shoulder. Must be a real hoot, living with an author, but you do it so very well.

And finally, to all the girls who've ever been doubted or not believed. I know how that feels. These books are for all of you.

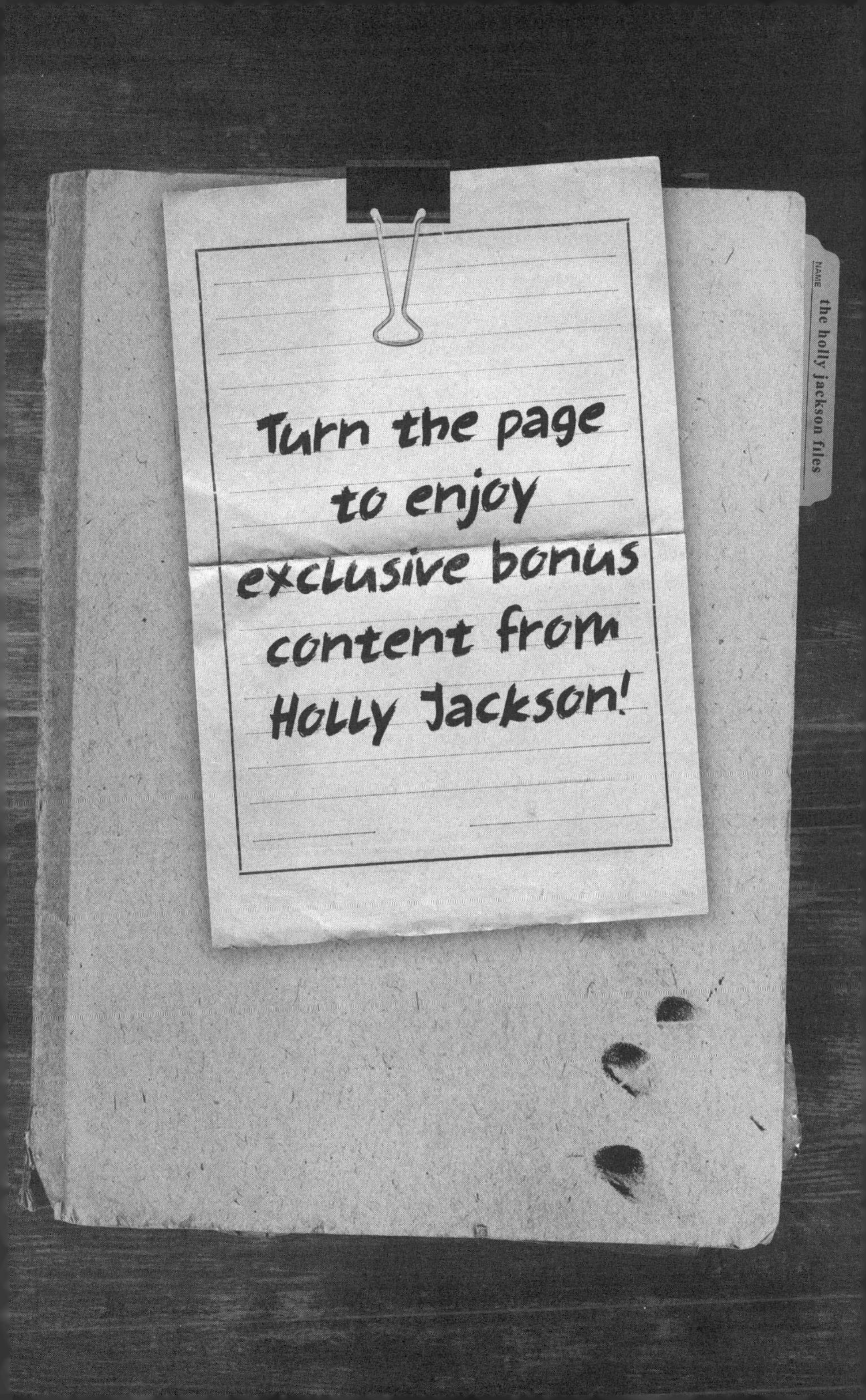
Turn the page to enjoy exclusive bonus content from Holly Jackson!
NAME
the holly jackson files

Title Brainstorming

Odd girl out

- No good girl
- No harm can come to a good girl
- Twice the girl I/she used to be

[Try to get rhyme in there, if we have alliteration and then expression]

- Girl alive
- May the best girl win/kill
- May the best girl live.

May the Good Girl live.

Keep a good girl down.

Good Girl down/gone

- Where no girl has gone before
- A changed girl
- Don't kill a girl when she's down
- Girl of her word.

Of Mice and Men. Of guilt and girls.

- Crooked <u>man</u>/girl
- Killer meets girl
- Killer's little girl
- Three for a girl, 2 for a kill
- good-time girl
- Go Go girl

nowhere to go

- Away with the missing (gone)
- Get away with murder
- lost/gone
- Where the missing go
- The Going and The Gone
- The Girl and The Gone
- Good Girl today, Gone tomorrow
- <u>Long Lost</u> Girl
- Long lost

A Good Girl and the long lost

- Lost and found

When the girl's away, the killers play

- The Gone and The Girl.
- The Missing and The Girl. <u>missing</u>
- The Girl, the town, and the Killer
- The Good, the bad and the Gone
- Guess Who, Girl.
- Grave / Great / Glass / Grass / Grave / Guilt / Grief / [illegible] / Glare / Greed / Given / Goodness
- Goody Two-Kills.
- To Kill a Mockingbird / Find
- Killer Kit The Killing Kind
- Small town.

One Girl, Two Gone

Good Girl Bad Blood

A Good Girl's Guide to Murder
Sequel Ideas

· first scene - naming her podcast / Youtube channel with Ravi - he comes up with the name - 'A Good Girl's Guide to Murder'.

· Then the story proper starts months later - around May. Much shorter timeline.

· Connor approaches Pip for help. His older brother (same year as Andie + Sal + Naomi) has gone missing. But the police won't investigate as he's an adult and has a history of running away. But the Reynolds family (mum, dad, connor, sister) consider he might be in trouble.
- Pip agrees to help and to live record (episodes released during investigation) for her podcast / Youtube Channel.

· Involves conflicting interviews with

family + friends. Naomi is interviewed because she knows him.

· Daniel da Silva + the police won't investigate – some conflict with Pip about this.

· Now that she is releasing episodes as she investigates – Pip gets tips and info / ideas from listeners writing in too.

· Pip has to work out Connor's brother's password to his laptop – she gets the idea after interviewing a friend.

· And the laptop has lots of leads – catfishing network.

· Could the secret between Howie Bowers + Stanley Forbes come into play here: Why Stanley was paying off Howie + what secrets does Howie know about him.

- Unfolding at the same time that Max Hastings' trial is. Pip either goes to watch + report later for podcast or - if she is a witness - Ravi goes to help + report back to her.

- When Max is acquitted + moves back into Town, Naomi starts considering confessing to hit + run to put Max behind bars. Pip conflicted because she's trying to protect Cara - but she becomes over-protective = investigates the new girl Cara is seeing + uncovers secrets she hasn't told Cara. Cara gets mad that Pip snooped - not everything in life needs to be an investigation

New Midpoint

Check electoral register for Layla - Mead

Making profile to find Layla.
Pip + Connor go back to hers to try + find
the catfish + update last seen map.
In her room - door open. Ravi comes in saying 'hey
I was trying to call you + Pip says sorry my phone
was on silent for interview - how was trial -
Ravi gives a quick update on how it went = prosecution
finished + defence started. Then they start looking on all
social media sites and all devices for Layla - with variant
spellings - Leila - Leyla - Layla - there are too many - they can't
narrow down - Pip tries to do reverse image search of Stella's

Charlie comes to knock and shows them the doorbell cam footage

Interview with Charlie Green who
comes forward with footage of Jamie
stealing from him. Connor has left -
Pip + Ravi have just recorded Max update when
someone knocks on door + Dad calls up for Pip. Charlie is
asking for her. He says to P+R - I have to show you
something - I think it's to do with that Jamie you're looking 4
So Pip + Ravi go over - Flora is sweet and offers them
tea + biscuits. Charlie shows them his computer set up -
he's a freelance graphic designer. They have a motion sensor door

Nat
eyes down, looks sad but determined
eyes this way, towards Jury. Mouth bared, mid-speaking, face looks almost aggressive
Epps
Max
face engaged, like he's listening with interest, watching his lawyer
Jury in this direction

Cut Word count

Try to cut 4000 words minimum. ✓

Places to cut significant amount of words:

- Calamity party + videos ☑
- Article about podcast ☑
- Conversation with parents ☑
- Cracking Jamie's password ☑
- Looking through computer ☑
- Hillary F. Weisemann thread ☑
- Original search of Jamie's room ☑
- The memorial scene ☑
- Cara scene (cut some detail) ☑
- Tom Nowak thread (trim) ☑
- 2nd episode outtro ☑
- Trial update at start ☑

Otherwise, try to cut 50–100 words from every other chapter / interview / case notes part.

Part	Words cut	Part	Words Cut	Part	Words Cut	
Prologue	69	ch 8.	145	case notes 3	82	
Article	443	case notes 1	21	ch. 16	187	
ch 1.	92	ch. 9	190	Stella Interview	73 +16	
Trial update	277	ch.10	142	ch.17	~~197~~ 170	
ch.2	139	case notes 2	86	ch.18	61	5014
ch.3	311	ch 11	286	ch. 19	100+14	
ch. 4	233	int with George Th.	81	ch 20	68	
ch. 5	345	ch. 12	193	Interview with Adam Clark	57	
ch. 6	~~108~~ 109	ch. 13	218	ch. 21	109	
ch 7.	217	ch. 14	341	ch. 22	144	
Joanna Interview	301	Mum Interview	79	ch. 23	201	
Connor Interview	230	ch. 15	217	ch. 24	491	
(reach 2000 here) [2426]		(reach 3000 here) [4425]		(reach (4000 here) – now (5500) [6198]		

Part	Words Cut
case notes 4	15
Ch. 25	169
case notes 5	30
Ch. 26	86
Ch. 27	~~37~~
Arthur Interview	28
Ch. 28	72
Ch. 29	30
Ch. 30	6
Ch. 31	+11
Ch. 32	+~~138~~ 146
Ch. 33	4
Ch. 34	48
Ch. 35	35
Ch. 36	29
Ch. 37	22
Ch. 38	31
Ch. 39	11
Ch. 40	10
Ch. 41	+34
Ch. 42	
Ch. 43	

(reach 5000 here) now: 6,800

(reach 8000 here) now 7000

aim for 93/94k total [95 Max]

total: 92,429

Don't miss the final chapter in the *New York Times* bestselling A Good Girl's Guide to Murder series by international sensation Holly Jackson!

By the end, you'll never think of good girls the same way again. . . .

Published by Delacorte Press, an imprint of Random House Children's Books,
a division of Penguin Random House LLC, New York.

ONE

Dead-eyed. That's what they said, wasn't it? Lifeless, glassy, empty. Dead eyes were a constant companion now, following her around, never more than a blink away. They hid in the back of her mind and escorted her into her dreams. *His* dead eyes, the very moment they crossed over from living to not. She saw them in the quickest of glances and the deepest of shadows, and sometimes in the mirror too, wearing her own face.

And Pip saw them right now, staring straight through her. Dead eyes encased in the head of a dead pigeon sprawled on the front drive. Glassy and lifeless, except for the movement of her own reflection within them, bending to her knees and reaching out. Not to touch it, but to get just close enough.

"Ready to go, pickle?" Pip's dad said behind her. She flinched as he shut the front door with a sharp clack, the sound of a gun hiding in its reverberations. Pip's other companion.

"Y-yes," she said, straightening up and straightening out her voice. *Breathe, just breathe through it.* "Look." She pointed needlessly. "Dead pigeon."

He bent down for a look, his black skin creasing around his narrowed eyes, and his pristine three-piece suit creasing around his knees. And then the shift into a face she knew too well: he was about to say something witty and ridiculous, like—

"Pigeon pie for dinner?" he said. Yep, right on cue. Almost every other sentence from him was a joke now, like he was working that much harder to make her smile these days. Pip relented and gave him one.

"Only if it comes with a side of mashed rat-ato," she quipped, finally letting go of the pigeon's empty gaze, hoisting her bronze backpack onto one shoulder.

"Ha!" He clapped her on the back, beaming. "My morbid daughter." Another face shift as he realized what he'd said, and all the other meanings that swirled inside those three simple words. Pip couldn't escape death, even on this bright late-July morning in an unguarded moment with her dad. It seemed to be all she lived for now.

Her dad shook off the awkwardness, only ever a fleeting thing with him, and gestured to the car with his head. "Come on, you can't be late for this meeting."

"Yep," Pip said, opening the door and taking her seat, unsure of what else to say, her mind left behind as they drove away, back there with the pigeon.

It caught up with her as they pulled into the parking lot for the Fairview train station. It was busy, the sun glinting off the regimented lines of commuter cars.

Her dad sighed. "Ah, that fuckboy in the Porsche has taken my spot again." "Fuckboy": another term Pip immediately regretted teaching him.

The only free spaces were down at the far end, near the chain-link fence where the cameras didn't reach. Howie Bowers's old stomping ground. Money in one pocket, small paper bags in the other. And before Pip could help herself, the unclicking of her seat belt became the tapping of Stanley Forbes's shoes on the concrete behind her. It was night now, Howie not in prison but right there under the orange glow, downward shadows for eyes. Stanley reaches him, trading a handful of money for his life, for his secret. And as he turns to face Pip, dead-eyed, six holes split open inside him, spilling gore down his shirt and onto the concrete, and somehow it's on her hands. It's all over her hands and—

"Coming, pickle?" Her dad was holding the door open for her.

"Coming," she replied, wiping her hands against her smartest pants.

The train into Grand Central was packed, and she stood shoulder to shoulder with other passengers, awkward closed-mouth smiles substituting *sorrys* as they bumped into one another. There were too many hands on the metal pole, so Pip was holding on to her dad's bent arm instead, to keep her steady. If only it had worked.

She saw Charlie Green twice on the train. The first time in the back of a man's head, before he shifted to better read his newspaper. The second time, he was a man waiting on the platform, cradling a gun. But as he boarded their car, his face rearranged, lost all its resemblance to Charlie, and the gun was just an umbrella.

It had been three months and the police still hadn't found him. His wife, Flora, had turned herself in to a police station in Duluth, Minnesota four weeks ago; they had somehow gotten separated while on the run. She didn't know where her husband was, but the rumors circulating online were that he'd managed to make it across the border to Canada. Pip looked out for him anyway, not because she wanted him caught, but because she needed him found. And that difference was everything, why things could never go back to normal again.

Her dad caught her eye. "You nervous about the meeting?" he asked over the screeching of the train's wheels as it slowed into Grand Central. "It will be fine. Just listen to Roger, OK? He's an excellent lawyer. Knows what he's talking about."

Roger Turner was an attorney at her dad's firm who was *the best* at defamation cases, apparently. They found him a few minutes later, waiting outside the old redbrick conference center, where the meeting room was booked.

"Hello again, Pip," Roger said, holding out his hand to her. Pip quickly checked her hand for blood before shaking his. "Nice weekend, Victor?"

"It was, thank you, Roger. And I have leftovers for lunch today, so it's going to be an excellent Monday too."

"I suppose we better head in, then, if you're ready?" Roger asked Pip, checking his watch, his other hand gripping a shining briefcase.

Pip nodded. Her hands felt wet again, but it was sweat. It was only sweat.

"You'll be fine, darling," her dad told her, straightening out her collar.

"Yes, I've done thousands of mediations." Roger grinned, swiping back his gray hair. "No need to worry."

"Call me when it's done." Pip's dad leaned down to bury a kiss in the top of her hair. "I'll see you at home tonight. Roger, I'll see you in the office later."

"Yes, see you, Victor. After you, Pip."

They were in meeting room 4E, on the top floor. Pip asked to take the stairs because if her heart was hammering for that reason, it wasn't hammering for any other reason. That's how she rationalized it, why she now went running anytime she felt her chest tighten. Run until there was a different kind of hurt.

They reached the top, old Roger puffing several steps behind her. A smartly dressed man stood in the corridor outside 4E, smiling when he saw them.

"Ah, you must be Pippa Fitz-Amobi," he said. Another outstretched hand, another quick blood check. "And you, her counsel, Roger Turner. I'm Hassan Bashir, and for today I am your independent mediator."

He smiled, pushing his glasses up his thin nose. He looked kind, and so eager he was almost bouncing. Pip hated to ruin his day, which she undoubtedly would.

“Nice to meet you,” she said, clearing her throat.

“And you.” He clapped his hands together, surprising Pip. “So, the other party is in the meeting room, all ready to go. Unless you have any questions beforehand.” He glanced at Roger. “I think we should probably get started.”

“Yes. All good.” Roger sidestepped in front of Pip to take charge as Hassan ducked back to hold open the door to 4E. It was silent inside. Roger walked through, nodding thanks to Hassan. And then it was Pip’s turn. She took a breath, arching her shoulders, and then let it out through gritted teeth.

Ready.

She stepped into the room and his face was the first thing she saw. Sitting on the opposite side of the long table, his angular cheekbones in a downward point to his mouth, his messy swept-back blond hair. He glanced up and met her eyes, a hint of something dark and gloating in his.

Max Hastings.

TWO

Pip's feet stopped moving. She didn't tell them to; it was like some primal, unspoken knowledge, that even one more step would be too close to *him*.

"Here, Pip," Roger said, pulling out the chair directly opposite Max, gesturing her down into it. Beside Max, across from Roger, was Christopher Epps, the same attorney who'd represented Max in his trial. Pip had last come face to face with this man on the witness stand; she'd been wearing this exact same suit while he hounded her with that clipped bark of a voice. She hated him too, but the feeling was lost, subsumed by her hatred for the person sitting opposite her. Only the width of a table between them.

"Right. Hello, everyone," Hassan said brightly, taking his assigned chair at the head of the table, in between the two parties. "Let's get the introductory bits out of the way. My role as mediator means I'm here to help you reach an agreement and a settlement that is acceptable to both parties. My only interest is to keep everyone here happy, OK?"

Clearly Hassan had not read the room.

"The purpose of a mediation is essentially to avoid litigation. A court case is a lot of hassle, and very expensive for all involved, so it's always better to see if we can come to some arrangement before a lawsuit is even filed." He grinned, first to Pip's side of the room, and then to Max's. A shared and equal smile.

"If we cannot reach an agreement, Mr. Hastings and his counsel intend to bring a libel lawsuit against Miss Fitz-Amobi, for a tweet and a blog post shared on April thirtieth of this year, which they claim consisted of a defamatory statement and audio file." Hassan glanced at his notes. "Mr. Epps, on behalf of the claimant, Mr. Hastings, says the defamatory statement has had a very serious effect on his client, both in terms of mental well-being and irreparable reputational damage. This has, in turn, led to financial hardship, for which he is seeking damages."

Pip's hands balled into fists on her lap, knuckles erupting out of her skin like a prehistoric backbone. She didn't know if she could sit here and listen to all this, she didn't fucking know if she could do it. But she breathed and she tried, for her dad and Roger, and for poor Hassan over there.

On the table, in front of Max, was his obnoxious water bottle, of course. Cloudy dark-blue plastic with a flick-up rubber spout. Not the first time Pip had seen him with it; turns out that in a town as small as Fairview, running routes tended to converge and intersect. She'd come to expect it now, seeing Max out on his run when she was on hers, almost like he was doing it on purpose somehow. And always with that fucking blue bottle.

Max saw her looking at it. He reached for it, clicked the button to release the spout with a snap, and took a long, loud sip from it, swilling it around his mouth. His eyes on her the entire time.

Hassan loosened his tie a little. "So, Mr. Epps, if you would like to kick things off here with your opening statement."

"Certainly," Epps said, shuffling his papers, his voice just as sharp as Pip remembered. "My client has suffered terribly since the libelous statement Miss Fitz-Amobi put out on the evening of April thirtieth, especially since Miss Fitz-Amobi has a significant online presence, amounting to more than 300,000 followers at the time. My client has a top-tier education from a very reputable college, meaning, he should be a very attractive candidate for graduate jobs."

Max sucked from his water bottle again, like he was doing it to punctuate the point.

"However, these last few months, Mr. Hastings has struggled to find employment at the level to which he deserves. This is directly due to the reputational harm that Miss Fitz-Amobi's libelous statement has caused. Consequently, my client still has to live at home with his parents, because he cannot find an appropriate job and therefore cannot pay rent to live in New York."

Oh, poor little serial rapist, Pip thought, speaking the words with her eyes.

"But the harm has not been my client's alone," Epps continued. "His parents, Mr. and Mrs. Hastings, have also suffered from the stress, and have even recently had to leave town to stay at their second home in Santa Barbara for a couple of months. Their house was vandalized the very same night Miss Fitz-Amobi published the defamatory statement; someone graffitied the front of their home with the words 'Rapist, I will get you—' "

"Mr. Epps," Roger interrupted, "I hope you are not suggesting that my client had anything to do with that vandalism. The police have never even spoken to her in connection with it."

"Not at all, Mr. Turner." Epps nodded back. "I mention it because we can surmise a causal link between Miss Fitz-Amobi's libelous statement and the vandalism, as it occurred in the hours proceeding that statement. Consequently, the Hastings family does not feel safe in their own home and have had to fit security cameras to the front of the house. I hope this goes some way in explaining not only the financial hardship Mr. Hastings has suffered, but also the extreme pain and suffering felt by him and his family in the wake of Miss Fitz-Amobi's malicious, defamatory statement."

"Malicious?" Pip said, heat rising to her cheeks. "I called him a rapist and he *is* a rapist, so—"

"Mr. Turner," Epps barked, voice rising, "I suggest you advise your client to keep quiet and remind her that any defamatory statements she makes now could be classified as slander."

Hassan held up his hands. "Yes, yes, let's just everyone take a breather. Miss Fitz-Amobi, your side will have the chance to speak later." He loosened his tie again.

"It's all right, Pip, I've got this," Roger said quietly to her.

"I will remind Miss Fitz-Amobi," Epps said, not even looking at her, his gaze on Roger instead, "that three months ago my client faced trial in court and was found *not guilty* on all charges. Which is all the proof you need that the statement made on April thirtieth was, in fact, defamatory."

"All that being said"—Roger now stepped in, shuffling his own papers—"a statement can only be libelous if it is presented as fact. My client's tweet reads as follows: *Max Hastings trial final update. I don't care what the jury believes: he is guilty.*" He cleared his throat. "Now, the phrase *I don't care* clearly places the following statement as a subjective one, an opinion, not fact—"

"Oh, don't give me that," Epps cut in. "You're trying to fall back on the opinion privilege? Really? Please. The statement was clearly worded as fact, and the audio file presented as though it were actually real."

"It is real," Pip said. "Wanna hear it?"

"Pip, please—"

"Mr. Turner—"

"It's clearly doctored," Max spoke up for the first time, maddeningly calm, folding his hands in front of him. His eyes focused only on the mediator. "I don't even sound like that."

"What, like a rapist?" Pip spat across at him.

"MR. TURNER—"

"Pip—"

"OK, everyone!" Hassan stood up. "Let's take this down a notch. We will all get our chance to speak. Remember, we are here to make sure everyone is happy with the outcome. Mr. Epps, could you take us through the damages your client is seeking?"

Epps bowed his head, pulling out a sheet of paper from the bottom of the pile. "For special damages, considering my client should have been in employment for the last three months, at a monthly salary level we would expect for someone in his position, this would have been at least five thousand dollars. This places the financial loss at fifteen thousand dollars."

Max sucked at his water bottle again, the water sloshing around his throat. Pip would have liked to take that fucking water bottle and smash it into his face. If there was to be blood on her hands, it should be his.

"Of course, no monetary figure can be put on the pain and mental anguish suffered by my client and his family. But we feel a sum of eight thousand dollars should be adequate, bringing the total to twenty-three thousand dollars."

"Ridiculous," Roger said, shaking his head. "My client is only eighteen years old."

"Mr. Turner, you should allow me to finish," Epps sneered, licking his finger to turn the page. "However, in discussion with my client, it is his opinion that his ongoing suffering is caused by the fact that the libelous statement has not been retracted and no apology issued, which would actually be of greater value to him than any monetary damages."

"Miss Fitz-Amobi deleted the post weeks ago, when your initial letter of demand was sent," said Roger.

"Mr. Turner, please," Epps replied. If Pip had to hear him say *please* like that one more time, she might just smash his face in too.